POWDER RIVER

Also by Ralph W. Cotton
While Angels Dance

POWDER RIVER
A Jeston Nash Adventure

◆ ❋ ◆ ❋ ◆

Ralph W. Cotton

St. Martin's Press 🐾 New York

Library of Congress Cataloging-in-Publication Data

Cotton, Ralph W.
    Powder river : a Jeston Nash adventure / Ralph W. Cotton.
       p.   cm.
    "A Thomas Dunne book."
    ISBN 0-312-13146-1
    1. Powder River Expedition, 1865—History—Fiction. 2. Oglala Indians—Fiction. 3. Dakota Indians—Fiction. I. Title.
PS3553.O766P68   1995
813'.54—dc20   95-5223
                                            CIP

First Edition: May 1995

10 9 8 7 6 5 4 3 2 1

For Mary Lynn . . . of course, and for Richard Pack
and Jay Back.

Roads we've wandered; sights we've seen.

Special thanks to Pete Wolverton at Thomas Dunne Books, for
liking my yarns, giving these outlaws a home, and letting them
speak their piece . . .

Note to readers regarding the Catahoula cur in *Powder River:*

The Catahoula cur, as it is referred to in this story, is actually a
UKC breed known as the Louisiana Catahoula. Some say the breed
originated when Native Americans crossed Spanish war dogs with
the American red wolf. Catahoulas are among the finest animals in
the world, and I use the word *cur* only because the breed was not
officially recognized during the 1800s.

See them prancing,
They come neighing,
They come, a Horse Nation.
See them prancing,
They come neighing,
They come . . .
—NATIVE AMERICAN FOLK SONG

◆ ✳ Foreword ✳ ◆

Over the years, I've asked myself many times what possessed my friend Quiet Jack Smith and me to travel into Powder River, smack into the middle of the mighty Sioux Nation, but I've yet to come up with a good answer. "Dealing horses to the army" is what I usually tell everybody else, but then as quick as I can, I always smile and change the subject. There were no *good* reasons for our going there or doing what we did—but I've always felt that if a man needs *good* reasons for everything he does, he'll die in a rocking chair with nothing to remember but yesterday's weather. There are some things you do without really knowing why, and I reckon for me, riding up to Powder River will always be one of them.

Jack and I were restless young men just back from a war we'd lost. We'd been whipped by the Northern army, but still felt cocky tough and confident, and ready for another round. Maybe *that*, as much as anything else, had something to do with us vacationing in the midst of an ongoing Indian war.

I knew very little about the Sioux Nation except what I'd read in the newspapers and periodicals I came across during the last days of the great civil conflict. I'd spent many a night huddled near a low flame as cannon fire streaked the horizon, and I'd taken my mind off the ugliness of "our" war by reading about that other war somewhere off in the high Northwest. Names like Spotted Tail, Bull Bear, and Strike the Ree danced in flickering shadows on the printed page; but aside from the evil they conjured in the hearts and minds of roving journalists, I always thought any of them would make a real fine name for a racehorse.

I'd known an old rounder during the war by the name of Cletis

Avery. He'd lived with a band of Sioux just east of the Black Hills, back when the Dakotas were still the Great Forest and everything west into Wyoming Territory was virtually untrekked by lathed boots. Remembering his stories had me looking for a reason to go there anyway, so as crazy as it sounds, when Jack approached me with one of his fast-money schemes, I jumped at the chance like a fox at a possum.

I'd watched old Cletis die in the last year of the war, and I thought it peculiar that the words of a dead man came to my mind as Jack Smith, Big Shod, and I rounded the trail and led a string of horses through a smell of woodsmoke and rain in an early morning haze. I remembered old Cletis's words . . . but I had no idea what they meant at that time. "Until a man finds something he's willing to die for," I remembered him saying as I gigged my bay mare and led the string at an easy gallop, "he's a man with no reason for being alive."

Part I
Prancing They Come

◆ ✳ 1 ✳ ◆

The road into Crofton lay deeply rutted and swollen with mud as civilians busied themselves packing, tying down loads, and glancing between us and the Big Horn Range. They watched us and our string of muddy horses in curious disbelief; but when their eyes searched the mountains they did so cautiously, in fearful anticipation.

Shod took the lead rope from me and turned the wet horses in to the livery corral; Jack and I kept the herd closed until the last of them splashed past us, then dropped the rail gate, latched it, and rode on up the middle of the mud street.

"Yep," said Quiet Jack, grinning at a young woman and sweeping off his soaked hat in a grand gesture. "I feel better already, now the rain's let up."

"I thought it never rained up here," I said, wringing my bandanna and draping it back around my neck.

"Where'd you hear that?" Jack chuckled as his face followed the young lady along the boardwalk. I just stared at him. He knew where I'd heard it; I'd heard it from him.

We slowed our horses almost to a stop, and watched a wagonload of bodies creak past us on its way out of town. The dead lay stacked like cordwood. Beside the wagon, four soldiers sloshed through the mud carrying shovels.

"Maybe it's worse here than we thought," I said quietly. We'd heard talk all the way from Missouri that Red Cloud's Sioux had allied with the Cheyenne and Arapaho and were killing anything that moved between here and Fort Phil Kearny. The fort was still under construction and heavily harassed. St. Louis oddsmakers put smart money on the fort never being completed.

We turned our horses and reined up to a hitch rail outside a rough-cut saloon; and I slipped down, hitched my reins, and attended to a loose stirrup as Jack stepped up on the boardwalk and through the open door. The rattle of a banjo danced in the air, above men's voices and a woman's laughter.

In a few minutes, I noticed Big Shod standing on the boardwalk and I nodded toward the saloon. "Jack's inside," I said, then turned back to attending my stirrup. Big Shod hesitated a second before going in.

A few seconds later, the banjo stopped midchord, and I looked up at three soldiers backing out the door with their hands near their sidearms. "Jesus! Here we go," I whispered, hastily running a new strip of rawhide around my broken stirrup.

"Tell him yourself!" Jack's voice boomed as he and Shod stepped out on the boardwalk and stopped three feet apart. Jack hooked his thumb in his gun belt near his forty-four and watched for a response. The young lieutenant looked scared and puzzled. Civilians weren't supposed to act this way. He glanced at the two privates beside him for support, then back at Quiet Jack.

Jack smiled, but it was a smile of warning, more like a wildcat showing its fangs. "Don't tell me to do your talking for you," he said. He leaned near the lieutenant. "And never"—Jack raised a finger for emphasis—"never . . . tap me on the shoulder from behind unless you're ready to meet Jesus." Jack was not known for beating around the bush, and six weeks of living in the saddle had him red-eyed and testy.

The young lieutenant cleared his throat, trying to look unshaken. He knew he'd grabbed hold of a panther; now he tried to let go without looking cat-shy. "Be that as it may," he said, pointing at Shod, "he can't drink at the bar with my troops." I hurried with the stirrup, keeping my hat low on my forehead. Being wanted for killing a crooked sheriff back in Missouri kept me a little meek of presence and shallow of voice. Of course, having Quiet Jack around made up for it.

"Then you shoulda told *him*, not me," said Jack, nodding toward Big Shod. I watched out the corner of my eye and breathed a little easier as Jack glanced at Shod. If Jack meant to kill these soldiers, he wouldn't have taken his eyes off them. He'd made his point. He knew it when the lieutenant's face turned white and his hands drew chest-high. Now he was teasing them. "Hear that, Shod? These *boys* don't appreciate your company, but they're too bashful to tell you." He'd emphasized "boys" just to aggravate.

Big Shod stood three heads taller than anybody I knew. He glared down at the soldiers as he spoke to Jack. "Ya-sur, boss," he mimicked. His voice was cannon fire from within a deep cave. The soldiers leaned back instinctively as Shod leaned forward. Big Shod was two hundred and seventy pounds of steel-woven muscle wrapped in shiny black, with veins in his forearms that looked like knotted rope. His head was as bald as a cypress stump, and trimmed in a pair of wire-framed spectacles that appeared always on the verge of sliding off his nose.

I finished my work quickly and dropped the stirrup just as a column of cavalry rounded the far corner and headed toward us at a slow pace. From within their ranks a harmonica played a weak and broken version of "Gary Owens."

"Time to go," I called over my shoulder. I never tarried long around anything connected to the government, especially if it carried guns. I'd been that way since the war, since riding with Quantrill. Killing that crooked sheriff had only strengthened my resolve.

Jack paid me no mind. "Didn't you *boys* just invest a few years of burnt powder and dead Yankees to free this feller?" He tossed Big Shod another glance. Big Shod just nodded, still glaring at the soldiers above the dirty wire-frames.

Now the lieutenant grew bolder as the column drew nearer. His hand slid to the safety flap on his holster. Jack grinned and let his hand fall to his side. "There could be a thousand coming, it won't help you a lick. They can write your mama about it . . . but it'll only make her cry."

The lieutenant's face flashed red; his hand tensed. I saw him think about it . . . bite the inside of his lip, rub his holster strap . . . but then he let go a tense breath. "Te-hut," he barked as he and the two privates spun to face the column of troops. The two privates stood wide-eyed. You could see their heartbeat in their faces. Jack glanced at me and winked. I cursed him under my breath.

"Lieutenant," the stocky major called out. He was a serious-looking feller with a red-gray beard. "Is there a problem here?"

"No-sir," replied the young officer. "This colored boy came in the saloon—"

"I came looking for my associate," Big Shod's voice overpowered him.

"I see," said the major. He rested his hands on his saddle and gazed at the distant horizon. The sky was a low boiling pot of gray lead streaked with swirls of white. "And you found him?"

"That is correct," Shod said. His voice sounded as clear and distinct as a schoolmaster's. The major turned his face curiously at the sound of Big Shod's polished words. Jack chuckled under his breath. I stood between the horses studying my thumbnail.

"What is your business in Crofton?" The major's eyes drifted across the three of us. Crofton was a thrown-up shack town with one saloon and a whorehouse in a big ragged tent. I reckon we were a hard-looking crew even for that place. We'd been living among eighty head of muddy horses since we left the buttes seven days ago—five weeks on the trail before that. Sweat and mud streaked our clothes and faces. We were armed to the teeth and our guns were the only clean things about us.

I stared at Jack, waiting for him or Shod to say something, but they just glared at the soldiers until I finally stepped forward from between the horses and looked up from under my low brim. "We're taking horses up Powder River, up to Fort Kearny. I'm a dealer out of Kansas. These fellers work for me."

"Powder River?" Muffled laughter rippled through the column of troops. The major glanced around, silencing them, but ready to laugh himself. "Do you realize what's going on up there? Didn't you notice a load of bodies—?"

"I've got a contract," I said, ignoring his question. "And I've got time and money invested. I'm taking 'em in."

"Major, sir," the young lieutenant butted in, "these men are belligerent and their attitude is quite obstinate."

"Watch your language," Jack chuckled under his breath. That's the thing about Quiet Jack. When you least need it, he throws in his two cents. Other times, when you need him to say something, he draws up like a cinch.

"I'm Beatty . . . James Beatty," I said straight-faced. My real name was Jeston Nash, but I was wanted for murder under the name Miller Crowe. Because I resembled my cousin, Jesse Woodson James, of Clay County, Missouri, lots of folk mistook me for him. It was one more reason I tried to go unnoticed. "I'm bringing these horses in under the authority of Colonel Henry Carrington, Eighteenth Infantry."

The major looked suspicious as I stepped forward handing up the requisition from inside my wet riding duster. "Horses?" His brow narrowed.

I said a silent prayer as the paper passed to his gloved hand. It was a flat-out forgery Jack had bought from Mysterious Dave Mather back in Hayes City. Mather was a slippery sort, and this horse scheme was all his and Jack's idea. Mather said he and a couple of Texas outlaws used the forged paper to bring in a string of horses a year earlier and had made a ton of money on the deal.

"Horses? For Carrington's *infantry?*" The major pinched the bridge of his nose and shook his head. "What will poor dear Carrington think of next? He has a marching band, you know." His face took a strange twist. "Plays snappy . . . I mean *real* snappy music, I'm told."

"These are top stock," I said quickly, feeling my face turn red as I shot Jack a dark scowl. "They've been properly broken and cared for." That much was true. We'd stolen them here and there from some of the better stables and auction barns across upper Missouri—thieving in the dark of night. I was known to have a keen eye for good horseflesh. These were fine animals.

The major glanced through the requisition, flipped it over, checked the back side, folded it, and flipped it back down to me. I felt the tension lift from my shoulders as I stuffed the paper back inside my duster. He nodded at the lieutenant. "That will be all." He nodded in the direction of the army camp a mile out. "You and your men report to your company." Then he turned back to me as the three soldiers scurried away. "You'll find few decent folks left between here and Fort Kearny, mostly Indians, outlaws, and bounty hunters." A suspicious smile twitched his lips. "I see you're not Indian. If it weren't for that requisition, I might wonder if you were one of the others."

"I'm a businessman, nothing else, Major . . . ?"

"Trapp," he said, "Major Leonard C. Trapp, Eleventh Cavalry."

I would remember his name if we got on the spot. He'd examined the forged dispatch without questioning it. If need be, I would mention his name down the line. Once we got the horses in, we would sell them for top dollar, clean and simple. "This is strictly business, Major Trapp. I've no hankering to mix it up with Red Cloud's bunch, or anybody else."

"I see." He studied my eyes for a few seconds, then called out over his shoulder. A soldier rode up from the rear of the column leading a sorrel mare with a blanket-wrapped corpse draped across her saddle. Blue, stiff hands hung from beneath the blanket. Flies swarmed in the wavering stench as Trapp reached out and flipped up a corner of the blanket. I swatted a fly from my face as I stepped forward.

I wasn't sure what Trapp's point was in showing me the swollen corpse; maybe it was meant to scare me. I'd seen worse during the war along the Missouri border, but I tried to look real shocked. "Mercy," I said.

"This is one of the Pope Gang," said Trapp. "The Sioux got to him before we did. Ever seen or heard of the Pope brothers?" He eyed me real close.

"No, I don't reckon I have." I stared at the back of the corpse's head. A flap of scalp hung down, covered with flies. The ears were gone; white rib bones and spine glistened up his back. From the jagged carving pattern, I would say he was still alive, screaming and kicking, when the skinning started. I winced, feeling the skin on my back tighten.

"They're rotten dogs . . . the Popes," said Trapp. "They prey on anybody crossing between here and Piney Creek. They've hit our payroll twice in the past year." Nodding toward the corpse, "We tracked him three days across the lower shoals. This is what we found." Trap watched my eyes a few seconds longer. I stared back, wondering what he meant by it.

"Like I said, Major, we're in and out . . . business only."

"Very well," he said, slowly tipping his finger to his ha glancing past me and across Jack and Big Shod, "carry on. watched in silence until the patrol rode off down the mud street and disappeared out toward the army camp. Thunder grumbled and rolled in the western sky.

"Infantry?" I just stared hard at Jack, but felt foolish myself that neither of us had bothered to think of how it sounded.

"Nothing's perfect." Jack chuckled and nodded at the whore-house in a ragged tent. From where we stood across the mud street, I saw a cloud of flies swarm above a pile of broken whiskey bottles, getting in their licks before the next round of storms. "Let's talk about it in a more sociable climate," Jack said. "I'm on vacation here." He'd been calling this his vacation since we left Missouri. I didn't ask why.

I glanced at the big ragged tent. "Jack, you could catch something in there that you couldn't scrape out of your belly with a broadaxe."

"The major said *carry on,* and I'm going to, right now." Jack lifted his eyes and brought them down on mine with a look that said, the only way out of town was through that whorehouse tent.

I took a deep breath and scratched my damp dirty neck. My boots had been on my feet so long, I figured the best way out of them was with a paring knife and a hide scraper. I could swat flies and whores with my hat long enough to get a hot bath.

"That's a big tent. Reckon they've got a hot bath a man could slide into?"

"If they don't, they'll make you think they do," Jack said, as we stepped off the boardwalk.

I glanced back at Big Shod. "Come on, let's take a break."

"I'll tend the horses," said Shod, stepping down and spinning his reins from the hitch rail.

"You ain't real smart, are you?" Jack spoke under his breath as we started across the mud street. "First you send him in a saloon where he ain't welcome, now an army whorehouse?"

A Catahoula cur ran up beside me, sniffed my muddy boots, and sneezed. I leaned without stopping, patted the dog's bony head, and nudged him away just as he cocked a leg and shot a stream at my boot. "Surely to God, Jack, anybody who could stand it is welcome to a bath in a place like that." I shook my boot.

"Yeah? Well, what makes you think he'd only want a bath? S'pose he wanted to pin something down. S'pose . . . like any man with any mind left after snuggling up to a rifle barrel every night for six whole weeks—"

Jack's words slammed shut in his throat as a shot rang out, and we spun toward the livery corral with our guns drawn. I caught a glimpse of Shod in the corner of my eye. He'd stepped up into the saddle, and now he spun his horse, rearing it up as he jerked his rifle from the scabbard. Then more shots rang from the corral, and Jack and I bounded forward, dove through the flap on the tent, and rolled to our feet.

Whores snatched blankets around themselves and scurried to the rear of the tent. One of them screamed as a pair of muddy boots climbed her naked back, trampled her into the mud, then tore through the back flap. "Goddamn-ya!" Mud sprayed from her lips.

"Get back," I yelled, waving my arm at Shod as another volley of shots exploded; but he reined toward the corral as he cocked his rifle one-handed.

"Aw-hell, Jack." I stomped my foot. "He's riding right into it!"

"What's wrong with him?" Jack flipped off his hat and slapped it against his leg. "Alls I wanted—"

"Come on," I said, switching the forty-four to my left hand and jerking the thirty-six from my shoulder holster, "he's going in!"

The muddy whore threw a chamber pot at us, but we were out and gone when it hit a pole and the front of the tent collapsed. We fired at the livery barn thirty yards away, splashing water as we ran to our horses. Shod was over halfway there when a volley erupted, and his horse went down in a spray of mud.

Jack jumped into his saddle. I stayed in the street, covering Shod with both pistols, blazing away as he rolled from the downed horse. Bullets slapped into the mud around him as he rolled behind a water trough. Jack jumped his horse to the middle of the street, pulling mine behind him. When I grabbed the reins, he covered the livery barn, and in a second we splashed toward Shod.

"Damn it, Shod," said Jack, when we dove into the mud beside him. He threw his arm over the trough and emptied his forty-four into the barn. "All you had to do was take cover!"

"They're coming out," Shod yelled. The barn door blasted open and three riders in long dusters pounded out, full run, firing in every direction. I saw a soldier tumble from the roof of the saloon. Another fell from a boardwalk. I glanced around quickly, searching for Trapp's patrol. Nothing. "Never when you need them," I yelled.

Then a shotgun blasted from the door of the saloon and one rider flew from his saddle, slamming into the rider beside him. Now one lone rider splashed on as the other two tried to stand and shotguns tore them apart.

I intended to lie still beside the trough with Jack and Shod as the rider splashed past us, but I saw the horse he was riding was one of ours and I lost my head for a second. "No!" I bellowed, and before Jack could stop me, I jumped to the middle of the street and put my last three bullets in the rider's back.

I snapped back to my senses, watching him roll in the mud, his duster tails flipping like a windmill. "Aw-naw. Not over a stolen horse." I breathed through clenched teeth, feeling a sickness ripple in my stomach.

For a few seconds the town fell silent, then from back up the street, the naked whore stuck her face through the flap of the sagging tent. "Goddamn-ya," she screamed.

"What's wrong with her?" Jack stood up, slapping mud from his duster. "Does she think *we* caused all this?"

Shod stood up and stepped over beside me. I stared at the body in the street and swallowed hard. "I don't know," I whispered.

"Yee-hi, damn good shooting." An old man ran toward us waving his hat and laughing across empty gums. I glanced at Jack and Shod with a puzzled look. Jack just shook his head. Now faces ventured from behind wagons and doorways. "I see'd the whole thing," yelled the old man, jumping up and down in the mud. "He just shot the holy-go-to-hell out'n Gyp Pope . . . shore did! This man, right cheer." He reached his hand all the way up past my head and pointed down. His voice was so loud, it echoed.

I ducked from under his finger and walked toward the body twenty yards away, hoping the old fool would shut his mouth, but he raved on and on like a town crier. So much for going unnoticed, I thought.

A soldier appeared beside me and glanced down. "Good shooting," he said, then disappeared. I stood over the body lying in the mud. Facedown, spread-eagle, the man convulsed and turned his head to the side, staring up at me with his mouth gaping. Blood frothed from his lips. His hand stretched out, straining for the pistol only inches from his fingertips. "Good shooting, you rotten—" He choked on his words. I reached out a foot to kick his gun away; but my other foot slipped in the mud and I ended up kicking him in the face . . . then fell on him.

"Now he's beating the living hell out'n him," the old man yelled. "Somebody stop him. He's gone crazy!"

Jack and Shod ran up and pulled me to my feet. "Damn, Mister Beatty," Jack chuckled. "The man's had enough."

"I fell, Jack! I'm sorry I even shot him, let alone—"

"You should be," said a clerk wearing an apron and carrying a shotgun. "I'd hate to be in your boots when his brother Parker gets ahold of ya."

"He ain't afraid of 'em," the old man yelled, running up beside me. He raised three gnarled fingers high in the air. "I see'd it all. Three times right square in the back, then stomped him . . . kicked his *goddamn* face in."

"Shut up!" I pulled the old man's arm down. Three soldiers and a handful of clerks gathered around us. The muddy whore came running up wrapped in a blanket, carrying Jack's hat in one hand and a bottle of whiskey in the other. "I'm sorry," she said, panting, handing Jack his hat and offering him the bottle. "I thought you all were with that son of a bitch that ran over me."

"God forbid," said Jack, with a smile, eyeing the rise and fall of her breasts beneath the blanket. He reached for the whiskey bottle, but I hooked it from between their hands and shoved my way through the crowd.

The old man spread his arms and shrugged, *What'd I do?* as I stomped past him to the livery barn.

I didn't even answer as I walked to the barn, eyes fixed straight ahead with the bottle hanging from my hand. We hadn't been in

Crofton an hour and already I'd been questioned by the military, shot at by gunmen, pissed at by a dog, cussed at by a whore, announced to the town by a loud-mouthed old lunatic . . . and, worst of all, I'd shot a man . . . shot a man in the back.

Inside the barn, I stared into a dark empty stall and threw back a long drink of strong whiskey. Less than an hour, and I already had that gnawing feeling you get when you sense that whatever your plans are, you've just caught a glimpse of them slipping downhill . . . headed to hell in a handbasket.

2

There was something about killing a man for stealing a horse that I myself had stolen less than three weeks ago that would not settle. I stood in the barn and tried washing the picture away with hard jolts of whiskey; but it lay etched in my mind, bloodstained beneath a swirl of burnt powder.

I heard someone behind me and glanced over my shoulder at Jack as he reached around and took the bottle from my hand. "Over a stolen horse?" he said quietly.

"I know," I said. "I acted without thinking. Now I wished to God I hadn't." I reached my hand around without turning, and Jack slapped the bottle in it. I took a shot and kept the bottle.

"Well . . . I wouldn't take it too hard," Jack chuckled. "According to that whore, the Popes ain't a real Christian bunch."

"Yeah," I said, "and I just shot one of them. Three times, in the back. Over one of our stolen horses"—I threw back another drink, felt it burn deep—"while he was just trying to get away."

I handed Jack the bottle. "Yeah," I heard him chuckle, "then kicked him . . . while he was dying."

"Jack," I said, slow and even, "I slipped . . . I didn't *mean* to kick him."

"I didn't figure you did. I'm just saying that's how his bunch will call it. By the time word gets to them, it'll sound like you did everything but torture him with a branding iron. You know how this stuff goes."

"Yeah, I reckon I do." I nodded back over my shoulder toward the street. Outside, the old man's voice sounded like a scratchy trumpet blowing on and on about the shooting. "All it takes is some old geezer like that—"

I caught a glimpse of Shod walking into the barn and turned around as he came toward us with his rifle hanging from his hand. He shook his head. "It's hard to believe, but Gyp Pope is still alive."

Jack shook his head. "How the hell?"

Shod shrugged. "I don't know, but some idiot is out there cracking his head with a pistol barrel."

"Jesus! What next?" I pulled down my hat and saw Jack pitch Shod the bottle as we stomped from the barn. Shod just looked at the bottle and pitched it back.

"Here he comes," yelled the old man as we stepped from the barn. The bodies of the two dead outlaws lay in a bloody heap near the corral gate. They looked like chopped meat that had been patted back together. Some of the townsmen had tied the wounded man to a board and propped him against the corral fence; they stepped back as we walked closer. I heard someone cuss and saw a bearded man in buckskins come from the horse trough hefting a bucket of water. He swung it back and sloshed it in Gyp Pope's face before we could stop him.

"Here's the one done it," I heard the old man yell from in front of the crowd, and saw him jumping up and down in the mud. The Catahoula cur appeared out of nowhere and licked a bloody puddle near the outlaw's feet.

"Now, where's your brothers?" The feller in buckskin grabbed Pope by the hair, pulled his face up, and shook his head back and forth. The dying man choked and strangled on the blood and water. A fresh gash from a pistol barrel glistened on his jaw.

"Go to hell," Pope wheezed.

At the bearded man's feet, the Catahoula cur stopped licking, growled, and snapped at his buckskin trousers. Without looking down, he dealt the dog a sharp kick in the ribs; the animal sailed four feet and landed in the mud with a hoarse yelp.

Dark blood ran from the outlaw's mouth as the bearded man pulled out his pistol for another swipe. "I said . . . where's your brothers?" On the ground, the dog's eyes shined above snarling fangs as he crept closer, lowered on his front paws and growling so deep, his whole body trembled.

Just as the big feller drew back his pistol, I stepped in, grabbed his arm, and slung him away. "Leave him be!" I bellowed so loud, the Catahoula slipped and slid across the mud and dove under a shack.

"You the one shot him?" The big man stepped back glaring at me, his pistol hanging from his hand.

"Shore did," yelled the old man. "Three times, right in the back! Then beated the fire out'n him!"

I glanced at Jack and nodded toward the old man. "See if you can shut him up."

"What'd I do?" The old man shrugged as I turned back to the big feller in buckskin.

"Why're you asking?"

" 'Cause I've been tracking his bunch for a month."

"Lawman?"

"No," he sneered, "bounty-man. I caught him and the other two hiding in the livery barn. It ain't right, you shooting him after me putting in all that time."

I let out a breath. "I'm not claiming any bounty."

"Good, 'cause I am." He dropped his pistol in his holster, stepped forward, and reached for the outlaw's hair. I caught his arm and shoved him away again. Thirty feet away, I heard the dog snarling beneath the shack.

"But you ain't knocking him around!" I thought I saw the man's hand twitch near his gun, so I drew mine and pointed it straight at his chest. "Don't even think it!" I cocked my forty-four with a quick snap of my thumb.

"Easy now," I heard Jack say as I stared into the bounty-man's eyes. I saw that he was *still* ready to go for his pistol. Cocking a gun in this feller's face was like pouring butter in my boot; it didn't help me a bit, and he couldn't care less. He looked close at my cocked forty-four, then back to my eyes. A trace of an evil grin crawled through his white beard.

"He's fixin' to kill again," the old man yelled, and the crowd stepped back slowly.

"Easy," Jack repeated.

"Stay out of this, Jack!" I spoke from the corner of my mouth. I saw I had my hands full; I didn't need Jack singing background. The big feller's hand moved an inch closer to his gun.

"Okay," Jack said, and his voice dropped low, "but . . . your gun is empty."

I felt the hair curl on the back of my neck. The big feller took a step forward as his hand moved to his holster with all the time in the world. "So's mine," Jack whispered.

"Hold it," I said, letting down my gun and spreading my arms. "This is all a big mistake." I tried a sheepish grin.

"Damn right it was." The bounty-man's voice curled down, like a snake letting out its breath.

As I saw his gun start up from his holster, I heard a rifle cock behind me.

"Mine's loaded," said Big Shod, and I drew a long breath. The bounty-man opened his hand, stared at the long rifle barrel, and let the pistol drop back in his holster. I stood silent for a second until my heart quit thumping against my shirt. Then I stepped forward, bold as brass. "Now . . . let me tell you something." I jerked bullets from my belt, shoving them in my gun with a trembling hand.

"Now he'll kill him!" the old man yelled. The big feller stepped back as I stepped forward.

"I ain't claiming the bounty, but I'll turn him over to these lousy soldiers before I let you beat him." I glanced toward two soldiers in the crowd. "No offense."

"So what, you kicked him," the bounty-man growled.

"I didn't mean to—"

"Yeah? You didn't mean to shoot him, didn't mean to kick him. What *did* you mean to do?"

I glanced again toward the soldiers. "Alright, he's all yours."

The soldiers shrugged. "What're we suppose to do with him?"

"Turn him over to your provost marshal and tell him there's no bounty due."

"I'll kill you," the bounty-man growled.

"Shouldn't we take him to the hospital first?" The soldier lifted his cap and scratched his head.

"That won't be necessary," Shod said behind me. I glanced toward Shod and saw his grim expression. "He's dead now."

I felt a sickness crawl across my stomach as I turned and walked away. "I'm not through with you," I heard the bounty-man yell, but I kept walking. "Not by a long shot! Hear me? Do you hear me? I'll track ya down and kill ya!"

Shod had rode out to the army camp with the two soldiers and dropped off Pope's body at the provost marshal's office while Jack and I grained and watered the horses. He returned about the time we'd finished. "So what did they say?" I spoke to Shod's back as he swung down from the saddle. "Did you tell how it happened?"

He turned toward me, took off his hat, and slapped mud from his shirt without facing me. "They said it was obviously a case of self-defense, judging from the number of holes in his back."

Jack muffled a laugh; I felt my face redden. "What's so funny?" I stared between the two of them.

Shod shrugged and dropped his hat back on his head. "It was either that or call it suicide." Now Jack didn't even try to hide his laugh. I felt my neck boiling under the skin. Shod held up a hand. "Seriously, Mister Beatty," he said through a trace of a smile. "They said it was the only way to avoid a ton of paperwork. They also said you would have to get Major Trapp's permission before leaving tomorrow . . . something about trouble up the Bozeman Trail."

"Damned army," said Jack. "You'll soon have to get permission to scratch your behind."

I turned and pulled a clean damp shirt from my saddlebags. "I'll handle Trapp. The sooner we're away from here, the better I'll like it." I took out a rolled-up pair of damp socks and slapped them loose against my leg. "I heard it never rains up here," I said, squinting at Jack. He chuckled and looked away, scratching his jaw.

"I think it would be wise if the two of you stayed and faced the Pope Gang right here," Shod said. He took off his spectacles and rubbed his eyes. "That way the army would—"

"What do you mean, 'the two of us'?" I turned toward him with my shirt and socks hanging from my hand.

Shod hooked his spectacles back behind his ears and adjusted them on his nose. "After all, gentlemen, I'm just the hired help here.

You can't expect me to meddle in your personal problems."

"Well, I'll be damned." I shook my head. "If you hadn't rode in there like Sherman into Georgia—"

"Oh, I see," said Shod. "I caused you to shoot Gyp Pope in the back?"

"—we wouldn't be worried about the Pope Gang."

"I'm not 'worried' about them, Mister Beatty . . . not for half a dollar a day. That's my point. But you have to admit, it would be better facing them right here with the army behind you than out there on your own."

"That does make sense," said Jack, reaching into my saddlebags and taking out the bottle of whiskey. "But I don't like nobody telling me where I can and can't go, specially after I've already made plans. I'm kinda like Red Cloud in that regard." He threw back a shot and let the bottle hang from his hand. "Besides, this is a working vacation for us. We've been curious to look at the countryside."

"You're kidding." Shod shook his head as if to clear a jumbled thought.

"Naw-sir, sight-seeing ain't no joking matter. Once we get rich selling horses, we might tour on up to Milk River. Might eat a moose." Jack winked, cocked his hat, and headed through the door with our only bottle of whiskey. Shod stared back and forth between us until the door closed.

"Is he serious?" Shod spread his hands.

I smiled, slipped out of my muddy shirt, and slung it over a stall rail. "Don't worry about Major Trapp." I dipped water from a rain barrel and poured it over my head. "I'll handle him first thing in the morning, then we'll light out of here."

"Just like that." Shod shook his head. "You'll say what? 'Pardon me, Major, but my friend and I are on vacation. We're curious to see the countryside'?"

"Yep, just like that." I slung back my wet hair. "You can go or stay, whichever sets well with you. It's your choice. But once we set out to do something, we see it through, no matter how craz—I mean . . . *tough* it sounds. I said I'm taking them horses to Fort Kearny and I'll do it if I have to pack 'em on my back. That's just how it is."

"But we could take care of the Pope Gang right here, *then* take the horses to Kearny. Doesn't that make *good* sense?"

"I don't know about *good* sense, but like Jack said, it ain't in our plans. If we run into the Pope Gang, we'll just shoot 'em real smart like and keep on going. As far as permission, I'll have Trapp eating out of my hand come morning." I patted the leather wallet in my pocket. "You watch. I know how to speak his language."

"Perhaps I shouldn't dwell on this, but isn't it bad enough riding into an Indian war, let alone having a band of outlaws gunning for you?"

"It's a minor setback. But we'll handle it." I dipped more water and poured it up and down my arms. "Besides, I'd rather face a gun battle out in the bush than cooped up here like sitting ducks. I'm a country boy, Mister Shod. I'm more at home out there."

"But there are troops here—"

"Yeah? Where were they today? They probably heard the gunfire and thought it was pigs farting." I scrubbed my hands up and down my arms. "What you've got here is a bunch of slack-shouldered draftees and galvanized Yankees. Half of this bunch were war prisoners 'til last year. The real soldiers are still licking their wounds and getting measured for a wooden leg. Any good officer is still laid up drunk in Virginia—shooting frogs along the Potomac."

Shod shook his head and reached for the dipper. "What perception."

"It's the truth." I dried my head on my dirty shirt and slung it back over the rail. "That's why they're losing up here. That's why General Conner's cavalry troops left here walking last year, holding their butts with both hands."

Shod poured water over his bald head and rubbed it around with both hands. "General Conner has been a distinguished Indian fighter his entire career."

"Then somebody forgot to tell the Sioux, 'cause they whipped him proper. Now he's sitting up in Utah with his chin in his hand, wondering where it all went wrong."

Shod took off his spectacles and scrubbed them with his thumb and finger. "I fail to see how any of this pertains to us."

I leaned against a bale of hay and peeled off my boots and dirty socks. "Because you seem so all-fired set on sticking close to the army." I held my socks at arm's length and dunked them up and down in the rain barrel. "I'm just pointing out, the army ain't faired so well."

"All the more reason—if the Sioux are beating the federal army, armed troops in great number, what chance do the three of us have, especially with a gang of outlaws on our backs?"

I stalled for an answer, and was grateful to hear the door creak open behind us. We turned toward the door as a portly little feller carrying a bowler hat stepped in. He stopped with a cake-icing smile and raised the hat to his chest as if we might take his picture. "Excuse me, gentlemen, I'm looking for Mister Beatty?"

"Right here. What can I do for you?" I stepped forward as Shod slipped back inside his dirty shirt.

"I'm Reverend Addison? Pierson Addison? Of the God Across the Plains Ministries? I'm sure you've heard of us."

"Naw-sir, Reverend . . ." I extended my hand, glancing toward Shod. He shrugged. "But we're not from around here." I smiled. The Reverend Addison worked my hand like a pump handle. "Oh, we've been taking the word of the Lord to the poor heathen Sioux for over two years now."

"Then I reckon they're the better for it, Reverend. What can I do for you?" I tugged my hand until he finally let go.

"One of the soldiers told me you have horses for sale. It's imperative that I get my converts away from here to the shelter of Fort Laramie. As good as I've been to Red Cloud's people, they're still destroying my entire ministry." He bowed his head.

"I'm sorry, Reverend, but I'm afraid we wouldn't have enough horses to accommodate your flock. You see, these horses are headed up to Fort Kearny."

He cleared his throat. "Actually, there's only one convert and myself. We would make do with one horse. I'm certain Little Swan doesn't mind riding double. That's her name." He tossed a hand. "What a beautiful child, bursting with spirit. I was telling Major Trapp only this afternoon what a wonderful child she is."

I slid a glance past Shod and back to the reverend. "You know Trapp? I mean, do you know him *well*?"

"Oh, of course." Now he tossed both hands. "He has been one of my strongest supporters. We never miss a chance to dine together when I'm in Crofton."

"Well, Reverend, in that case maybe we can work something out. I have to talk to Major Trapp in the morning about taking my horses up to Fort Kearny. It sure would help if you talked to him first, your being his friend and all."

"Mister Beatty, I would consider it an honor to speak on your behalf."

I turned to Shod with a wink. "Mister Shod," I said with sugar dripping off my words. "Would you please gather the good Reverend Addison a couple of horses?"

"Oh no, please, Mister Beatty," said the reverend, making a steeple of his fingers. "One horse is plenty. Little Swan is light as a feather. I can sit her right up on my lap all the way to Fort Laramie."

"Are you sure?" I watched his chubby face blush red as Shod went out to the corral. "I can spare two. Seeing it's for such a good cause and all."

"You're too kind, Mister Beatty. But one is sufficient."

In a second, Shod returned with a tall chestnut gelding. When I handed Reverend Addison the lead rope, I leaned toward him with a smile. "Now, you'll be certain to mention us to Major Trapp?"

"Consider it done." He winked. "I'm certain after I speak to him, you'll leave here with my prayers and the army's blessings."

"So there, Mister Shod," I said in a fake show of religious tranquility, spreading my arms and gazing toward the ceiling, "the Lord doth provide for honorable men of good intent."

Shod squinted and rubbed his forehead.

◆✳ 3 ✳◆

The next morning I struck out early to the army camp, huddled in my duster with my hat pulled low against a fine mist of rain that grew heavier as a dark sky closed from the west. Thunder grumbled somewhere above the clouds; thin streaks of lightning twisted and curled, and danced like the devil's daughters high atop the Big Horn Range. By the time I swung out of my wet saddle and spun my reins around a hitch rail, I heard a heavy wall of rain sweeping in across the grassland behind me.

"I thought it never rained up here," I said to a stocky corporal as I stepped from the mud up onto the boardwalk outside the command shack. I took off my hat and slapped water from it.

"Where'd you hear that?" He laughed, looking me up and down like an old hand eyeing a greenhorn.

"Friend of mine," I said, turning, shaking my duster. I ran my hand across my face and knocked on Major Trapp's door.

"Yes, enter!" I heard Trapp mumbling under his breath as I swung open the door and stepped in. He looked up from a stack of paper, nodded, and looked back down.

"My wrangler says I need to see you before heading up to Kearny," I said, stepping over in front of his desk.

"Humph." He glanced up and back down, scribbling with a pen. "You're not going anywhere."

"Well, not this minute." I smiled and gestured toward the ceiling. "The rain—"

"No . . . you're not going anywhere *period*, and that's final." He dropped the pen and leaned back in his chair with a determined smile. "You could've gone yesterday, right after we talked, but now the order's come from Fort Kearny. No civilians . . . no way, no how, unless you have a minimum of thirty armed men. That's the new playing rules."

I stared at him for a second. "For how long?"

He folded his hands behind his head. "Until Red Cloud's Bad Faces finish their sweep. It's for your own good. I don't care how many lunatic preachers you send to influence me."

"Lunatic—? Hell, he said he was your friend. He said you and him were—"

"Friends? I'd give half a month's pay to see somebody castrate him with a rusty hog scraper. He's one of the reasons the Sioux won't believe anything we try to tell them. These preachers come in here wanting to save everybody's soul on Sunday, then spend the rest of the week stealing everything they can get their hands on, including wives and daughters."

I spread my hands. "But he said he was some kind of missionary. Said you and him—"

"Oh, he is. But they never came around until the Indians started getting their annual annuity payments. Now you can't cross the trail without stepping on God Across the Plains, or Jesus Up Your Tepee, or some such rigamarole. Most of them wind up with their throats cut for selling bad whiskey or giving some squaw the clap. Hell, decent preachers don't last the summer up here."

"Well . . . I didn't know. I just thought he needed help."

"Yeah, and you helped him. You helped him steal somebody's daughter more than likely. He tricked her into going with him. Now he'll use her 'til he gets tired of her, then sell her to some tavern owner or whorehouse." Trapp raised his hands with a dark grin. "All in the name of the Lord."

"I had no idea."

"Of course you didn't. See, you come around up here where you don't belong and wind up meddling in everybody's business. Things are bad enough without outsiders coming in peddling their goods, whiskey, guns, religion"—he gestured toward me—"horses." He gave me a curious look. "What's so important about taking horses up there anyway? Do you have some kind of idiot death wish?"

"They're for the army, Major," I said, feeling my face redden. "It's how I make a living. And like I said before, I've no hankering to mess with Red Cloud or anybody else." I chafed the back of my neck. "Tell you the truth, I'm kinda on a spot here."

"Yes, I know about the trouble yesterday—good shooting, by the way—but I have my orders."

"Then you oughta realize, I'm just as safe out there as I am here if the Pope Gang comes calling."

"It's not just the Popes you have to worry about." His jaw tightened. "Now, listen close." He mouthed his words slowly. "There's, a, war, going, on. Are you stupid or something? This town is disappearing, wagonload at a time." He poked his thumb south. "All in *that* direction. Doesn't that register? Any fool can get into Powder River. The difficulty will be getting out."

"Look, Major." I leaned forward. "I'll go broke feeding them if I can't take 'em—"

"Go home, Beatty!" He shook his head, exasperated. "Horse dealer. That's about one step above a thief and one step below a maniac."

I ignored his remark. "I just need to get in and out as quick as I can. I know this place could be a bare spot in the road by the time I get back."

"Um-hmm, and when it's gone, so are we." He waved a hand across his office. "There will be nothing left between here and Fort Laramie. You'll be going to hell and locking the door behind you."

"I know it's craz—I mean *risky,* but it's no different than sitting here waiting on the Pope bunch."

"That's not the point."

"Then what is? You said it's 'for my own good.' "

"The Popes aren't likely to make a move while my troops are here, and if they did, we'd back you up. Of course, we *will* be riding out come evening. We're heading up wide of the Bozeman and bringing in some settlers. Could be three or four weeks."

"See?" I threw my hands in the air. "I lose either way. At least let me choose—"

"Will that be all?" He cut me off, shook his head, and leaned forward over the stack of paperwork. "I'm very busy here."

I studied him a second, then took a hundred dollars from inside my duster, dropped it before his face, and stepped back without saying a word. He snatched it without looking up. "Well now, thank you," he said as the money disappeared into his tunic. I smiled and nodded as I turned toward the door. That's how it's done, I thought, clean and simple, no beating around the bush.

"By the way," he said as I reached for the door. "I'm posting guards around the livery barn. You can sell your horses here if you wish, but if you try to leave with them, you'll be arrested."

"Now, wait a damn minute! What about that money I just gave you? What do you think that's for?"

He shrugged. "You gave that snake Addison a horse. I suppose you're just a simple-minded, 'generous' kind of person. If I thought otherwise, I'd have to arrest you for attempted bribery." He winked and smiled. "So I appreciate it. Thank you very much."

I took a step toward his desk. "Guard," he said calmly, and the stocky corporal ran in with a rifle at port arms. "Show Mister Beatty out of camp." He leaned back with his hands folded across his stomach. "But feel free to call again, Mister Beatty, if I can be of further assistance."

I stomped out, boiling mad, and saw a private standing beside my horse, holding my reins in his hands. Water dripped from his garrison cap; he stifled a laugh. "For sure, come again, lad," the corporal said playfully as I snatched my reins from the private's hand. "We're your public servants, we aim to please." I heard him murmur something to the private and the two of them laughed as I rode away.

By the time I got back to Crofton, the rain had slowed to a drizzle; thin streaks of sunlight peeped through the low sky and sparkled like diamonds on the muddy street. I spun my reins around a hitch rail, splashed down in the mud, and over to the saloon. "There he goes," I heard the old man yell, "fightingest devil this side of hell."

Some of the town's men had taken time off from packing to tie the other two outlaws' bodies to a board and prop them against the front of a shack. Overnight, the rain-soaked bodies had turned the color of bruised fruit. "I see'd him kill all three, quicker than a goddamn rattlesnake!" the old man yelled.

"What happened?" Jack eyed me up and down as I walked in and dropped into a chair, slapping water from my hat. He sat riffling a deck of cards. Two grizzled old teamsters and the Catahoula cur came and peeped through the door as I pushed back my hat and stared straight ahead.

"...And that's it?" Jack shrugged after I told him about Trapp and the hundred dollars. "He just thanked you?"

"That's the whole of it," I said. "Called me simple-minded." I slapped my hand on the table.

Jack chuckled. "You've been called worse."

I stared at Jack. Two soldiers and a yellow-haired whore shot us a quick glance, then turned back to the bar. "All three," I heard the whore whisper. "Beat one to death with his pistol barrel."

Jack pitched the cards on the table. "Didn't he know it was a bribe?"

"You better believe he knew it." I rapped my fingers over and over on the tabletop. "I should've shot him."

"Yeah, I wish you had," Jack said. "Why stop with the Pope Gang, and C. W. Flowers, when you can stir up the whole federal army?"

"What's that supposed to mean?"

"It means you can cause more trouble in the shortest time than anybody I've ever seen." Jack took a deep breath that ended with a muffled laugh. "You've shot my sight-seeing plumb to hell."

I took a deep breath and stared at him. "Jack, none of it's my fault."

"I know, but let's just look at everything that 'ain't' your fault." He raised a finger. "You've killed Gyp Pope for stealing a stolen horse. Didn't just kill him . . . naw-sir . . . back-shot him, then stomped the hell out of him while he was dying. His brothers will feel *real* good about that."

"Jack, I didn't stomp—"

Jack raised a hand. "I know, but that don't matter. It looked like you did." He spit a stream of juice and raised another finger. "Then . . . you nearly tangled with one of the meanest bastards twixt hell and Texas—"

"You reckon that really is C. W. Flowers?"

"That's what Queenie said."

"Queenie?"

"Yeah, ain't that a pretty name?"

"What'd she say?"

"She said if you owed me any money, I oughta collect it real quick." Jack laughed, "God love 'em, that's all they think about, ain't it?" While Shod and I had spent the night in the livery barn washing off in the rain barrel, Jack had helped fix the tent and visited Queenie. Now he was clear-eyed and chipper, wearing a fresh-washed shirt. His hair was smartly parted and his smooth-shaved jaw smelled of witch hazel.

"I reckon," I said. "Do you think he'll hold any hard feelings?"

"Aw-yeah. According to Queenie, he'll be on you tighter than a wood tick. That's why you ain't welcome in the tent. He's the one that killed the Quince brothers, One-Eye Jake and Marvin. He brought back their heads in a gunnysack."

"Great. I feel a lot better—"

"Of course, he'll have to beat the Popes to you . . . according to Queenie." Jack spit, shook his head, and grinned.

"That's . . . *real* good. You all must've had just a wonderful conversation. I'm glad to see you're so cheerful about everything."

"Yeah, I told her you wasn't worried. I told her you're Wyatt Earp, leader of the Earp Gang."

"Well . . . Shod caused it all, riding into a gun battle just to see about them horses."

Jack shrugged. "Ain't that what we're paying him for—to look after the horses?"

"He should've used better sense."

"Then you oughta tell him so. Tell him next time you poke an empty gun in a bounty-man's face, to just keep his nose out of it."

I studied the tabletop for a second, then looked up at Jack. "Yeah, I reckon I can't say too much. He did real good, didn't he?"

"Yeah," Jack grinned. "I figured he would. That's why I favored hiring him." He tugged at the cuff of his clean shirt. "You didn't do too bad yourself. That was some good shooting 'til you run out of bullets. Course, it would've looked better on you if he'd been riding backwards . . . or you'd been standing in front."

I pictured Gyp Pope flying from his horse and rolling in the mud, same as I'd pictured it all night in my mind. "That was the strangest thing," I said, shaking my head. "I don't know how it happened. I ain't that good a shot."

"I know," said Jack, "I've seen you shoot." Cutting a fresh plug of tobacco, he shoved it into his jaw. "I'm surprised you didn't gun down a bunch of innocent bystanders."

"Now, wait a minute, Jack. I ain't *that* bad a shot." I stared out through the open door and watched sunlight glisten on the mud street. "Am I?" I snapped my eyes toward Jack.

"Are you what?" Jack spit a stream. He'd gazed off to the bar. The whore led the two soldiers out the back door, giggling and slapping them as they pawed at her.

"Am I that bad a shot?"

"You ain't the best, let's put it that way." Jack tugged at his clean collar and brushed a piece of lint from his shoulder.

"I dropped three, straight through his washboard, on a running horse. I'd like to know who could do any better."

"Uh-huh." Jack rolled the plug of tobacco around in his jaw. "That's it, get cocky about it . . . now that your shooting's been insulted. Yesterday you was dragging the bottom about killing him."

"I know, but he's dead . . . and I can't change it."

"But his brothers ain't." Jack held up a finger. "And somewhere along the line we're going to run into 'em. You can count on it. Them and C. W. Flowers."

I stared at him. "You got a problem with that?"

"Naw . . . what do I care?" He spit another stream. "But I'm wondering if we oughta pay Shod something extra from here on. We might be asking a lot of him."

"He took the job. He knew what it paid."

"It's just something we might wanta consider, is all. We're heading into some rough country with some long odds against us. I'd hate to lose a good gun over a half a dollar a day."

"You're not wanting to go, are you?" I studied Jack's face.

"It ain't the smartest thing we've ever done." He grinned and picked up the cards. "But it'll be something to talk about for a long time. I just don't want to go back to Missouri telling everybody how you got killed. It'd ruin my vacation."

I nodded. "Then offer him a dollar more."

"That's good, 'cause—"

I nudged Jack as I glanced up and saw Shod walk up to the door and stop. Jack looked around and motioned him in with a wave of his hand. "Hell with the army if they don't like it." Jack shot the bartender a hard frown; the bartender ducked his head and busied himself behind the bar as Shod walked over to the table.

"I checked on the horse Gyp Pope was riding," Shod said, sitting down at the table. "It's lame. And the other two horses kept going. They haven't been found. Someone evidently caught them and kept them." He looked back and forth between Jack and me. "I hate to tell you, but there are armed guards at the stable. They said we can't take the horses up to Kearny."

"Don't worry about them," I said. "I'll figure something out."

"You're kidding," Shod said with a puzzled smile.

Jack slid a clean glass across the table and filled it for Shod. Shod just stared at it as Jack took a drink from the bottle and passed it to me. I set it down and slid it to the middle of the table.

"We was just talking about what happened yesterday," Jack said to Shod. "About how it might get a little tense from here on."

"It certainly could," said Shod.

Jack nodded his head. "You were right in what you said last night. A half a dollar a day seems a little slim for what this could turn into."

"Are you offering me an increase in pay, or telling me I should be seeking other employment?"

"Whatever suits you. But if you ride out, you best travel by night and hide by morning. By now, you're the wild-eyed cannibal that helped kill Gyp Pope."

"And was ready to throw down on C. W. Flowers," I added.

Shod pushed his hat up his forehead with a puzzled look. "You're still determined to go?"

"Sure," I said, "why not?"

"They're holding the horses?" Shod leaned closer across the table, as if we were playing a guessing game.

"I'll figure something out."

Shod rubbed his chin and straightened his spectacles. "I still think we would be better off facing the Popes here. But obviously you're not going to listen."

"It ain't in our plans," I said.

He shook his head. "Of course not, I know ... your travel itinerary through an Indian war. I hope you remembered to bring fishing poles."

"I glanced between the two. "Like I said last night, you can go or stay."

"How much of an increase are we talking about?"

"Dollar a day." Jack rapped his knuckles on the table.

Shod smiled and pushed his spectacles up his nose. "Being educated doesn't mean I'm a fool, Mister Smith. I can bump horses for half a buck a day, but killing or being killed is worth a full share of the business . . . whatever business it is. Wouldn't you agree?"

I leaned forward and stared at Shod. "How long have you been putting this together?"

"Ever since I've been the last man on the bottle." Shod glanced at his whiskey glass, then back to me. "I gave it some careful consideration after our talk last night. I know there's more going on than taking a string of horses to Fort Kearny, and I don't buy the vacation story. You gentlemen couldn't be that stupid."

I squinted at Jack, and shook my head. Selling horses *was* all we'd planned on doing, that and maybe hitting a bank or two on our way home. I figured the vacation part was just Jack's way of making a little joke of it.

"If you want me to side with you, I'll side with you," Shod continued. "But let's stop talking about chicken feed. If I'm in, I'm in for a third." He glanced between the two of us. "And I want the conversation to quit changing every time I enter the room."

Jack and I glanced at each other. "We've seen you've got guts," said Jack. "Are you any good with a gun?" We both eyed him close.

"Yes." Shod's eyes didn't waver.

"And you don't mind killing?" I leaned forward.

"No . . . not if it's necessary."

"Then I reckon you're in," said Jack.

"Very well, gentlemen," he said. "Now, do you want to tell me what you were discussing when I came in?"

I pushed up my hat and looked across at him. "The weather," I said.

"That's more like it," Shod said with a grin, pushing his spectacles back up on his nose. He reached over, took the bottle from Jack's hand, turned back a shot, and passed it to me. Staring at him, I wiped my hand across the top, took a short sip, and handed it to Jack. Jack held the bottle up, gauged the remains, then turned it up and killed it.

◆ ＊ 4 ＊ ◆

As we started out of the saloon, the two old teamsters stepped through the doors with their ragged hats hanging from their hands. The Catahoula cur whined but stayed outside wiping the boardwalk with his wagging tail. "Begging ya pardon," said one of the teamsters. His scraggly head leaned almost against his shoulder. "We hear'd ya got horses for sale." His face was covered with hair, fear, and a streak of mud. "We's hoping maybe you'd help us out—"

"Riding horses," I said, cutting him off. "They're too expensive to be pulling freight."

I started around him, but his partner, a squat little feller with tobacco stains in his beard, stepped right before me. His lips trembled as he spoke up to me. "Mister, all I got is rolled up in that wagon, and we run our horses plumb to death getting here. Ya gotta sell us some . . . ya gotta." He threw back his coat with a rough and trembling hand, revealing a rusty pistol. "For I'll fight ya iffen I have ta."

"Easy now, feller." I raised a hand slowly between us and glanced between Jack and Big Shod. They kept from smiling. "I don't want to fight you, but them horses are promised to the army. Nothing I can do about it."

"Come on, Tack." His partner tugged at his sleeve. "We've played out our string. Reckon we'll die right cheer."

Shod smiled. "Don't worry, the army will get the two of you out of here."

"Mister." The one called Tack stepped toward Big Shod. "My woman's laying dead in that wagon . . . wrapped in a wet blanket." His voice quivered. "Reckon the army'll tote her back where I can bury her in a soft place? Fifty years, mister . . . *fifty."* His eyes filled; he started to break down. "I'll not watch 'em roll her in a ditch." His whole body shook. "Not as long as there's—"

"Hold it! Just hold everything." I tossed my hands and looked away—couldn't stand seeing the old feller shame himself. Wiping something from my eye, I turned back to Jack and Shod. "Reckon we can spare a couple of horses?"

"Certainly," Shod said quietly. Jack cleared his throat and nodded.

"Four," said Tack's partner. I looked him up and down. "It's a big wagon." He shrugged and leaned toward me in a whisper. "His woman's belongings and such . . ."

When we got to the livery barn, I cut out four of our horses, strung them together, and handed Tack's partner the rope. These horses would bring a hundred apiece from the army, but we'd settled on fifty just to help them out. "Lord bless you," said the old man as he wrapped the rope around his crusty hand.

"That'll be two hundred dollars," I said, with my hand out.

Tack fumbled inside his coat, pulled out twenty dollars, a pencil stub, and a wrinkled piece of paper.

"What's this?" I said, as he laid them in my hand.

"Put on there where you want us to send the money to, and we'll shore do it."

"On credit? Nobody mentioned credit . . ."

"I know," said Tack, "but God bless you for understanding."

"Alright," I said to Jack and Shod as the teamsters' wagon rolled away. "From now on, we only deal with the army . . . in cash. No more sad stories."

"I meant to tell you," Jack butted in. "I promised Queenie and the girls last night that we'd sell 'em enough horses to get them out of here."

I just stared at him.

"How many . . . for how much?" said Shod.

"Nine of 'em." Jack shrugged. "For a hundred apiece, same as we'd get from the army."

"That's okay," I said. "Beats taking them to Fort Kearny. But from now on, let's stick to the plan." We turned and headed back to the saloon.

"There he goes, folks," we heard the old man yell from behind us; I stopped and gritted my teeth. "Stalking the streets like a wildcat, ready to *kill* and *kill* again!"

Jack and Shod walked on as I snatched up a chunk of dried mud, spun around, and threw it at him. He ducked behind a woodpile, then stuck his head out with a bewildered look. "What'd I do?"

"Leave him alone . . . you murderer," a whore called out from the ragged tent.

"I feel like holding his head down in a water trough," I said, catching up to Jack and Shod.

"That would just prove his point," said Shod.

"What's wrong with him anyway?" Jack glanced back as we stepped up on the boardwalk. "Is he cussing you, or praising you, or what?"

"I don't know, but I swear he's driving me nuts!"

"You've certainly impressed him." Shod grinned. "You're lucky he doesn't play a guitar."

As soon as we stepped inside the saloon, six big fellers turned facing us from the bar. On the floor near their feet, a wild-eyed prisoner lay shackled to an iron ball. "Are you Beatty?" the tallest of the bunch asked. He wore a long fur coat, pulled open to show a pair of black-handled Walker Colts. A half-moon scar ran beneath his left cheek.

"Who's asking?" I felt Shod and Jack drift to the side as I took a step forward. The other men eyed us close. The one on the floor just stared with a crazy grin.

"Jake Howard, federal marshal." His left hand moved up and rested on the bar. He offered a firm smile from behind a drooping mustache. "I hear you've got horses for sale."

I glanced at Jack and Shod. There was no way I would sell stolen horses to a federal marshal, especially Long Jake Howard. "We've got a deal with the army to deliver them to Fort Kearny. They need them real bad." I was ready to flash the forged paperwork, but decided against it as I stepped closer to the bar.

"So do we . . . just as bad." He flipped out a leather bag and dropped it on the bar. "We've already looked them over. Name a price. We're taking eighteen just as quick as we can get them. Some for us and some for supplies."

"I'd like to help, but they're going to the army, and that's that."

"I said . . . name a price." His voice kicked up a notch and his men spread farther along the bar. Two of them stepped out in the middle of the floor. The bartender just remembered something he'd forgot out back.

I felt my hand tense beside my holster. "I told you—"

"Two hundred a head," I heard Queenie say as she stepped around from the door and shoved a wad of money in my shirt pocket. "There's the nine hundred I owe you for the horses—less expenses." She nodded toward Jack and winked.

We watched, slack-jawed, as Queenie stood at the bar and Jake counted out eighteen hundred dollars for "her" nine horses. "I still need nine more," said Jake, as Queenie stuffed the money up under her dress and walked past us with a smug grin.

I glanced at Jack and Shod. For two hundred a head, I'd sell horses to the devil in hell. After what Queenie just did to us, I felt I needed to make up the loss. "Okay," I said, letting out a breath. "Nine more at two hundred a head."

Long Jake nodded toward the door—"Go get the horses"—and the two men in the middle of the floor headed out for the livery barn.

I stepped to the bar. "Let me buy you fellers a drink," I said. Jack and Shod walked over beside me.

"No, thanks," said Jake, "we're in a hurry. Only idiots would hang around here." I watched him pick up the leather bag and shove it back inside his coat. "So you boys are headed for Fort Kearny?"

"That's right."

"You've got guts instead of brains. But I heard the railroad's passing the hat around, starting a *Kill the Injun* fund." Jake Howard shook his head. "I suppose they'll soon have Red Cloud stuffed and mounted." He flipped out a receipt book with a pencil stuck in it. I felt my stomach drop. "I gave her all the cash we can spare, but you won't need it where you're going." He started scribbling. "If any of you *ever* make it back alive, take this to any federal marshal's office ... identify yourself, and they'll pay you straightaway." I stood speechless as he folded the scrip and shoved it into my hand.

I heard the prisoner cackle out loud as they pulled him to his feet. Hefting the iron ball in his arms, he winked and laughed right in my face as they drug him away. I turned to the bar like a man in a trance. "Gentlemen," I heard Shod say softly. "I've been your partner for one day and already lost more money than I've *made* in the past two years."

I pulled out the money Queenie shoved in my pocket and spread it on the bar. "Expenses?" I shook my head slowly. "Jack, there's less than four hundred dollars here. You couldn't have spent that much."

Jack cleared his throat and folded his hands on the bar. "Horses ain't the only thing in short supply."

When we left the saloon that evening the rain had come and gone again, but the evening sky was still gunmetal gray and hanging low, still growling from the Big Horns like a galled bear. Water dripped from roofs and cut narrow streams through the mud street.

The Catahoula cur fell in beside us, walking slow and stiff-legged, growling with his hackles up and watching the other side of the mud street. "Hold it," I said, stopping Jack and Shod with my arms before we stepped off the boardwalk. "That dog's spooked about something." We spread out slowly along the boardwalk as the cur stooped low, ready to pounce toward a stack of nail kegs against the side of a shack. I nodded at Shod and Jack, drew my pistol, and stood in a crouch. "I know you're there, Flowers," I yelled across the street. "Show yourself and let's get at it."

I ducked as a shot spit past my head and slapped the front of the saloon. Before I could get off a round, the Catahoula sprang from the boardwalk with bullets kicking up mud around him. He tore across the empty street snarling like a crazed panther. We heard a scream and saw a gun sail past the dog's head as he charged through the pile of barrels, then disappeared down the alley, snapping at Flowers's back.

We stayed crouched with our pistols drawn and listened to a long fading scream and the echo of the growling dog. In a few seconds, the cur bounced out of the alley wagging his long tail, and pranced toward us with a bloody rag hanging from his mouth. In the distance we heard a sobbing voice fade away. "I'll get you for this. I'll kill you . . ."

I reached down to the dog—"Good boy"—and tried to take the rag. But he growled low and shook it, like a bullfighter waving a cape. "Easy, boy." I jumped back. "You keep it. It's all yours."

"Hear me, you bastard?" The sobbing voice sounded even farther away. "I'll kill you . . ."

A few faces poked out of doorways. The old man stuck his head out from behind the woodpile. "You," I shouted, "don't open your mouth!" I swung my gun, and he jerked back out of sight.

"Not a damn thing . . . that's what," the old man grumbled.

"Leave him alone, Earp, you murderer," said a voice from the ragged tent. I looked at Jack and he chuckled under his breath.

"See, Shod?" I waved my hand about the street. "See why I want out of here?"

As I spoke to Shod, I noticed a big feller step down from a wagon and start across the mud street. I paid no attention until he stopped fifteen feet away and started rolling up his shirtsleeves. "So you're Earp." His forearms looked like fence posts. "You're the coward that beat my uncle Andy to death with a pistol butt."

"My goodness," Shod said under his breath. "What is it about you?"

"I ain't Earp," I said, raising a hand to stop him from coming forward.

"I heard what that whore called you." He stood cracking his knuckles.

"That's a joke," I said, "just a joke . . ."

"Step on out here." He cracked his knuckles louder. "We'll laugh about it together."

"Kill 'im, Wyatt," yelled the old man. "Goddamn 'im! Kill 'im with'n your bare hands!"

He started forward and I threw my hand to my gun. "Don't do it, mister. It's all a mistake, but I'll kill you, so help me." There was no way I'd go toe to toe with this thick-backed ape.

He stopped and turned all the way around to show he wasn't armed. "It's man to man, Earp. Your big gun ain't going to help you this time. I'm taking a piece of your skull back to my poor aunt Mildred."

"This is crazy," Jack growled, and spit. "Shoot him. We'll blame it on Earp."

The big ape stepped forward. Seated beside me, I heard the Catahoula cur growl low, his voice muffled by the rag in his mouth. "Alright, mister, I tried warning you." I threw my arm up, pointing straight at him. "Sic him, boy!" I yelled to the dog.

"Oh no," I heard Shod say as the bony cur sprang straight up and hit the street running with his hackles raised and his teeth shining. The bloody rag flew up in the air.

Wide-eyed, the big ape froze for a second as the cur came toward him with a long string of saliva flying back from its fangs. Then he jumped to the side as the cur shot past him, out across the street with a vicious growl, and disappeared through the alley. A terrible howl echoed back to us; I stood dumbstruck.

"I hope that wasn't your best plan," said Jack. "Now he's really pissed off."

"Hell with it." I started to draw my pistol and drop him, but I heard a rifle cock in the alley beside the saloon.

"Everybody freeze up," said Long Jake Howard as he and his deputies reined slowly out of the alley and spread out in the middle of the street. "We heard shots. What's going on here?"

I felt a large drop of rain fall on my hand as I let it drift away from my pistol. I let out a tense breath. "Marshal, this feller thinks I'm Wyatt Earp. I didn't want to kill him, but—"

"And I'm not even armed," said the big ape, raising his hands waist-high. Rain began pelting the street like silver darts.

"What about the shooting I heard?" The marshal looked up at the rain. Lightning winked and disappeared above us. Thunder followed.

"Well, Marshal, that's a whole other thing. That was C. W. Flowers trying to shoot me for killing Gyp Pope yesterday."

Long Jake stared at me with a puzzled expression. Rain dripped from his flat-brimmed hat. "You shot Pope in the back, then kicked him to death. Now you're fixin' to gun down an unarmed man?"

"He sicced a dog on me, too," said the big ape. I watched his hair fall wet against his forehead. His shirt clung to his thick shoulders.

Jake Howard shot him a glance, then back to me. "Have you ever been in a fair fight?" His deputies stifled their laughter and huddled against the downpour.

"Now, damn it, Marshal!" I pointed my finger up at him. He calmly lowered his rifle in my face. Water ran down the small of my back.

"Don't raise your voice to me," he said politely. "I'm a living legend."

"So is this coward," said the ape. "But look at him. He won't step out here face-to-face—"

"Go away," said Jake Howard. "This isn't Wyatt Earp."

The ape pointed a thick finger, "He's been claiming to be."

"Excuse me, Marshal." Shod stepped forward. "May I say something here?" He visored his hand above his spectacles against the pounding deluge.

"Of course not," said the marshal with a patient smile. "You better stay real quiet." He reached and flipped up his collar; water dripped from his nose as he turned back to me. "Are you impersonating Wyatt Earp?"

"No, Marshal. Somebody made a little joke about it, is all."

"Earp will be real happy to hear you're making little jokes about him." He uncocked his rifle and laid it across his lap. "We can't even leave town without running into some kind of crap." He nodded skyward. "Now, more of this."

Beside me, I heard Quiet Jack turn and walk back toward the saloon. I looked around just as Marshal Howard called out, "You there. Where do you think you're going?"

Jack turned slowly outside the saloon door. "I can't swim," he said, holding out his hand and letting water run off his palm. "I'm getting out of this."

"Maybe you don't understand," said Marshal Howard, raising his rifle toward Quiet Jack. "I'm still talking here."

"Maybe *you* don't understand," said Jack. "I've got enough sense to get in out of the rain. If you need me, I'll be inside where it's dry."

I took a slow step from between the two of them as their eyes met and locked across the boardwalk. For a second, a dead silence hung above us, save for the growl of thunder and the pounding rain. Then Marshal Howard's thumb slid back across his rifle hammer.

Jack's eyes narrowed; a peaceful grin twitched at his lips. "Cock that hammer, Long Jake, and I'll put your *legend* to sleep."

The deputies seemed to stop breathing. Long Jake sat tense, like a coiled viper. His hat brim drooped from the weight of the water. "What's your name, young man?"

"I don't use one," said Jack. He nodded upward. "And I ain't gonna stand here and drown explaining why."

"Want me to straighten him out, boss?" said a deputy.

"Shut up," the marshal said, seeing something in Jack's eyes that told him not to push it. Jack stepped away slowly and through the saloon door.

"Just watch him," said Long Jake, and the deputy slid from his wet saddle and walked slow toward the door. The prisoner sat on his horse holding his iron ball on his lap, staring straight up in the rain and grinning like a fool.

"I reckon he's right." Marshal Howard smiled cautiously and slung water from his hand.

I let out a breath and wiped my hand across my face. "Marshal, same as yourself, I'm just trying to leave town. You know I'm heading up to Fort Kearny. We ain't broke any law, and we ain't looking for no trouble."

"Who's your friend?" He nodded toward the saloon.

"Like he told you. He don't care for names. Now, we ain't done nothing—"

"Marshal," said Shod, "if you'll permit me—" We heard a quick slap and a heavy thud from just inside the saloon door.

"Both of you shut up," said the marshal. We watched as Jack stepped from the saloon with the deputy's arm looped across his shoulder. A trickle of blood ran from a knot on the deputy's forehead, and his legs were trying to walk in every direction. Jack walked him to his horse and hefted him up into his saddle. We all just watched. Thunder jarred the earth.

"I told you where I'd be," said Jack, above the relentless downpour. "There was no cause to send him in. It was rude of ya."

"He's knocked ole Greasy cold as a wedge," said a deputy. The prisoner laughed out loud.

Long Jake held up a hand. "Everybody be still."

Jack walked back inside the saloon. The deputy wobbled in his saddle with bloody water running from his chin. "You're lucky I'm in a hurry," said Jake, shoving his dripping rifle into his scabbard. "I'm sure if I looked, I'd find your pictures somewhere." His duster tails clung to his horse's flanks. "But since you haven't broke any laws that I know of—"

"What about hitting ole Greasy?" said a deputy.

"—and you did sell us some fine horses. I'm letting you go. Now, get on up to Powder River. The quicker somebody kills you, the better off we'll all be." A bolt of lightning hung for a second above us, writhed like a golden snake, then shot down behind a wooden shack beyond the big ragged tent. Thunder followed it as if to drive it into the earth.

"What about ole Greasy?"

"Shut up," snapped the marshal. "Don't you realize, everybody and their brother will be out to kill these idiots." He turned back to me and tipped his hat. Water poured. "No offense."

◆ ✳ 5 ✳ ◆

Night had fallen by the time the storm passed. Now the dark damp air felt gentle but crisp as I watched Shod take out a pair of gloves, push them over his hands, and pull them tight with his teeth. "We came here to take horses to Kearny," I said, "and from here on, that's what we're going to do . . . nonstop." I looked back and forth between Jack and Shod. We stood beside a plank shack and watched the flicker of an oil lamp through the cracked door of the livery barn. "Now, let's get out of this miserable mud hole while we've still got enough horses to ride and enough sense to know how to ride them."

We crept near the edge of the corral and looked around for the guards. "I hope this Queenie isn't setting us up," Shod whispered.

"She's charged us ten horses," I said, clinching my teeth. "She better not be."

"If you can't trust a whore," said Jack, "who can you trust?"

I glanced at him; he was serious.

"Perhaps we could have bribed them," said Shod, not knowing what had happened with Trapp.

"Bribery is a tricky business," I said, shooting Jack a glance. "Trust me."

We slipped into the large corral among our herd of horses, and as Jack and Shod let down the rail gates, I eased up and peeped through a cracked door. One soldier lay passed out in a pile of hay, naked as sin. Beside him a young whore sat buttoning her dress, quietly humming a tune. Two empty whiskey bottles lay beside her. She must've seen my shadow stir at the door, because she looked toward me and held her finger to her lips.

I leaned back from the door as she slipped out. It was the yellow-haired whore I'd seen in the saloon. "The other two are passed out in the hayloft," she said. "Queenie and Vera are with them. You must be Wyatt Earp. We've heard all about you. Vera is dying to meet you, but Lucy says you're cold-blooded. Is it true?"

I glanced around and watched Jack and Shod slipping the horses from the corral and gathering them a few yards away. "Don't be spreading it around," I whispered. "I'm touchy about it. Besides, I'm not supposed to be here."

"Okay." She smiled, then leaned closer. "We're lucky we got our horses from you earlier today."

"Why's that?"

"They just put that up a little while ago." She pointed to a warning notice nailed to the side of the barn, and giggled as she slipped back through the door. I turned and snapped it down. It said: "These horses are the confiscated property of the United States Army. Any attempt to remove them without written authorization will be considered an act of theft against the federal government; and the perpetrator or perpetrators will be prosecuted by a military court, to the fullest extent of the law."

"I'll be damned," said Jack. "We just stole those horses . . . for the second time . . . what's left of them."

"This ain't right!" I snatched the notice back from his hand and wadded it up as we led the string out across the swollen creek behind Crofton.

"It's within their legal authority," Shod said, riding up. "If the government needs them in a time of crisis—"

"There ain't a thing right about *confiscating* a man's horses, crisis or not." I pulled my hat low on my forehead. "It's just another word for plain thievery."

Jack chuckled and gigged his horse forward. Thirty yards away, the Catahoula cur slinked along with us, sniffing from tree to tree just inside the woods line as we made our way through the dark wet night. His back looked straighter now that we'd left town.

By the time we'd gone twenty miles, the sky overhead had turned deep and clear; a quarter moon shone bright from within a purple dome. Another ten miles and I heard tall dry grass swish against our horses' legs. When we stopped near morning, the ground was firm and dry, turning to rock and sprinkled with clumps of buffalo grass. We did not sleep, but instead, sipped coffee and rested our horses until a thin sliver of sunlight split the eastern sky. When we started to push on, I saw the Catahoula cur dart in and out of our string of horses like a sergeant readying troops for a field march. "Reckon he thinks he's on the payroll," Jack said, as we mounted up. "Or maybe he just likes bossing something around."

By noon we came upon a family of settlers in a rickety wagon headed the opposite direction. The man's eyes were red-rimmed and shiny with fear. A tired-looking woman sat close behind him with a shotgun cradled in one arm and a curly-headed baby nursing her breast in the other. Three more kids gathered near her skirt. Flies swarmed in a wavering stench of warm milk and wet diapers.

"Cut his mules loose, and stick a couple horses against the wagon." I just let out a long breath and shook my head. "I reckon if we're giving 'em away to preachers, whores, and lawmen . . ."

The settler threw back a drink from one of our canteens and passed it quickly over his shoulder. Water trickled through his beard. Shod cut away sharp toward our string of horses.

"Lord God . . . I don't know how to thank you, mister," said the man's trembling voice. His mules staggered from exhaustion as Jack started unhitching them. "We was just going to go till they dropped, then walk from there. Far as I know, we're the last ones out."

"What kept you?" I said. "Didn't you know Red Cloud is on a killing spree?"

"Had a short spread up off the Bozeman—nineteen head of cattle. Now they're gone. We're lucky to be alive. If it weren't for the woman and youngins, I'd stay and fight 'em off." He shook his head and stared at his worn-out boots. "I just couldn't bear to leave . . . just couldn't . . ." The woman's rough hand came up over the seat and rested on his arm. He patted her hand and slid down to help Jack and Shod hitch up a fresh team.

I took a round of dried shank and a canteen of water from our supplies, walked over and pitched them up on the wagon seat.

"This'll get you to Crofton," I said. The youngins stared at me, wide-eyed, like a litter of dumb rabbits. The baby turned from the moist breast with a toothless laugh as the woman ran her finger across its chin, wiped a streak of milk, and stuck it in its mouth without looking up. I shook my head. "Settlers . . ."

"We always got along with the Sioux 'til the army started building that blasted fort," I heard him telling Jack and Shod as I gazed out across the stretch of grassland. This was big country. I saw why the government wanted it, and why Red Cloud wouldn't give it up. "I figured when Red Cloud just told us to leave instead of killing us right off, maybe there was a chance of staying." He shook his head. "I sure figured wrong. Now that Dull Knife's Cheyenne is riding with him, Red Cloud has given 'em free run. They've gone plumb loco." He chafed the back of his neck with a rough hand. "I can't figure it out. We'd been friends with Red Cloud and his bunch for the longest time. We traded coffee and beef to them for the *longest* time."

"They're telling you that you ain't welcome here anymore," I said. "Is that too hard to understand?" As soon as I said it, I regretted it. I saw the hollow desperation in his eyes. He swallowed hard.

"The Injuns don't want us up here. The folks back east don't want us there. You tell me, mister. How's a man s'posed to scrape up enough to fill his youngins' bellies? We got to live somewhere."

I stared at him in an awkward silence and listened to the flies buzzing. "I know," I said quietly. "You have to overlook me. We just came out of Crofton. It's a madhouse." I offered a smile.

"I know how you feel." He let out a long tired breath. "I don't do well in that town myself. Rains every time I'm there. What brings ya'll up here anyhow?" He gazed across our string of horses.

"Business," I answered.

"We're tourists," I heard Shod say under his breath. Jack chuckled.

"We're taking horses to Fort Kearny." I shot a hard glance toward Jack and Shod.

The settler tried to smile. "So ya'll ain't exactly welcome here either."

"No, but we're just here on business. We ain't getting in nobody's way."

"Well, they'll kill you . . . that's what," said the settler. "If you think Red Cloud will stand still for you taking horses to the army, you're crazy. You see how he's drove us out, and we're neighbors." He shook his head. "He'll skin you fellers alive."

"Thanks for the warning, but we'll be alright." I saw Shod slap the exhausted mules on the rump. They staggered away. "It ain't my place to say so, but you'd do well to take your family south. You've got better odds at getting rich on a New Orleans gaming table than you do at staying alive up here."

"You might be right," said the settler, finishing up with the horses. "But we'll be back as soon as it's over, just like everybody else. Once they all kill each other off, one way or the other, we'll be coming."

That evening we came upon three horsemen in buckskins and they circled wide as they passed us. Their horses were loaded with battered mining gear. "You staring at us . . . hunh? Are ya?" One yelled, his voice hissing like a snake as his hand went to his holster. I heard Jack and Shod cock the rifles across their laps, but the three men rode on without taking their eyes off us. Their eyes looked the same as the settler's, red-rimmed and tortured by fear. "Think you're something, don't 'cha?" yelled one, pointing at our horses. "They'll make quick work of your *fine* horses."

"Don't stare at us, goddamn ya!" said another. But we watched until they rode out of sight. One of them slumped in the saddle; an arrow stub stuck from his back in a circle of dried blood.

"There's a real unhappy bunch," I said. "I'm surprised we didn't have to fight 'em."

Jack chuckled. "I'm surprised you didn't give 'em some horses."

"No more charity and no more bargains, Jack. And we better keep a close eye. Anything we run into from here on will be the last devils thrown out of hell."

When we pitched camp, we tended a low fire and took two-hour turns at keeping watch. Like the old guerilla days, we staked our string of dealing stock ten yards away and slept sitting up with the reins to our riding horses in our hands.

At midnight Jack nudged me with his boot. I stood up, wrapped my blanket around me, and walked over to the edge of camp, just out of the dim firelight. Jack stepped beside me with a hot cup of coffee. I leaned against a tree and sipped it. "Something's stirring about a hundred yards out," he said in a low whisper. "They've moved closer past ten minutes."

"Why didn't you wake us?" I whispered.

"No hurry."

"No hurry? Jack, I've got a bounty-man and a gang of killers to worry about, not counting that we're in Indian country here."

"It ain't Indians."

"You don't know that, Jack." I glanced around the campsite. "Reckon it could be that dog?"

"Naw . . . he's with the horses, spread out on his back with his pecker pointing to heaven."

"Then it has to be Indians."

"Huh-uh." Jack shook his head.

"How the hell do you know?" I was starting to get put out with Jack's cavalier attitude.

" 'Cause if it was, I wouldn't have heard them."

"That's great, Jack. That's the kind of craziness that gets a feller killed." I took a couple quick sips and pitched the coffee from the cup. "If we're lucky, it's only Flowers or the Pope Gang."

"You're really starting to worry too much," Jack chuckled under his breath. "You need to relax." We listened into the woods surrounding us. "See what I mean?" he whispered. "It's the sound of one rider, two at most."

He was right. The sound was low, steady, and coming from one direction. I glanced at Jack and nodded my head. He knew what to do.

For the next half hour I leaned against the tree and listened to the sound grow closer. When the sound stopped I slid quietly down the tree and listened to the silence, hoping Jack was right about it not being Indians. We'd had run-ins with hostiles down in the Indian Nations, back during the war, but nothing like this.

Up here it was Sioux and Cheyenne, enough of them to have the army tiptoeing around Montana, and enough to impede the laying of track for the largest railroad in the world. At least that's the way it read in the newspapers. Red Cloud's warriors had grown steadily in numbers, and he'd served notice: This was his hunting ground and all whites would leave or die. Here I sat, white as last Christmas.

Deep down I knew I had no business being here, heading farther into this dangerous place from which sane and decent folks had already fled; but it seemed that the more I saw others leaving—going the other way as fast as their fear would carry them—the more intent I became on seeing why. I felt like a man fascinated by fire and drawn closer and closer to the flames. I knew it could hurt me, but I had to touch the heat and feel it burn.

I couldn't ask for a better partner than Jack Smith when it came to nerve or handling a gun. Nobody could outshoot him, at least nobody ever had, and nobody could outnerve him . . . nobody at all. We'd taken on Big Shod as a hired hand, and I knew nothing about him except he was big enough to shoulder an ox. We'd hired him six weeks ago coming out of Nebraska Territory—another of Jack's ideas. Now he was a full partner.

The second I sensed something stir beside me, I started to swing my rifle around. But I froze as the cold barrel of a forty-four pressed below my ear. "Got-cha!" growled a rough voice as he stepped around before me. From beneath his frayed hat brim, I saw his eyes dart toward the campfire, then back to me. Big Shod still sat wrapped in his blanket with just the top of his hat sticking out. Jack's blanket lay piled on the ground. "Where's the other man?" the voice growled low.

I stared straight into his shadowed eyes. "He's about four feet behind you getting ready to shoot your head off."

His eyes narrowed as if I might be bluffing. But before he could say a word, Jack stepped from the brush behind him and tapped him on the head with his rifle barrel. "See how it works?" I said. Reaching real slow, I started to push his gun away. He held firm.

"No!" he said in a louder voice. "Here's how it works." I glanced out the corner of my eye to see if Big Shod had stirred. He sat still as stone. I wondered if he would wake up when the bullets started flying. "Kermit!" he growled over his shoulder and behind Jack, "Blow his head off!" He spread an ugly smile across bad teeth as he cocked his pistol. Behind him, Jack chuckled under his breath. Behind Jack the woods lay silent. "Kermit, damn it, boy," the man said, wanting to look behind him. Still no sound except Jack's dark laughter.

"Last I saw your friend," said Jack, "his boots were flapping two feet off the ground, and a big old feller was holding him up by the throat."

The ugly smile faded and the man's jaws went slack. "Aw-hell," he said. His voice sounded ready to apologize for some slight mistake. He offered no resistance as I took the gun from his hand.

"Goddamn it," he whined, "I ain't had no luck in the longest time. Now I reckon you'll kill me, won't you?"

"I reckon so," I said, pointing his gun against his chest.

He sighed and shook his head. "I knowed it, by God, I just knowed it."

Big Shod walked in from the brush with a skinny young feller hanging from his hand. The feller gagged and wiggled like a fish on a line. "What do you suggest I do with this one?"

I glanced toward the campfire. Big Shod's blanket still sat propped up, like he was sleeping with his rifle across his lap. It'd even fooled me.

"Aw, mister, don't kill him," the voice before me pleaded. "He's just a kid. He was just doing what I told him to. I swear to God."

"Yeah," I said as Jack stepped around beside me, "but you sure came in here to kill us. Now, be a man about it."

"Aw, mister, I couldn't have killed you. There ain't a bullet in that gun."

"Oh, really." I recocked the hammer and pulled the trigger right against his chest. Nothing. It just snapped on an empty chamber. I shrugged and lowered the gun.

"See?" he said. "We're just so hungry, we had to try something. My boy Kermit has one shell in his shotgun, but we wouldn't have killed nobody if we could've kept from it."

I nodded to Big Shod. He turned loose of the boy's throat, and the boy fell to the ground like a bundle of rags. Jack reached out a hand and patted the old man's coat for any weapons. "See?" said the old man. "Clean as a whistle." He seemed proud to have told the truth.

"Where's your stores," asked Jack, "and your horses?"

"Got neither," he said. "Indians picked us clean over the past winter. All we got's an old mule we rode in on."

Jack glanced at me and managed a serious expression. "We can use a good mule."

"Aw, come on now, mister, please don't kill us," the old man wailed. The young man sat rubbing his throat and staring wide-eyed.

"How've you managed to stay alive?" I asked, gazing between the two of them. "Why haven't the Indians killed you both?"

The boy, Kermit, struggled to his feet, and Big Shod patted him for weapons. The kid looked up at Big Shod the way a man looks up at a grizzly bear.

"We've stayed ahead of them," said the old man. "This is big country, and I know it well. It's hard to get caught as long as you keep quiet. Besides, they didn't try too hard. Things weren't so bad 'til the army started building that blasted fort. That's when Red Cloud went nuts . . . sent out Crazy Horse and the warriors." He looked at each of us. "You're not after the bounty on Red Cloud, are ya?"

"Bounty?" I glanced at Jack and Shod.

"That's ridiculous," Shod said. "There's no such thing."

Jack shot the old man a dark smile. "I better go get *my* new mule," said Jack.

The old man's shoulders dropped; he shook his bowed head. "Mister, please, you don't have to kill us."

I glanced between Jack and Shod; they just stared with no expression as the old man fell to his knees and threw his hands to his face. His hat fell off; he shuddered. "Alls we was doing is trying to stay alive here. I've never harmed a soul. I do right by everybody—I just got no luck. Don't kill us for *that*—"

The Catahoula appeared out of nowhere, sniffed the old man's leg, and growled. "Easy now . . ." I patted the dog's head. A dark stain ran down the old man's leg, and he babbled and wailed as I pulled him to his feet. *"Jesus,"* I said, stepping back to stay dry. His boy, Kermit, stared wide-eyed between Big Shod and the Catahoula cur.

Jack picked up the old man's hat, shoved it against his chest, then smiled at me. "Last devils thrown out of hell?"

Part II
Cowboys and Indians

6

Now that I'd shaken the mud of Crofton off my boots and was able to do some clearer thinking, I realized that fear and self-interest had turned the town a little crazy. Craziness showed itself in the eyes and actions of everybody I met, but while I was there, I was standing too close to see it. While I was in it, I was no different from the rest. Now that I was out, it was clear as a bell. Crofton was the place rats swam to from the sinking ship. It was that point of a terrible nightmare where the sleeper realizes he has to wake up or die.

Nobody wanted to think it or say it, but the United States government with all its military resource was on the verge of losing a war within its own borders; losing it to a bunch of ragged Indians on wild ponies. It was unthinkable, unspeakable, yet deep down everybody knew it; it was the core of the craziness, and Crofton lay at the edge of reason, like a wounded coyote snapping at its own guts.

I never saw a man work as hard and talk as much as Ben Bone. His son, Kermit, was a fair hand at wrangling horses. Anytime I wanted him to work a little harder, I put him with Big Shod. He seemed real impressed that Shod had plucked him up by his throat and held him there for nearly a half hour. Old Ben must've figured the more he talked, the better we would like him. I never told him we wouldn't kill him and his boy, so he never shut up.

We'd fed them that night, telling them it was their last meal. They ate like they believed it. The rest of the night, whoever was standing watch would walk past the tree where we kept them tied and point a cocked gun at them. We would stand there awhile like we still hadn't made up our mind. It was cruel, I reckon, but they had come upon us at gunpoint. We owed them something.

Fact is, except for the circumstances, I was glad we ran into Ben and Kermit Bone. Ben knew the country and said he spoke Sioux. Since the rest of us didn't know either, I decided to keep them along and watch them close. When we got to Powder River, it was Bone who guided us through the long stretches of quicksand. We didn't lose a single horse.

"Here's how it works," I told old Ben the evening we made the Powder River crossing. "You carry your guns, I'll carry the bullets." Jack and Big Shod had gone with Kermit to tend our stock. I watched Ben work up a low fire and break out cooking utensils. The sound of the river rushed behind us.

"That's just fine," old Ben started in. "Nothing suits me better. I trust your judgment on that more'n I do my own. I was just saying to Kermit how much—"

"You can ease off the *bull*," I said. His babbling was starting to get on my nerves. "If you do well leading us to Fort Kearny, I reckon we won't kill you."

"Sure enough?" Ben let out a breath and sat on a pile of driftwood. "You know, I feel real bad about me and Kermit doing what we did. It ain't like us at all."

I just squinted and nodded my head. "This country makes a man do peculiar things," he went on. "I just wish we'd met up with you boys sooner. If me and Kermit had been with you to begin with, you wouldn't had to hire that . . . you know."

"No," I said, "I don't know." Old Ben kept an open ear for anything that might get him inside our personal business. We saw it, but never let on. The night before, he'd asked where Jack and I were from. We both lied. I'd said Alabama; Jack said Pennsylvania.

"That black boy," said Ben. "You being a southerner, I know you can't have much use for the likes of him."

"He does his job," I said. "He's my . . . partner."

"I ain't butting in," said Ben Bone, "but I can't see the two of you lasting long as partners. I reckon your other partner, the *Yankee*, must've brought him in."

Ben was picking at anything he could find. Jack Smith was really from New Jersey, not Pennsylvania. He'd come from an upstanding

Northern family. Why he'd hooked up with Quantrill's guerilla forces and fought for the South was anybody's guess. But he and I had spilled blood together and saved each other's hide more than once. There was no room for Ben Bone to fester anything between Quiet Jack and me. But Big Shod was a whole other thing.

I wasn't about to admit it, but Ben was partly right. I didn't like taking Shod in as a partner. I don't know why. I hadn't even favored hiring him, but once he joined us, I accepted it. Now, if Ben Bone could see a distance between me and Shod, I had to wonder if Shod saw it too.

"Don't concern yourself with my business, Mister Bone. I can always change my mind about turning you loose at Fort Kearny."

Old Ben sprang up from the pile of driftwood and busied himself with the coffeepot. "I shouldn't brought it up, naw-sir . . . I knowed I shouldn't."

"Tell me what you know about the Pope Gang." I motioned toward the driftwood and he sat back down, slowly.

"The Pope Gang?" His eyes narrowed and turned wary. "You ain't got no business with that bunch, do you? You ain't no kin, are ya?"

"Just curious." I shrugged, not wanting to slant any information he might have. I'd seen that Bone could change direction quicker than a Kansas twister.

"Well, they're a damn rough bunch. I'll tell you. Not that I'm talking bad of them, you understand, not if they're your friends or kinfolk."

"They're neither. I'm just curious about them."

He let out a breath. "Tell you the truth, they're some mean sons a bitches. They've stayed alive up here with all that's going on. That tells you something."

"They're on terms with the Sioux?"

"Naw, they're just bad enough to hold their own, and the Sioux are cowardly without the odds in their favor. Red Cloud's warriors would run from a dead bulldog, in my opinion."

"Well, they've sure impressed the hell out of Washington."

Bone raised a finger. "If the government had any sense, they would come through here and not leave an Indian standing. I mean kill 'em all, bucks, squaws, papooses, the lot of 'em. Indians are low cowardly, lying, cheating—" He stopped and raised a finger. "And the Sioux is the lowest of all." He thumbed himself on the chest. "I know. I've tried dealing with 'em. They're lazier than a Mex and dumber than a darky."

"Hey! My mama's a Mexican." I heard a slurred voice in the brush behind me and spun up with my pistol drawn and cocked. Bone disappeared down into the driftwood.

"That's right," said another voice. "And my pappy's a—"

"Hold it there!" I glanced around for Jack and Shod as two drunks came stumbling out of the brush, leading their horses.

"Hold it right there!" I pointed my gun, but they just staggered closer. One reached for his gun and missed, pulled his suspender loose and almost fell. His trousers dropped on one side. The other stepped back and pointed at his friend, reared back and cackled like a fool. "Did you—did you see that? You scared Run-around half out of his britches." I heard Jack and Shod running from up the trail. They came sliding to a stop with their guns drawn. Kermit peeped around from behind a tree.

"Look, Harvey," said the fat one, holding his trousers up with one hand and holding his reins and a gallon jug in the other. "We've caught 'em in a bad mood."

"Who the hell are you? How the hell did you get in here?" I shot Jack and Shod a cold look. They shrugged.

"Awww, we've gone and star-artled you," the lanky one belched as he wobbled forward. "I'm Harvey Kid Cull. This here is Run-around Joe Philipé. His mama really is Mexican, but my pappy ain't no . . . you know"—he glanced at Shod and almost turned sober—"colored gentleman." Shod smiled and lowered his rifle. Jack walked up and motioned to the jug.

"Help yourself, shore-nuff." Run-around hefted the jug to Jack and almost fell again. His horse jerked sideways. Jack caught him by the arm and steadied him.

"Damn, boys," Jack chuckled, "how do I get to where you're at?"

"Huh-uh, Jack," I said. "We've too much going on to—"

Jack threw back a long gurgling drink. When he lowered the jug, his eyebrows pinched together across his nose. A dark blue shadow started at his forehead and drew down his face like a window shade. His mouth fell open. "Whoa-Lord-God!" He caught his breath and blew it out. "This stuff would make a jackrabbit spit in a rattlesnake's eye."

"Let me see that a second." I reached for the jug. Shod shook his head.

"I don't know," Jack chuckled, "we've got a lot going on."

"Just a taste." I grinned.

"Watch it," Cull said, his face split in a one-toothed grin. "It's made from bull-juice and melted hammerheads."

Shod stepped forward. "Surely to goodness you're not—"

I tossed back a short swallow and felt my knees jerk. Through a watery veil, I saw Ben Bone stand up slowly from the pile of driftwood and venture forward. "Give me that," said Shod, "before you spill it."

"Hits everybody in a different spot," Cull cackled. "I saw a man's ears fold over once."

"Who are you people?" My voice sounded like it was squeezed through a straw.

Shod sniffed the jug. "Whew." His eyes watered. He threw back a drink.

"We come up from Texas or somewhere. Just run a herd up to Montany with the Reedleman drive. We're the only ones to get a herd through all summer."

"Shore did," said Run-around Joe. "We's tougher than a boot full of rocks."

I glanced at Shod. He held the jug against his chest and tried breathing deep. His eyes looked like a Holy Roller who'd just seen Jesus; his spectacles dangled crooked on his nose.

"Now we're gonna stay drunk 'til hell wouldn't have us." Cull reached for the jug.

"Shore am." Run-around nodded.

"Haven't you had any trouble with Red Cloud?"

Bone eased up close to Kid Cull, grinned, and nodded to the jug. "Get out'n here, ya got-dawn weasel!" Cull stomped his foot and Bone jumped back. "Not a lick of trouble out'n Red Cloud." He grinned. "Shot at a couple outlaws trying to carve out a steak.

They're so hungry up there, they'd eat the ass out of a running wildcat."

Run-around Joe stepped forward and almost fell. He looked all around. "Don't Red Cloud live around here?"

"Come on," I said, motioning toward the pile of driftwood, "let's get some coffee."

Jack grinned and shook his head. "Cowboys . . ."

We sat around the low flame, sipping coffee and listening to our stomachs growl. Both Kid Cull and Run-around Joe had passed out on the driftwood while we cooked a pot of beans and tried to eat. When Kid Cull woke up, he raised the lid on the beans with a shaking hand, turned stark white around the eyes, then lowered it with a nervous rattle. "Here," I said quietly, nodding to the coffee-pot, "try this first."

He had to use both hands to pick up the metal cup. To keep him from scalding himself, I took the cup, filled it, and after trying to hand it to him twice, I set it down near his feet and let him pick it up best he could. After a couple of sips, he rubbed his face and nodded toward Run-around Joe. "Is he dead?"

I grinned. "Naw, just sleeping."

"That's just as good, poor ole boy."

I glanced at Jack. He just shrugged with a puzzled look.

Cull took another sip. "He's knocked up some whore down at Sugar-Kay Bartlett's. Then his pa got kicked in the nuts by a red bull. They talk like he'll never straighten up all the way—" He stopped and looked around as if struck by some revelation. "Say, who are ya'll anyway?" His shaking hand slipped toward his holster.

"It's alright," I said. "You fellers just staggered in and passed out on us. No problem."

"Thank God. For a second I thought you's Injuns."

"Speaking of Indians," said Shod. "How have you two managed to stay alive?"

He shrugged. "I don't know, just drunk, I reckon. I don't really drink too often. But him with that whore pumped up and his pa packing his balls in a water bucket . . . I just felt sorry for him, poor sum-bitch, I oughta kill him. He spent his money and mine on fifteen gallons of 'wonderful stuff.' Got it buried in the rocks out yonder. Now we can't go home 'til it's gone. My wife and baby's waiting in Texas or somewhere without a pot to piss in, and I got seven dollars to show for the summer." He took a sip. "Ya'll from around here?"

"Missouri," I said. "We're running a string up to Fort Kearny."

He shook his head and made a trembling one-toothed grin. "Then ya'll is crazier than us. Least we're drunk and can't help it."

I grinned, and saw Shod shake his head. "Why don't you sober up and light out of here? This ain't the place to be right now, drunk or sober."

"Hell, I know it. But we can't go 'til we've drunk up the whiskey. That'd be like throwing away our pay."

"How much you want for a couple canteens of that ole door-slammer?" Jack leaned forward with a smile.

"Jack . . ."

"It's my vacation," Jack chuckled. "The hell you expect?"

"Aw, mister, cut you off a couple from that jug and drink it up. That's all it's good for. Quicker it's gone, the quicker I can go home and fight with the wife. Run-around can marry that whore and go help his pa straighten his back up." He stood up, stretched, and nodded toward his friend. "Poor sum-bitch. I wouldn't be in his boots for a hundred dollars."

He walked to the jug, took two long swigs, and handed it to Jack. "If ya'll don't mind." He lay back down in the driftwood, curled up in a ball, and went back to sleep.

"Can you believe that?" Shod nodded toward the two drunken cowboys. "I take back everything I've said about vacationing in an Indian war."

Bone managed to take a couple of sips of the whiskey before Jack filled his canteen. He drew up a piece of driftwood and sat down across the fire from Shod and me. After a few minutes of staring into the low flames, he spoke in a quiet voice. "So, Mister Shod, where did you say you're from?"

"I didn't," Shod replied.

The whiskey must've had Bone feeling brave. "Why, I bet you're from one of them abolitionist states, ain't ya? One of them that heaped the war on fellers like Mister Beatty here?"

I watched Shod out of the corner of my eye. I knew exactly what Bone was doing. I was curious to see just how far he would take it. "What is this?" Shod asked, eyeing Bone. I stared straight into the fire.

"Just making conversation, that's all," Bone said with a smug grin. "Hell . . . you fellers are partners. I reckon you talk all the time about where you're from and what you believe."

I heard Jack chuckle from across the fire. Kermit lay piled against a saddle, asleep a few feet from the cowboys.

"Oh, I see," said Shod. "You haven't said a dozen words to me since we caught you trying to ambush us. Now you've had a couple of drinks and you want to make conversation. Is that it?"

"Yeah," said Bone. "No harm asking where a man's from, is there?"

"Ordinarily, no," said Shod. He sighed a long breath. "But in your case, I take offense at anything you could possibly ask. So, if you persist in your attempt at conversation, be advised that I will reach over and squash your head like a little ripe grape."

Bone's eyes bulged; he swallowed hard. Jack turned up a shot from the canteen, then pitched it to me. "Nothing's nicer than a little fireside chat." He grinned.

I took a short sip and held my breath a second. Passing the canteen to Shod, I watched him tip back a drink without taking his eyes off Bone. When Bone reached for the canteen, Shod capped it and pitched it to Jack. "I can see how drinking could definitely get you killed, Mister Bone."

We sat staring into the low flames. I felt the whiskey weave around my mind and draw my eyes deeper into the flickering fire. The canteen came to me again, but I passed it on, already feeling a warm powerful surge.

The night fell silent except for the sound of the river. I reminded myself that we were sitting in the middle of the last hunting ground of the mighty Sioux Nation; and that no matter what was to come in the days and weeks ahead, what was happening here tonight was the only thing that mattered for now. I had arrived in the land of Bull Bear, Red Cloud, and Strike the Ree. Day by day, mile by mile, they were becoming more to me than good names for racehorses.

Against all odds, warnings, and better judgment, I came here to deal horses, short and simple; yet, through a whiskey glow I felt some deeper reason try to surface, and I reached inside my mind like a man searching for diamonds in the dark. There were *other* reasons beneath the surface, and for a second I felt myself brush against them, but as I tried to pick them up, they slipped through the cracks in my consciousness and tumbled away. Something wild, innocent, free, and elusive permeated this time and place. But it only caressed my spirit briefly . . . then disappeared.

For some reason, I had to speak, and I did so quietly. "So where *are* you from, Shod?"

There was a long silence, then finally, "Michigan," he said softly, speaking into the low flames as if something had swept through him as well. "But I attended college in Delaware. After college, I served in the Union army, cleaning slop ditches and hauling bodies—" He stood, dusted the seat of his trousers, and filled his broad chest with a deep breath of night and silence. "Like any educated man would do." He rubbed the toe of his boot back and forth in the outer ashes and studied them as if thinking of something more to say. Finally he shrugged. "I suppose I'll stand first watch, if there are no objections."

"None at all," I said quietly. "Wake me in a couple hours."

"Of course." He turned and walked away toward the string of horses.

"I reckon he thought he was too damn good to shovel shit and haul dead meat," said Bone, after Shod was well out of sight. I reached across the fire as Jack handed me the canteen of whiskey, but instead of drinking, I capped it and let it fall on the ground beside me.

"That's sure one uppity"—Bone's eyes slid around; his voice lowered—"*you know what*, if you ask me," Bone said in a hushed voice as I leaned back against the pile of driftwood.

"Nobody asked you," I said.

I heard Jack laugh and I glanced toward him as he lay back and pulled his hat down over his eyes. "No matter where I roam," he said, "it's just like home to me."

"Alls I'm saying is, he ain't the kind of man you can trust if the going gets a little dangerous," Bone said, still glancing about and ducking his shoulders. "He'll cut and run, you watch." He shot me a somber stare. "You're lucky me and Kermit showed up . . . sure are."

I leaned back against my saddle and just lay there for the longest time, staring at Ben Bone, listening to the silence of night, and the rush of Powder River.

◆ ❋ 7 ❋ ◆

The next morning, I stared at the two cowboys who sat holding their heads and gagging as Bone brewed a fresh pot of coffee. "From now on, Jack," I said quietly between the two of us, "no more drinking until we're out of here and headed back to Missouri."

"You do what you want," Jack chuckled, "but I'm on vacation."

"I mean it, Jack. Look at them. What will become of them?" I shook my head. "They'll never make it. They'll die here, drunk and penniless." I raised my hand toward the jug of whiskey. "That's all for me."

"Coming down a little harsh on your fellow man, ain't ya?" Jack smoothed back his hair and dropped his hat on his head. "You don't know. They might be the *only* ones to make it. They could wind up rich and become chairmen of the temperance league."

"Do what you want," I said, waving Jack away. "I'm staying sharp-eyed until we're out of here."

"Don't s'pose you could use a couple more drunks, could ya?" Cull called over to me without looking up. "We don't know much about sheep, but we're good hands."

I glanced at Jack. "See what I mean?" Then, "It's horses," I said to Cull. "We're running a string of horses."

He waved it away. "Hell, never mind. If I can't tell what you're running, I got no business trying to run 'em."

"We don't need any help, but you're welcome to ride along if you'll stay sober. It'd be safer."

"Naw, thanks anyway," said Run-around. He stood up and spread his hands as if to steady himself on a wobbling planet. "We better stay close to them jugs 'til they're gone."

"You can bring them with you."

"Naw . . . I'd hate to take a chance on breaking 'em if we run into trouble. 'Sides, we already made plans."

Shod walked up and cocked an eye toward me. "We can certainly appreciate that."

"I hope you know what you're doing," I said. "It could get a little tense around here."

"If we don't, we'll figure it out as we go." Harvey Kid Cull stood and rubbed his face with both hands. He looked all around the ground. "If you see any Indians, you might tell 'em we're just here getting drunk. We ain't looking for no trouble." He looked around more. "Was I wearing a hat?"

Run-around looked down, joining the search. "One of us was. I don't know which . . ."

"It's on your head, damn it." I stepped forward. "Why don't you ride along with us a few miles anyway. You ain't in no shape to be wandering around out here."

"Naw, we'll just drink our way from gully to draw. We'll do alright."

We gazed up on our left. Scattered pine and spruce towered above yellow cottonwood across rock ledges and up the rising slope from the valley. Ahead, the valley came to a narrowing point at the end of vision. To our right, Powder River curved along like a large brown snake, shrouded in a silver mist.

"If it was mine, I reckon I'd die for it, too." I studied the ridgeline and saw an eagle sweep in from nowhere, spread its wings against the air as if putting on brakes, and suspended itself in an updraft. "Lord yes," I whispered, "I truly would."

"And that's what old Red Cloud is fixin' to do." Jack's voice sounded as hushed as my own. "Course, he's gonna leave a smear of blood across it." He stared up at the eagle and out across the sky. "Can't blame him."

I took in a breath of cool morning air. "If it was mine, I reckon I'd kill for it too."

"Yeah," Jack chuckled, "I seen how attached you get to other people's property. I'd hate to see how you'd be with your own."

I let out my breath. "Come on, Jack . . . I didn't mean to kill Pope, and you know it. Something just took over inside me and I pulled the trigger."

"Maybe that's how it is with Red Cloud," said Jack. "Maybe he just sees all of us as a bunch of wild men riding off on his horses."

"But his horses ain't stolen like ours are."

"Don't fool yourself. The Sioux stole this land from somebody, same as the government is stealing it from them. Land don't just happen to you. You either steal it yourself, or buy it from somebody who stole it." He spit a stream and ran a hand across his mouth. "Either way, it bears somebody's handprint. Nobody brought it with 'em when their mama spit 'em out on the ground."

"I reckon you're right," I said, watching the eagle shoot down past the tree line like a hunter's arrow. "But we're the outsiders here. When the Indians fight over it, it's like keeping it in the family."

"Yeah, and maybe that's how *they* justify killing each other for it. They think the Great Spirit made the land just for them. Course, I like to think the same thing about every whore in Kansas City." He chuckled under his breath, "And you think it about every horse twixt here and Missouri."

I grinned. "Got it all figured out, do you?"

"Naw-sir, just the parts that suits me . . . like everybody else." He spit another stream. "I'm still working on the rest. If you get right down to it, how could land belong to anybody unless they take it from somebody else?"

"Here we go," I said, pushing my hat up.

"It's the truth. When you can't buy it, beg for it, or trick somebody out of it, you just forget appearances and you take it." Jack swiped a hand across the air and held it closed. "Knock 'em in the head and run off with it. Works the same way for Congress as it does for a common thief." He spit the wad of tobacco out into the river and watched it swirl away. "Law of nature . . . man's nature. Let me hear you deny it."

I smiled and turned my horse back toward the camp. "Let me work on it awhile," I said over my shoulder. "I'll get back to you."

Big Shod stood strapping gear to Ben Bone's pack mule as I rode into camp. Jack stayed with the string of horses as they watered and grazed. Ben and Kermit Bone spread the remains of our campfire and covered the spot with driftwood. I was stepping down from the saddle to help Shod when something slapped the ground, raising a puff of dust. As I dived into a pile of driftwood, the shot echoed out across the valley.

"BEATTY . . . YOU LOUSY COWARD! I KNOW . . . WHO YOU ARE." The echo rolled over and over.

"It's Flowers," I called over to Shod. He and Bone lay hunched against a pine log. Kermit lay ten feet behind them, flat on the rocky ground. All three stared at me. "What's he talking about?" Shod's voice was low and cautious.

"Long story," I said. I knew Jack had heard the shot, and by now he would be trying to take position. I glanced at the rifle in my saddle scabbard. Another puff of dust flared up near my horse's hoofs. This time the shot struck a rock and whistled past us. My horse jumped farther away. "I've got to get a rifle," I said. "Cover me—"

"We're out of pistol range," said Shod.

"Just make some noise. It'll take him a second to know—"

"You're crazy," said Shod.

"Do it," I yelled, coming out of the driftwood and diving toward my horse. Shod's forty-four exploded behind me as I snatched the rifle and turned to dive back. Just then, above the roar of the pistol, we heard the raging snarl of an animal, and a gut-wrenching scream echoed across the valley. I froze near my horse and scanned the high ridgeline. "What the hell was that?" I watched for the glint of a gun barrel as the woods turned silent above us.

Shod slipped to his saddle, drew his rifle, cocked it, and steadied it across his horse's back. We walked our horses slowly into a clump of spruce, our rifles fixed on the ridge, while Bone and Kermit crawled along behind us.

After a few minutes of breathless silence, we heard an echo of laughter. "You won't believe this," Jack yelled from above us. But before we could answer, a quick thunder of hoofs roared in from out of nowhere, and we swung our rifles toward six mounted Indians surrounding our camp.

They stopped suddenly and sat still as stone. I'd flipped my rifle to my shoulder. "Don't shoot!" yelled Ben Bone. "They's Shosho-ni."

"Shoshoni?" I lowered the rifle slightly, but stayed ready to throw down.

"They've sided with the army against the Sioux and Cheyenne," Ben said in a hushed voice. A young warrior wearing an army tunic with the sleeves torn off nudged his horse forward. Starting toward us with a nasty expression, he glanced around our camp. "But walk easy with 'em," Ben whispered. "They can get real ugly. Army lets them get by with anything."

Stopping his horse near Big Shod, the Indian reached out with a feather-decorated muzzle loader and poked it at Shod's chest. His hand was not on the trigger and the rifle wasn't cocked. He tossed some words over his shoulder and the rest of the Indians laughed. Shod glared at him, glanced toward me out the corner of his eye, and tensed forward. "Stand still," I said to Shod. "If he makes a move, I'll splatter his brains out."

The Indian snapped his head toward me with a cold stare. "Damn it," said Ben Bone, "I should've told you, most of this bunch speaks English."

I squinted and kept my rifle before me. "Next time, let me know things like that," I hissed at Ben.

The Indian jumped his horse toward me and jolted to a halt less than three feet away. If it was meant to scare me, it worked, but I didn't budge. I came a hair from blowing his head off. Now his thumb was on the hammer of the flintlock. A Colt forty-four lay in his lap, hanging from a long strip of rawhide looped around his neck. Beneath my shirt I carried a forty-four in the same manner.

He shouted something in Indian, and I turned to Bone.

"Thought you said he speaks English."

"Does," said Bone, stepping closer to me. "He's just doing this to insult you . . . right, Two Hand?" The Indian made a smug grin. "He wants to know what the shooting was all about."

"Tell him I said 'go to hell.' " I spoke to Bone, but stared right in Two Hand's eyes. A flash of fire shot across the Indian's face. "If he wants to talk, tell him to talk to *me*. If he don't, tell him to shut up and get out of here."

"Easy," I heard Shod say beside me. But I knew that Jack was above us on the ridge. I knew his rifle was leveled, and knowing it made all the difference in the world.

"You might want to go along with this a little," said Bone. "Mister Two Hand here is big medicine."

I let out a tense breath. "Tell him some idiot has been following us . . . trying to shoot me. I don't know why."

Bone and Two Hand jabbered, then Bone turned to me with a strange look on his face. "Is it because you shot Gyp Pope in the back, nutted him with a glades knife, then slit his throat—?"

I glanced past Shod. He rolled his eyes. "No," I said, "that's a whole other thing." I caught a glimpse of Kermit; his hand dropped from his throat to his crotch.

"—or is it soldiers, because you stole a string of horses?"

"Neither." Jack's voice boomed out from the edge of the woods. All heads turned toward him as he came forward slowly, his rifle pointed at the Indians with one hand and his other closed at his side and dripping blood. "If he's got any more questions, tell him to write us a letter," Jack chuckled under his breath.

I felt a pounding start in my forehead, slow and steady like the beat of a funeral drum. I knew what came next.

Ben Bone jumped close to the Indian's horse with his hands up in clear view. "How is my friend Chief Washakie?" yelled Ben in a gush of words. "Does he still carry the long-knife I gave him?" The Indian's thumb slid from the hammer of the rifle and rested on the stock. Slowly he turned from Jack and faced Ben Bone. I tried to silence the funeral drum by breathing deep.

"Washakie is old and worthless, like yourself, old man."

Bone stepped back. "But still gives orders, and braises a man's hide if they ain't followed," said Bone. A sly smile crept across his face. I was surprised to see it, but he knew how to handle Two Hand.

"You have a sharp tongue," said the Indian. "It would look good on my lodge-pole." Behind him the rest of the Indians laughed.

I stood ready. Instead of Bone cowering from the threat, he stepped forward. I glanced over at Shod; his hand tightened on his rifle. Kermit stood slack-jawed and helpless. His shotgun lay empty, ten yards away.

"These boys ain't playing," Bone said to Two Hand in a low voice. The Indian backed his horse a few steps, ignoring Bone's warning. He pointed toward Big Shod. "He must come with us. His people are friends of our enemies, the Sioux."

"I don't think so," I said. Again the drumbeat started in my head as I gripped the rifle.

"We take him and *two* horses each," said the Indian, as if he hadn't heard me.

"Listen real close," I said. "Ride out of here, or all you're taking is a face full of lead."

Three rifles cocked from among the Indians surrounding us. Their horses shuffled about, restless. It was ready to happen; I felt it. The Indian before us raised his hand. I figured when he dropped it, I would get him and maybe another or two. Jack would get a couple before they knew what hit them. Shod would catch one, maybe two . . . and hell, that was all of them.

The Indian smiled as if it was my last warning. "We take him and *one* horse each." He tensed his hand as if ready to drop it and start the show. I felt sweat start to trickle down my upper lip.

"Are you sure he understands me?" I said to Ben Bone out of the corner of my mouth. The funeral drum pounded hard in my forehead. I took a close aim on the Indian's chest and he backed his horse toward his warriors.

"Easy," whispered Ben, "he's backing down. Don't do nothing to make him look bad. Appearance is everything to them."

When Two Hand had backed into his group thirty feet away, he handed his rifle and pistol to the Indian beside him and drew a painted stick from his riding blanket. In a flash he bolted toward Big Shod, waving the stick in the air. "Stand still!" Ben shouted to Shod. "He's only counting coup."

Ben's words came too late. As Two Hand reached out to slap Shod with the stick, Shod dropped his rifle and snatched him from his horse with one hand. "Don't!" yelled Ben Bone. But Shod swung him high in the air, his ass in one hand, his neck in the other. "He's only"—Shod slammed him down—"counting!" He cocked his knee like breaking kindling. There was a snap like seasoned hickory. "Coup . . ." Ben Bone's voice trailed into silence as Big Shod rolled the broken body from his knee and glared at the rest of the Indians. They stared in disbelief, for a second, then backed into the woods and disappeared.

Two Hand lay on his side, his eyes staring through the veil between this world and the other. Quiet Jack walked over, reached out a boot, and nudged the Indian over on his back. The upper half of Two Hand's body flopped right over. It seemed like a second passed before the lower half followed. "Lord God, what a lick," Jack chuckled under his breath.

Kermit stared down at Two Hand, then up at Shod. He rubbed his throat as if remembering. Ben Bone shook his head and slumped down on a pile of driftwood. "Damn it, he was only counting coup."

"Maybe they oughta stick to counting their fingers. We ain't here to take any guff, right, Shod?" Big Shod turned away and walked to the horses. He looked ashamed. I shrugged toward Jack. "They ain't so tough when you get right down to it."

Jack smiled. "Don't get too cocky."

"Neither of you know what the hell just happened here, do you?" said Ben Bone. "Well, let me tell you—" He pointed in Shod's direction. "That big darky just killed a Shoshoni war chief in front of his warriors, while he was counting coup. They'll be on him 'til they get him; us too."

"They had their chance," I said.

"Humpf," Bone grunted, "you can thank the Sioux for keeping the Shoshoni from killing us just then."

Jack and I looked at each other, then at Bone. "What're you saying?" I asked.

"I'm saying the Sioux must be awfully close right now, and there must be a big swarm of them. That's why Two Hand's warriors pulled away. They knew the Sioux were close enough to hear the ruckus. And you can bet they heard that shooting a while ago."

I squinted at Jack. "There's just no letup, is there?"

"I reckon not," he said, staring down at Two Hand's broken body. "And look at this." He held out his closed hand and opened it a foot from my face. I jumped back at the sight of a bloody glob of meat.

"Jesus, Jack, don't stick something like that in a man's face. What is it?"

"It's the upper half of C. W. Flowers's left ear."

"Damn, Jack, what'd you do to him?"

"I didn't do nothing. That crazy cur nearly ate him up before he got away."

I glanced around the campsite. "Where is that dog?"

"Last I seen him, he was chasing Flowers and his horse out across the ridge."

"I've never seen a dog hold a grudge the way he does. It ain't natural."

"He's a black-brindle Catahoula. You ain't s'pose to kick 'em. It's bad luck."

"I've never heard that."

"Well . . . it's the truth. If you ever see Flowers, just ask him."

Shod and Kermit had the mule packed and the campsite cleared as Jack and I watched the ridgeline. "What about his body?" Shod gestured toward the dead Indian.

"They'll come back for him," said Bone. "Don't worry, you've done enough already."

I heard a rustle in the brush and swung toward it. "What's all the racket?" said Kid Cull, thrashing through the brush and staggering near the edge of the camp.

"I don't believe this," said Shod. "Somebody should stop them for their own good."

"I thought you left," I said.

"Did." He staggered and caught himself against a tree. "Made it a ways out and laid down to rest. Now I've lost Run-around. You ain't seen him, have you?" He gazed bleary-eyed at Two Hand's body. "Who's *she?*"

Jack and I slipped up into our saddles. I shook my head. "I reckon if you're drunk enough, it won't hurt too bad when they kill you."

I gigged my horse. "Enough socializing," I said over my shoulder. "Let's move out before we get more company."

We winded away slowly along the low bank of Powder River until we found a narrow stretch of flatland leading to the darkened shelter of a shadowed ridgeline. I glanced up towering rock walls and imagined that from high atop, we must look like a colony of fleas crossing the back of a large wild animal.

8

For three days we traveled among the shadow of rock ledges. To get to Fort Phil Kearny, we knew we would have to break cover and cross miles of open grassland. On the fourth day we held up along the wall of a deep basin and waited for the cover of darkness. "Don't you know they've already spotted us," said Ben Bone. We gazed across a sea of grass. "If not, they've seen where we've been. Might want to think about turning back. You'll never get them horses up to Kearny."

"Let me make something clear, Mister Bone," I said. "Maybe you know these Indians a lot better than I do, but when it comes to staying alive, Jack and I ain't no newcomers. Don't forget, we're the ones trapped you in your own game."

Ben Bone shrugged. "Alls I'm saying—"

I cut him off. "So far everybody I've met has told me I'm crazy for trying to deal horses to Fort Kearny, but every day that passes, I'm just a little bit closer." I glanced between Bone and Jack. "I reckon lots of folks thought Sutter was crazy when he struck out to California looking for gold."

Bone eased back. "I shouldn'ta said a word." He waved his hand. "Not a word. I didn't know you felt so strongly about it." He turned his horse back in to trees and rock shelter.

Jack handed me his telescope and I scanned the grassland. "So now you're comparing our string of horses to the California gold rush?"

I lowered the telescope. "Are you gonna start on me too?"

"No," Jack chuckled. "I'm just checking now and then to make sure you don't get too far away from yourself. You've quit drinking and started talking about the gold rush. I knew a feller once who quit drinking and thought his brother-in-law could fly. Shoved him off a cliff—nearly killed him."

I stared at Jack as he gazed straight ahead. "I was just making a point," I said, raising the lens once more. "Where would we be today if nobody ever jumped out and took a chance? That's what life's about, you know, following your own mind. It's what makes a man what he is." I glanced from the lens.

"Um-hmm." Jack cocked an eye. "Just don't go thinking this is California, or them horses are made of gold."

"I'll try not," I said, scanning back through the lens.

In the distance a party of four Indians topped a knoll and disappeared down into a gully. In seconds they came back in sight. The one in front was a lean, middle-aged man wearing a skin shirt, wool pants cut off at the knees, and skin moccasins. Behind him a bare-chested younger man with beaded armbands kept watch in all directions from atop a spotted horse. Feathers waved in the horse's plaited mane. Further back, an Indian woman rode with a small child cradled in her lap. The child's legs bounced lifeless.

I glanced around for Ben Bone, but he'd disappeared into cover. "Take a look at this," I said to Jack, handing him the field lens. He stared through the lens a few seconds, "Uh-huh." He drew out the word.

"What do you make of it?"

"Fine-looking woman." He grinned. "Now, if I was to follow my mind right now—"

"Give me the glass!" I snatched it and gazed out, searching for them again. "Reckon they're Sioux?" I found them and watched as they weaved up and down across a low rise.

"Maybe so," said Jack. "They're dressed a little fancier than Two Hand's bunch, except for the one in front. He looks like he just fell off a freight train."

I watched as they pounded on across the grassland. Their horses looked tired; white froth dripped from their mouths and blew back in long strings. I had just started to take my eyes from the lens when a handful of Indians came up out of the tall grass ten feet in front of the riders. "Ho-ly!" I said. "They're being ambushed."

"Here," Jack said quickly, reaching for the lens. "Let me see." I pushed his hand away.

The Indian in the skin shirt reared his horse and spun away just as an arrow grazed his shoulder. The woman cut sharp and pounded away toward a rock ledge in the distance. The bare-chested Indian rode into the ambushers and jumped from his horse into their midst, swinging a war axe. He disappeared down in a flurry of knives and clubs.

I watched the older Indian pull rein and fall back to cover the woman and child as she bolted past him. An ambusher jumped on the spotted horse and started after them. As the woman raced on for the rock cover, the older Indian pulled a single-shot rifle from his riding blanket and took aim slow and carefully toward the oncoming rider. The shot echoed in to us a second after the Indian flew backwards off the spotted horse and rolled like a bundle of sticks. "These boys work fast," I breathed.

"Let me see, damn it," Jack cursed.

"Hang on," I murmured.

Now horses rose up from the grass, and in a second the ambushers were mounted and in pursuit. But the woman and child were just topping a rise of loose rock and headed into cover. Rifles barked and I saw the older Indian sway, nearly coming off his horse. Then he righted himself and headed up the slope of loose rock. The seven or eight ambushers split into two groups. Part of them headed right behind the fleeing Indians and the others swung wide to the right.

I snapped the lens shut and handed it to Jack. "That's it," I said. "Show's over."

"I'll be damned," said Jack. "What happened? I could see them a little but not enough to make it out."

"Looked like a bunch of Shoshoni ambushed some Sioux. I see now how they work. They come up out of the grass like snakes."

"Kind of like we did back in the war?" Jack grinned.

"Yeah, come to think of it." I rubbed my chin and studied the wide stretch of grassland. "It ain't the kind of fighting they teach at West Point."

"That's good to know," said Jack. "If they all fight that way, it's no wonder the army can't get the jump on 'em."

"By the time the army figures 'em out, this war will be history."

"Yeah, but you'll never read about it. They'll bury this one under the White House. Indians ain't supposed to win."

That night we eased the horses down onto the grassland and pushed them forward. "Keep them pointed straight across," I whispered to Big Shod. "Jack and I'll circle ahead wide and work back toward you. If anybody is waiting in the grass, we'll catch them from behind." I glanced toward Ben and Kermit Bone. Ben nodded his approval.

Jack and I rode out toward the spot where the Indians had run for cover. We could be there well before daylight, and work our way along the bottom of the ridges to Fort Kearny. I figured if the Indians took cover there, so could we. We split up and swung a wide circle for a half mile. When I met Jack at the end of the circle, we worked slowly back through the grass ten yards apart. "Didn't I hear somewhere that Indians never attack at night?" Jack had whispered before we started back.

"I heard it once myself," I said. "Where did you hear it?"

"From an old Cherokee down in the Nations," said Jack. Cool wind whipped across the valley. A sliver of moon floated in a swirling cloud. Somewhere a cat squalled from among the rock ledges.

"I wouldn't swear to it," I said, reining away with my rifle across my lap.

Each time we worked back to Big Shod and the horses, I would let out a low whistle—a night bird call I'd learned in the war. At the end of our first pass, I reined up beside Shod, "How's it going?"

"So far, very quiet," he answered barely above a whisper. "I would feel better without those two behind me." He nodded over his shoulder. Ben and Kermit Bone rode at the rear of the string, thirty yards back.

"You want to switch with one of us and make a pass?"

"No, I'll manage. The horses are grazing their way across. As long as they're quiet, I can hear anything behind me."

"We should be across in five passes," I whispered. Shod nodded toward Jack's canteen. "Perhaps I'll try a little bracer. It seemed to make those cowboys invisible."

Jack handed him the canteen and he threw back a short drink. "Goodness." He slung his head back and forth. "That's it for me. Where did they get this stuff?"

"It's trade liquor," said Jack. "I ran across some back in the war. Illegal as hell, but the law's been overlooking it for years. It's put whole tribes out of business."

"I can certainly see how." Shod wiped his sleeve across his eyes. "I think I'll abstain from any mo-re of it," he belched.

"Too much of it will kill you." Jack grinned. "Or flatten your brain to where you can't find your butt with both hands."

I took the canteen from Shod, looked at it, and passed it to Jack. "I think that stuff's gonna pickle your brains, if you ain't careful. Maybe you oughta leave it age a few days."

"There's an idea." Jack threw back a long drink and stiffened up across his shoulders. "Since that's my last one for a while, I thought I'd make it a good one." His eyes watered.

I shook my head as Jack and I reined around and headed out again.

We made another long sweep, and coming back for the third time, my mare stepped sideways and nickered low as I braced the reins to keep her from bolting. I readied with my rifle in one hand as my mare swung sideways, and I nudged her forward easy as Jack heard her and came riding over. He stopped with his forty-four cocked and raised shoulder-high. I slipped from my saddle quiet as a ghost, crouched down, and stepped forward through the tall grass. Fifteen feet into the grass, I froze at the sight of the dead Indian from the earlier skirmish.

His beaded armbands were gone; so were his ears and half his scalp. His mouth had been slashed open from ear to ear; his jaw bones broken to cut out his tongue. For all the gruesome killing I'd seen in my life, I couldn't help but gag and turn away. His testicles lay beside him in a bloody heap. A foot-long string of gut still connected them to his crotch. "He's had a rough day," Jack whispered beside me, and I almost fired before I realized it was him.

"Damn it, Jack! Don't do that," I said in a loud whisper. I stood up trembling, taking the reins to my mare from Jack's hand.

Jack nodded at the mess on the ground. "You know that *had* to hurt."

I swung up in my saddle and tugged my hat brim. "These people are animals, Jack, low-down animals. No wonder the government wants them killed. They should be."

Jack swung up in his saddle beside me. "They didn't invite us here." He turned his collar up against the cool wind and holstered his forty-four. Behind us the cat squalled out again as we stared down at the body in the dim moonlight.

"What in hell would make them do something like this?"

"Who knows," said Jack. "Indians have strange ways. This might be some great honor."

"Honor?" I looked at Jack and hunched up inside my coat. He'd been nipping at the whiskey off and on since we left the camp along Powder River. I felt better now that he'd stopped.

"Yeah, for all we know, this ole boy might've spent his life looking for a chance to get his nuts cut out and slung on the ground."

Again, the cat squalled out from the rocks. This time it was answered from farther out in the night. "Jack," I said in a low voice, "I meant what I said earlier about a man following his mind."

"I know ya did," Jack answered, searching the darkness.

"Reckon it was true what Mather said about him coming up here last year and making a bunch of money?"

"Hard to say. Mather's not an easy man to pin down." Jack stared at me in the darkness. "Thinking about turning back?"

"I've thought about it ever since we left Crofton ... but I just can't do it for some reason. I sat out to do this and I've gotta see it through."

Something moved in the grass and I almost drew my pistol before I recognized the Catahoula cur slinking along toward the distant wailing of the cats. He stopped for a second and raised his nose in the air, then lowered his whole body and slipped through the grass as quiet as a spirit. I noticed his shoulders had broadened since we'd been on the trail, and his tail no longer curved back under his belly. Now it stood up in the shape of a living question mark.

"Besides," I said, nearly in a whisper as I reined my mare around and tapped her gently forward, "we've gone too far to turn back now." I watched the dark outline of the Catahoula slip farther away in the moonlight, until I saw only the slightest ripple of grass in his wake. Again a cat called out somewhere in the distance, and its voice curled down on the end as silence wrapped around us.

◆ ❋ 9 ❋ ◆

Before dawn we'd climbed the slope where the Indians had fled the day before. Daylight cast a thin distant glow as we rounded the horses into a deep ravine no more than sixty feet wide and a half mile long. "This is a damn good place for an ambush," said Ben Bone, glancing up the rock walls.

"And a damn good place to hide a string of horses," I said back.

As Jack rode ahead to scout the ravine, Kermit and Big Shod drew ropes across the rear of the herd, boxing it in. I rode forward far enough to keep an eye on Jack's back in case he ran into trouble. This place was as safe as any, under the circumstances. Apparently everybody and his brother was roaming Powder River, and everybody but us was bent on killing somebody . . . even the Catahoula cur. He'd returned before morning and lay stretched out on his back with flies circling his belly. A patch of yellow fur stuck from under one of his long nails; his coat looked slick and shiny.

Not risking a fire, we ate beef jerky and hard biscuits, washing them down with water from our canteens. Ben Bone stayed close by my side all morning, studying the top of the rock walls. "Don't you reckon Kermit and I should load these guns up?" said Bone. "It makes good sense, don't it?"

I squinted into the sun's glare and studied the far end of the ravine. "Yeah, it does."

Ben Bone grinned. "Then you'll give us some bullets?"

"Naw . . . I reckon not."

Bone sat shaking his head as I walked to the other side of the herd and sat on a rock. I sipped from my canteen and watched flies swarm in a dark spot on the ground ten feet in front of me.

I thought of the Indian yesterday as I watched the hungry insects gather on the ground. That must've been the way it looked out in the tall grass. A swarm of Shoshoni thirsting for blood as they ripped out the Sioux brave's tongue and testicles. I reckon God must've sat above that terrible scene and watched in curiosity, the same way I sat and watched the blowflies swarm on the dark spot of . . . blood?

Suddenly my spine stiffened as a chill shot up my back. "Blood? Oh no!" I spun around from the rock as a flurry of feet and fists came charging into my chest. Even as we pitched backwards rolling in the dirt, my free hand going to my boot for the glades knife, I saw the trail of blood leading under a cliff overhang.

Struggling in the dust, I heard Ben Bone and Shod running through the herd to help me. I caught a handful of shiny black hair, as fists pounded my face. I yanked back on the hair . . . saw the exposed throat . . . slung back my knife . . . a high arch . . . one slash . . . one would do it. I was a split second from opening the throat, but I saw the face of the young woman from yesterday, and I had to stop my arm all at once like slamming on a wagon brake.

"Kill her!" yelled Bone as he and Shod slid to a halt. They crouched near us, Shod reaching out and pulling her off me. Dust swirled; it burned my face where she'd clawed me. She struggled against Shod's grip like a gnat against an elephant.

I ran my hand across my cheek and saw the thin smear of blood. I remembered the trail of blood behind me . . . the older Indian from yesterday?

"Get down!" I yelled, and we dropped behind the rock, peering over in the darkness beneath the cliff overhang. She started to yell a warning, but Shod's hand went across her mouth, covering most of her face. I'd dropped my knife and drawn my forty-four. I pointed it at her. "Who all's in there?"

Her eyes were wide above Shod's hand. Her face was turning blue. "Shod, she can't breathe! Let her breathe."

He took his hand from her face and she gasped for air. She swayed forward and I caught her shoulders. "She can't speak English," said Bone. He leaned close and babbled something in Sioux.

"No one," she gasped, without looking at Bone. I squinted at him. "I'm wrong." He shrugged.

I glanced over the rock, then back at her. "No one? Then we'll go in shooting." I cocked my pistol, started to stand. She grabbed my arm.

"My father, he is there, and my son." Her hands gestured quickly as she spoke, as if speaking sign language at the same time. "My father, wounded. My son, sick."

"Armed?" I watched her face for any sign of deception.

She drew a long line in the air with her hand. "Big fifty, buffalo."

"Great," I said, letting out a breath. "He's got a damn buffalo rifle. That's what I saw him shoot yesterday. He's good."

"Who's good?" said Quiet Jack. He'd walked up without us hearing a sound. He leaned on the rock and stared into the dark crevice. He hooked his thumb in his belt as if he would lean there awhile.

"Get down, Jack!" I pulled at his pants leg. "There's an Indian in there with a fifty-caliber rifle."

"Whooa!" said Jack, hitting the ground beside me. He glanced past the young woman, then snapped his head back toward her. He looked her up and down with a devilish smile. "Well, howdy, ma'am, I'm Mister Smith, call me Jack . . . and you?" He held out his hand. She just stared.

I shoved his hand down. "Jack! We've got a situation here."

"I believe you," he said, still smiling at her.

"Listen, damn it." I was getting really tense. "You ever seen what a big-fifty does to a man, close up?"

"Huh-uh," said Jack, still smiling at her. He'd started leaning close to her to say something, then snapped his face toward me curiously. "Have you?"

I was really getting tense. My face burned from the scratches. My hands shook and my head thumped. "No . . . I ain't! But some have, and I know it'll kill a buffalo . . . and . . . Look, Jack." I let down and wiped my face. "Will you just pay attention here?"

"Some have?" He smiled at me.

"You know what I mean."

Kermit Bone showed up wiping sleep from his eyes. "Get down, boy!" I shouted. Kermit stumbled in a confused circle, then dropped down in the dust.

Jack chuckled under his breath, "We could've seen what a

big-fifty does 'close up' if you'd left him alone."

Shod glared at Jack. "If he starts shooting, he'll draw in every Indian within ten miles."

Ben Bone stared into the dark crevice rubbing his chin. "Who carries a big-fifty?" His voice trailed.

Deep in the shadow of the crevice, a four-foot gash in the rock wall led into a small cave. Once inside, I held the woman in front of me with my arm around her throat and my knife in my left hand beside her ear. In my right hand I held the small torch. "I swear I will," I shouted into the darkness. "I'll kill her deader than hell. Hear me?" There was no way I would've killed her, but I needed leverage.

"He, no hear," she said in a near whisper, "too weak."

"Yeah, we'll see," I threatened. "I'm a killer!" I raised my voice into the cave. "Hear that? I'm a killer here. Don't try anything."

Ben Bone stepped in behind me. I nearly swung on him as he brushed against my arm. "Give me the torch," he said quietly.

We walked farther into the small cave and heard the sound of labored breathing. "He, weak," she said, "much blood." A few more feet, the torch glow came upon the wounded Indian leaning against the rock wall. His rifle lay near his hand beside him. Two feet away, the small boy lay rolled in a ball, shivering like it was dead of winter.

I turned the woman loose and she ran to her son. Ben stepped closer and held the torch over the wounded man. The Indian's eyes drifted as if lost in a fog. Bone kicked the big rifle away. "Lord-a-mercy." Ben's voice quivered. "Look who we've gone and captured."

I stepped forward. "Who?"

"I'll kill him and the reward's all mine," yelled Bone, snatching his pistol from his belt. The woman screamed and grabbed Bone's leg. He kicked her away and spread an ugly grin, the grin I'd seen that night in the woods. "Yiii!" Bone yelled as he pointed the pistol. His face twisted into a terrible death mask. He pulled the trigger repeatedly. Each time, the hammer snapped on an empty chamber. I just shook my head as I reached down to help the Indian. In his excitement, Bone forgot he had no bullets.

"Damned idiot," I growled over my shoulder. The woman carried the boy over and laid him beside the old man.

"Goddamn it!" Bone bellowed. He bent double as if stricken by a cramp, and stomped the ground. "No . . . luck! Not for the longest . . . goddamn time!"

"Who is your father?" I asked her softly, ignoring Bone's ravings. I helped her with the pile of leaves and dirt she'd used as a poultice on her father's gaping shoulder wound. She looked into my eyes with hesitance and concern, as if telling me might bring about his death.

"He is called 'Makh-pie-sha' Red Cloud, chief of the Sioux Nations."

◆✳ 10 ✳◆

"Let me make sure I've got this straight," said Jack. He chewed on a mouthful of beans and used his spoon to punctuate his words. "This is *the* Red Cloud? It's not some third cousin or something like that. He's the one that *points* and *tells* above all the Sioux?"

"Right," I said. I picked at my plate a few times and finally set it aside. I sipped at the coffee and stared at the ground.

"What's he doing out here?" Jack reached over, picked up my full plate, and set it next to his coffee. He kept on eating.

"She says, they're coming back from a medicine lodge. I reckon from the kid being sick. According to her, he travels this way all the time. It's his country, he can go where he wants. Who'd ever recognize him in that ragged getup? He looks like something that would beg biscuits at your back door."

"So every Indian in the world is hunting him right now?"

"Yep. The Sioux are looking for them 'cause they've been missing over a week. And the Shoshoni are real eager to lift Red Cloud up on a spear and claim the reward. Bone says there's a railroad man offering a handsome reward for whoever kills him."

"How much reward?" Jack cocked an eye.

"Forget it. We ain't bounty hunters."

"I know," said Jack, "I'm just curious how much money we *ain't* going to collect for *not* turning him in." He dropped his empty plate and picked up my full one. "Old Bone seemed real disappointed not getting to kill him this morning. Reckon it's just the reward money?"

"I don't know. Why?"

"Just curious."

"Don't trust Bone?"

"That far," said Jack, spitting a bean on the ground.

"Same here."

Big Shod and Ben Bone walked up from across the front of the herd. Shod carried a saddle blanket over his shoulder. He stopped and looked down at us. "He has lost a lot of blood, but I think he's going to live."

"The boy?" I asked.

"His fever is breaking. I'm certain he'll be fine by morning."

"Good." I nodded. "Surely if Red Cloud's bunch shows up, they'll cut us some slack for saving him and his grandson."

"Depends on who shows up," said Bone. "Right now there's four war chiefs under Red Cloud. There's Crazy Horse, Sitting Bull, Gall, and Standing Bear. Horse, Bull, and Gall are loyal to Red Cloud, but Bear would cut his own mother's throat if it made him chief of all the Sioux. If we run into his bunch, we're in trouble. He might even want to kill them, and lay it on us."

"Politics." Jack shook his head. "Always politics."

"And you're wanting to kill Cloud and get the reward," I said, squinting at Bone.

He shrugged. "If we're going to be blamed, we just as well get something for it."

"There's no reward for Red Cloud," said Shod. "Where did you hear such a thing?"

"By God, there is too." Bone leveled his shoulders. "I heard there's a railroad man from Kansas City offering—"

"That's insane," said Shod. "And it's also illegal."

"It's the damned truth," Bone barked. "I say kill 'im and see if we ain't offered a reward."

"Makes sense, don't it, Jack? . . . Shod?" I glanced between the two. They just nodded to go along with me.

Now Bone got excited; his eyes lit up. "Then I can kill him?"

I let him think I was considering it as I sipped my coffee. Finally I took a long breath. "Naw . . . I reckon not."

"Goddamn it!" said Bone, swinging his arms. "See? See about my luck?"

"Another thing," I said. "I don't know why you're so anxious to see him dead, but if something happens to him because of you or that lop-eared boy of yours, I'll kill you so quick, you'll think you died yesterday." Ben Bone slinked away shaking his head and slapping the empty gun at his waist.

I stared after Bone. "Watch 'em," I said to Jack and Shod, "watch 'em close."

Jack belched and pitched my empty plate at my feet. He scraped up a handful of brown dust, wiped his plate and spoon clean, and held them over the fire. "Good business would be to kill the old man, collect the reward, screw the young woman, sell the kid back to his tribe, forget the horses, and get the hell out of here." Jack picked a fleck of bean from his teeth and flipped it away. "That's the smart way." He nodded.

I knew Jack was just blowing off. "What's screwing the woman got to do with business?" I asked, scraping up dust to clean my plate and spoon.

"Tradition," he said. "Everybody's screwing the Indians."

I laughed; Shod walked away. "What's his problem?" I asked.

Jack shrugged. "No sense of humor, I reckon."

Inside the small cave, the Indian woman sat pressing a damp piece of cloth to the boy's head. Next to the boy, Red Cloud lay covered by two saddle blankets. His breathing was near to normal. He was still unconscious. I'd taken the big-fifty and handed it over to Shod for safekeeping. It weighed a ton.

"I don't know what to do about you folks," I said down to the woman. She stood slowly, smoothing the front of her doeskin dress.

"I cannot say. Only my father can give you your freedom." Her hands worked as if painting a picture of each word.

"Wait a minute," I chuckled at her words. "Maybe you don't understand. We're not the prisoners here, ya'll are." I caught myself using my hands, same as her.

"Prisoners?" She smiled. "You have many horses, few warriors. We have many warriors and horses. You come on our land, take horses to our enemies." Her hands moved quicker and stronger.

"Buffalo man kill Shoshoni war chief, Two Hand. Now Shoshoni kill you . . . my people kill you." Her hands clasped together. "Prisoner?" She stopped talking and stared at me.

When she'd clasped her hands together, I felt like my nuts had been smashed between them. I rubbed my chin. "Maybe we can work something out." I tried to smile. "We did save their lives, don't forget." I pointed at the boy and Red Cloud.

"I will speak to my father," she said firmly.

I was stepping back away from her. For some reason, I took off my hat and held it at my chest as I moved backward toward the cave entrance. "I sure thank you, ma'am, I really do."

I stomped from the cave to where Jack stood watch at the front of the herd. I was mad at myself for bowing and scraping with my hat in my hand, and I felt foolish because I didn't even realize I was doing it until I stepped out of the cave.

"What's the matter?" asked Jack, seeing I'd turned surly since going into the cave.

"Nothing," I snapped. "I'm just negotiating their release."

"Um-hmm," said Jack, "she burnt your ass."

I stomped to my mare and jerked my rifle from the scabbard. "I don't understand a damn thing about these crazy people or this crazy country," I called over my shoulder. I started back toward Jack, fifteen feet away, to stand watch. "I'll tell you another thing. I ain't sitting and wait—"

Kermit let out a scream from the front of the herd. "Up there," yelled Big Shod, pointing to the top edge of the ravine as he dove over a pile of rocks. I jumped behind the rock in front of the cave as another arrow whistled in and stuck in the hard ground. Jack was already behind the rock scanning upward through his rifle sights.

Kermit lay screaming in the dirt, squeezing his leg. An arrow had struck just above his knee; it stuck out on both sides. Another arrow whistled in and landed beside him. I saw Shod appear from behind the rocks. Jack and I fired shots up the wall of the ravine to cover Kermit and Shod. The horses jumped around, ready to bolt through the rope corral.

Ben Bone slid in beside us and pointed toward Kermit. Shod had drug Kermit behind the rock pile and was tying a tourniquet around his leg. "See?" said Bone, jabbing his finger in the air. "Same as me . . . no goddamn luck!"

Two more arrows whistled into the ground before us. We

couldn't see a damn thing up the ravine wall. "We can't just sit here," I said to Jack. I turned to Bone. "Why no gunfire?" I heard an arrow whistle in and shatter on the rock before us.

"Young bucks maybe," said Bone. "Probably a hunting party of young bucks. They wouldn't have rifles yet."

"Then I'm riding out of here after them," I said. "This is bullshit."

"I'll go too," said Jack.

"No, stay here and keep a lookout. If we're not back soon, light out." I turned to Bone. "You, come with me."

"No!" He shook his head. "Not with my goddamn luck."

"Fine," I growled, "I'll go alone. Jack, if I don't come back, stab both his eyes out and cut his legs off."

"Sure." Jack shrugged. Another arrow thumped into the ground.

"Now, goddamn it," said Bone, swinging his head back and forth, "I'll go, but you've seen my luck. At least give me some bullets."

I squinted up into the sun. "Naw . . . I reckon not."

◆✳ 11 ✳◆

When Ben Bone and I left the ravine, we'd cut sharp and headed back along the ridge. "It's Shoshoni," Ben yelled above the thunder of our horse's hooves. I glanced around at the arrow he pulled loose from his saddle as we'd made our run. He held it over toward me as we pounded on. "Here's how you can tell."

"I don't give a damn!" I yelled. "Cheyenne, Sioux, Shoshoni, to hell with them all!" I gigged my mare harder and pulled away from him.

"Wait! I've got no bullets," he pleaded.

"Then you better keep up, damn it."

The four Indians spotted us at three hundred yards across the flat grassland. I had my rifle in my hand. I knew it was useless to try a shot from this distance on horseback, but I fired a round to draw them away from Jack and the others below. I recocked and fired again as they slid up on their horses and raced away.

We cut right behind them, out across the grassland. "If they get away, they'll bring others," yelled Bone.

"They ain't getting away."

Their horses were fast and with a good lead. We had chased them over a mile when I realized that if we spent out our horses, we could land in a trap. It was the oldest trick in the book. If they could get us to spend our horses in a hard run. All they had to do was have fresh riders waiting on both sides. They would lead us in, then disappear; the other riders would drop from both sides and leave us holding our guts in our hands. That's how we'd done it in the war. It worked.

I'd just started pulling up on my reins when we heard rifle fire from the other side of a grassy knoll. I glanced at Bone.

"Army!" he yelled. His face split in a grin. "Now we'll hear about it." A hard volley echoed and Bone hooted and laughed. "Kill 'em, goddamn 'em!"

"Wait," I yelled above the sound of the rifles, "it might be a trick."

"Trick, hell," laughed Bone, "there ain't that many Indian rifles in this whole territory."

"I mean us," I said, lowering my voice. "Look beside you, straight ahead." We reined up hard and slipped over the edge of a low shoulder. I saw movement in the grass on both sides of us on the road ahead. Now Bone saw it too. "No wonder you've got no luck," I whispered as we slipped from our saddles and eased our horses into a shadowed gully. We crawled back to the edge and watched the grass bend as Indians eased back, quick and quiet. "You're right . . . it must be army rifles," I whispered. "But we were heading to heaven the hard way, if we'd gone on. The army must've spotted it."

Bone stared at me, slack-jawed; and I realized that all he knew about Indians was how to back-talk them in their own language. I'd seen enough of Powder River to know the only way to stay alive here was to settle down and start thinking like an Indian. So far, they'd gotten the upper hand on everything the army threw at them. They must've been doing something right.

We crept to the edge of the knoll and looked down. The four Indians had run smack into a cavalry patrol just before trapping us in a cross fire. They'd managed to cover behind some rocks near the edge of a dry creek bed, but given the odds, they wouldn't last long. I saw two arrows whistle out from behind the rocks, then a barrage of rifle fire shattered chunks of stone in all directions.

"Christ," I said to Bone, now that I could see the Indians closer, "they're just snot-nosed kids."

"You saw what they done to Kermit," growled Bone. "Kill all them little devils, before they grow up and make more."

"This is madness!"

In a second the firing stopped. "Throw out your weapons," demanded a barrel-chested captain from the center of the line of soldiers. There was a moment's hesitation, then bows and quivers of arrows came hurling over the rocks and landed in a puff of dust. "Now, come out with hands in the air."

"Good," I said. It was over. These kids would be taken prisoner, but it beat the hell out of dying before their next birthday. I wondered what kind of warriors would use their children to spring a trap. "Only the kind that didn't intend to lose," I thought. "And that's the only kind that don't."

Seeing the four of them standing there in front of the mounted soldiers, I was grateful we hadn't gotten close enough to shoot them during our chase. The oldest looked no more than twelve, the youngest maybe ten. They stood there wide-eyed, as if ready to wet themselves. The soldiers laughed. I even grinned myself. I wondered if their daddies would chastise them for getting caught.

I had just started to stand and yell down to the soldiers when an explosion of rifle fire thundered. The four kids seemed to fly apart like sugar cookies thrown against a wall. Their blood erupted in a fine red mist, and they flew back against the rocks and melted down like candle wax.

I stood, speechless, stricken, my arms spread to my sides. Not even in the war had I seen the likes of this. "Yee-hiii!" yelled Bone from beside me. "Killed them . . . every damned one!" He stepped back as the soldiers turned the rifles in our direction. I still could only stare at the torn and mangled kids.

"Identify yourselves," ordered the captain. I turned my face toward him slowly. Even at thirty yards, I could see where blood had splashed from the rocks and left dark spots on the soldiers and their horses.

"Beatty," I called down to them, "James Beatty." My words sounded thick and distant to me. I heard Bone cackle in laughter behind me. I couldn't see him, but I could feel him jumping up and down.

"He's a goddamn liar," yelled Bone. "His name is Miller Crowe, and I'm Ben Bone, the man what caught him cold!"

"How the hell does he know that?" I thought. I started to spin around and yank his tongue out, but I felt the back of my head ring and saw the soldiers and horses swirl before me. "Aw-naw," I said, or think I said, as I felt the tall grass catch me like a mother's arms.

"I tell you," I heard Bone's voice through the pounding fog in my head, "I tracked the sum-bitch for a week. Thinks he's slick, but I just waited for the right chance."

"Bone," said the captain, "you couldn't track shit if it was on your shoes. This man saved your life back there. We saw them sneak in. That's why we hit from the other direction."

"By God, I'm claiming the reward, on him and Red Cloud and any of that bunch that's worth anything."

"There's no bounty for Red Cloud, you idiot. That's just some stupid rumor that's been circulating."

"There's a railroad man offering a reward, and I aim to get it."

"You're disgusting," said the captain.

Lying on the ground, I barely opened my eyes and saw many pairs of boots standing before me. I knew, without looking, my gun was gone from my holster and my glades knife from my boot. I feigned unconsciousness and listened to Bone rattle on.

"I might be disgusting, but I'm destined to be *rich*-disgusting."

"You're destined to be *dead*-disgusting if you lead me into a trap looking for Red Cloud."

"He's there, so help me hell."

"Better be. Or I'll put you on the sick list."

"Is, goddamn it, if we get a move on."

I heard the captain call out, "Dog, you and Dirty Jaw get Crowe here on a horse and tie his hands behind him." He leaned down and lifted my head by my collars. "And I bet you haven't heard a word, have you?" he said close to my face.

"Aw-hell, Captain," Bone whined, "why can't I just shoot him? I caught him."

"Go ahead," said the captain, and I felt my guts pucker up. "It's your style."

"I told you, I've got no goddamn bullets! Will you *please* give me some bullets?"

"Got none to spare."

"Goddamn it!" yelled Bone as two pair of moccasins appeared

before me, pulled my hands behind my back and tied them tight. I saw Bone's boots stomp the ground as he raved, "Why can't I ever get any goddamn bullets?"

Dog rode beside me at the rear of the column while Dirty Jaw scouted ahead. "Maybe Bone's luck will change now that he has caught you." Dog was a serious sort, who would only speak if he looked you in the eye. I'd known Cherokee like him down in the Nations. You knew right away you were talking to a man you could trust.

"I'll change his luck," I said, as the back of my head throbbed.

"He really has had a run of bad luck," said Dog.

"I've heard him mention it," I said. Without asking, I could tell by looking, Dog wasn't full-blooded Indian, not from around here anyway. His cheekbones were not as high-set, and his eyes were more green than brown. Dog was a lower Nation's half-breed. They'd lost themselves years ago. Now they'd mixed their blood to survive, and picked up enough white to make them crazy and enough Indian to make them wild. They kept it masked, each side from the other.

"He had you believing the Sioux kids were Shoshoni, huh? Anybody knows the only Shoshoni up here are the braves working for the army."

"Yeah," I said. I felt foolish and out of place here among men who knew this country and its many peoples. "But that was a cowardly thing, killing them youngins."

"Worse than gutting a sheriff in his sleep?" asked Dog, looking straight in my face. I reckon the news of my killing that sheriff had traveled around the world.

"You had to be there," I murmured to myself. I wasn't admitting a thing.

At the entrance to the ravine, Dog took out a strip of raw hide and gagged me with it. The column moved forward slowly as if inspecting each rock and drift of dust. When we got to the spot where I should've seen horses, there were no horses, no ropes, and not even a hoofprint in the dust. From the front of the column Bone raved like a lunatic as six soldiers came back from beneath the cliff overhang. They shrugged and shook their heads.

Dog led my horse to the front of the column and jerked the gag from my mouth. "Tell him, goddamn it!" Bone started right in. "And tell the truth! Tell him you're Miller Crowe. Tell him who was here with you!" He started to reach for me. I raised a foot to kick his brains out. Dog jumped his horse between ours.

"Hold it," the captain barked. "Bone, how do you know this is Crowe?"

"Two Hand told me. We was talking Indian between us and he told me it. I kept quiet and waited for my chance." Bone pointed at me and sneered. "Some say he's the horse-man for the James Gang."

"How would Two Hand know?"

"A feller named Flowers told him. Flowers had been tracking him. Then a big dog bit Flowers's ear off, 'cause Flowers kicked it back while they was fighting in Crofton."

The captain looked him up and down as a wave of laughter rippled across the column. "Have you been drinking?"

"Hell no!"

"He's lying, Captain," I said quietly. "Lean over and smell his breath."

"No, thanks. I can smell it from here."

"Now, goddamn it! I had a couple shots of 'wonderful stuff,' but I'm telling you the damn truth."

"Did you get it from a couple of drunken cowboys, Kid Cull and Run-around Joe?"

"He sure did," I said.

"That explains it." The captain rubbed the back of his neck. "We have orders to arrest them and get them out of here for their own good. They ran a herd north with Thump Reedleman. He said they've been blind drunk ever since." He let out a breath. "Bone, that stuff would cross a billy goat's eyes. It's old-time trade whiskey—liquid brain damage . . . and you're not that stable anyway. I believe you've slipped a rim."

"I'm telling you the truth, Captain. They're here somewhere!"

"I should go ahead and kill you for putting my column in danger. But I will wait and see what Two Hand says about it."

"Then you'll be waiting forever, Captain." Bone pointed at me. "His black-giant partner broke Two Hand in half back at the Powder crossing."

More laughter rippled. The captain silenced it with a cold stare. "Black giant?"

"I swear . . . a giant! He's bald and wears little eyeglasses and talks better than a ten-dollar lawyer. He broke him so bad, Two Hand's ass was where his belly oughta be."

The captain squinted and bit his lip. "Dog," he finally said, very calmly, "if Bone opens his mouth again, put a bullet between his eyes and get him out of *my* misery." Dog nodded and pulled back the hammer on his rifle. Bone's face turned blue and froze.

The captain turned to me. "Were you here earlier with a string of horses, a group of wranglers, Red Cloud, his daughter Stands Alone, and her son?" He shot Bone a look he didn't learn at West Point. "Anybody else?"

Bone shook his head, and his eyes pleaded.

"No, sir," I said straight-faced. "I was here with Ben Bone, but that was before I realized he was a drunken lunatic."

Bone turned colors I'd never seen on a living person. He strained and gritted his teeth till spit run down his chin. Dog smiled with his cocked rifle hovering in Bone's face. He smiled even more as he reached out and tweaked Bones' nose with the barrel.

"Sergeant," said the captain, "is there any sign of a cave inside the crevice?"

"No sir." The big Irish sergeant shook his head. "There's a boulder under there that would take a team of ox to move."

I glanced at Bone and almost smiled. Any minute he would have to let go and fly into another raving fit. I believed it would be his last one. He and I knew how the boulder got there. Big Shod.

"I see," said the captain. He glanced around the upper edges of the ravine. Darkness was closing fast; it seemed to concern him. "Prepare to advance in column of twos," he said. "Bone . . . I've decided not to kill you for some reason, but for your own good, I'm placing you under military arrest. We'll settle this back at the fort. Dog, tie him up and gag him."

He turned to me as Dog slapped a leather gag around Bone so hard, you could hear it pop. "I'm going to ask you one time and one time only. Are you Miller Crowe?"

"No sir, Captain."

"Are you sure?"

"I ought to know, Captain. I'm Beatty . . . James Beatty. I'm a horse dealer out of Missouri. I did come up here with a string of horses, under the authority of Colonel Carrington, but I lost a bunch of 'em in quicksand and the rest got stolen . . . and my wranglers got killed. Now, that's the whole of it. I only took up with Bone because he said he knew the country and the Sioux. But as you saw by that ambush that was about to happen back there, he don't know squat."

"Bone is just a greedy old bastard. Everybody around here knows it." He pushed his hat up an inch. "What made you realize you were heading into an ambush back there?"

"Just common sense, Captain. I'd started pulling up when I heard your rifles."

He considered a second, looking me up and down. "Dog, cut him loose, but watch him."

I glared at Bone. "Captain, can I have my gun?" Bone's eyes widened and he whined behind the rawhide gag.

"Yes, back at the fort."

"My knife? Right now, just for protection?"

"At the fort," the captain said in stern reply. I decided not to push my luck.

I glanced around as we rode forward out of the ravine. Bone had upset the captain's maneuvers. The captain was worried. He was too far out for this time of evening. I found some comfort in knowing that he even thought of it at all. Red Cloud's warriors would not trick this man, not even with their children's lives. He had learned the Indian's ways of war, to kill anything that was a part of the enemy. The high plains had taught him the art of merciless brutality, and I wondered what his knowledge had cost him, somewhere in the darkness of his military mind.

They'd all disappeared. In the two or three hours since I'd left, Jack, Shod, Kermit, eighty horses, and the three Indians had vanished without a trace, like smoke in a breeze.

Darkness had sat upon us by the time we'd cleared the ravine and rode half a mile across the grassland. I heard the Catahoula howl, and the lonesome call of a night bird as we rode past grassy knolls and in and out of dark gullies. I tensed in my saddle for just a second, wondering if anybody else knew what it was. Jack was a good hand at staying alive. I heard the sound again and knew that Jack had control. But the soldiers didn't recognize the sound, and Dog and Dirty Jaw didn't seem to care. We rode on in the soft clanking of army rigging, and the scuffle of the horses' hooves.

◆✳ 12 ✳◆

We arrived quietly at Fort Phil Kearny, just the way I'd imagined I would. Except, instead of leading a string of horses, I rode in between two armed soldiers at the rear of an army patrol. Dog reined up beside me as the patrol shuffled through the main gate in a cloud of brown powder. "You carrying any money?"

I looked him up and down. "Why're you asking?"

"Because if you are, don't try offering any bribes to Carrington. He's very strict and 'by the book.' It would only make things harder on you."

"Thanks," I said, "but I know better than to try and bribe an army officer." I thought about Trapp and my lost hundred dollars.

We reined up near a half-finished livery barn. As I slipped from my saddle beside the two scouts, Dog nodded toward the front of the column and we saw Bone jumping up and down with his arms tied behind him. Someone loosened his gag, and though we couldn't quite make out his words, apparently they weren't very pleasant. The young captain said something to the big Irish sergeant, and we heard a loud pop as the sergeant's fist snapped out and sent Bone flying backwards.

"So much for Bone," said Dog. "If he thinks Mad Johnson won't have him killed just because we're in the fort, he truly is crazy."

Mad Johnson? "That's what you call the captain?"

"If you get to know him, you'll understand why."

"After seeing what happened to those Indian kids, I've already got a pretty good idea."

"But he knows how to get the job done," said Jaw. "You've got to give him that."

"If it takes killing half-grown kids, I ain't sure it's worth it."

"The Sioux have done just as bad to white children. To hell with them . . . that's war."

"You're Indian, Jaw. How can you feel that way toward your own people?"

"I got here because my Crow ma was raped by a Cheyenne warrior before any white man gave a damn about what was going on up here. You have no idea who my people are. My people are whoever pays the best." Jaw spread a bitter grin. "Or the ones who're winning. I'm in the war business, and it's always booming." The two of them hooted with laughter.

"Well, I'm glad you took no offense. I'm just trying to figure out how things really stand around here. I've got to tell you, this upper plains bunch is more than just a little puzzling to me."

"Aw," said Dog, "you'll get used to it after you've been here awhile. It just takes awhile to know who's who. Don't try to think too much about anything but staying alive. That's the way Mad Johnson does it. That's why he's the best."

"Yeah," I said, "and I bet that's the way he got his nickname."

"See?" Dirty Jaw slung back his head and laughed. "You're learning already."

"It could be as long as a year before anybody comes to identify you. With Red Cloud's war going on, only a fool would venture up here unless they had to." Colonel Henry Carrington leaned back in his desk chair and tapped his chin with the quill pen. He was a finely trimmed little man with sharp eyes and a tightness about his chin.

"Surely to goodness you're not going to hold me that long because Ben Bone, a raving maniac, says—"

Carrington cut me off with a snap of his eyes. "I don't really care if you're Miller Crowe. If Kansas City or the state of Missouri has a charge against you, that's their problem. I've got more to deal with—" He stopped his words and looked away a second. "I am concerned that you've been found carrying an army requisition dispatch with my signature forged on it. There was one floating around last year. But once we chased away some grifter and a couple of his outlaw buddies, I thought that would be the end of it."

I thought of Dave Mather's story and felt my neck heat up. Mather and I were going to have a serious talk if I ever got out of here. "For the fifteenth time, Colonel, we were slickered by a fast-talker back in Crofton. He sold me the herd and the requisition. Said if I had the nerve to bring that herd up Powder River, I would make top dollar. I swear."

"So you just jumped right in?"

"Yes. I know I was stupid, but damn it, the paper looked real enough."

"An infantry commander ordering a hundred saddle horses? I must say it has a certain flare of originality."

"Eighty," I said. "Most of 'em stolen by a bunch of outlaws before I made it past the crossing . . . Two good men dead. Look, how was I supposed to know? Hell, I showed the paper to a Major Trapp in Crofton; he never questioned it."

Carrington leaned forward in his chair. "Trapp had the authority to confiscate the horses. But between you and me, I'm glad you took off with them. Trapp doesn't like me, you know. He thinks because I appreciate good snappy marching music that somehow I'm not competent to command this expedition." He waved a thin hand. "Actually it's more than that, but be that as it may. I just wish you could've brought them up here. We generally only contract with designated horse dealers, but right now I do have two companies of cavalry who are in immediate need of some well-broken saddle horses."

"Is that so." I eased back in my chair. "Well, maybe I can find them, if you let me out of here."

"I admire your spirit, but those horses are long gone by now. Of course, if you could bring up another string . . . off the record, I'd buy them."

"If I found some, I could be talking over a hundred a head, as risky as it is."

He waved a hand. It seemed like his mind just slammed shut on the subject. "You'll have to talk price with Captain Fetterman. I'm infantry, he's cavalry." Carrington leaned back and eyed me closer. "So you shot Gyp Pope on the fourteenth, is that correct?"

"Sounds about right," I said. "Why're you asking?"

"Because the day after you left, the Popes hit our payroll for the third time, seven miles from Crofton."

"Damn," I whispered under my breath. "I was that close to the Pope brothers?"

"I know what you're thinking," said Carrington. My eyes snapped up at his. I was thinking, If only I'd known, Jack and I could've knocked out that payroll ourselves and to hell with the horse scheme. This whole bunch was either over my head or twisted deep in my imagination. Either way, I would've settled for the payroll, and ran back to Missouri.

"And what you're thinking is right," said Carrington. "You're lucky to be alive. If they could've found you, they would've skinned you."

"Praise the Lord," I whispered, but I was thinking that between Jack and me ... quick ambush ... snatch the money. I shook my head to put it out of my mind. "How'd they know where to hit? I thought with the war up here, payroll deposits were top secret."

"I personally think they're getting inside information. We've asked Washington for help"—he shrugged—"but ..." Carrington's fist bumped the desktop. "Trapp's men found three troopers' bodies on the sixteenth, floating downriver where they'd crossed. They'd been skinned and gutted ... poor bastards."

I whistled low. I'd done some far-handed things, but I could never do what had been done to the body I'd seen in Crofton. Then again, I couldn't have done what was done to those kids. Maybe it was something Powder River does to people, because I *could* do what I did to Gyp Pope, no denying that. "Colonel." I shook my head. "You people up here are truly puzzling."

Carrington stood, walked to the window of his half-finished office, and stared out at the construction workers on the north wall. "Of course, I'm not from around here, Mister Beatty." I breathed a little easier, hearing him call me Beatty.

"I served behind a desk until Powder River. Actually I'm an attorney by calling." His voice dropped as if he didn't want it to go past the room. "I was sent here to build three forts along Powder River. Washington hired a newspaper man by the name of Edward Taylor to head a peace commission—Rosy Ed, I call him." He made a tight little smile. A funny sound rattled in his throat. "Can you imagine—a newspaper man? With a stroke of the pen he convinced them everything was just fine and dandy up here. I even believed it." He waved his hands. "I brought my wife!"

"Freedom of the press, I reckon." I couldn't think of nothing else to say.

"Needless to say, she got upset with *me* when the arrows started flying. As if I could just scold them and send them away. I'll be lucky if she doesn't leave me, on top of everything else going wrong."

"Um-um." I shook my head. "Women . . ."

"Come to find out, Taylor's only treaty was signed by a bunch of small tribes who aren't even from here! 'Sure,' they told him, they wouldn't make war on the Bozeman Trail. So he sent them on their merry way with a wagonload of gifts. They must've laughed themselves silly."

"What a bunch of pranksters," I said, hoping to lighten the air. It didn't help.

"Meanwhile every warrior who could ride, walk, crawl, or slither has gone up to join Red Cloud for one grand and final bloodletting. And here I am with a handful of green troops and carpenters. I'm supposed to teach them to shoot without killing each other, learn to ride without breaking their necks, and oh, by the way, fight Indians when I find the time"—he chuckled under his breath; it was that dark ironic sound like Jack Smith always made—"while we build these stupid forts straight through the heart of the Sioux Nation."

"Every job has its drawbacks, Colonel." I cleared my throat. "Not to change the subject, but if I'm free to go, I believe I might round you up some horses." He had to buy my story about the forged paper if he expected to do any business with me.

"They called us Carrington's Carnival, because we hauled in two hundred wagons full of building material, and I brought along an excellent marching band." He shook his head. " 'Carrington's Carnival.' Imagine how that looks on my military record. We only just sent our families home last week." He shook his head. "What were we thinking? Most of our rifles are old muzzle loaders—they look terrible in a parade. We only have three cannons, and I'm the only one who knows how to fire them."

It must've been a long time since he'd spoken to anything but a blue uniform. I sat back and let him ramble. "So here I go." His fingers danced back and forth like little make-believe legs. "I run over here and shoot the cannon, run over here and measure a wall, then over here to rehearse with the marching band. It all seems so ridiculous." He shrugged. "I asked for some cavalry and they sent me Fetterman. He wants to kill anything that moves and have it mounted. Then—now, listen to this—they said that Fetterman wasn't supposed to arrive here officially until November. So rather than cause extra paperwork, I'm not supposed to keep a record of his patrols until he 'officially' gets here."

"I don't know what to say," I said, shrugging, but he didn't even hear me.

"And I've tried explaining to Red Cloud that all we want is to build forts, to protect travelers along the Bozeman Trail. No one is trying to live here. Oh, a few scattered settlers maybe, but all we want is to cross through here." He shrugged. "It's not like we would bother anything."

"Well . . . if horses are any help, I believe—"

"I welcomed him here, gave him—all of them—coffee, sugar, tobacco." He rolled his hand. "You know, the kind of things they like . . . things they really enjoy."

"You just can't please some people." I shook my head. "But as far as horses—"

"I even had the band out there playing snappy, I mean *real* snappy, tunes—"

"Colonel, can I go?"

"—but no, Mister Big Chief Red Cloud doesn't want us going through 'his' hunting ground."

"I mean, if I leave here, I can probably come back with some horses."

"You know what he said?"

"What's that?"

"He said, if *he* was living in *my* yard, would giving *me* a cup of coffee and a cigarette make me want *him* to stay?"

I had to stifle a short laugh. But Carrington wasn't joking.

"Then he had the nerve to say the band music was like everything else about the white man, 'loud and endless.' "

"Now, that was plumb rude." I slapped my leg. "I couldn't blame you for wanting to get a bunch of horses and—"

He fanned his hands before him as if wiping a wall. "Of course, I can't blame Red Cloud altogether. As it turns out, while I was leading my 'carnival' up here, Rosy Ed Taylor and Colonel Maynadier, the so-called Great Peacemaker"—he wiggled his fingers—"were back at Laramie promising Red Cloud we would stay out of Powder River. How did that make me look?"

I made up my mind. If he ever quit rattling on, I was going to ask one more time if I could leave. I was leaving either way. I just hoped I could do it legally and strike a deal for the horses at the same time.

"He even made a personal remark about my ears." Carrington seemed to brood just remembering it.

"Your ears?"

"That's right." He nodded his head quickly. "He said he could not trust a man with ears as small as mine." Carrington's hand drifted up the side of his head.

"Well . . . he had no cause to get personal. I'd say that's a flaw of character."

"And that's what I'm supposed to deal with." I thought he was going to get emotional.

"To tell you the truth, Colonel, most of this military strategy talk is way over my head. I'm just a common horse trader. But if you'll give me the go-ahead, I promise you I'll bring you some crack riding horses, somehow, someway. Then you can tell them all to go kiss your ass."

"I don't understand." He shook his head as if to clear it.

"Well, it's pretty damned clear to me that some high-hatted brass somewhere would just love to see you fail here."

"Do you suppose?"

"Sounds like it to me. Have you pissed anybody off up along the Potomac?"

"No." He stopped and considered it. "But General Cooke never has liked me. I've always thought that."

"Well, there you are. It's hard to get something done when your boss is always on ya."

He raised his finger, gazing away. "You know, he's always saying snippy little things in his dispatches."

"Oh?"

"Yes, you know, like why haven't I been more aggressive. Why don't I send out more patrols. He even hinted once at having me relieved of command—asked how I felt about Fort Casper. Probably has an old classmate he wants to put here. You wouldn't believe how much of that old West Point glad-handing goes on."

"No fooling?"

"Believe me . . . the stories I could tell. And I can't even get my brother-in-law a job with the Indian Commission." He waved a hand. "But you don't want to hear my troubles . . ."

I let out a breath. "Can I leave, Colonel?"

"Leave?"

"Yes, leave. I'll get you some horses, but you'll have to let me go."

His shoulders shook as he chuckled, "Go? Go where? Beatty, you've got everybody in Powder River wanting to kill you, including that idiot Bone. I suppose that's why I've enjoyed our conversation. You're the only person I've met in months who has as many problems as I do." He broke into a crazy, trembling little laugh, as if he was afraid someone would hear it. Then all of a sudden he straightened up, wiped his eyes, cleared his throat, and tugged at his tunic. Now he was back to "business as usual." "Of course, if you think you can really procure us some riding horses, then by all means, go. Go with my blessing."

That night I lodged as a guest of the U.S. Army. In the horse stable near the south wall, Dog, Dirty Jaw, and I pitched our saddles in a row for pillows and wrapped in blankets, not only for warmth, but to keep from swatting flies all night. I'd lain there awhile wondering about Jack, Shod, the Indians, and my stolen horses. Since I'd heard Jack let out the night bird whistle, I knew they were all right. Finding them could be a whole other thing.

After telling Carrington they'd been stolen and my wranglers killed, it would be hard explaining how I got them back. But now I knew that if I could find Jack, selling the horses to the army was a done deal. Ben Bone had screwed things up, but not for long. Now that I had my pistol and rifle back, and my glades knife back in my boot, Ben Bone wasn't going to believe how bad his luck would get.

Dog had told me before we turned in that Bone was in the army sick tent in a restraining jacket and under heavy medication. He said Bone was babbling about Miller Crowe, Red Cloud, black giants, bullets, boulders, and "no luck." I would medicate the son of a bitch when I got my hands on him.

✦✳ 13 ✳✦

I awoke next morning to the sound of rifle fire from the north wall. A flaming arrow thumped into the ground just inside the barn door; but before I could make a move, Dirty Jaw stomped over from his bedroll, jerked the arrow from the ground, and stuck it in a rain barrel. He kicked some burning hay from the doorway and walked back to his blanket. I heard a scream and a crash from the north wall and jumped to my feet. "Think we better get out there?" I yelled.

Dog rolled over, frowned, and rolled back away. Dirty Jaw had rolled back up in his blanket. "Do what you want," he said. "We're off today."

I splashed water on my face from the rain barrel and walked to the wall. I'd taken my rifle from my saddle scabbard and carried it cradled in my arms. A line of soldiers milled outside the mess tent, smoking and waiting for breakfast as if nothing was going on. "Bullshit," I thought, "if they ain't worried, neither am I."

An arrow whistled in and stuck in the side of a water barrel. When a thin young private leaned to pull it loose, "Leave it alone," called a thick-necked sergeant, "or the damn thing will leak." The kid stepped back in line and shrugged.

Bullets thumped against the wall and I flinched as I approached it. "Good morning," shouted Carrington above the melee. He stepped toward me with a determined smile. A rolled-up set of construction plans stuck from under his arm. Yesterday evening he seemed lost in the dark irony of his situation; now he seemed as spry as a squirrel. I wondered if Jesse, Frank, or anybody back home would believe a word of this. I made up my mind; I wouldn't tell them.

"Need some help?" I called above the racket of gunfire. Indians whooped and screamed from the tall grass outside the partially finished wall.

Carrington cupped his chin in his hand considering my offer. I begin thinking he was as crazy as Ben Bone, but in a different way. "How are you with a crosscut saw?" He was serious. I just stared and pointed at the wall.

"Out there, Colonel. Do you need any help with that bunch?"

He waved a hand, dismissing the ruckus behind him. "That's every day; means nothing."

"Nothing?" I let my rifle hang from my hand.

"I realize how this must look"—Carrington smiled—"but I have three forts to build. I may have sounded a little overwrought last night, but I can't let things like this get me down."

From the catwalk atop the wall, soldiers pounded out rounds into the tall grass. At their feet, other soldiers scurried about, measuring, cutting, and driving nails. A measuring stick fell at my feet. I jumped, thinking it was an arrow. Carrington picked it up and pitched it to a soldier on the catwalk. "Be a little more careful, trooper," he called out.

"Morning patrol!" yelled a voice from the tower above the main gate.

"Oh, good." Carrington beamed. "Here comes Fetterman, who isn't stationed here yet, bringing in the patrol he hasn't been on." Outside, the Indians turned more aggressive. In seconds the gates swung open in a hail of arrows and rifle fire as a dozen mounted soldiers came sliding and pounding into the fort.

Dust billowed. A horse went crazy as an arrow grazed its rump. It ran bucking, crashed through a hitch rail, up on the boardwalk. The rider flew away into a stack of nail kegs. The horse charged through a group of soldiers and into the sick tent. "Goddamn it!" yelled a voice from inside as the tent rocked and quivered. I could have sworn it was Bone's voice.

A lean, swaggering captain jumped from his horse and stomped toward us, slapping dust from his shoulders. "Secure that animal!" he bellowed, pointing at the sick tent. Carrington had pulled the plans from under his arm and unrolled them.

"About my getting you some horses," I said. I wanted out of there, even if it meant riding through the Indians.

"Colonel!" boomed the captain's voice as he stopped right in Carrington's face. "I need some cavalrymen out here. These lousy foot soldiers are dangerous on a horse. They can't ride without poking each other with them blasted muzzle loaders."

"Good morning, Captain Fetterman." Carrington beamed. He rolled the plans up and stuck them back under his arm. "I was just going over the drawings for the enlisted men's barracks."

"There won't be any enlisted men left if I don't get some cavalry troops here."

Outside the wall, the Indians had quieted down. Fewer rifles barked from the catwalk. "I know we have some problems in that area," said Carrington.

"Problems? Shit! We're going to be burying our problems."

"That's a good one," chuckled Carrington. He gestured toward me. "This is Mister Beatty. He's the one who killed Gyp Pope."

The young captain looked me up and down quickly. "So . . . you're the one that smacked him with a broadaxe."

"Well," I said, "the truth is—"

"Good for you." He snapped back toward Carrington. "Get me eighty good cavalrymen, that's all, and some horses, I mean *good* riding horses, and I'll put the Sioux Nation out of business." His voice dropped a notch. "As soon as I get here in November, that is."

"Mister Beatty here is going to talk to you about horses."

"I didn't smack Gyp Pope with a broadaxe—"

"Surely!" growled Fetterman. "Eighty good men—"

"Gentlemen!" Carrington held his hands chest-high.

"I just don't want people thinking I hit him with a damned axe. All I did was shoot him, and I didn't even mean—"

"Please, gentlemen!"

"—with good repeating rifles, and horses that can run without falling—"

"We need to discuss all this in my office. We're distracting the workers out here."

Fetterman stomped on to Carrington's office while Carrington took his time, looking around the construction crews and making notes with a carpenter's pencil. I walked on, watching him over my shoulder. When I stepped up on the boardwalk, Fetterman stood restlessly fidgeting with the doorknob. He leaned near my ear. "That's the slowest human being I've ever seen. By the time he finishes taking a shit, he's hungry all over again." He snickered through clenched teeth. "Don't say I said it."

"I won't," I snickered back. I'd decided to go along with whatever craziness they had in mind, until I could get out and find Jack and the horses.

"The men all hate him. They call him 'little cannon.' Get it?" He gigged me in the ribs. "He thinks they're saying it because he's the only one who's had any howitzer training. They're really saying it because of how his wife bosses him around. She made him drag her up here, you know. Probably feared he would be short-wicking one of these squaws—as if any of them would have him. I'd do a better job here; everybody knows it . . ."

"All done," said Carrington, stepping up to join us. He poked his notes inside his tunic. Fetterman glanced at me and rolled his eyes as Carrington took the time to smooth the front of his uniform. When Carrington turned one last time to look around the fort, Fetterman blew out a breath, snatched out a pocket watch, waved it at me, and shook his head. "Think I was kidding?" he said just above a whisper.

"Hmm, what's that?" Carrington turned to us with a smile. Fetterman cleared his throat as he pocketed the watch. "I was saying what a fine job you're doing with this place. I bet the little lady would be proud if she saw it now."

"You really think so?"

"No question, Colonel. She would love it." Fetterman threw his hand around his throat and made a face as Carrington stepped through the door and led us inside. "Don't say I said it," he whispered again as Carrington stepped behind his desk and we took seats before it.

"Now then, Gentlemen, where to start?" He rubbed his hands around on top of his desk as if admiring the polished finish. "We have plenty of wood and hay, so perhaps we won't be sending out work details today or tomorrow."

Fetterman glanced from me to Carrington with a puzzled look. I wondered if the colonel had forgotten I was in the room. "And now that most of the settlers are either dead or chased back to Crofton or Fort Laramie, maybe we can channel our efforts toward building the kind of fort that will last long after we're dead and gone."

"Begging the colonel's pardon," said Fetterman. "I believe you asked us here to discuss horses?"

I took a deep breath. The whole bunch were starting to really get on my nerves. "I could come back later."

"No, of course not." Carrington straightened up in his chair. "I was simply making small talk. Now then, Mister Beatty, please tell Captain Fetterman what you have in mind."

". . . I swear, Dog, that's what he told Carrington. 'Eighty men and he would put the Sioux Nation out of business.' Can you believe that?"

Dog shook his head and wiped the biscuit around in his plate. "I believe anything anybody says about them. See why I'm leaving? They're all idiots up here. Except Johnson, and he's crazy. Fetterman wants Carrington's job so bad, he can taste it. God help them if he ever gets it. He could screw up a steel ball."

We sat on nail kegs inside the barn and ate in the glow of a coal oil lamp. Rain pounded just outside the open door. It blew across the fort yard in gray sheets and whipped against the tents.

"Where you from, Dog?" I'd made an agreement with Carrington and Fetterman three days ago. I still had to get back to Fetterman to work out the price, but other than that, I could leave any time. When Dog told me he was leaving in a week, I decided I had a better chance of finding Jack, Shod, and the horses with somebody who knew the country. I figured they'd gone with Red Cloud and taken shelter somewhere until Red Cloud was back on his feet. I knew Jack wouldn't turn Red Cloud loose unless they came to some kind of favorable terms. After all, we'd saved his life and the life of his grandson.

"Down in the Nations," he said across a mouthful of biscuit and gravy. "Signed on for a year; needed the money. Started out at Laramie. That's where I met Jaw. He's on terms with Chief Big

Mouth and the Laramie Loafers Sioux. They got me on scouting. But I didn't know these fools were all working for the railroad."

I spooned more of the elk stew. "You really believe that?" He'd told me earlier, Fort Phil Kearny and the other two proposed building sites were just smoke screens, decoys to distract the Indians while the Union Pacific laid tracks westward. It was just one more theory from one more person who probably had no more idea what was going on than I did. Everybody had their notion, but nobody really knew. Powder River was a hell of a conversation piece if nothing else.

"No big secret." He shrugged. "You think the army would send these idiots if they really meant to build permanent forts?"

I shook my head and concentrated on the elk stew. "They are a *different* bunch, I'll say that."

Dog reached out, poured more stew from the small pot onto his plate, and dipped his biscuit into the steaming gravy. "I think Carrington's here because they ran out of books for him to mark back at Omaha. He's a schoolteacher, you know."

"He told me he'd been a lawyer."

"Ex-lawyer, ex-schoolteacher." Dog shrugged. "I'll tell you one thing. He'll be an 'ex-officer' when Red Cloud's through with him."

"I sort of think he's been screwed by somebody. You've got to have somebody pissed off to draw this kind of job."

"Naw, he's just one of those people keeps stepping on the rake and getting smacked by the handle. They just needed someone to draw fire off the railroad workers, and Carrington just stepped right on it. Look at what they sent up here, green troops, no rifles or ammunition, can't ride a horse, can't shoot straight—"

"He seems to think it's because of bad information that came from a peace commission. He says that the newspapers back east heard from the peace commission that everything was settled and started telling people to roll on up here."

"That could be, but it's hard to believe. Of course, it's hard to believe they would send him in here with only five companies of troops when they send at least twelve to places like Laramie, where there ain't been a shot fired in years." Dog spit out a sliver of bone and shook his head. "Army . . ."

A young soldier splashed in from the rain and stood before us dripping water. "Yeah?" said Dog.

The boy couldn't have been over sixteen. "I'm supposed to fetch a horse?" He seemed unsure if he'd come to the right place.

"They're the big furry things with long tails." Dog pointed at the stalls without getting up. I shook my head and laughed under my breath as the boy ran back and forth among the stalls.

"All I can say is that Powder River is one big test." Dog kept on eating. "Maybe the army ain't sure what they're doing. Maybe they're just figuring what they'll need to do later, once the railroad's finished."

The kid came back leading a red gelding. Hair was missing from around the horse's eyes and mouth. Dog stepped out, took the rope from the boy's hand. "Don't take him, he's a straw-horse."

"Huh?" said the kid. He squinted and scratched the top of his head.

"He has a crooked spine. If you ride him very far, he'll fall down from the pressure. He's here to graze around the colonel's house. Keeps the grass short."

Dog tied the bald-faced gelding to a barn post and sat back down. "Besides," he continued as if he'd never stopped, "the government wants this land, but not just yet. They don't know what to do with it yet. But wait 'til the rails come through. There's gold up the Bozeman Trail, and the government needs it bad."

"Son," I said, as polite as I could, "that's a pack mule." The young soldier looked embarrassed as I took the rope and led the mule over beside the gelding. I sat back down and took a biscuit from the platter. "I wonder if Red Cloud sees it that way." I dipped the biscuit in the elk stew.

"It's his people's land," said Dog, as the young soldier came forward again. "Cloud is the only person with an honest interest here." Dog reached out and took the rope from the boy's hand. "That's *my* horse."

"So he don't see none of it." I shook my head, gazed into my stew as Dog tied his horse next to the mule and the gelding.

"No," said Dog, looking around at our now-crowded area. He moved the pot of stew closer to me and pulled his nail keg away from a swishing tail. "All Cloud sees is that his country is being invaded. The Sioux have been pushed from east of the Black Hills all the way to here. They're just starting to realize that there's really no place for them anywhere. This government is going to push 'til there's nothing left, so they might as well stop here, where there's still enough game to live on, and enough room to fight. The Sioux have to do something. Where else can they go?"

"Sounds like Red Cloud is going to kill a bunch of whites before it's over." I shook my head and watched as the young soldier backed a large Belgium workhorse out of its stall. "Jesus," I grinned. "Where do they find these kids?"

Dog stood up, stretched, and stared at the young soldier, "I better go help him before we run out of room here."

Part III
Higher Plains

◆✳ 14 ✳◆

The night before we left Fort Kearny, Fetterman had me summoned to his tent. The same dumb boy who'd come for a horse brought me Fetterman's message. "I'm going to be a horse soldier," he'd said as we splashed through the mud. "My pa was infantry, and his pa before him. Now it's time we step up. I had a feller write me a letter to send home and tell 'em."

"That's good," I'd said. "Always remember, they're the ones with shorter ears." He'd looked puzzled as we stepped into Fetterman's tent.

"You mean horses, or horse soldiers?" The kid actually felt his ears. I just stared at him. I wondered if he had any idea what was waiting for him out in the dry winds of the high plains. I felt like stopping right there and telling him.

"That will be all, Private," said Fetterman. The kid disappeared into the rain, still wondering. I heard his boots splat through the mud and disappear into the night.

"So you really are a horse dealer?" said Fetterman. He didn't even offer a drink from the bottle of rye on his footlocker. I glanced toward it two or three times. He ignored me.

"That's right." I shrugged. "Didn't we go over all this the other day?" I wouldn't look toward the bottle again if I died choking of thirst.

"Yeah, but I needed time to think things out. You know most of the money is coming out of mine and Carrington's pocket. I don't suppose I can appeal to your patriotism to go easy with us on the price?"

"Not a chance, Colonel. It's strictly business to me. This ain't no war to protect the homeland. From what I've seen, this is just the government's idea of target practice, except this time they've stepped in shit and don't know how to get it off their boots."

He cackled and threw back his head. "Yeah, you're not far off there. But I'm thinking about these young soldiers. They'd have a better chance on horseback."

"Better chance at what, breaking their necks before the Indians kill 'em? You've got some that don't know a horse from a tall hog. Your best defense is that the Indians will die laughing."

His cackle turned to a roar; he slapped his leg. "You're funnier than hell. Where do you get that stuff?"

"Just watching and listening, I reckon." I saw he was just smoothing me out to cut a good deal for himself. But it wouldn't help him. I was the man with the horses, and he was the man with his nuts in a bear trap. He must've seen it wasn't going to work.

"Then let's not mince words," he said. "I will pay a hundred and fifty . . . No!" He stopped and cleared his throat. "Make that a hundred a head for all the broke and trained saddle horses you can bring me."

I looked deep into his eyes, saw madness mixed with a trace of suicide, both brought on by a deep need to outfight a tribe of half-naked Indians, who so far had beat him, hands down, and defied all concepts of military strategy.

"Poor, crazy fool," I thought, reaching out and picking up the bottle without asking. "I will charge a hundred and *fifty* . . . No!" I threw back a shot. "Make that *two* hundred a head for eighty horses broke and trained."

"Where will you get that many horses?"

"Watch your language." I smiled. "Is it a deal or not?"

"Two weeks?"

"Better make it three," I said, as if time or deals meant anything in this country. I'd raised the bottle and took another deep swipe. He watched with a whipped look as I lowered the bottle and set it gently back on his footlocker. I let out a breath as the fiery amber cut through the dampness in my chest like liquid sunshine.

"It's a deal." He glanced at the bottle as if gauging the damage I'd done. "I hope you know what you're doing. I need them bad, and quick."

"So much for horses," I said with a cavalier grin. "How much for some soldiers who can ride them?"

He'd looked puzzled, then hurt, then all at once broke into an insane fit of laughter. "I get it!" he raved between choking, laughing, and turning red. "You'll cause me to bust a gut!" The crazy bastard.

The next morning, Dog, Dirty Jaw, and I rode slowly out of the fort as a twenty-piece military band blasted loud enough to wake the dead. Carrington stood smiling with his hands folded behind him, swaying and tapping his boot. Fetterman gave me a snappy salute, nodded toward Carrington, grinned, and rolled his eyes.

"Why don't they just hang a target on our backs?" I said. Dog and Jaw just smiled.

"It's not as bad as all that," said Jaw. "They're only killing whites."

"That's good to hear," I said. They both laughed.

"They won't bother you while you're with us," said Dog. "The big boys in Washington want you to believe that Cloud's command is a bunch of bloodthirsty savages, but that's just so you don't notice what's being done to them."

"Yeah," said Dog. "The Sioux have let whites live here for years with no more trouble than you'd have anywhere else."

"But now Washington wants to take over, so they play the Sioux as murderers," said Jaw. "If it wasn't for these damned forts, everybody would be getting along." He grinned toward Dog. "But then we'd be out of a job."

"Politics," I said.

"Always is," said Dog.

I noticed as soon as we left the fort, they got rid of their army shirts and cavalry saddles. Now they rode bareback, bare-chested, and slung Indian blankets around them against the morning air.

"We play it either way," said Dog as we turned our horses and headed for Powder River toward the Red Wall. That's where they said you would go to hide a string of horses and a wounded Indian. I didn't mention that the Indian was none other than Red Cloud De

Oglala, leader of the Bad Faces Sioux and Chief of Chiefs over Powder River.

"If we need work with the army, we throw on our scouting clothes. If we feel like wintering with the tribes, we take them off."

"Just like that? Nobody ever gives you any trouble?"

"Sure, all the time," said Dog. "Both sides call us the Laramie Loafers."

Jaw grinned. "We're a whole tribe under Chief Big Mouth. They look down on us, but not when they want something done—"

"It gives us an edge." Dog smiled. "We get a chance to bend things a little . . . sometimes. When the army wants to get a few chiefs together and sign another treaty, they send us—"

"Or if the tribes need to cut a deal for coffee or guns." Dog thumbed himself on the chest.

"Real slick," I said. "So you two see and hear what you want to, like the other day at the cave? I know ya'll had to see something."

They glanced at each other and laughed. "Sure, we saw traces of hoofs," said Dog, "but why tell them?"

"It'd been a long day," Jaw chuckled. "The last thing I wanted was to fight a bunch of pissed-off Sioux, 'specially in those dry creek beds."

"Hell, Mad Johnson probably saw it himself, but he'd already killed those Sioux kids. He probably figured it was a good day's work. Besides, it gave him a good reason to torment the hell out of Ben Bone, and it was a lot easier than taking out after your wranglers."

"Jesus," I said, "does anything make sense up here?"

"Nothing I've seen. But think what it would've done to Jaw's chances of joining the Sioux if we'd tangled with them that night."

"You're joining Red Cloud's Bad Faces?" I looked at Jaw in surprise.

"Either them or Standing Bear's bunch . . . just 'til winter," said Jaw. "Living with the tribes in winter is miserable. Everything starts smelling like bear grease and dog piss. There's never enough to eat, soldiers shooting at your ass . . ."

"I reckon it's rough," I said, dismissing the subject. I'd found that thinking or talking too much about this Powder River bunch caused my head to hurt.

Three days later, we'd stopped at a path in the deep woods. Jaw turned, placed his hand to his chest, then swung it away. "Watch out for your hair, White Dog," he called out. "You too." He nodded to me before disappearing into the fog-shrouded woodlands. I sat with my arms crossed on the saddle horn. Rain poured, running from my hat brim in a long stream as I nodded my head.

"Think he'll be alright?"

"Sure, he'll hook right up with the Sioux."

"Just like that? After serving with the army?"

"Cloud needs all the help he can get. Stick a feather in your hat and you could probably join."

"It's a big crazy game up here," I said.

"And everybody plays it," laughed Dog.

"You too?"

"Um-hm." He smiled.

We were many days getting to the Red Wall. We kept out of sight as much as possible, staying in rock shadows by day or traveling the flatlands by night. Much of our time was spent backtracking and slipping out of our trail. I'd nearly come out of my skin when we came upon a party of Cheyenne near a river crossing. They were part of a Southern Cheyenne tribe, still neutral, but I had no way of knowing. I thought it a good idea if everyone would wear something on their back saying whose side they were on.

They recognized Dog right away. I felt like a greenhorn outsider as I watched them speak Indian and make hand signs among themselves. At times I could tell they were talking about me, and I watched their eyes real close. Dog's eyes were always steady and deep, the eyes of an "honest man." "They want to know if you were with the buffalo man who snapped Two Hand in half."

"What did you tell them?"

"I told him your buffalo man was killed by the Sioux. They're disappointed. They wanted to meet him."

I hoped he was telling them wrong. "What else?"

"They want to know where we were going." He turned back to them, speaking and making signs. An older brave stepped near me, raised a painted stick high in the air, and made three circles as he spoke to the sky.

"What did you tell them?"

"Up Bozeman Trail for the summer," Dog whispered. The Cheyenne nodded among themselves. One of them held a fist chest-high and slowly laid his other fist on top of it.

I nodded with them; I liked Dog's style. I felt at ease traveling with him. He knew enough to stay alive, a rare gift in Powder River.

We shared a camp that night with the Cheyenne. When we woke up three hours before daylight, they'd already vanished. "They've stayed out of the war so far," said Dog, "but you never know when that could change. They could drift back in here with some Sioux and turn it into a hair-lifting."

"But you're on terms, ain't you?"

"Yeah, but even that could change if they caught me off guard. It's better to tell someone you're a friend while you're on equal ground. If I tried talking to the Sioux after they'd cornered me, they might figure I'm just talking to save my life."

"Makes sense." I grinned. "If you want to be friends with the Sioux, you need to catch *them* off guard and tell them."

"I know it sounds crazy, but that's better than telling them while their knife is at your throat." We rode away quick and quietly, going over a mile in the direction he'd told the Cheyenne, then swinging back after making a wide circle through some rocks. Two hours later, we sat overlooking a wide sunken valley at the base of Red Wall.

"I've got one more question," I said as we gazed across the valley. It had rained the night before, but come daylight the sun quickly dried the silver haze. I'd taken off my wet duster and spread it across my lap.

Dog smiled and pointed his rifle out across the valley. "Right over there," he said. He dropped his horse back behind mine as if to help me see better. "There's an opening in the wall beside a big white rock. Just follow the trail around through the canyon. If they're in there, they'll find you."

"Thanks," I said. I reined my horse around facing him. "But that's not what I wanted to ask you." I smiled; I would sure miss Dog. I'd thought of asking him along, but I knew it didn't fit his plans. I'd wondered what his plans were back in Kearny when he asked me to come along. Now, after watching him talk with the Cheyenne, I answered a question I'd asked myself the first night I'd met him.

"What then?" His horse stepped back and forth restlessly. He drew a tight rein.

I glanced around the wide cliff and up at the sky. "I was wondering why you waited till we got to this spot."

"For what?" said Dog, his eyes steady and clear; a slight smile twitched at his jawline.

"To kill me, as I ride off." My eyes were just as steady and clear. My smile was firm and certain.

Dog shook his head as he eased the rifle barrel slowly in my direction. "How did you figure?" he said, still smiling but with a look of regret. I watched his barrel move fraction by fraction.

I shrugged. "I wondered the first night we rode into Kearny. Nobody asks a man if he's carrying money, unless they're thinking about getting it. I wondered more the day you and Jaw told me how you played the army back and forth. I figured the only way you'd tell me all that was if you knew I wouldn't be around to repeat it."

"You're not as stupid as you look." Dog smiled.

"Thanks. I also watched how you lied to those Cheyenne, straight-faced and all. Then turned right around and told me you lied to them." I shook my head slowly. "Sloppy, on your part."

"Thanks for telling me. It must be my white blood. I'll work on that." His eyes glanced at the pistol in my holster as his thumb cocked the hammer and the rifle crept closer. He was wondering if I was fast. I could've told him I wasn't, never had been. It wouldn't have mattered if I was. I'd already learned not to fire a shot in this land of a thousand echoes, not unless you wanted to draw everybody within ten miles.

My left hand was on the saddle horn holding the reins. My right hand lay across my lap on the wet duster, a long way from my pistol. He was wondering, I was watching. The funeral drum began to pound in my head.

"Money? Is that what it is?"

"Yeah." He shrugged, looking a little embarrassed. "I've never met a horse dealer who didn't keep a roll stashed somewhere on him." He was very calm; he knew he still had the drop, or thought it.

"It's in my boots. I never carry it anywhere else, traveling."

His rifle stopped. "You sure are being a sport."

"If you want it, it's yours." I shrugged. "You don't have to kill me for it. You can take it and let me ride away." Again he watched my hands. Did I have a pistol in the folds of my riding duster on my lap? I raised my right hand slowly and laid it on top of my left on the saddle horn, just to show him I didn't. His hand relaxed slightly. Now I would hear his true intentions.

"No, I won't kill you." His eyes said he meant it. The eyes of an honest man. They were even deeper and more clear than before. Now his smile spread, opened up, wide and sincere. That's when I knew he was lying; he meant to kill me sure as hell.

"Which one first?" I let my hand drift cautiously toward my right boot. He caught on and stopped me.

"No, the left."

I hesitated with a worried look. Finally I nodded easy. "Okay, left it is." I brought my right hand up and lowered my left. He stared intently. It was like gambling to him. I saw a light come on in his eyes.

"No!" This time he was sure. He'd caught my trick. I stopped with a puzzled look. "The right!" His rifle swung toward me and he grinned like a sly dog. "Take off the right boot first." I shook my head and reached down. He glanced up and away for a split second as if congratulating himself, then his eyes snapped back suddenly at the whistling sound. His whole body jerked once; his eyes held a look of great revelation, that turned to confusion, then a startled plea for a second chance. The handle of the glades knife glistened against his bare chest. A trickle of blood seeped beneath the brass hilt and ran down in a jagged red line.

His hands went to the knife handle, not on it but near it, like the hands of a gypsy hovering near a crystal ball. His body jerked once more; his fingers quivered. He looked back up at me, his future revealed, then melted down the side of his horse.

"I'm sorry," I said softly. "I truly am." Wind across the valley roared in a deep echo as it swept the caves and canyons. I kneeled beside him and watched the knife handle rise and fall with each fading breath, an inch from his heart. He raised a weak hand to his hair. "No," I said. "I wouldn't know how even if I wanted to." He seemed relieved.

I let out a deep breath and shook my head. Above the valley a hawk lay in an updraft, suspended in air. Dog stared at it a second through distant eyes. He raised his hand to the knife handle and looked up at me. His eyes were not clear, or deep, or offering pretense. There was no need for either honesty or deception. We'd become two strangers waiting for a train, each headed in a different direction, each in our silence, making our travel plans. He tried to nod his head. I saw what he asked, took a firm grip on the handle ... twisted it once ... quick, through bone and flesh, a half inch, and his heart stopped.

◆✳ 15 ✳◆

I spent a strange day riding into the Red Wall, thinking about White Dog . . . about killing him. By noon, all traces of last night's rain had vanished, and the valley became a furnace. Hot wind whipped up dust devils from within the grass; they danced past me, stinging my face, licking at my clothes, and tangling my horse's mane.

It was foolish, the knife trick I'd played with the half-breed. I should've back-shot him as soon as I had a hunch about his intentions. I reckon I was hoping to the end that he would prove me wrong. Either that, or else I was getting as loco as every other fool I'd run into lately.

I hadn't intended on burying him. I'd planned to leave him where he fell, same as I'd done others during the war and since. But I'd rummaged through his belongings there on the windy cliff, and afterwards, well . . . I just figured I owed it to him.

I carved layers of sod with my glades knife. When I'd pulled a spot wide enough and long enough to cover him, I laid him in it, spread his blanket over him, and pressed the sod down good and firm. I carried in a few rocks and laid them over him; that was that. I said no words, for there were none to say. I'd killed him, before he could kill me.

Among his personals I'd found an envelope. Inside, there was a lock of black hair tied in a pink ribbon. I figured it was his mother's. With it was a wrinkled letter that had gone yellow from weather and time. He must've carried it everywhere. It wasn't signed and it was just three words poorly written. "Make us proud," it said. I buried it with him, kept his rifle and ammunition, and turned his horse loose in the wide valley.

I followed the advice of the man I'd killed, riding across the valley and bearing left around the red cliffs. By midafternoon I was deep inside a stone corridor and feeling as if the world was shutting down behind me. My horse's hoofs sounded too loud against rock and hard ground. I tried to ride easy and quiet. I don't know why.

There's no worse feeling than being alone after taking a life. There is a silent presence. A spirit pleads as if in obligation to share what's gone on since the moment of death. It's crazy. I have felt it many times. The mind argues with itself and all life around it as if to justify the act.

And it's different killing a man close up with your hands, with the flick of cold steel. In the heat of morning I'd felt the warmth of his body on my hand as I slid the blade from his chest. I'd smelled him, his clothes, his hair, his presence, and heard a sigh from within his chest, though he was already dead.

Come dark, I built a small fire, laid out a rolled blanket, and propped Dog's rifle against a rock. I hobbled my horse in a mound of grass and climbed a sharp slope twenty yards above the campsite. From a recess in the face of the slope, I had a clear view of all beneath me. With my rifle across my lap I slung my riding duster about my shoulders and went to sleep thinking of White Dog, and Gyp Pope . . . and others who'd fallen along the way.

When sunlight crept across my lap, I got up, climbed down the slope, and cleared all traces of my campsite. By midafternoon I rode up a low rise and looked behind me. The hard land lay peaceful and silent, and I sat there for the longest time, just thinking.

It was foolish, I reckon, but I sat wondering how long Red Cloud and the Sioux could hold this land. Could they hold it any longer than the ones they'd taken it from, or the ones before *them?* And once the white people—my people—took it, how long would they hold it, and who would someday drive them from it? It was foolish thoughts; the thoughts of a man alone, small and quiet in the face of this harsh slice of heaven.

I reined away from the low rise and wandered off deeper into the land. I looked at what was going on up here as an outsider. What I saw was a swirl of faces, from Queenie the whore to the president of the country; they, and everybody between, were acting in what they thought was their best interest. The settlers, the teamsters, the army and miners, everybody snatched for a handful of something.

I was no different. I came here wanting to sell stolen horses and make a fast dollar, I thought. But hell, it went deeper than that. Whatever I and all the others really wanted lay somewhere in the silence high above the canyon walls. I had to shake my head clear of such foolishness and go about the business at hand.

◆✳ 16 ✳◆

"Guns and knives," he said, from within a gray beard that seemed to cover his entire face. His words were without expression or air, the voice of a man who hadn't spoken to anyone in a long time. I stared at him from against the woodpile as a three-legged dog limped back and forth threatening me across broken teeth.

"I've been wandering around for two days," I said. "If I meant you harm, I could've ambushed you from that ledge." I nodded toward the rock overhang above his shack. I'd heard the distant belch of a shotgun the day before as I'd sat there in deep thought. When I followed the direction of the sound to the ledge, I'd come upon the shack below.

He'd rigged a false ledge of loose boards, covered it with dirt and rock in case some dumb bastard came snooping around. It worked. One step and I'd bounced sixty feet down rock and scrub trees. Then I'd been bitten by a three-legged dog as I lay unconscious.

"As it is," he said, curling his lips like he wanted to say more.

"What?" I saw the swirl of lunacy in his eyes as he leaned slightly toward me pointing my pistol at my chest. "Just one more," I thought, "in a country overblessed with maniacs."

"As it is?" He cocked his head sideways. Somehow I was supposed to understand.

"Uh, yeah," I said, "as it is."

He'd missed the forty-four hanging from my neck by a strip of rawhide beneath my shirt. When I got a chance, I could close his eyes and ride on, but I hoped I wouldn't have to. He was just a crazy old coot with a biting dog. "Can I have some water?" I pointed toward a rain barrel.

He looked at the rain barrel curiously as if seeing it for the first time. "Water," he said.

"Yeah," I thought, it had been a long time. I wondered what strange conversations had gone on between him and the dog before he'd finally shut up altogether. I moved real easy, careful of spooking him. Since he hadn't said no, I decided to see how far I could go before he stopped me. The dog stayed right at my feet, growling.

"Seen any horses through here lately?" I poured a dipper of water over the back of my head and let it run down in my face. "I'm looking for a string of horses." I sipped from the dipper. "A white man and a black man." Sometimes talking normal to people like this would cause them to come around. It's like their mind shuts down from lack of use. Least thing can restart it. "I reckon you ain't," I answered for him.

"Guns and knives," he said, pointing my pistol at me. It wasn't cocked. My glades knife was in his belt; my rifle leaned against the woodpile. Somewhere above us my horse would graze until I returned for her, or get thirsty and wander off.

I wiped water from my face with my hand and slung my wet hair back. "I need it back now," I said, reaching for my pistol like it was no big deal. He stared at it and turned it over in his hands. I carefully placed my hand on his and raised the gun in the air. I eased it from his hand and dropped it in my holster. "Knife too." I motioned at his belt. The dog growled at my feet.

"As it is," he mumbled, shaking his bowed head, "guns and knives." He slid the knife from his belt and handed it to me.

"I know," I said, "crazy things, ain't they?"

"As it is."

I wiped dust from my rifle and checked it over good. "Did I hear a shotgun coming from here yesterday?" I stared at him a second, then shook my head. "Forget it," I said.

He walked away around the side of the shack and came back carrying a muzzle-loader shotgun. He carried it by the barrel with the stock dragging in the dirt. When he held it out to me, I noticed the trigger was gone, replaced by a strip of leather. I took it and leaned it against the woodpile. "You need to get to town more often." I smiled.

That afternoon I climbed the ridge, found my horse, and rode three miles around until I found a steep path down to the shack. I took some jerked strips of elk from my saddlebags, and the old man ate like he was starving. I flipped a piece to the dog; he grabbed it and ran limping away, as if I might change my mind.

"Are you out of stores?" I asked. He just stared at me, puffing and snorting as he worked on a mouthful of elk. "I know." I raised my hand. "As it is."

The next morning I rode out early and shot a young buck deer. I brought it back, quartered it, and cooked it over an open fire. The rest of it, I hung in the curing shed next to the shack. While the meat sizzled and flared, the old man and the three-legged dog stared as if watching a holy event.

"Sure enough, I was . . . goner." He reached a weak hand to carve off a chunk of venison. It still sizzled over the fire. I shoved his hand away and stabbed a sharp stick into the roasting meat.

"Carve around it," I said. He did, with a trembling hand, and I handed him the stick with steaming meat on it. "Easier on the hands, ain't it?"

He grinned and tore into the hot venison. "I reckon . . . was starving . . . you came along." He'd come around quick. His mind still skipped a beat now and then, but words were coming back to him. The dog grabbed anything that hit the ground, then disappeared with it.

I'd gone through his supplies and found nothing but a handful of dried roots and less than a pound of beans. He'd barely made it through the winter and lost his mind by early spring. Isolation and hunger works quick on the mind. Now he was snapping back.

"Found some rabbits . . . but missed them . . . last shot."

"Well, I'm going to leave you a rifle and a belt full of ammunition. If you're wise, you'll head south before next winter."

"May-be," he said, but I knew he was lying. He would hang on 'til his world stopped. The shack would rot into the ground around him and they would disappear into the dirt. I reckon it was his choice.

"What's kept Red Cloud's bunch from killing you?"

"No reason . . . to. Cloud . . . ain't that bad. Nobody . . . comes here. Army's . . . the problem."

My job was to fill in the missing words.

"You asked . . . horses?"

"You remember me asking?"

He nodded his head. "Remember hearing . . . couldn't answer." He pointed up over the ridge. "Two weeks back . . . hundred maybe . . . big dark man."

"That's my bunch." I poured boiling coffee and set a cup at his feet. He drank it as steam billowed from both corners of his mouth. I had to look away.

"By God, you're hurting me," I laughed.

"Good coffee."

"Yeah, I'm known across Kansas for my coffee."

"I . . . bet," he said, eyeing my tied-down holster. He was coming along real well.

"How long have you been here?"

He considered it, scratching his beard and gazing up at the sky. "Since right . . . after Antietam." He wanted to say more, but the words weren't there yet.

"You fought for the Union?" I watched him, hoping the conversation would loosen the hinges that had rusted shut in his mind.

"Yeah," he said finally, nodding his head slowly as if he hadn't thought of it for a long time. "Stood the . . . first charge." He thought of it some more. I began to get the picture of a man still licking his wounds from a battle somewhere deep inside his head. It was a battle that still raged. Maybe up here in the high plains, he'd learned to silence it from time to time. "Served as sergeant under General Burnside." I watched him shake his head as words began to draw shape from the pictures in his mind. "After the first charge, we ran through a field . . . of guts and brains, 'til our pant-legs were soaked with blood. Took three charges before we broke the line at Sharpsburg." His eyes glazed and traveled off. "Then A. P. Hill's Rebels . . . hit us at the bridge . . . stopped us cold . . ."

"I reckon it was pretty rough." I wanted to keep him talking as long as I could, until his mind loosened up.

"Yeah." He focused back on my face with a mused expression. "The rifle fire was so heavy, it sounded like a sleet storm. Over twelve thousand dead and wounded. Afterwards . . . I just walked away . . ."

"And you wound up here?" I spread my hands across the horizon.

"Lot of us did . . . between here and Red Wall. The Sioux call us the 'Walking Dead.' Most of us have either drifted away, or starved . . . or prayed down the end of a gun barrel. Red Cloud and the Sioux don't bother me." He studied the ground at his feet. "They go on a killing spree now and then, but it's nothing to fear. It's the killing in my head that I have to worry about."

The next morning I gave him Dog's rifle, pistol, and bullets, and showed him how to use the repeater. After three rounds he could snap a limb from a tree. He turned the rifle back and forth in his hands, inspecting it. "I'm lucky you didn't have that when I fell in here," I laughed.

"Real sorry," he said, shaking his head.

"Forget it." I waved my hand. "You should have enough ammunition here to last you the summer. Next rabbits you run into are in big trouble."

When I was ready to swing up in my saddle, the three-legged dog came from behind the woodpile wagging his tail. He stood watching as if to bid me farewell. I reached out to pet his head before I left. Sniffing my fingertips, seeing no food in my hand, he bellied down in a low growl. I jerked my hand away, barely missing a flash of broken teeth. "Good dog," I said, shaking my head and checking my fingers.

Falling in on the old man and his three-legged dog had shaken me back to reality. Whatever reason I had for being here, staying alive was a big part of it. There were places in this land where a man with enough bullets could hold off an army till he died of old age, and I figured there were people here prepared to do *just* that. Who the hell was I to question what was going on? The ground was full of people who'd done that.

I imagined eyes behind every rock and above every ledge. They could see me, I couldn't see them. I had no choice but to ride on.

Most of my life I'd ridden the shadows, trying to keep from being found. This was a whole other thing for me.

By evening I'd crossed a wide range of grazing land and started back up a low rise of loose rock. I'd seen hoofprints of many horses traveling in close order. They were not Indian horses, for they wore shoes, and they were not carrying riders, judging from their shallow impressions.

I followed the prints as I climbed the loose rock and watched them fade and disappear as the loose rock turned into a hard solid surface. For over an hour I rode leaning from my saddle studying the ground for any trace of hoofprints. Only when I'd nearly given up and raised upright in the saddle did I see the Catahoula cur bouncing along quietly with his nose to the ground as if helping me search. "Well, I'll be damned," I said aloud, feeling a little embarrassed. I had no idea how long he'd been with me.

I reined toward him, and he stopped long enough to turn his head and raise a front paw, then loped away toward a high wash of dirt that led upward into a narrow valley. When he disappeared, I followed his tracks up a slope of dirt and loose rocks, and didn't see the eight mounted warriors until I topped the ridgeline and stared at them from ten feet away. I jerked to a halt and froze. My hand started instinctively to my holster, but I stopped it. At this distance all I could do was hope and pray they knew Jack and Shod and what we'd done for Red Cloud.

Two warriors bolted forward, one on either side. Their hands went across me like a swarm of locusts, gathering my weapons. One reached out, slapped me on the chest, and smiled. He ripped open my shirt and pulled the loop over my head. My hat flew away as he snatched my forty-four from my neck. I stared straight ahead at the one in the middle. "I am good friend of the Sioux," I said, trying to use my hands the way Red Cloud's daughter did. "I saved the life of Red Cloud." He made no expression. I waited a second. "You speak English?"

He spoke to the warriors and they laughed. Behind him I heard more hoofs running up the low rise toward us. "What did you say?" I smiled. Evidently my words had struck a humorous chord.

Three horses topped the rise behind them and begin circling to the front. I heard a familiar voice. "He said, you sound like a man scared out of his wits . . . who'd do or say anything to save his neck."

"Howdy, Jack," I said in a breath of relief.

◆✳ 17 ✳◆

"You have seen what happened to others, still you come. Why?"

Red Cloud sat across the low fire on a stack of blankets and hides, just high enough above us that we had to tilt our heads.

"Business." I glanced at Jack and Shod, wondering if Red Cloud understood what I meant.

"Your 'business' is to come into my country . . . to bring horses to my enemies?"

I shrugged. "I can't deny that's why we came here. I reckon we hadn't looked at it that way."

Red Cloud drew a firm smile across his tired face. He looked better now than when I saw him last, but he still had a ways to go. "None of your people look at it 'that' way. I don't understand. I do not come to your country and cut roads where you do not want roads. Yet you people keep coming even after I tell you not to."

I glanced again between Jack and Shod. "Mister Cloud, we can't tell you why our people do what they do. We just deal horses. It would take somebody higher up to tell you why the government is doing what they're doing up here. Every time I hear it, I hear a different version. Tell you the truth, I don't think anybody knows."

"You come while others flee. You saw the trap my warriors set for you and Bone the Fool. You are alive at the top of my country where the army wants to be, but cannot. Your warriors"—he gestured toward Jack and Shod—"hide me from the soldiers and return me to my people when they could have given me to the army. Who is higher than you? You killed a man for a horse that did not belong to you . . ."

I glanced at Jack. He shrugged. "We talked a little—"

"You and the loafer, White Dog, traveled through our warriors and then you killed him. You saw through his trap. You fight like one who has fought against many. You sleep in the cold and watch from above your campfire, so your enemies cannot see you. You feed the crazy one who waits alone for death with his crippled dog. And you come here led by a dog who belongs to no one, but who leads you as a friend. Why has the spirit brought you here, 'Miller Crowe'?"

"Crowe?" Shod breathed the word and stared at me as if seeing me for the first time. I snapped my eyes toward Jack.

"I didn't tell him *that*," he said.

"You try to hide from your name, but you cannot. Your name travels around you. I heard it from one who heard it from the White Beard who kills for money. He hunts you for killing Gyp Pope."

"Yeah," I said. "It's been a busy trip."

Red Cloud spread his arms. "But now you are here at the top of my country, where your enemies will be my enemies, and you can rest and sleep on soft skins without looking over your shoulder. When you have rested, we will talk and make smoke together."

By the end of the week, though I wasn't going to complain, Indian food was shooting through me like a dose of salts. As I came back from the woods one night holding my belly in both hands, I heard a rustle in the grass a few yards away. I dropped to the ground, crawled a few yards, and peeped over the edge of a low rise.

Red Cloud stood tall and still, gazing out into the darkness, his shadow drawn long in the moonlight. His voice sounded low and deliberate as he spoke to the empty night. "Find someone else's country where you can do what you think you must do. You are not welcome here. We are—" He stopped and drew a breath and started over. "Find someone else's country where you can do what you—"

He stopped when my belly made a long curious sound; and instead of being caught crawling around like a snake, I stood up quickly as he turned toward me. "Evening," I said quietly with a raised hand. He stood silent as I walked over—"real pretty country"—and gazed out across the valley.

"I heard sound, like small cannon," said Red Cloud.

"Yeah." I felt my face redden. "I ain't felt good all day."

"White man's food, does me, same way." He drew up his shoulders beneath his blanket and gazed out with me. A shooting star crossed in a slow arch that seemed to take forever. Seeing it, he let out a long breath. "I say words to the night, to know how to say them to Little White Chief Carrington."

"I'll go—" I said, not wanting to disturb his practice.

"No. Stay. Tell me what to say, so they will understand me, and stop coming."

"I wish I could, Mister Cloud . . . I truly do. But you're wasting your breath."

"Better my breath than my people's blood."

"I hear you. But you'll waste both, and they'll still keep coming. They think they're supposed to . . . like it's meant to be or something. They call it 'manifest destiny.' "

He nodded to me, then gazed out. "I have seen that about the whites. They think all things belong to them. They only hear their own words."

"Yeah, it's hell, but it's born in us. We think we've got free run, and everything else is under us. We've been that way since God was a gardener. It makes us crazy."

"At first they come, bringing gifts. They looked at our country and liked what we have. And we were friends . . ."

"Ain't that *always* the way." I shook my head. My stomach growled low; it hurt really bad.

"Then they come, to help us, but we need no help. Then they come to teach us their ways. But we have *our* ways . . ."

"Just like Sunday school."

"Then they come to have us make words on paper. We need no words on paper. So they left us . . ."

"Never seen it fail," I said.

"Now they come, only to kill us . . . to kill our food, to kill our country. They say we should be in another place. A place that is not our country."

"I know, I know."

He stopped and faced me. "Why, are you, agreeing, with me?"

"No offense," I said. "But I'm just doing it to shut you up."

His eyes flared in the moonlight. "To shut, me up?"

" 'Cause like I said, you're wasting your breath."

"Then we will spill blood."

"Now you're talking! Shoot it up and get it over with. The quicker they kill you, the sooner they can start feeling bad about it. In a hundred years . . . they'll *really* be sorry. Some will be plumb pissed off about it, but see if they offer your land back."

"You talk strange."

"I just finished fighting a war against the same bunch. They all live by a big river in a bucket of mud. They kicked our ass real smart like. Now all you hear 'em say is what a terrible thing it was."

"The war to free the slave people, like your buffalo man?"

"If you believe that, you're as stupid as they think you are. That war was about business, same as any other war. The push to free the colored folk only became a hot issue when it looked like England might jump in and deal with the South as a separate country. Congress don't give a damn about the colored people no more than they do about you or me or any little feller. The war has been over more than a year and they still ain't gave the colored folk their citizenship. Even if they do, it'll be a hundred years before they can vote. You just watch."

Red Cloud looked puzzled. I caught myself rambling on. "Hell with it, Chief. I don't know what I'm talking about, no more than you do. Let's just say it like this. The colored folk might've gained freedom on paper, but it was mostly for show. That big feller back there couldn't even drink in a saloon."

"Then why did you fight among yourselves?"

"Beats the hell out of me. They call it 'progress'—it means 'gone crazy wanting more.' The South had something the North wanted, so they found a reason to go to war. Ain't that always the way." I shook my head. "It's dog eat dog where I live, Chief. And I've learned to be as big a dog as the rest."

"If I could go there and speak to the Chief of Chiefs, I could tell them what you say. Then they would listen and do different."

"I appreciate your confidence, Mister Cloud, but if you do that, they'll either hang you or put you in a circus. Either way, you've seen your last shooting star without it bumping into something."

"You have much bitterness inside you."

I let out a breath. "Naw, but I've sure got my share. I fought guerilla, for a lost cause . . . same as you're doing here. I reckon it's still in me . . . makes me think different. I reckon that's what brought me up to the top of your country. That and just restlessness."

"No. The spirit led you here. I am sure of it. But we must find out why."

"That's what I'm starting to ask myself. All I can say is, 'I came to deal horses.' "

He turned to me with a wise smile. "Are you making 'progress'?"

"I reckon I asked for that," I said, looking sheepish.

Red Cloud shook his head and studied the stars. "Such strange people. How do I talk to such people? How do I deal with such people?"

"You don't. You can't dabble in mud without getting it on your fingers. So don't talk to them. If they talk, don't listen. If they preach, don't pray. They hand you something, don't take it. Feed you something, don't swallow. Just say '*No.*' "

Something rolled over in my stomach and made a sound like a broken bed spring. I pressed my hand against it. "Your country is being held by an occupation force, but it won't last forever. Stay guerilla, whatever the cost. Demand justice. Make the bastards kill you . . ."

Red Cloud stared at me a second reading my eyes. "Would you die to see justice?"

I let out a breath and felt my stomach growl. "Naw, I reckon not, but that's a different thing. I'm nothing but a two-bit outlaw—"

"I see. That is what you made of yourself." Red Cloud glanced away. "Would you die for money?"

"Well . . . I've come near it a few times."

"Honor? Would you die for honor?"

"Hell no! But we're not talking about—"

"Thank you." Red Cloud smiled and raised a hand. "You have shown me how to repay you for saving my life."

"What?" I looked at him curiously, then smiled. "Letting us take those horses to Kearny would be thanks enough."

"So you can make money?"

"Well, yeah, to tell the truth. I care a lot for money."

Red Cloud gazed into the dark sky with a wise smile and drew his blanket around him. "But I will repay you with much more."

"That's very kind of you to offer, but money is plenty." I smiled and gazed up with him. My stomach made a long squeal and fell hard.

"Sounds like somebody stuck a hog," Jack said, stepping up beside us from out of the darkness. We turned facing him. My stomach lunged up in my chest, then dropped again, like a load of hot rocks.

"Ya'll excuse me," I said in a strained voice. I started into the woods in quick short steps.

"Whatever he's been telling you, Chief, don't take it too serious," I heard Jack say to Red Cloud. I heard him chuckle. "He's just got the shits."

"I understand," said Cloud, in a low voice.

The next morning, Shod, Jack, and Kermit stood around me as I scrubbed my long johns in a creek. "Whatever you said to him, it certainly has him fired up," said Shod.

"Just politics and religion," I said without looking up. "I should've kept my mouth shut."

"Well . . . he's ready to cut a deal." Jack chuckled under his breath. "Maybe you work better on an empty stomach."

I picked up my boots with two fingers and sloshed them around in the creek. The Catahoula cur walked up beside me, looked at my wet boots, and stuck his nose in my face. I patted his head and nudged him away as he tried to lick me. I noticed he was looking slicker and better fed. "What's he saying?"

"He didn't go into detail," said Jack, "but it sounds like he's giving us 'our' horses and a bunch of his, to take to Fort Kearny."

"Congratulations," said Shod. "Once again you've impressed someone."

I glanced at Shod; his expression said nothing. Kermit stepped closer and peeped around over my shoulder.

"Can I have five damn minutes alone?"

Kermit snapped back. Jack chuckled under his breath and nudged Shod. As they walked away, I slung water from my boots and shoved my bare feet in them. When I'd hung my socks and long johns over a bush, I started up the creekbank with the Catahoula cur beside me. I tried to remember what I'd said to Cloud last night. I felt embarrassed about most of it. I hoped he didn't think I was crazy.

A toothless old Indian yelled something as I walked to Red Cloud's tepee; his voice reminded me of the old man back in Crofton. I glanced at him and he made a sign with his fingers like many horses running. A group of Indians smiled and nodded their heads. "What's wrong with him?" said Jack, as I joined him and Shod in front of the tepee.

"Hell, I don't know."

"You seem to draw those kind," said Shod, and I just stared at him as Stands Alone stuck her head through the flap and beckoned us inside. She left when we entered.

When we were seated, Red Cloud glanced at my wet boots. "Feel better?"

"Much." I nodded, avoiding Jack and Shod. "Thank you."

Two warriors joined us. We watched as they seated themselves beside Red Cloud, on the ground just below his pile of hides and blankets.

"This is Crazy Horse and Band of Iron. We will make smoke together." I studied the two Indians' faces as Red Cloud filled a long pipe and touched a burning twig to it. Band of Iron had the expression of a man waiting to be told what to do, but Crazy Horse stared with a fixed jaw. His eyes swirled between a whisper and a scream, like a man ready to wrap death in small packages and send them to everybody he knew.

"I have thought of your words," said Red Cloud, leaning forward, and passing the pipe to my hands.

"Yeah." I cleared my throat. "About last night. Don't listen to me. I'm just a damned outlaw. I don't know nothing. I'm out there knocking my nuts together every day, just keeping from getting killed or caught."

Red Cloud looked puzzled. Jack and Shod stared down and shook their heads. Band of Iron patted himself on the crotch, made two fists, and bumped them together to show Red Cloud what I meant.

"Umm," said Red Cloud with a wince, "I understand."

I shot Jack a smug glance and handed him the pipe. The smoke I'd inhaled dropped against my raw and tender intestines and I felt them twist and groan. "But you spoke from here." Cloud patted his stomach.

"That's for sure—"

"You did not think of your words, the way the white chiefs, and even *I,* have done. For that, I say you are a man to be listened to. A man who speaks from his inside."

"Don't take it too far. I wasn't in the best of shape—"

Red Cloud silenced me with a toss of his hand. By now the pipe had gone full circle, and my stomach whined pitifully as Red Cloud took a long draw and delivered it to me. The tepee swirled in a brown-gray fog. My eyes turned wet; sickness crawled at the back of my throat. I inhaled a heavy chunk of smoke and shoved the pipe to Jack. He looked at my face and chuckled under his breath.

"If you were fighting a large army with few warriors, how would you fight?" Cloud glanced past Crazy Horse, then stared at me for an answer. I saw he was testing me.

I swallowed hard. "I reckon I'd draw off a few of them at a time. Make 'em chase me. Keep 'em mad, keep 'em scared. I'd stretch them out along narrow trails, then jump out and kill 'em one and two at a time."

Crazy Horse stiffened up with a curious gleam in his eyes. "See," said Red Cloud. "This man knows our ways of war."

"Nothing new," I said. "We fought that way along the border. It's the way—the only way—a small army stands a chance. It's better to win a *lot* of little battles than to lose *one* big one."

"The white army knows this. Why do they fight the way they do?"

"They've got no choice. It's all worked out on paper before they get here. They're fighting here in your land. They don't know where to hide, and they have so many dumb kids to get killed that they don't even care. They'll get you the hard way. They'll kill your food supply and keep pouring in troops. They'll buy some of you off with treaties and lies, divide you, starve you . . . They'll win. Make no mistake—"

"We will never be beaten," Crazy Horse hissed. "We will fight—"

"I know," I said. Red Cloud watched as I spoke to Crazy Horse. "They'll never beat you inside, but they will beat you. I'd be lying if I told you what you're wanting to hear."

The pipe came back around. I inhaled a deep draw and felt my insides shudder. Red Cloud nodded at Crazy Horse, then turned to me. I felt my stomach swell up in my throat.

"You will take the horses we took from Star Chief Conner's troops, back when the moon was cold. You will sell them to the army and buy guns for me from the Laramie Loafers."

I gagged and threw my hand over my mouth. My eyes filled with water. I nodded and tried to swallow. It didn't help. I stood up wobbling. "I have your word that you will do this for me?"

I couldn't say a word for fear of getting sick right in their laps. I nodded my head up and down vigorously, felt my jaws cramp and my eyes water as I spun toward the open air. "Good," said Red Cloud, "it is done."

◆✳ 18 ✳◆

"I couldn't just sit there and blow puke all over his tepee."

"Of course not," said Shod. "So instead, you've agreed to sell him guns to use against the United States Army." He rubbed his bald head. "The list grows longer."

"What's that mean?"

"It simply means I'm wondering about this partnership of ours."

I dipped my bandanna in the creek and wiped my face with it. Now my head thumped like a club on an oak bucket. "Look, Mister Shod, you don't owe me a thing. I can pay you right now, a dollar a day since we left Crofton, or a third of the string—"

"Thank you ... but we're a little 'up-country' to start negotiating a buyout."

"Then shut up about it, boy!" I was sick and rattled; I lost control. Shod's nostrils flared and his eyes turned into warning labels on a bottle of poison. I knew it was a mistake and I already regretted it. I was just too sick to stop myself. Kermit jumped away as Shod's hand slapped his holster, then stopped.

"So finally it comes out," Shod breathed. He let his hand fall away from his gun and stared with a mused look. " 'The man who speaks from his inside.' "

"I didn't mean it . . ."

"Sure you did—"

"But you've been on my ass in a sneaking way ever since I got here. Now, we ain't kin and we ain't the same color. You're too big to fight and too smart to argue with, so leave me the hell—"

"Just the way I like it," said Jack, walking up with a rope thrown over his shoulder. "Everybody pissed at everybody else."

I looked up at Shod, spread my hands, and let out a breath. "Damn it, Shod—" He turned and walked away.

"Kermit, who're you mad at?" Jack grinned. Kermit glanced between us, shrugged, turned and followed Shod toward the horses. The Catahoula cur sat looking back and forth.

"If he's on you about selling guns to the Indians, he's right."

"Don't start—"

"They'll hang us a bunch of times, then talk bad about us when we're gone."

"Jack, I was just trying to get out before I puked."

"Cloud thinks you gave your word."

"Then I'll explain."

"Let me know before you do. I want a two-day head start."

"Damn it, Jack. What am I gonna do? I'm sicker than a dog. I went and said all that bullshit last night." I held my thumping head in my hand, felt sweat trickle down my nose.

Jack reached out and slapped me on the back. "You'll feel better after a big ole bowl of breakfast," he chuckled.

Stands Alone walked up with a gourd of fresh water in one hand and what looked like chopped-up tree bark in the other. She smiled at Jack as she offered them to me. "Swallow this," she said. "It will make the rumbling go away."

"I'll try anything." I reached out a trembling hand, took the concoction, and threw back a long drink of water. She watched for a second as I felt my face draw tight across my cheekbones; but in a second I felt my stomach calm down, and she turned to Jack as I let out a long breath.

"Is good, it is done." She gestured toward the strip of woods on the other side of the creek. "You asked to see pretty spot?" Her eyes flickered with the slightest suggestion.

"I can hardly wait." Jack grinned.

As a guest of Red Cloud's Bad Faces, I was free to wander about the sprawling camp. In doing so, I soon realized there were well over five thousand warriors. And this was no ragtag band of drifters. This was a well-fed, well-mounted light cavalry force with the capabilities of sustaining themselves for a long and bloody campaign. Under

Red Cloud's command, there was a sense of organization that, according to Band of Iron, had never existed this strong among the Sioux Nation.

Army wagons, stolen during raids around Fort Kearny, carried in loads of fresh game throughout the day, and the women stayed at the large cook fires from daylight to dark, constantly preparing meals. War parties came and went with regularity, keeping pressure on Fort Kearny and the Bozeman Trail as if following a long-range battle plan.

Here was a nation committed to war, going about their business with coordinated determination. Even the children stayed busy cleaning the weapons seized by the warriors and brought back to be distributed among newcomers who arrived daily.

While nothing more was said about us saving Red Cloud's life, hospitality centered around us wherever we went.

One evening, as I stood looking across an endless herd of horses, I watched Dirty Jaw come riding by with three other braves. When he saw me, he cut away from the group and reined up near me. I dropped my hand near my holster in case there were any hard feelings over my killing his friend White Dog; but he saw my move and made it a point to keep his hands chest-high in the reins.

"So you made it to the top of Red Cloud's country." He smiled and swung his horse around. I watched him close as he slid from the Indian saddle and stood before me. "I wondered how it would go between you and White Dog. Did he die well?"

I stared at him a second before answering. "He's dead, however 'well' that is." I took a step back and eyed him close. "You don't seem very broken up about it. I thought he was your friend."

"Sure was . . . my best friend. We rode many a mile together." His smile broadened. "But that don't make you my enemy, does it?"

"You tell me."

He waved a hand as if to wipe away any memory of White Dog. "Naw, I've got nothing to settle with you. Fact is, I'm the one who'll be bringing the guns to you from Laramie. I'm looking forward to working with you."

"I don't know that I'll do it. I've got to think about—"

"Oh, you'll do it," he laughed. "I've got no doubts about that."

"What makes you so sure?"

He leaned forward and rubbed his thumb and fingertips together in the familiar sign of greed. "Money, what else? I told Cloud you'd do anything for money. You might say I gave you a good reference."

I gazed at his sly expression and felt a flash of shame. "You had no cause to say that about me. If I do it at all, it won't be for money." I stared at him. "Did he believe you?"

Jaw shrugged. "Who knows what goes on in his mind. But he knows that's why I'm doing it. I made it plain that my interest is in cashing in on some traveling money." He grinned again. "Cloud understands. He knows the way of the world outside of here."

I just shook my head as I thought of the children back in the camp, saw the seriousness in their eyes as they sharpened knives and wiped blood from the seized army swords. "And you call yourself an Indian?"

"Huh-uh. I'm only half. And even that half has dipped a long time from the white man's well. It's not my war." He stepped back toward his horse, seeing that his conversation was not welcome. "I can't stop it or change it. But I'll do my best to get rich from it."

It crossed my mind that I would've preferred it being him that day overlooking the wide valley instead of White Dog. But then, Dog was no different. He'd posed as a friend for the chance to rob and kill me. "But Cloud knows all that," he continued. "He even spoke up for me to some of the other chiefs. He said he believed they could put all their trust in me as long as there was money involved." He slid up on his horse.

"Then I reckon he also knows you'd cut his throat if the army paid you enough to do it."

He smiled as he turned his horse and headed away. "One job at a time," he called over his shoulder. "See you when I get the rifles."

As I watched him ride away, Band of Iron came riding out of the herd of horses and pulled up beside me. He must've seen the look on my face. "Pay him no attention. He is a blind wolf. He misses what he knows is here, but can no longer see. Because of it, he snaps at everything . . . to grab on to anything."

I looked up at him. "That's just a long way of calling him a 'no good son of a bitch.' "

"There is no short way to tell of a man's spirit. If there was, we are all no good sons of bitches." Band of Iron's eyes gleamed. "I learned that from the books brought here by the Steel Shirts when my father's father was a boy. It is called phil-os-ophy."

"I know," I said. "But I've never heard it said quite that way." I stepped up into my saddle and sat beside him, gazing across the herd. There was something in the smell of sweet grass and horses that reminded of home, of home a long time ago. Here at the top of Red Cloud's country, I felt a yearning for something I hadn't known in years. There was something sad and peaceful here at the heart of the Sioux Nation, something wild, innocent, simple, and complete. Here was a circle within a circle, a quiet spot within the thunder of life.

"You are troubled about getting rifles for the enemies of your people?" Band of Iron spoke after a pause.

"It goes against a lot of things." I gazed out across the herd. "But it's not for money. I don't need money that bad. If I get the rifles—"

"If?" Band of Iron's voice flattened. "You have given your word."

I stared at him a second, wondering how to explain it. When I started to tell him, he raised a hand and stopped me. "The books the Steel Shirts brought were good, and many of my people learned to read them. They told of how people can live together in peace. I asked my father once, whatever became of the great books." Band of Iron stopped and waited for my response.

"And?"

"He told me, 'My people burned them in the Moon of the Great Cold, to keep from freezing.'"

By the time we'd rested and got ready for our trek to Fort Kearny, at least another eight hundred warriors had drifted in to join Red Cloud's war. Many had left their brick reservation houses, abandoned their ten acres of cropland, and arrived in wagons loaded with corn. They wore ill-fitting suits given them by the agency, and hid their close-cropped hair beneath flat-brimmed hats. Some had submitted to reservation life after barely escaping the gallows during the uprising of '62. Now they shed the white man's world like moths shedding heavy cocoons, ready to follow Red Cloud in one last spree of bloodletting.

"Jesus," I said to Jack and Shod, as we watched a stolen mailman's buggy pull in and spill out four young warriors. One of them ripped the shirt from his chest and threw it in a fire with a loud war cry. "Red Cloud must have some 'powerful medicine.'"

Shod pushed up his hat and watched the newcomers pull rifles from beneath the buggy seat. "If oppression is 'powerful medicine,' I suppose you're right. But I think it's more a matter of the right person, in the right place . . . at the right time. Red Cloud just happened to be here when these people felt their backs against the wall. The government would do well to take notice and learn from their mistake, or someday it will be the colored race doing the same thing."

"I wouldn't count on it," I said, as I threw my saddle and bedroll up on a roan gelding.

"On what?" said Shod. "The government learning from their mistakes . . . or colored people rising up against oppression?"

I let out a breath and shook my head. "Why is it, any damn thing I say, you right off think I'm trying to—"

"We better get a move on," Jack cut in, "if we want to get that string across the river before dark." He deliberately led his horse between Shod and me.

I turned back to tying down my bedroll as Shod went to help Kermit with the horses. "Okay, Jack, you heard it. I didn't say a damn thing out of the way."

"No, but after what you said the other day, you can't blame him for being on the defense a little."

"Maybe you're right. But I don't like being around somebody if I have to watch every word I say. I've got nothing against colored folk, and I never liked slavery. Hell, I'm glad they got their freedom. I'm all for it."

Jack chuckled and spit a stream. "I reckon Shod and his family would be *real* pleased to hear it."

"What the hell do you mean by that?"

"Nothing." Jack spit again. "You've got it stuck in your head that all coloreds were slaves—stableboys and chambermaids. So I reckon there's no point trying to explain it to you."

"Explain what?" But before Jack could answer, Band of Iron rode up with a blanket roll tied behind his cavalry saddle and a lariat slung around his shoulder.

"I will ride with you for a ways."

I glanced between him and Jack. "Suits me," I said. "But I oughta tell you, I've been offending everybody lately."

Near the fire, one of the newcomers swung a sword above his head and let out a battle cry. Band of Iron smiled and spread his hand toward the camp full of armed warriors. "I stopped being offended by the white man . . . many moons ago."

◆✳ 19 ✳◆

Three days out of the Red Wall, we split the string into two groups. Jack and I kept forty horses. Shod, Kermit, and Band of Iron traveled fifty yards ahead with the other sixty. Some of Red Cloud's horses bore a cavalry brand. They were thin and carried themselves low and tired—I reckoned he hadn't had time to rest them and fatten them up—but the others, the Indian horses, bounced along in stride, slick and clear-eyed, tossing their manes like show ponies.

My stomach remained tender from all the Indian food, but two weeks of rest and gallons of Stands Alone's herb tonic had me feeling crisp as a new dollar; and traveling with Red Cloud's blessing and Band of Iron to prove it, we made good time pushing the string toward Fort Kearny. We still had to watch out for any Shoshoni prowling about, and there was always the chance of running into the Pope Gang or the U.S. Army; but other than that, and bears, cats, and rattlesnakes, we pushed right along.

I nearly jumped out of my skin when a band of seven Brulé Sioux warriors appeared from out of nowhere; but they were met by Band of Iron, and after he explained our situation, we brewed coffee and drew around a low fire chewing tobacco. The leader was Brown Horse, a peaceful-looking feller with a broad mouth that seemed always on the verge of a smile. His small tribe was among the ones who'd met part of General Conner's invasion forces over the past winter, and though outnumbered seven to one, they'd sent the soldiers back to Laramie, wounded, ragged, starved, and scared out of their minds.

"You are Man With Many People's Horses?" He spit a stream over his shoulder.

I looked around at the faces in the flicker of fire. "I prefer Beatty . . . Jim Beatty."

Band of Iron rattled something in Sioux and all the Indians looked at me and smiled. "Bee-Tee-Jhem-Bee-Tee." Brown Horse nodded.

"That's close enough." I smiled.

Over the rest of our trip, Brown Horse's group stayed close until we neared the forks of Piney Creek. He seemed to feel it necessary to think of names for everybody. Quiet Jack became Man Who Has Known Stands Alone. Shod became Buffalo Man Who Lifted Two Hands, and Kermit became Boy Who Speaks Only To Spirits.

I felt bad about the run-in I'd had with Big Shod, and it seemed the more I tried to clear the air and put it behind us, the worse it got. Shod said he'd forgotten about my racial remark, so I reckon I was the one who couldn't put it away. But he was still concerned about me being Miller Crowe—I couldn't understand why.

"If I *was* Miller Crowe . . . and I'm not saying I am, what difference would it make? We gave you a job . . . we made you a partner. We ain't held your color against you. How many people would do that?" I really wanted to let him know that I held him no different than I did anybody else. But I saw his nostrils flare as he turned his face away for a second and watched Kermit at the head of the string.

"You're right, of course," he replied. "That certainly was white of you." He gigged his horse away before I could speak.

"What's the use?" I said to Jack, as Shod rode away in a flurry of dust. "We'll never see eye to eye on anything. Black is black, and white is white. Maybe that's how it's supposed to be. There ain't a damn thing I can do about it." We reined left of the string of horses, keeping between them and the rising slope of spruce and heavy pines.

"I reckon you're right," Jack chuckled. "But maybe it'd help if you fixed him a mess of chitlins."

"Why don't you just say what you mean instead of talking in circles all the time?"

Jack shook his head and spit a stream.

One of Brown Horse's braves reined up hard from a full run, kicking up dirt and leaning into the reins. "Rider coming." He pointed toward the front of the string as Kermit and Band of Iron swung them around a curve in the high trail. To the left, the land broke off and dropped at a steep angle, a hundred feet. "He sees us; still he comes. One white man." He ran his hand across his chin. "Beard like snow."

"Flowers?" I glanced at Jack.

"Why not?" He shrugged. "I figured you'd see him again. According to Queenie—"

"CROWE . . . YOU DIRTY ROTTEN COWARD. COME FACE ME."

"Yeah, that's him." I took out my forty-four, checked it, and slid it loose into my holster. Beside me, the Catahoula cur dropped his head, drew his tail between his legs, and slinked away into the woods. I couldn't get over how good he was looking. "I reckon I'm on my own," I said to Jack. "I think it's time we settle up . . . for once and for good."

"You're still weak." Jack nodded toward the soft blanket and bearskin I'd fitted to soften my saddle. "I'll kill him for you if you want me to."

I shot Jack a glance and gigged forward. "This will only take a minute."

"There you are, you son of a bitch," said Flowers. He glanced around. I reckon he was looking out for the dog. The Indians gathered in a wide circle; Flowers stood in the center. His face looked lopsided from missing an ear. Shod and Kermit steadied the front of the string. Jack galloped up behind me. "This time it's me and you, no tricks, no dogs, no nothing. I'm asking you to call it fair and tell this bunch to stay out of it. This ain't for bounty. It's man to man."

"Part of these horses are Red Cloud's. I'm running 'em for him. I reckon if you win, they got every right to kill you." I just said it to rattle him, to give me an edge. What difference would it make to me, if I was dead?

"That figures, you cowardly bastard." Flowers spread his feet shoulder width . . . scraped his heels in the dirt . . . opened and closed his fingers, and relaxed with his hand poised near his holster.

I eased from my saddle, feeling the drum starting to beat in my head. Walking slowly toward him in the middle of the road, I slipped the leather glove from my right hand and dropped it in the dirt. Cool air ran between my fingers as I stopped at ten yards and wiped my hand on my shirt. "Let's do it," I said quietly, and the world fell silent around me.

I saw his lips move, but I heard no words. I stared into his eyes and watched for the slightest flicker. He could've been praying or cussing; I had no idea. I saw an eyebrow arch; a gleam came alive in his eyes. I felt my hand close around the handle of my forty-four . . . felt it swing up as his hand did the same. He came forward a step and his eyes widened, his gun swinging up quicker than mine. I tried to speed up—I couldn't. But his gun hand swung away in a crazy broken motion and he slammed forward, struck from behind.

His shot flew out across the valley. Mine whistled past his head as he hit the ground, screaming, with the Catahoula cur ripping strips of shirt and meat from his back.

"God Almighty!" Jack bellowed behind me. I tried pointing my gun at the rolling thrashing bundle of limbs, fangs, and fur. The Indians spread out as Flowers and the dog rolled through them. Flowers kept banging his pistol on the dog's back, and a round exploded each time he did.

The dog had him pinned, mauling his face, his shoulder, and going for his throat. Flowers tried pointing the gun in the dog's face, but the big cur grabbed his hand and slung it back and forth like a loose rag. Then they rolled again, and Flowers disappeared over the edge of the cliff in a long fading scream as the dog flipped up from the ground, shaking himself in a cloud of dust. He peeped over the edge, shook himself again, and turned toward us with two fingers sticking from his mouth. "Jesus Christ!" One finger hung down the dog's chin, the other stuck straight out as if giving directions.

"Dog Who Points the Way," said Brown Horse, and the Indians nodded and mumbled among themselves.

"Lord God," I said, walking slowly toward the Catahoula cur. "Spit 'em out, boy." But the dog growled, shaking his head. Flower's bloody fingers waved back and forth as if correcting me.

"Don't that beat all." Jack's voice sounded low and breathless. We all stood watching as the dog trotted up the wooded slope, his head held high like a holy man pointing to the promised land. "Don't ever kick that dog!"

"I won't," I said in a hushed voice . . . and I meant it.

◆❋ 20 ❋◆

"Every lunatic in this country must lay around waiting to hear a gunshot." We'd topped the high trail and started across a stretch of jagged flatland when we saw the wake of dust. I cocked my rifle and crouched down beside Shod behind a small boulder. Brown Horse and his warriors had disappeared with half the string. They would close in from behind if need be. Kermit and Band of Iron held the other half in the shelter of a rock canyon just below ground level.

"Army," said Shod, as he dropped back down after peeping over the rock. Ten feet away, Jack lay flat on a large boulder ten feet above us.

I peeped up over the edge and dropped back. Two Pawnee scouts rode straight toward us from fifty yards away. Ten yards behind them, I saw the face of Mad Johnson leading his column, gazing around in every direction. "It's the crazy son of a bitch that killed them Indian kids. We better get ready to spread a good story."

"That's your department." Shod grinned.

I stepped up on the rock and waved my arms in the air. "Over here." I hoped Band of Iron would see what was going on and hightail it out before Johnson's patrol got too close. I could explain a lot of things, but not having one of Red Cloud's warriors wrangling horses. "Thank God it's you," I yelled as the Pawnees drew closer. I glanced down at Shod; he shook his head. "We were afraid you were more of them damn murdering Sioux." The Pawnees just stopped and stared with their rifles propped straight up from their laps. Shod stood up and raised his hands chest-high.

"I was just telling your scouts," I called out to Johnson as he rode in closer, "I'm glad it's ya'll instead—"

"Shut up," he said in a low voice. His column sat restless behind him, studying the terrain.

"Now, just a minute, Captain."

"If he says another word"—he glanced at the Pawnees—"put a bullet in his head, right about here." He tapped his forehead and turned to Shod and me. Shod lowered his hands. One of the scouts gigged his horse forward and rode to the edge of the rock canyon. In minutes, Kermit joined us with his hands in the air. Three soldiers brought out the string of horses. Band of Iron had slipped away. Jack never made a peep from atop the large boulder.

"So Bone was right," said Johnson. "You do have a string of horses and a giant colored boy with you." He turned to Kermit. "You're Bone's kid, aren't you?" Kermit shrugged.

Johnson raised a boot across his saddle, leaned on his leg, and took a deep breath. "All right," he said, letting out his breath and studying the horizon, "somebody start talking."

"Here's the whole of it, Captain," I said. "There was three wranglers with me and I did have a string of horses like Bone said. But the rest of it was craziness—the part about Red Cloud, his daughter, and all. But after Carrington let me go, Fetterman told me if I could round up some horses, I could sell them to him. Now, that's just what I did . . . as you can see."

"Where's your third wrangler?"

"Poor feller." I shook my head. "They killed him—a bunch of Sioux. Cut off two of his fingers and threw him over a cliff 'bout five miles back. That's what the shooting was about."

"That's not bad, Crowe—"

"Don't start that Crowe stuff again, Captain. Carrington will tell you I'm Jim Beatty—"

"—but let me tell you what's going on in my world. Two old teamsters arrested in Laramie. They had four stolen horses, said they got them from you."

"Try to help a man, and what do you get . . ." I shook my head. "We didn't know the horses were stolen . . . Ask Carrington. We were slickered. But I just let the old fellers have them horses to haul his dead woman out of here." Laughter rippled across the soldiers and scouts. Johnson shot them a cold stare.

"The dead woman story," said Johnson. "Tack's been using it for years. The nearest he's ever come to a female is when his mother spit him out in the dirt." More laughter; another cold stare.

"How would I have known? I tried to help; this is the thanks."

"Do you know Long Jake Howard?"

I felt my stomach crawl. "I've met him . . . yes, sir."

"He says you sold him eighteen stolen horses. He's not real happy. He's coming back up from Laramie to kill you."

"There again . . . same situation. But I only sold him nine. Queenie sold him the rest."

"I know, and she says she got them from you—all stolen. There's also a settler and his family in Laramie, but he says he found two horses roaming around near Crofton. I figure he's lying for you just to show his appreciation."

"You can ask Carrington," I said. "Carrington will tell you—"

"Are you kin to Carrington or something?"

"No."

He turned to Shod. "Are you as big a liar as he is?"

"Of course not." Shod seemed offended by such a suggestion.

Johnson dealt him a curious glance. "Where did you learn to speak like that?"

Shod glared at him. "Chopping cotton, Captain, where else?"

Johnson almost smiled. "How much of what he's saying is true?"

Shod glanced at me with a strange expression, then let out a breath. "All of it, as far as I can tell. I hired in with him a few weeks back. It's been quite an experience. If I was him, I'd blow my brains out."

"Don't worry, Long Jake has sworn to do that." Johnson gazed down and shook his head. "I probably should kill you, all three of you, actually. But . . . that's not my job. I'm here to comb the countryside and sweep up the trash." He glanced toward Kermit. "Your father is at Fort Kearny. He's an idiot, you know." Kermit just shrugged.

"Captain, sir," said one of the soldiers. "Some of these horses have cavalry brands. Some are Indian, and some look like they came from a horse show."

Johnson lifted his leg and dropped it back to his stirrup. "Why is it I'm not surprised?"

"I can explain," I said.

"That doesn't surprise me either. Round them up," he said to the soldiers. "We'll escort them to Kearny." He shook his head and turned his horse. "I love this fucking job."

That evening, Johnson sent for me as the soldiers settled in to their guard positions. When I walked up, he looked up from a plate of beans and picked a tooth with his fingernail. His revolver lay in his lap; his hat hung from his empty holster. His wild head of black hair glistened in the glow of the low fire before him. "Where you from?" I could see right off he was only making conversation after a hard day's work.

"Pennsylvania," I said with a straight-faced smile. His right hand calmly picked up the revolver, cocked it, and pointed it in my face. His left hand scooped up a spoonful of beans.

"Go again?"

I shrugged. "Kentucky?"

"Umm." He smacked his lips and considered it a second. "Yeah." He nodded his head. "I'd say Kentucky." He waved his pistol toward a rock beside him, let down the hammer, and laid it back across his lap. I eased down on the rock and let out a breath.

"Know what a Nebraska breakfast is?" He smiled across a working mouthful of beans.

"Naw-sir, I don't reckon."

"That's a bowl of squaw-guts, served warm while she's still screaming." He stopped for a second, waiting for me to respond. I didn't know how. "It's a joke," he laughed. "We're off duty now . . . we can relax."

"Oh, a joke," I said. "I get it." I stared at him as he scooped up beans. I wondered what kind of strange music played on the tight strings in his dark mind. "I reckon I've so much on my mind, I can't see much humor—"

"Don't worry after working hours. That's my rule. Besides, we'll all probably die out here . . . so laugh it up." He nearly spit his beans. I tried a cautious chuckle. I couldn't come out and tell him, but on this patrol we were all resting in the arms of angels.

The Sioux weren't about to hit and ruin my deal with Red Cloud.

I knew Jack had heard the conversation and got to Brown Horse and Band of Iron before we'd rode out of sight. Johnson didn't know it, but he could dance naked across *this* night and nothing would happen to him unless he stepped on a rattlesnake.

"Ever been in a war?"

"Yeah," I said, "stars and bars." I wouldn't mention it was with Quantrill, fighting guerrilla along the border. I didn't know when this bastard might snap.

"No kidding?" He set the plate on the ground and wiped a sleeve across his mouth. "Did we kick your asses, or what?" He had a big playful grin.

"That's a fact."

He gazed away and sucked his teeth. "God . . . how I wish I could've died in that war. It was truly something, mortars flying, waves of men clashing head-on . . . the way God intended war to be."

"It was a wonderful thing," I said, knowing his gun and mind could explode at any second. "I know I sure miss it."

"Not like this rotten, stinking mess." He waved his arm to clear the rotten, stinking mess away from him.

I watched cautiously as he picked up the revolver, scratched his head with the barrel, then wiped his hand around the tip of it like you would do a canteen before taking a drink. The poor bastard didn't realize how close his mind was to sucking a mouthful of fire from the end of that gun. "This isn't war. This is soldiers scraping scum off their boots." He dropped the pistol in his holster beneath his hat. I breathed easier.

"Well, looks like that scum is sticking pretty tight. I'd bet on the Sioux, from what I've seen so far."

He nodded. "I know you're a fool, a liar . . . a thief, and"—he tossed a hand—"all such as that." He let out a sigh. "But I have to agree with you, we'll lose this one, lose it big."

"Umm-hmm," I grunted.

"And you know why? I'll tell you why." His voice dropped low as if it were a secret. "We're wrong here . . . got no business here."

"Oh?"

He leaned closer. "Of course, you didn't hear me say it—"

"Naw-sir."

"—but this is kind of like attacking a large farm or ranch somewhere."

I just stared.

"See, here's Red Cloud, running a spread from the Black Hills to the Big Horn Mountains. All the elk, and deer, and buffalo . . . it's his stock. It's what he feeds his family, the same as my father's cattle in Maryland. See what I mean?"

"Sure."

"And all Red Cloud is saying is, 'Stay the hell off my farm.' But nobody listens. They don't realize . . . or want to . . . or something." He ran a hand back through his hair.

"Yeah, I get it," I said. "And what would your daddy do if I came cutting a road through his land, killing his cattle and chopping his trees?"

He cocked his thumb and put his finger against my forehead. "Bang," he said. Shadows from the fire danced in his eyes. He took another long breath. "Yeah . . . but that's Red Cloud's sad story. I'll be glad when we gut the son of a bitch, so I can go home for a couple of weeks."

"That's the spirit," I said, gazing out across the night. The night was not nearly as clear and peaceful here as it was at the top of Red Cloud's country. Here, I saw no shooting star.

Part IV
Red Cloud's Farm

◆❋ 21 ❋◆

Mad Johnson's craziness must've settled in me with my beans and biscuits, for I went to sleep thinking of Red Cloud's farm, and woke up the next morning with it still on my mind. Maybe if he "worked" his spread, we would've seen it different. If he had his braves rope, brand, and herd the elk, deer, and buffalo, we would have understood. If they'd worked up a sweat clearing, cutting, building barns with stalls for their stock, and taking them to slaughter pens and county fairs, it could've been a whole different thing. Fences would help, maybe a corral and loading pen here and there. If we could just see him doing something, anything; making "progress" of some kind. I had to stop thinking about it.

"Shod," I said quietly over a cup of army coffee, "I'm keeping my word to Red Cloud. I'm taking him rifles."

"You've completely, lost touch, with, any, spark, of intelligence." He sliced his words smooth and thin.

"Hear me out," I said, motioning him back down. "Just imagine Red Cloud as a big farmer somewhere . . . say, Maryland."

"They, will, hang you."

"Only, his farm runs from the Black Hills to—"

"No, Mister Beatty, or Crowe, or God knows . . . whoever you are. I will *not* go along with this madness. Innocent people will die."

"Innocent people *are* dying! Red Cloud's farmers—I mean *braves* . . . all his people. Are they guilty?"

"You know what I mean," Shod said. "Our country is at war with him, and like it or not, those people are the enemy."

"You saying it's right?"

"Of course it isn't. But it's a reality. We have laws. And we are loyal Americans; I am, at least."

"Just a minute, ole buddy." I waved my finger in the air. "When your bunch was slaving in the fields . . . wasn't that a reality? I recall that was legal as hell—"

"That law was changed. That injustice was rectified—"

"Horse shit! Ain't a damn thing changed, and it won't in a thousand years. Not if you count on the law to do it. It's right here." I banged my fist on my chest. "Now, you're a hell of a lot smarter then me—"

"That's correct . . . and I'm out. You can hang by yourself." I sipped my coffee and watched Shod jerk the cinch on his saddle. He stopped as if considering something, then turned back facing me. "Is Mister Smith going to go along with this?"

"Why, sure." There wasn't a doubt in my mind. Jack would jump at anything this crazy. "If he don't, I'll kill the whole idea; fair enough?"

Shod stared up at the thin line of morning on the eastern edge of heaven. He shook his head. "I must be losing my mind."

The whole day we crept along rock walls and in and out of gullies and plug washes, off the trail and across country fit for mountain goats. Three times we spotted a handful of Brulé Sioux, but always at a distance and only for a few seconds. I had no doubt it was Brown Horse's warriors. I figured he didn't want things to look too quiet; it might raise suspicion.

By late evening, as we followed the open trail to the fork of Piney Creek, I heard the sound of a night bird and knew that Jack and the Sioux had us covered.

"Clever how you two have that worked out," said Shod, in a low voice.

"It comes in handy."

"You and Mister Smith are extraordinary, in your own way."

"We get by."

Shod smiled. "I had hopes that by now I would have gained your confidence enough to be a partner, I mean a *real* partner."

"You are."

"No, I've never been included, not in what you're *really* up to. I realize once we settle up on the horses and guns, you two will go your way, and I'll be back to a dollar a day somewhere."

"I know how this disappoints you, but we ain't up to nothing."

"Sure." He shrugged. "I shouldn't ask."

I cocked an eye. "Why're you so damned interested in our business . . . *if* we had any?"

"You can't imagine how hard it is out here for a colored man. I can wrangle, poke cows, handle a gun, I can do it all, but I'm seldom given an opportunity. I have a college degree; even that doesn't help."

"So you figure throwing in with folks like us would give you an edge? You're looking to tie into some quick money?"

"What choice do I have? I'm not good at shining shoes and cleaning spittoons."

"Well, I'm sorry if you've read us wrong, but we ain't up to nothing but dealing these horses."

"No offense, but I believe the two of you rob banks more often than old folks go to the bathroom."

I laughed. "You've missed your mark this time."

"Well, I don't want to intrude, but I wish it could've been different. I won't bring it up again."

"Shod, if it means anything, I can't think of a man I'd rather have on my side robbing a bank . . . if I was robbing banks . . . which I ain't."

"Thanks," he said, and he gigged his horse away to the front of the column. I reined up and let the string of horses drift by until Kermit brought up the rear. Stepping my horse in beside his, I pushed my hat up my forehead. "We're heading into Fort Kearny in a little while. I reckon you're free to go your own way if you've a mind to. Your pa is somewhere around there, but if you'll take some advice, you might want to strike off on your own. No offense, but your pa ain't the best influence a man could follow." Kermit looked at me and shrugged.

"But suit yourself," I said, wishing I'd never opened my mouth. I was not one to be giving advice, and if I was, Kermit was too dumb to listen. I reckon it was one more mouthful of wasted breath; there was a lot of it drifting around Powder River.

◆❋ 22 ❋◆

". . . THANK YOU, JESUS! THANK YOU, JESUS!" Captain Fetterman spread his trembling arms. "God bless this wonderful man!" I stayed on my horse a few minutes to let him get it out of his system. The way he acted, I was afraid he'd hug me. "These magnificent animals, glorious, majestic horses." He ran among them with his arms spread, stroking, patting—it was a little embarrassing. I glanced at Shod and Kermit. They just stared.

Mad Johnson reined up beside me with a crazy grin. "Fetterman when he's happy is something I don't care to see. Good luck, whoever you are."

"Wait," yelled Fetterman. "Where did you find this wonderful man?"

"Near Shaggy Ridge." Johnson grinned between Fetterman and me. "He crawled up from under a rock. It will be in my report." He saluted and turned his horse. "Question him if you can . . . It's fascinating."

Fetterman waved him away. "Pay him no mind." His face split in a wide smile. "You did it, by God . . . just like you said you would."

I slipped down from my saddle and slapped my shirt with my hat. Dust billowed. "Some of them have army brands, Captain. But I can explain." I caught a glimpse of Shod shaking his head.

"Nonsense, lad, don't you dare. We made a deal for horses, and I'm damn glad to get them." He pulled my arm. "Let's get a drink and negotiate."

"Negotiate? We already agreed—"

"Come on." He pulled me along, laughing and slapping my back. I glanced back at Shod and Kermit, and shrugged. They turned the horses toward the livery barn. "It's not very often that someone beats those horse-thieving Sioux at their own game. I want to hear all about it."

Inside his tent, I plopped down on a wooden stool and dropped my hat on my knee. I looked at the bottle on his desk and wiped my mouth. "Come to think of it, a drink don't sound bad right now."

I drew a deep breath as he fumbled in a desk drawer, searching for glasses, I figured. "Yeah, it was a bit hairy there for a while, I have to admit. There I was, Indians every—"

"I don't want to hear your bullshit," he snapped. I watched him pull up a folded paper and slap it on his desk. "I want to settle with you and get you out of my face."

I sat there with my mouth hanging open as he unfolded a letter and slid it to me. I picked it up cautiously. It said: "These horses are the confiscated property . . ."

"The *hell* if they are!" I sprang up, slinging the stool one direction and the paper another. A cocked forty-four pointed straight at my nose as I stepped forward. I froze.

He shook his head and laughed, the same crazy laugh I'd heard the night we made the deal. "You sharp-eyed little turd. You came in here, drank my whiskey straight from the bottle, talked to me like I was a damned *civilian,* insulted my troops, and dared—DARED— talk *price* when my men's lives were in danger. Tell me what I owe you."

"Easy, Captain." I saw he was crazy enough to pull that trigger and laugh above the explosion. "You've won. I don't like it, but I know when I'm licked."

"That's dandy," he said, beaming like a full moon. He tilted the pistol up and let down the hammer. "Now, march your ragged ass out there and tell your buck nigger and Bone's idiot kid that you just got screwed by a 'MILITARY MAN.' "

I felt the skin draw tight across the back of my neck, and I had to swallow hard to silence the drumbeat in my temples. I would buy Red Cloud's guns for him if I had to go to New York and rob a bank to do it. I forced a deep breath and stepped back toward the flap. "Tell me one thing," I said, calm and even. "Do you blue-belly pricks ever keep your word to anybody, about anything?"

"No, but we don't have to." His brow lifted in feigned astonishment. He leaned forward across his desk. "We're your government—" His face split once more in a wide ugly grin. His teeth were polished tombstones, and he jiggled his pistol in the air. "Carrying guns!"

Shod rubbed his bald head. "I find it peculiar that he associated the incident with a sexual act."

"What?" I was still boiling. "What're you talking about? Are you with me here?"

"I simply mean . . . the way he said, tell us that you'd just been—" Shod chopped off his words with the edge of his hand, then shook his head. "Forget it, it doesn't matter."

Beside us, Kermit leaned against a stall rail and nodded to the ground. I glanced between them and spread my hands. "Am I talking to myself here?"

"No," Shod said quietly, "but you're not far from it." He took a deep breath. "It's over; we might as well accept it."

"So you're giving up?"

"You're incredible!" said Shod. "There's nothing left. It's over. What does it take to convince you?" He flipped a blanket on the hay-piled floor and stretched out on it. Kermit turned and stared into an empty stall.

"I can't believe this."

"Right," said Shod. He rolled over on his side and laid his hat over his face. "Wake me if anything changes."

I left the barn mumbling to myself and kicking rocks. For over an hour I roamed around the dark fort, watching silhouettes move inside tents lit by glowing lanterns. Shod was right, but I couldn't give it up. In this land full of wild-eyed losers, I reckon I just couldn't quit until I won *something*. I couldn't see that the only way to *win* here was to *leave* here.

When I'd cooled off a little, I sat down on a stump outside a dim-lit tent and in seconds I felt my eyelids fighting against a heavy weight. I didn't even have the strength to drag back to the barn.

When I first heard Mad Johnson's voice, I thought he'd slipped into my dream to turn it into a nightmare; but as it sounded clearer,

I realized he was in the tent behind me. "Don't worry about my part," I heard him say just above a whisper. "I'll get it out through one of the Laramie Loafers."

My senses perked up. I eased down flat to the ground and ran my finger under the edge of the tent. "It's quite a pile," I heard another voice say softly. "There's no time to sit on it—"

"Don't worry," Johnson cut him off. "It's as good as done."

I raised the bottom edge enough to peep under, and up at Johnson and a bearded feller in a long-tailed riding duster. On a table between them lay a pair of bulging saddlebags; I knew they weren't whispering about their laundry.

I heard the bearded feller muffle a laugh as he patted his hand on the saddlebags. "Take good care of it, Mister Johnson."

Johnson smiled. "You can count on it, Mister Pope."

My breath slammed shut in my throat as I watched Johnson raise the lid on a small footlocker and drop the bags inside. Pope stood back and nodded his head. He was a tall, mean-faced man with eyebrows that met above his crooked nose. I caught a glimpse of a gold tooth as he sliced a wicked smile, stepped back, slipped through the flap of the tent, and disappeared into the night. Johnson stepped quietly to the flap, peeped out, then stepped back to the footlocker. I watched, not believing my luck, as he took out the saddlebags and pitched them under his cot. "Thank you, Jesus!" I thought it so loud, I hoped no one had heard me.

"Do you *ever* sleep?" Shod rubbed his eyes and stared down at the saddlebags beside him.

"The mother load, Shod." My voice trembled; my hands shook. "I'm talking moth-er load!"

"But how?"

"I waited 'til he went to sleep, split his tent, took it, and slipped away like a sidewinder."

"He's in with the Popes . . ."

"Up to his eyeballs. Can you believe it?"

Shod touched his hands to his temples. "We need to think about this. We need to talk about some things."

"Think? You must be crazy. You said you wanted in on something. Here it is, 'partner.' All you have to do is help me stay alive 'til we get to Jack and Brown Horse, 'cause Johnson and the Pope Gang are going to be on me like flies on a billy goat."

"No doubt." He flipped open the bag and ran his hand across the money. "It has to be the army payroll. There's nothing else around—"

"I don't give a damn if it's the president's petty cash. It's ours now. Let's roll up and get the hell out of here."

"Absolutely." He smiled. "But what about the guards on the wall?"

"Are you still asleep, damn it? They're looking for somebody busting in . . . We're busting out."

"We really need to—" Shod bowed his head and rubbed it. He let out a breath as if he was having a hard time deciding. "Oh brother," he sighed.

"Come on, Shod! Wake up and get a grip." I nudged him. "It all fell in our laps."

Shod and Kermit dressed and gathered their gear in the darkness while I paced back and forth on sharp nerves, tapping the saddlebags I'd thrown over my shoulder. It flashed across my mind as we slipped away into the darkness that here on my shoulder was the *deeper,* more *meaningful* reason I'd come to Powder River. Now it was clear. Some crazy merciful God of horse dealers, outlaws, and fools had pointed at me from afar and bequeathed to me the brass ring of life. "Thank you, Lord," I whispered, darting my eyes skyward into the darkness as Shod slipped off to scout our getaway. I could barely contain myself.

"Kermit," I whispered, standing in the shadows beside our horses with our reins in our hands, "when this is over, I swear, I'm buying you a *brand*-new hat, any size, style, or color." Kermit stared at me blank-faced.

Shod slipped back from the north wall and took his reins from Kermit. "This is amazing," he said. "There's only one guard at the small gate, and he's snoring." The north gate was only four feet wide and used to carry out garbage. I'd seen it during my last visit. Fetterman hadn't even bothered to post guards around us or the horses. He must've figured we wouldn't be trying to leave with Red Cloud's warriors prowling about.

"Then let's round up every horse in the place and take 'em with us, just for the sake of good manners. It's easy picking."

"You're out of your mind. We've got the money." Shod checked the cinch on his saddle and stepped up quietly. "You need to talk to someone about why you're always wanting to steal horses."

"Alright." I handed Shod the saddlebags. "But you two go on. I've got to take a few, just to show Fetterman that we ain't school kids."

Shod opened his mouth to say something, but changed his mind and shook his head. I reckon he saw my keyed-up condition. I watched as he and Kermit slipped quietly away, then turned with my arms outstretched toward the stables. "Come to Daddy," I whispered in a low strange voice.

I know it sounds crazy, and I wouldn't have believed it myself if I hadn't been there; but there are times when luck comes in a large wave, and when it does, the only thing to do is ride it without question or hesitation. I realized something was happening that night that would never happen again in a thousand years, and like a gambler on a winning streak, I reveled in it.

As Shod and Kermit waited fifty yards from the small gate, I led out string after string of horses. I stole so many, I got tired of stealing them. When the guard quit snoring, I snuck over, tied him up, drew a bandanna around his mouth, and just kept on stealing—stole until I ran out of anything to steal. It was a horse thief's heaven and I was seated on the throne. By the time I got down to the bald-faced straw-horse, I'd lost count. Shod finally had to yank me by the arm or I would've started on the milk goats.

"I mean it, you've got to get a grip on yourself," said Shod. "It will be daylight soon . . . They'll see you."

"So what?" I was dazed from it. "They can't chase us unless they do it on foot."

"Do you realize how many horses we have here?"

"Bunches." I grinned, lightheaded. "Just bunches and bunches."

"That's it, we're leaving. If you're smart, you'll come with us."

I hesitated a second, then swung my horse beside Shod and

motioned for Kermit to ride up and take the lead. Our string of horses was now ten horses wide, and from where we sat on the moonlit night, the front of the herd seemed to stretch a half mile. "Don't ever say I can't steal a horse or two." I beamed.

"I hate to burst your bubble, but you know we can't hold these horses long, not all of them anyway."

"I know. I just want Fetterman to get the point. I might've been screwed by a 'military man,' but I want him to know he just got the same thing, straight up, from a no-'count *outlaw*."

"Both of you are *sick* men," Shod said above a whisper.

"What's that supposed to mean?"

He gigged his horse and we started our push toward the fork of Piney Creek. "If you have to ask . . ." Shod just shook his head.

◆✳ 23 ✳◆

By the time we'd topped the high pass, I'd gained control of myself. Many of the horses had wandered away—we just couldn't hold them all—but it was worth risking a hanging just to be able to look down from the ridge and watch the troops chase them in the valley below.

Jack and Brown Horse fell in with us near the top of the pass, and Brown Horse's warriors helped Kermit wrangle the remaining horses out across a stretch of high flatland. Band of Iron had ridden ahead to meet Red Cloud farther along the Bozeman.

"This was better than you putting a bullet in him," said Jack. We watched Fetterman stand up and wobble in a two-wheel cart, shouting orders as a red ox trudged along, pulling the cart across the valley.

Five yards behind him, Carrington sat on a swaybacked jackass with one hand on his hip, holding the reins high, military style. He had to be wondering how this would look in his monthly report. Two soldiers tackled an Indian mustang around the neck. The mustang bounced them off the ground three or four times, then slung them off and cantered away. "Serves 'em right . . . confiscat—*stealing* a man's horses the way they did," I said. I didn't see Mad Johnson in the valley; I figured he was more concerned with the payroll money.

We stood up from the edge of the ridge and Shod slung the saddlebags over his shoulder. I nudged Jack. "He ain't took his hands off that bag of money since I handed it to him." I grinned. "Reckon he feels better now?"

Shod heard me, smiled, and patted the bags. "This is what I meant by 'partner.' "

Jack slapped dust from his shirt with his hat. "It'll get a lot lighter when you take out enough to buy Red Cloud's rifles."

"I'll buy him a bunch of rifles if I have to pick them up at the factory gate. The more I look at this mess, the more I realize, Cloud's the only decent son of a bitch north of Laramie. He's the only one that belongs here."

"Does that include us?" Shod hefted the bags across the back of his saddle.

"Naw-sir," I snapped, "because we came here with the best intentions. If everybody would've done like they said, we'd've been gone long ago."

"Be careful, Mister Smith," said Shod, "or he'll start telling you about Red Cloud's farm."

Jack chuckled, "His 'farm'?"

"Some other time," I said, stripping the saddle from my tired horse and throwing it across the back of one of the fresh horses we'd kept from the string. I slipped the bridle from his muzzle and slapped his rump—"Go join the army"—and he trotted away as I slipped the bridle on the fresh mount.

"We'll have Johnson and the Popes on us before long. We better take what we need to buy the rifles, and stash the rest."

Before we rode off, I spooked the remaining horses to cover our tracks and keep the soldiers confused. All the horses scattered except the straw-horse—the bald-faced gelding. He just stood in a patch of grass, as if he was still grazing in Carrington's yard. "Poor bastard's been hobbled so long, he don't know freedom when it smacks him on the rump." He followed us as we headed for the flat grassland.

An hour later, we pulled into a stretch of high pines, took out money for the rifles, and buried the saddlebags under a heavy rock. We were headed back to our trail when Jack held up a hand and we froze behind him. He listened for a second, then held up one finger. Shod and I slipped our pistols from our holsters and slid down from our saddles.

We crept to the edge of the pines and into a brush pile, hearing the slow steady sound of hoofs coming along our trail. Shod peeped up, then dropped back beside me. He shook his head and pushed up his hat. "You're going to love this."

"Army?"

"Ben Bone."

"I'll-kill-him!" I tore through the brush, my gun cocked arm's length, my hat flying off behind me, and Shod right on my heels.

"Don't shoot," yelled Shod as I hit the trail screaming. Seeing me, Bone fell backwards off the mule, just as Shod's hand swung over my shoulder and clamped around my gun.

"Turn me loose! I gotta kill him!" I struggled against Shod's grip. Bone peeped around the mule, terror-stricken.

"Can't you see he's not worth shooting?" Shod bounced the palm of his free hand off the top of my head. My eyes crossed, then snapped back.

Shod snatched my gun and held it over his head. I swiped at it and missed. Bone stepped from behind the mule with a ball-peen hammer raised in the air. "Thank God it's ya'll. I feared it was Indians."

"You'll pray to God it was Indians—"

I leaped for my gun, missed, tried to snatch Shod's from his holster, but he jumped away. "Jesus Christ," said Jack from his horse behind us. "Can you-all keep it down a little?"

"Thanks, Mister Smith," whined Bone, already sucking up.

"Give me my gun." I jumped back, pointing my finger in Shod's face. It was like pointing up at sunshine on top of a smokestack. "I ain't fooling."

He let out a breath, uncocked my forty-four, and handed it over butt-first. "Use your head," he cautioned.

I cooled down and dropped my forty-four in my holster. In my rage, I'd forgotten the thirty-six under my arm and the other forty-four under my shirt. "I'm sorry . . . you're right." I turned toward Bone and his raised hammer. Stepping forward, I leaned, jerking my glades knife from my boot. Sunlight shot from the blade like a message from heaven. "I'll just gut him—gut him like a hog."

Bone stepped back, threatening with the hammer. "And I'll holler 'til they hear me in hell."

"Let's just feed him to Red Cloud," Jack chuckled. "Take his hammer."

I stopped a foot from him and held out my hand. "Okay, hand it over."

He drew it back farther. I snapped my fingers. "Come on, I won't hurt you." I let down my knife. "Just give it here."

"You mean it?"

"Give it here." He slowly brought down the hammer and laid it in my hand, head-first. I closed my fist around it, slung it back, and popped him in the forehead, just enough to raise a bloody welt.

"Goddamn!" He bent double and threw a hand to his head. "You said—"

I patted him on the back. "Yeah, I know. But I lied. Truth is, I'm going to hit you, kick you, maybe cut you a little, every time I think of what you did to me . . . right up 'til I pitch you in Red Cloud's lap. I might even help him skin you."

"Mister Smith, Mister Shod," Bone said in a pitiful voice, "how's my boy? How's Kermit?"

"I shot him," Jack said with an evil grin. "What about it?"

Bone looked up and his expression changed before our eyes. "Why, hell, not a thing, Mister Smith. If you shot him, it's just 'cause he deserved it. He weren't no-'count . . . never was."

Shod stared down at his saddle and shook his head. "Mercy." I cracked Bone on the back of his head. He yelped. I kicked him in his knee. "Let's get started."

We rode out through a stretch of pines, just off the trail. I kept Bone riding beside me, every once in a while poking him in the ribs or cracking him on the knee with the hammer handle. I was glad I didn't kill him. He wasn't worth it. But I had to pick at him, the way a yard dog has to pick at a hurt rattlesnake.

"So what brings you this way, Mister Bone?" I tapped the handle against his ear. He hunkered away and flinched.

"You won't believe me, but I came looking for ya'll as soon as I heard you stole all them horses. I felt bad about what I done, even worse now, knowing Kermit let you down. I'm shamed."

"Well," I said, bonking the back of his head. "Don't be 'shamed.' Jack was only teasing you."

"Teasing? That ain't a thing to tease about. That boy is the light of my life."

"Shut up, Bone!" Shod's voice was low, like muffled thunder. I laughed, seeing that Bone was even starting to get to *him*. "And why don't you leave this imbecile alone. We need to concentrate on the Pope Gang."

"You worried about the Popes?"

"Certainly; anybody with any sense would be."

"Not me." I drifted back beside Shod.

"My point exactly—"

"I figure you can just hold all their guns way up in the air. They'll be jumping, grabbing . . ."

"Hold it! What's that smell . . . that sound?" I heard the tension in Jack's voice and we stopped for a second, then crept ghostlike around the turn of a clearing, and froze, unprepared for the grisly scene before us.

The buzzing of flies was deafening as they whipped and swarmed about the bodies strung from low tree limbs, and nurtured their maggots on the bodies on the ground. Soldiers, civilians, women, and children, their swollen, dismembered corpses decorated the clearing like a stage show from hell.

"Holy mother of—" Shod whispered. I pulled my bandanna up over my nose and stepped my horse among them. In the center of the clearing, I saw the head of Major Leonard C. Trapp, 11th Cavalry, scalped, and jammed down on a thick tree branch that stuck from the ground. His eyes were gone, the sockets filled with flies, and he seemed to be crying white tears as maggots spilled down his cheeks. Thin branches fluttered on the limb beneath his head. The leaves looked like funny green hands waving at us.

I backed my horse quietly, as if afraid to disturb the dead. We sat outside the small clearing, brushing at flies and searching the woods in all directions. "It's the worst I've ever seen," I said above a whisper. "What kind of people would do something like that?"

"The kind you're prepared to deliver rifles to," said Shod.

Jack sat silent as stone, his hand working back and forth slowly on the stock of his rifle. Ben Bone leaned and swatted flies from his boot. "It's Standing Bear's bunch. They did it to show what the army done last year at Sand Creek . . . 'cept that was Injuns . . . these are whites."

"What should we do?" Shod spoke to no one in particular. "Should we bury them?"

I rubbed my face. "How do we know who's who, they're so—"

"Burn 'em," Jack cut in. His voice had a bitter snap to it. "Burn 'em all."

"We can't risk a fire, the smoke—"

"Then forget 'em." Jack turned his horse roughly and gigged it toward the woods. "Let the earth claim 'em, and forget how they died."

I watched as Jack rode away, and I knew what he was thinking right then. He was thinking the same as I, that we should take the money and leave this place of madness, this place where craziness reined. We should go, right now, leave . . . run if we had to; but shed ourselves of this place and never look back or think of it again.

I pitched Bone's hammer out into the woods. He watched me and seemed relieved. "One mistake and you're a dead man," I told him, calm and serious. Bone nodded and swallowed hard. I glanced between him and Shod. "Let's find Red Cloud and finish our deal."

"Surely you're not going to bring him rifles, not after this." He waved a hand toward the clearing.

"No. I'm going to give him the horses and the money for the guns. Then I'm out of it."

Shod turned and followed Jack. I slapped Bone's mule on the rump and rode behind him. The Catahoula cur peeped through the bushes and came up beside us, trotting along with his nose to the ground. I hadn't seen him since the day he rolled Flowers over the cliff. His coat shined; his eyes glistened like fire.

◆✳ 24 ✳◆

The next day, we came to a bend in the trail where the earth narrowed around us. Two of Brown Horse's warriors appeared high up in the trees, one on either side, and it felt as if they closed a gate behind us as they waved us in. In another ten minutes we came upon the string of horses, and Brown Horse rode up at an easy gallop.

When Bone saw Kermit standing beside the trail, he rolled off the mule and ran to him with his arms spread. Kermit looked ready to turn and run; but Bone threw his arms around him in a bear hug. "My boy," bellowed Bone. Kermit's eyes bulged; his body turned into a thin sausage, squeezed in the middle.

"Where you find that asshole?" Brown Horse drew a quick circle in the air and poked his finger in it.

"You know Bone?" I watched as Kermit's feet touched the ground and he stepped back. Bone stepped in to hug him again, but Kermit ducked away.

"He sell bad whiskey to Crazy Horse's warriors. Make them bad sick."

"That sounds like him. I brought him as a present. He tried to shoot Red Cloud, back when Cloud was wounded."

"Good present," said Brown Horse. He rode off to the front of the string, watching Bone the way a fox watches a crippled chicken.

That evening, we stretched out the string a half mile long and let them graze along through a narrow valley. The army horses were so tame, they traveled like a loose military column. The others, some of the saddle horses and Indian mustangs I'd taken to Fort Kearny, followed their lead. The bald-faced gelding stayed off from the rest, grazing in short circles as if still tied to a stake.

"It's three more than I had when I got there." I crossed my arms on my saddle horn and watched the string of horses drift along. Far in the distance, Brown Horse and his men led the string.

"Shame we couldn't kept 'em all," said Jack. He spit a stream.

"Yeah, but I reckon I showed Fetterman we ain't to be fooled with."

"That's important to you?"

Shod didn't realize it, but he and I were headed for a blowup between us. I was getting more and more jawed by his high-minded schoolhouse ways. I ignored him.

"But they're back in the saddle by now," Jack said quietly, wiping his mouth. We'd all been a little quiet and tense since coming upon Trapp's patrol. Even Brown Horse and his braves seemed edgy; I figured they wondered what we were thinking about Standing Bear's gruesome handiwork, maybe wondering if we held it against *them*. They knew that the slogan "The only good Indian is a dead Indian" was real popular in the white man's world. I reckon it didn't take much to stir something up.

Shod had just turned to ride back to Kermit and Ben Bone when I heard something like a large hornet streak past him. He slapped his hand to his neck just as blood spilled down his shirt collar. Then another one whistled in, but this one landed against his horse's neck with a soft thud and the animal reared high and collapsed beneath him.

"Shoshoni!" Bone screamed. But I'd already seen the feathered arrow sticking from the downed horse's ribs, and I jumped out of my saddle, over my horse's neck, bulldogging her down and snatching my rifle from the scabbard. I hit the ground sheltered by my horse.

Seven Shoshoni stormed down from the woods, spreading out to surround us as I swung my rifle over my horse and pounded out rounds. Behind me, I heard Jack's forty-four barking, and screams from the other side of the narrow valley. Kermit and Bone disappeared. Shod came crawling beside me quickly as rifles tore up the ground behind him. He had his pistol out, firing. The Indians flew from their horses like twigs hit by high wind, and the horses veered and fell beneath our volley of fire.

Shod snatched bullets from his belt to reload. I saw Brown

Horse's warriors coming to help us, but I knew it'd be over by the time they arrived. The last three Indians came in quick, as I dropped my spent rifle and snatched my pistol and rolled up on my knees.

Shod gave up reloading, snapped his chamber shut, and put two shots in an Indian on his right. I heard Jack fire over my head and another rider flew away. The last one's horse rose into the air before me, going over my head, and I fired almost straight up into the leaning rider. His cavalry sword flashed past my head, and his face exploded over me as his horse sailed down to the ground behind me and kept going. Then, as quickly as it had started . . . it was over.

Brown Horse's warriors jolted to a halt, sliding sideways in a spray of dust and rock. I stood up, my hands trembling. Snatching bullets from my belt, I glanced behind me, saw Jack standing, facing the other way, and let out my breath. Shod stood, holding a bandanna to his neck. "How bad?" I asked in a shaky voice.

"A graze." His voice sounded as weak as my own.

"Warriors!" Brown Horse proclaimed. He threw his fist in the air and brought it down toward us. The others looked at the dead Shoshoni scattered across the narrow valley and whooped among themselves. I rubbed my face and saw Kermit and Bone walking among the bodies with their arms spread, truly stunned. The Catahoula ran out, sniffed at a bloody head, lowered down on his front paws, and growled.

Jack's pistol appeared in the corner of my eye and exploded. The body seemed to relax; the Catahoula sniffed again and pranced away. "That's closer than I ever like to get to a cavalry sword," I said quietly.

Shod looked at me and tried to smile. It was a crazy, dizzy smile, then I saw the wide spread of blood on his shoulder as he spun limp to the ground. "Damn it." I tried to catch him, but fell with him. "Help me, Jack, he's shot plumb through." Now I saw the hole as I rolled him on his back. It'd caught him just beneath his collarbone and blew out under his shoulder blade.

"I'm fine," said Shod, "I need to get . . ." His voice trailed away.

While the warriors kept watch along the trail, Jack and I tore strips of rags, dressed Shod's wounds in a hurry, and got him into his saddle. He lay slumped on the horse's neck as we pushed hard toward Tongue River. That's where Band of Iron would be waiting with Red Cloud's bunch. We could get help for Shod and protection against the soldiers.

"From here, all enemies will be behind us." Brown Horse pointed three fingers out across the trail below. "Take the buffalo man to Red Cloud. I will bring horses. My warriors will protect the trail behind us."

I glanced at Jack. "He's right," he said, "Shod needs more help than we can give 'im here. If he takes a fever, he'll die real quick."

I shook my head. "I never seen a big feller go down so hard from a shoulder wound."

"I know."

"Reckon he ain't as tough as he looks."

"Nobody is," said Jack. "Maybe he ain't used to getting shot up ever now and then." We turned our horses back toward the string.

"Then he better think twice before staying in this business."

"He won't stay in this business." Jack cut a plug and shoved it in his jaw. "He might act like he wants to make a quick dollar, but once he gets a big taste of it, he'll spit it out."

Back at the string, I took Shod's reins and led him behind me. He slumped in the saddle and mumbled under his breath. "Poor feller," I thought to myself. He'd surely be embarrassed after this was all over.

♦ ✳ 25 ✳ ♦

"You have learned how to stay alive in my country, while many want to see you dead." Red Cloud gazed across the low flames as we sat in a small clearing beneath the bend in Tongue River. "Now your heart is heavy, from what you have seen."

"I reckon there's something about seeing young-pup soldiers and women and babies slaughtered that don't set just right . . . you could say."

"You saw the Madman Chief Johnson kill our young ones."

"That was just as bad," I said.

"And in the war you fought against the government. Did you see many die?"

"Sure. But somehow that was different."

"Different when whites kill whites? Different than when Sioux kill whites?"

"I don't know." I pitched the money on the ground near the low fire. "Maybe that's how I am. If it is, I can't help it. All I know is that them dumb settlers didn't come up here to get them and their youngins butchered like animals. I reckon the government leaflets forgot to mention that you'd be here waiting." I shook my head. "Anyhow, I can't make it set right. More guns mean more killing."

"More killing of your people." Cloud leaned close to the fire and riveted his eyes on mine. *"No* guns mean more killing of my people."

I dropped my eyes from his for a second. Picking up the stack of money, Red Cloud wiped it and held it close to his face, turning it, examining it. He smiled as he ran his fingers across the crisp new bills. "Big Chief in Washington, makes pretty pictures on his paper.

Shows people who are proud, who have done many things. Picture promises to do many more things."

"Yeah." I breathed deep. "It's real fine stuff, and I'd love to have a wagonload of it. But about buying you some rifles—"

Red Cloud pitched the money back on the ground before me. I looked at it, saw it flicker in the firelight. "Once I traveled to the Missouri country to look at treaty. It was a big trip." He stirred a stick in the fire.

"They fed us from on top of a long table. Played music to help us eat. Then we traveled to a place where many big animals lay in traps for people to look at."

"A zoo," I said.

"Zoo . . . thank you. In zoo, they showed us a bear from my country."

"Now, that was *real* good planning." I shook my head.

"On his trap, they made words to tell people to stay away. But people reached out anyway. One man who had drank much whiskey, reached into the bear's trap. The bear tore his arm from here to here." Red Cloud clawed his fingers down his arm.

"Some damned drunk." I shook my head again.

"Soldier told me that the bear must be destroyed. I asked why. He said because it hurt 'business.' I did not understand. He said people would stop coming if they feared the bear. I said why put a bear in a trap, tell people to come see it, put words on trap to tell them to stay away, then kill bear because people do not listen?"

I chuckled under my breath. "What did he say?"

"He took out a watch and said he had to be some other place. That we would talk about it later. But we never did." Red Cloud stopped and looked puzzled. "What is, '*smart prick*'?"

I grinned. "It can mean a lot of things . . . Why?"

"When he left, that is what he told other soldiers about me."

I watched a trace of a smile work at the edge of his lips; I let out a sigh and picked up the money. "He might be right," I said. "Mister Cloud. There ain't many people I'd do this for. I just want you to know . . ." I still wasn't sure I could bring him guns. I had wrestled with it ever since we'd left the first time. I agreed with everything he said; but once I got out of sight, too many other things told me not to do it.

"I trust you because you have much thought inside you. If you told me it was easy for you to do, I would not trust you."

Everybody's a mind reader, I thought to myself as I stood up. Red Cloud stood up with me and pointed off to the eastern sky.

"They live there. I live here. You live between us. That is why your thoughts are troubled."

I turned and walked to the group of braves gathered around a chunk of venison roasting over a fire. "Where is the buffalo man?" I held my hand high over my head and tapped my shoulder.

They nodded. "He is gone," said one, over a mouthful of food.

"Gone?"

"Gone." He sucked his fingers as he spoke.

"Gone where?" I spread my arms.

A brave laid his hand on his chest and swung it away. "He went out, in hurry, that way." He pointed south.

I reckon a lot of possibilities raced across my mind. He could've decided, after getting shot and grazed with an arrow, that he'd had it with Powder River. He could've decided nothing was worth this, and slipped out because he was embarrassed to tell me. But as these possibilities dropped off the edge of thought, I was struck by one solid, heavy conclusion. He'd gone to get the money. The son of a bitch!

Red Cloud appeared beside me as I jerked the cinch on my saddle and threw a short rope around a relief horse. He wanted to talk; I was in a hurry. "So it was a bad name, the name the soldier called me?"

I hurried a bit into my horse's mouth and spoke without looking around. "I wouldn't let it grieve me, Mister Cloud. They say a man's greatest compliment is the ridicule of fools."

He looked confused. "Tell me what these words mean."

"I'm sorry, but if I don't catch that low-down, lousy 'partner' of mine, I'm out of business."

Red Cloud was not a man to be hurried or put off. He took a hold of my bridle and stepped between me and my horses. I had to stop and take a breath. "When he said I was smart, he didn't mean it?"

"See, there's a good way of being smart and a bad way. He meant that you were being smart in a way he didn't appreciate . . . or something. These kind of words are hard to explain." I stared in his eyes. I didn't have time to explain it. "But like I said, Mister Cloud, don't worry about it—"

"The words I heard you say to Mister Smith about the army. Are they those kind of words? Words that mean a lot of different things?"

I couldn't wait. I had to get moving. It was a matter of money. Shod was after it. I had to stop him. It was my money, even if I stole it from someone who had stolen it from someone else. I had to control myself from shoving Red Cloud aside or trampling over him. I was making no "progress" standing here trying to make him understand something that didn't amount to a hill of beans. "What words?" I almost shouted. "What words was that?"

Three braves heard me raise my voice and they stood up slow, facing us. Red Cloud waved them down. I reminded myself how easy it would be for him to leave my head on a tree limb waving little green arms. I calmed down and smiled. "What words do you mean, Mister Cloud?"

"I heard Mister Smith tell you the army would hang you for helping me, and you said, 'Fugem-fugem-all.' "

The way he said it sounded like an Indian chant. I stepped around him slowly, taking the reins from his hand and picking up the rope on my relief horse. "Oh, that. Well, that means . . . when you have no regard for a person at all. You don't hear them or see them—"

"I see. It is how the army thinks of my people, and how you think of the army?"

"Yeah, something like that." I rechecked the cinch before stepping up in the saddle. "Now I really have to go, Mister Cloud." I gigged my horse and jerked the rope on the relief horse.

He stepped back. "May the spirit ride with you." He stepped back again and raised a fist in the air. "Fugem-fugem-all."

I heard some of the braves repeat his words as I turned my horse and threw my fist in the air. In minutes I pounded out around the trail and across the woodlands beneath Tongue River, hearing nothing but the wind in my face and the sound of my horse's hooves.

I rode all night and part of the next day, not bothering to follow Shod's tracks. He had to go in the same direction. He would follow the trail until he got close to Jack and the string of horses, then cut up into the ridgeline and swing around them. I would save ten miles by riding straight through.

I'd stopped and swapped my saddle to my relief horse when I heard a sound in the brush and spun toward it with my forty-four cocked. One of Brown Horse's braves stepped forward, saw what I was doing, and helped me without saying a word. He slapped the spent horse on the rump and it loped off into the woods as I swung up in my saddle. "How far back are they?"

He drew a line in the air. I could only guess that it meant they were close. He made a clucking sound and a spotted horse stepped from the brush, quiet as a ghost. He swung up on its back and we pounded down the narrow trail.

An hour later, we swung into a sharp turn, topped a hill, and came upon the braves at the head of the string. They stepped their horses to the side and let us through. Near the rear of the string, I saw Jack sliding his rifle into his scabbard and drawing the cinch on his saddle. He turned as I came reining up sideways.

"Shod's gone. He slipped away while I—"

"So's Bone." Jack nodded back up the trail. "Saw his tracks, heading back."

"You don't think—?"

"The money? Yes. Bone and Shod, together? No way. They just both got greedy at the same time." Jack stepped up in his saddle.

"Bone's no problem," I said. "He's too stupid to find it. But Shod knows where it is. You can bet on it!"

"This is the awfulest bunch I've ever seen," said Jack, tapping his spurs. "I'm getting afraid to turn my back on my own shadow."

◆✳ 26 ✳◆

Daylight slipped over the horizon in a blue-golden haze as we led our horses quietly into the woods and past the rock where we'd buried the money. "They ain't been here yet," said Jack, leaning and examining the rock.

"Good. Let's lay right here and shoot their eyes out." We both turned at the same time and only saw a flash as Shod's rifle butt smacked Jack in the chin, then the barrel flipped around and jammed into my chest.

"What are you fools doing here?" Shod crouched with the rifle cocked. His voice was a rough whisper that made me whisper in reply. Jack lay cold as a wedge.

"You've got some damn nerve, you double-crossing—"

"Shut up!" He poked me with the barrel, reached, flipped my gun from my side holster, and dropped it on the ground. "I thought it would take you at least another day to start after me." He flipped my pistol from my shoulder holster and dropped it. "You *are* smarter than you look."

"I reckon it's true what they say about all you—"

"Say it, and I'll pound you straight into the ground. You don't know what you're dealing with here." He started to reach down for my glades knife, but we heard rifles cock all around us and he froze, staring up at my eyes.

"Kill 'em," shouted Bone. "Send 'em all straight to hell!"

"Shut up, Bone," I heard the familiar voice say, and I stared over Shod's shoulder as the six riflemen stepped closer. The voice was the one I'd heard in Mad Johnson's tent the night I robbed him.

He stepped forward and smiled, the smile of a wolf over a

downed antelope. Morning light glittered across a gold tooth. The other gunmen spread out surrounding us. "Drop the long-arm, boy. Let's talk a spell."

"Way to go, Shod," I growled.

I heard someone breaking through the brush behind the riflemen, and in a second Mad Johnson stepped into the clearing. His hat was missing and he looked like a man with a lot on his mind. "Thank God," he said. He pointed straight at me. "That's him, Parker . . . the one who stole it." I noticed Johnson's holster was empty and the flap turned up. He looked scared. Behind me, Jack groaned.

"He's got a hog gutter in his boot," said Bone, as Parker Pope stepped closer. "Watch him."

Pope nodded toward Jack. "Get his gun, Bone, and shut your mouth."

Two gunmen stepped up to Shod. One held a rifle in Shod's face while the other stepped around, drew his hands behind him, and tied him. I saw Shod wince from his shoulder wound. "I hope it hurts," I said through clenched teeth.

"You're the one who shot my brother Gyp?" His eyes honed in on me. I figured I was going to die real soon. I took a deep breath.

"Yeah, I shot him in the back, kicked his face in, cut his head off—I even said some things about his mama." I braced, ready for the explosion.

"Kill 'im!" Bone's face turned into an ugly death mask.

"I like a sense of humor." Pope grinned. I heard Jack cuss and thrash on the ground. I nodded toward him.

"He didn't have nothing to do with it. He wasn't even there."

"I don't give a shit." Pope stepped over to Jack, speaking to me over his shoulder. "I didn't even like him. I owed him forty dollars. I'm glad he's dead."

"I liked him right well," said one of the gunmen.

Pope pointed his thumb. "That's my brother Clement. They were close." He nudged Jack with his boot. "Wake up and smell the morning."

"Who the hell are you?" Jack's hand cupped his swollen jaw. He crawled up on a log, shaking his head. "Where's my damn gun? Who hit me?"

"It's the Pope Gang, Jack," I said cautiously. "Go easy."

"I don't give a blue damn who it is. There was no call to crack me in my damn jaw." Jack glared up at Parker. Parker looked at him curiously.

"Who are you? You look familiar."

"Well . . . I ain't. And don't ask me nothing. My jaw hurts." Jack spit near Pope's feet.

"I like your style," said Pope. "I think I'll shoot you first."

"Well, fire away, you gold-toothed son of a bitch. I'm the only one knows where the money is." Jack winked and tried to smile. "So there."

"Jack," I said quietly, "they were watching. They know it's under the rock."

"Ha . . . just raise that ole rock and check her out, by God." I looked at Jack, thinking he'd lost his mind.

Pope spread an evil grin. "You're bluffing, and instead of shooting you, I'm going to skin you real slow—"

"Yeah? Give me two minutes, man to man. I'll teach you to bust my jaw."

"Jack," I said, "he didn't—"

"Shut up," Pope snapped. He spun toward Mad Johnson. "Roll it over, and you better pray it's there."

Johnson grunted with both hands under the edge of the rock, until it finally pulled loose and flopped over with a thud. "There it is!" He snatched it up. I thought it looked too flat, even after lying under the rock. His face turned chalk white. His lips trembled. "It's empty."

"Surprise, surprise," Jack laughed. "You bastards call yourselves outlaws?"

Pope spun toward Johnson with his rifle. "Tough break, soldier."

"No . . . please," shouted Johnson.

"Don't fire that shot!" I yelled, but too late. Johnson's head snapped as a long red ribbon curled out the back of it and exploded in the air. Shod jerked beside me as Johnson fell at his feet. "Jesus," I breathed.

"So . . . now. Where do we start?" Pope swung the gun toward Bone. Bone's face turned the color of death after a long illness.

"It's around here . . . it is, it is!" His trousers turned dark around the crotch. "This is where I found them, right cheer, down on the road!" His eyes rolled back in his head, his body bucked and quivered, and he fell to his knees with his hands fluttering in the air, talking in tongues.

"You're disgusting." Pope shook his head. He turned to Jack. "What's your deal? I know you've got one."

Jack rubbed his jaw and chuckled under his breath. "I oughta bust you in your head."

"Come on, Jack, for Christ sake!" I leaned toward him. Pope blocked me with his rifle barrel. Shod let out a breath and shook his head.

"Here's how it plays," said Jack, "short and sweet. You turn us loose and give us half the money." Pope's gunmen had stepped in close around. They all laughed. Pope pointed the cocked rifle an inch from Jack's nose.

"You're crazy, and I ain't going to dicker with you."

"Fair enough." Jack gritted his teeth, stared straight up the barrel. "Fire away . . . You don't need the money."

I saw Pope's hand tighten on the trigger. I started to jump against him, but a gunman held me back. "BANG!" shouted Pope, and everybody flinched except Jack. He just spit on Pope's barrel and laughed under his breath.

"You boys ain't tough. You've just been tickling your nuts up here in the high country. Now pull that ole trigger like you got some guts."

Pope snarled like a dog. His gold tooth gleamed. He glanced at his gunmen, then back to Jack. "A third, and that's my only offer."

We all stared at Jack as he reached slow inside his pocket, gazing off as if considering it. He took a plug of tobacco, bit off a chunk, and offered it to Parker Pope. Behind us, Bone babbled and honked like a goose stuck in a barn door. Pope took the plug, twisted off a chunk, and handed it back. I let out a deep breath, ready to talk in tongues myself. "You boys have spunk," said Pope. "Where you from?"

"We're from the hard end of Missouri," said Jack, spitting a stream and cupping his jaw. "We've been sight-seeing up in Red Cloud's country."

"Sight-seeing." Pope grinned. "That's good. Now let's chuck up that money and get on down the road. Where's it at, ole buddy?"

Jack nodded. "Right behind you, inside that stump."

"Get it!" Pope barked at one of his gunmen, then shot Jack a hard stare. I saw his gun hand tighten again. "So long, sport. It's been fun talking."

"It ain't here," said the gunman. Pope looked confused. Again his gun hand loosened. His expression softened.

"You ain't playing with school kids here, Pope." Jack grinned. "Sooner you settle down, the sooner you'll get your money."

I knew Jack couldn't have hidden the money over a few yards away during the time I spent struggling with Shod and trying to shoot Bone. But we'd been working our way up the wooded slope nearly ten minutes, and Jack showed no sign of letting up. The three men following us had all our handguns shoved down in their belts, except for the forty-four I had hidden under my shirt. Pope still had Shod tied up back in the clearing. I was waiting for Jack to make a move.

When Jack glanced over his shoulder at the gunmen, I knew he was judging distance, so I braced, ready. He stopped, turned suddenly—"Right here, boys"—and buried the toe of his boot in one gunman's crotch as I grabbed the other's rifle by the barrel and pulled him toward me. As he came forward, off balance, Jack stepped in with a straight punch. The man flipped backward, rolled down the slope a few feet, and landed against the tree like he was taking a nap. I had his rifle.

"Don't shoot," groaned the one on the ground at Jack's feet. He lay rolled in a ball, his hands clasped to his groin. But as I stepped forward to bust him in the head with the rifle butt, we heard all hell break loose down in the clearing. I dove to the ground, thinking it was Pope's men firing up at us; then I heard Indians yelling.

"See?" I said to Jack, crouched down beside me. "I told him not to fire that shot. Every damn time you pull a trigger—"

Jack jerked his gun and mine from one gunman's belt as I slipped over to the tree and did the same with the other. "Reckon it's Shoshoni?" I called over in a loud whisper.

"Why not?" Jack shook his head. "The way things have been running, it wouldn't surprise me if it was Chinamen riding camels."

◆ ❋ 27 ❋ ◆

In a few minutes we could tell the fight had turned into a mounted chase. We took the gunmen's boots and ran them off into the woods, then slipped back down to the clearing. The Popes had put up a good fight, but the odds must've been stacked high against them. Three gunmen lay stretched out with their bodies shot to pieces. Seven dead Indians dotted the path up from the trail. We looked around for horses. There were none.

Jack walked over to the log he had sat on earlier, bent down, rolled it a turn, and hefted up the saddlebags of money. He grinned. "Help me put it under the rock."

As he threw the bag on the ground beneath the rock, I heard a terrible wailing coming from the edge of the woods. "What's that?" I whispered, already drawing my pistol.

"Check it out. I'll finish up here."

". . . Don't kill me, don't kill me, whoever you are." I recognized Bone's sobbing as I stepped in the brush. He looked up, his face streaked with tears, his eyes dilated and shiny. He was scared out of his wits. "I love every *goddamn* body, Indians, whites, big colored fellers."

"Shut up, Bone!" I pulled him to his feet.

"We've always been friends . . . you know it?"

I cracked his forehead with my pistol barrel. He threw his hand to it. "Don't start that again," he wailed. "I always try to do what's right."

I smelled a rank odor and realized he'd soiled himself. "You're too low to live and too pitiful to kill. Get out of here!" I pointed my gun in his face, and he scrambled out through the woods, leaving a vapor of stink, like a kicked skunk.

Jack patted the rock as I walked back. "I took out some carrying-around money in case we need it," he said. "I don't see Shod nowhere; maybe he managed to crawl away."

"He won't be that lucky if I ever get my hands on him." I glanced around the clearing one more time, then we headed down to the trail and started our walk back up to Tongue River. I thought it peculiar that the only person we could count on, the only person in Powder River who wasn't ready to kill us for some reason or other, was Red Cloud De Oglala, the most feared, hunted, and hated man on the western slice of heaven. Somehow, we were right at home with his bunch. We could get horses there. We could rest on Red Cloud's farm.

"If I ever see him, I'm killing him . . . guns, knives, fists, however he wants it." I banged my fist against the palm of my hand. "To think I trusted that slick-headed, smooth-talking— They just ain't like us, Jack. That's all there is to it. You can't trust 'em."

"None of 'em, or just Shod?"

"That's the only one I know. But they're all the same. One black bastard is no different than the rest. They're all the same."

Jack shook his head. "Do I have to listen to this all the way to Red Cloud's country?"

"It's the damn truth. I might've just thought it before, but I believe it now."

"He let you down real bad, didn't he?"

I took a deep breath. "Yeah . . . just when I thought he was one of us. It ain't like Bone. You know right off you can't trust that back-stabbing snake. Shod was different."

"I thought you and Shod was headed for a run-in back before he got shot."

"We were. I was getting tired of his mouth, but there you are. You can do that with a 'partner.' " I stared at the trail ahead. "If I see him . . . he's dead."

"I thought he was a pretty good feller." Jack smiled and spit a stream.

"Yeah . . . well, let me tell you. It wasn't Pope that cracked your jaw. It was that 'pretty good feller,' Mister Shod."

"Hell, I know it. I just needed a reason to make Pope think I was mad at him." He spit again. "Makes it more personal—gets 'em rattled." Jack cocked an eye. "That's poker."

◆✳ 28 ✳◆

To avoid the many people who roamed the country wanting to kill us, we stayed just off the trail and hiked along through brush and timber for the rest of the day, then slept a few hours in a clump of pines. After midnight, we got up and pushed on, planning to travel only at night, now that we'd distanced ourselves from the scene of the battle.

We figured the Shoshoni would comb the area looking for survivors right after the fight; and it was best to "get" while the getting was good. But now we would travel in the cover of darkness, slip back to the Sioux, get some horses, and return for the money.

We'd just climbed a dark ridge and started around it when we noticed the glow of a low fire in the valley to our right. A camp meant horses—Indian, outlaw, army, it didn't matter what kind, as long as they had four legs and wouldn't nicker too loud when we led them away.

We belly-crawled closer and gazed down the last fifty feet at four Shoshoni braves sprawled around the fire. Twenty feet to their left, I saw a tail swish in the pale moonlight, heard a low nicker and the solid thud of a hoof scrape the ground. To the right, a guard sat nodding over his rifle barrel; before him, I saw two of Pope's men— what was left of them—and Big Shod hanging in the air from a low branch, his wrists bound by rawhide. In the flicker of firelight, I saw they'd worked on his chest a little with skinning knifes, probably just enough to make him scream. They must've saved the rest of him 'til morning. Pope's men were dead, most of their skin hanging in long strips, and one's belly spilling down his legs.

"Reckon you'll miss your chance at ever kicking his ass," Jack whispered.

I swallowed hard. "Serves him right. He had a chance at doing right by us. So now . . . to hell with him."

"That's right, piss on 'im. Just because he stopped Flowers from opening your head with a forty-four—"

"Don't start, Jack. He was out to rob us. Let 'em carve a few pounds off him."

"Damn right," said Jack, quietly checking his pistol and cocking his rifle. We lay there in silence for a few seconds watching Shod's bloody chest glisten in the firelight. He raised his head once as if in a plea to heaven, then dropped it. His eyes were swollen shut.

"You'll have to help me get him on a horse," I said, reaching down and slipping my glades knife from my boot.

"I got ya," said Jack.

"As soon as we get him out, he's on his own."

"Yeah," said Jack, "I know."

"Or I'll kill him."

"Right."

"I mean it," I said.

"Just go on; it's alright." Jack nudged me, and crept away to the horses. I crawled slow and easy toward the guard.

Ten feet from the edge of the firelight, I spotted another guard leaning against a tree with a rifle across his lap and a bottle of whiskey between his legs. He wore a stained army tunic with the sleeves ripped off at the shoulders. Crawling closer, I saw he was passed out drunk, and I eased the rifle from his lap and clubbed him one solid lick on the head.

Knowing there would be other Shoshoni in the area, I took a deep breath and went about my killing as quiet and deadly as a vengeful spirit. First the guard. I wrapped my arm around his face from behind as I lifted the blade up between his ribs, running it through his heart and lying back with him as his feet quivered, then relaxed in death.

Jack slipped in and crouched in the center of the small clearing, covering the sleeping braves with his rifle. But he wouldn't fire unless he had to. He watched me go from one to the other until my hands and chest were red with their blood.

"Whew," he whispered, as I stepped back from the last of them and wiped the blade across my leg. I just stared at him, my face drawn tight and my body trembling. We'd called it a "Missouri sunrise" back during the war. I'd learned it well.

I cut Shod down from the tree as Jack gathered the horses and walked them over as silent as a ghost. One of the horses bore a cavalry brand; it was probably Mad Johnson's. Carefully we raised Shod into the saddle. "Don't," he groaned, and I put my hand over his bruised and swollen mouth.

"Lay still, it's us," I whispered, knowing his eyes were too swollen to see. "You're the only one that gets to ride in a saddle, you rotten son of—"

"Help me out here," Jack whispered. We leaned him forward, ran the rawhide around the horse's neck, and tied each end to his hands to keep him from falling if we got into a chase.

"Slow and easy," Jack whispered, and we walked the horses out of the camp and nearly a half mile before we slipped up their bare backs and rode off down the edge of the trail.

By daylight, we stopped along a creek and eased Shod down from the horse. His chest was cut in even lines from his collarbone to his navel. The cuts were deliberately shallow, the way you would do a deer before skinning it. I reckon he was in for one hell of a morning if we hadn't showed up. I took off my blood-soaked shirt, swished it in the cold water, and wrung it over his face. "Time to wake up, Mister Shod, 'partner.'"

He turned his head slowly back and forth as the cold water ran over his face. "Oh no . . . not you two," he breathed, looking up for a second through a slit of an eye.

"Yeah . . . it's us, your guardian angels." I grinned, but I knew he couldn't see me. "You low-handed, double-crossing—" The more I spoke, the madder I got. I drew back a boot. Jack shoved me away.

"What's wrong with you? Let him get back to life before you go kicking at him."

"I lost my head." I took a breath and wiped Shod's face carefully with the wet shirt. "Sorry, Shod, 'partner,' I just couldn't help but remember what a lousy, rotten, back-stabbing—"

"Here, damn it!" Jack snatched the shirt from my hand and shoved me away. "I'll do it."

We rested most of the day, letting Shod get back some of his strength before heading the rest of the way to Red Cloud's farm. That evening we heard horses on the trail beneath us, and I lay beside Jack, peeping over the edge of a ridge. "What do you make of it?" I said, staring down at two Pawnee and a big man in full buckskins. Right behind them, four cavalry officers cantered along in full dress uniform carrying a flag. Behind them rode eight soldiers in a column of twos. They all wore a white strip of cloth tied around their arms.

"S'pose they're on some kind of military picnic?"

"If they are, they've more to worry about than ants."

"Cloud's gonna eat 'em for breakfast," Jack chuckled, "and use those white rags for napkins."

"Good. Maybe it'll take his mind off the rifles for a while." I still hadn't decided about getting the rifles.

We slipped along with them, until we reached the stretch of land below Tongue River. "They must be riding all the way in," said Jack. "Reckon they oughta be told?"

"There's sixteen years worth of West Point bobbing under them fancy hats. If you think you can tell 'em *anything,* feel free."

When they stopped at a creek for the evening, we lay in the woods and watched them carve a chunk of dried shank and stake it over a fire. Soon the smell of sizzling meat caused our bellies to growl. Even Shod raised his head and sniffed at it. "They're probably a half-decent bunch, if we gave them a chance. I don't see any I recognize, do you?"

Jack chuckled, "I don't recognize any of their horses, if that's what you're asking." We watched the Pawnee scouts turn the meat slowly.

As they carved off thick slices onto metal plates, the old man in buckskins picked up a pot of coffee and walked to the edge of the clearing. Looking up in our direction, he flipped open the lid and steam bellowed. "We got enough for the three of you," he said toward us. "We might have something to treat the big feller's wounds."

My mouth dropped open. "How the hell . . . ?"

"I don't know," said Jack, "but I'm too hungry to give a damn." He stood up and waved his rifle back and forth slowly. "I'm coming down."

We eased our horses down through the woods. At the edge of the camp, the Pawnee let Shod down from his saddle and jabbered about the cuts on his chest like craftsmen comparing their work. The man in buckskins smiled, turned, and walked back to the fire. We followed the wake of fresh coffee like sailors sniffing a whore. Around the fire, the officers stood up and dabbed at their mouths with cloth napkins.

"Please join us, gentlemen," said one with the wave of a perfect hand. His words were too smooth to grab; he had the smile of Jesus, protected by a fire red moustache and a dangerously sharp goatee. "I'm Colonel Richard Hunt McDowell . . ."

"Thanks," I said, staring at the meat on the fire. I wiped my hands up and down on my dark-stained shirt. It had dried the color of cheap wine. "I'm Beatty . . . James Beatty. This is Mister—"

I glanced beside me and saw only an empty space where Jack should've been. Hearing a rustle at the fire, I turned toward it and saw him tear off a strip of meat and shove it in his mouth.

He glanced over his shoulder with his mouth bulging. "Pleased," he snorted with a hand thrown in the air, then turned back to the fire.

The colonel smiled. "My fellow officers are . . ." Each time he said a name, a head nodded, as if he jerked a string beneath their chins. "We're traveling up to the Tongue River Reservation to visit Chief Red Cloud."

"Reservation?"

"Simply a figure of speech." He tossed his hand. "But come, you must be hungry. Replenish yourself, while my colleagues and I finish our discussion. We can chat later."

"I reckon," I said under my breath as I stepped over beside Jack. Tearing off a strip of meat, I glanced over my shoulder, then back to Jack. "Red Cloud's gonna love talking to this butter-tongued son of a bitch."

Jack grunted and chewed. Over to the right of us, the Pawnee scouts smeared salve on Shod's chest and tipped a canteen to his mouth. The old man in buckskins came up, pitched two metal cups to us, and stepped back with a crooked grin. "What gave you away was traveling upwind from us." I sniffed at my shirt, shrugged, and kept on eating. "No way," I thought; nobody's that good.

"I'm Bridger, Jim Bridger." He threw his head back. "If you ain't heard of me, you must've been living under a rock."

Jack grunted and nodded over his shoulder. I wiped my free hand and held it out. "I sure have, Mister Bridger; it's an honor."

He looked me up and down—"Oh, yeah"—searched himself quickly, pulled out a short string of wooden beads, and dropped them in my hand.

I just stared at him.

"We heard shooting two days ago. Was that you fellers?"

"No," I lied, "but we heard it too."

Bridger eyed me close. "That's Shoshoni cuttings on the big feller, ain't it?"

"Jesus," I said, truly impressed. "You can tell just by looking?"

"Don't be stupid, boy." He cocked both eyebrows on their outer edges. "We seen 'em doing it night before last, coming up off the trail. That's why I figured it was you fellers doing the shooting. They'd already skinned two others, gutted one."

"They why didn't you stop them? They're working for the army."

"Had no time. We're on a mission of peace here."

"Oh," I said. I was starting to see that whatever Jim Bridger once had must've been left out too long in the thin air of the high country. "Well . . . that's important too."

"You're right it is. I'm the only man Red Cloud will listen to, riding or walking." He snatched off his floppy hat and pulled a picture from it. "We're like brothers. Here's a picture we were going to have taken together"—I looked at the picture; it was Bridger alone—"but he couldn't make it that day. I went ahead anyway just for a keepsake." He held up two rough fingers pressed together. "We're just like that."

I grew tired of nodding my head; and I hungered for more food before Jack ate it all. "Meet my friend, Mister Smith," I said, and I turned to the meat as Jack shot me a dark stare.

"Smith, huh?" Bridger scratched his whiskers. "I knew a Head-splitter Smith up along the Canadian. He lived with a she-bear. They say him and that bear—"

"No kin." Jack sucked his fingers and rubbed them on his shirt. "Now, listen real close, Mister Bridger." Jack's voice was low and even, his finger in the air between them. "I don't want you talking to, asking or telling. I don't want you looking toward me, past me, or anywhere near me. You don't know any of my kin, or any kin of any of my kin. In short, don't mess with me. Are we clear?" Jack turned back to the meat.

Bridger turned to me. "The Smith I knew was *just* like that, contrariest man you ever seen, *riding or walking.* They say a bull buffalo gored him once from here to here." He sliced his hand across his belly. I nodded and kept on eating.

"Way to go, Red Cloud," I thought to myself as Bridger babbled behind me. The army must've known they were losing; sending in Jim Bridger was truly an act of desperation. Bridger had been a hell of a man in his time, legendary, but it was plain to see that his time was slipping fast. His brain had spent too many nights nestled on cold stones high up in the Rockies. How could the army have missed seeing it? Or did they? Maybe it was their way of showing Red Cloud his time was over, same as Blanket Jim Bridger's.

". . . A truly wonderful old gentleman," said Colonel "Jesus" McDowell. He spread his hands before him and closed them slowly as he spoke until they formed a sharp steeple pointing up at the dangerous goatee. "He is a virtual textbook on Sioux protocol. And they love him . . . they simply *do.*"

"I think he's suffering from a split in his main timber." I cleared my throat, trying to sound as well bred as he. "I simply *do.*"

He turned his head slightly with a puzzled look. "Oh? You mean to imply . . . he has said something to give you the impression— Oh my." He ran his finger and thumb down his goatee.

"He's nuts, Colonel. There, I said it. He's been around too long, and his mind's as stiff as hickory kindling. You and the rest of the army are bound to have seen it . . . unless you're all as crazy as he is."

He stood up slowly from a folding stool and tugged at the edge of his perfect tunic. Smoothing it, he walked over to the fire, faced away from me, and folded his hands behind his perfect back. "Are you a veteran, Mister Beatty?" Near us, Jack, Shod, and the officers snored softly, while Bridger and the scouts worked the ridgeline, keeping watch. Moonlight spilled like a vapor of medication on the quiet of night.

"That is correct," I said, trying to polish my words up to his standard.

"With whom did you serve . . . McClellan, Sherman . . . Grant?"

I cleared my throat. "Actually—"

"Oh, pardon me . . . the accent. I should've known." He took a breath. "Let's see . . . Lee? Jackson? Yes, Jackson. Of course, that's who it was, wasn't it? Ole Stonewall?"

"Well . . . the thing is. I actually—"

"Come, come, Mister Beatty. You can be proud to have served with any of those fine southern gentlemen." He turned from the fire with a smile; with his hands still behind his back, he stepped toward me, leaning lower and closer as he spoke. "The war is over; you have nothing to be ashamed of." Bringing one hand from behind his back, he poked a finger straight up. "Unless . . . of course, you rode with that despicable band of lawless trash along the border. In which case you should have been hanged, like many of them were and all of them should have been. And in which case you most certainly would not *dare* question the competence of a decent human being like Jim Bridger, or the decision of an educated, skilled spokesman . . . trained military professional in their attempt to establish peace with a group of heartless, murdering savages. Am I correct?" His perfect teeth flashed less than a foot from my face. His breath smelled like Washington—cherry blossoms and stale air.

"You're smooooooth," I said above a whisper, leaning back in fear of a deadly kiss. "And you're riiiight. I shouldn't have said a word.

But as I recall, that rebel trash along the border armed and outfitted themselves with the guns and horses of dead Yankees, and never stopped kicking ass, 'til you boys hollered uncle and damn near had to sign a separate treaty. How was it they said it? 'An act of kindness, so the country can heal itself.' Kindness, your fine feathered ass. Them ole boys had ya'll's hands shaking so bad, you couldn't piss without jacking yourselves off—"

"That will be quite enough!" He recomposed—"Thank you, Mister Beatty"—and turned his back once more. "If there's a point to—"

"The point's this." I got up, stepped right beside him, and threw my hands behind my back. I peered around with a smooth mocking smile. "If you think that border trash was a handful, you ain't gonna believe how hard Red Cloud is gonna jar your faith. I don't give a damn how many feebleminded mountain men you haul in with a string of beads to suck up to him. You'll leave here carrying your better parts in a wicker basket."

We stood nose to nose, until I realized how foolish it was to have said a word. I clenched my teeth. "I'm . . . sorry. I've got, an, uncle, who's a, preacher." I trimmed each word separate. "Sometimes, it just, spills out of me."

He cocked his head and smiled. "No kidding? I'm Presbyterian myself, and yet . . . I believe we're all God's children."

I just stared at him for the longest time, picturing his head on a tree limb, waving little green hands.

Part V
Dog and Pony Show

◆ ✳ 29 ✳ ◆

Even daylight seemed to jump up quickly as our stately group rode by. I'd never seen a flag as large or as bright in color as the one that led us into Red Cloud's country. It bellowed and rolled in a flurry of stars and stripes as wind licked it, and it slapped and pushed at the officer carrying it, sometimes ready to knock him off his horse. But he held on. I couldn't help but wonder if they should be waving a large white flag and wearing a red, white, and blue cloth around their arms; but after last night's conversation with Colonel Mc-Dowell, I wasn't about to mention it.

"And another thing," I thought to myself, as we traipsed along behind. "Who the hell am I to question the mental condition of someone like Blanket Jim Bridger?" The man was a legend. He'd led wagon trains, scouted the high country, and saved the lives of God knows how many. All these things he'd done while I was still hanging from a teat. Now I felt low.

I gigged my horse and rode up beside McDowell, in front of the riders, right behind the bellowing banner. He acknowledged me with a curt snap, then stared straight ahead into the flag. "Colonel," I said above the wind in the heavy cloth, "about last night. I sure feel bad about what I said . . . you know, about Bridger?"

He smiled without facing me. "I have completely forgotten the incident, Mister Beatty."

"Well, thank you, Colonel." I stayed beside him, listening to the slapping sound of the flag and watching sunlight sparkle on the brass eagle atop the pole. Glancing around at the sharply creased and perfectly fitted blue and gold-trimmed uniforms, I wiped my hand on my grimy shirt and started to fall back to Jack and Shod.

"Give me your perception of Red Cloud," said McDowell, without facing me.

"My what?" His words had been broken by the sound of the flapping flag.

"What do you think of him? How do you know him?"

"That's a long story. But I think he's a man who wants somebody to listen to him and understand what the hell's going on."

"Can you speak intelligently without using profanity?"

I shrugged. "Well . . . I can *try*."

"Good. That's all I require of you. Now, you were saying?"

"Seems to me, Red Cloud knows his people have been fu— scr— that is, beaten out of most of their land. All he's saying is that it has to stop right here. This is where he eats. He can't pull back no farther. Without the wild game between here and the Black Hills, his people will starve." I leaned close to him. "You never fu— mess with a man when it comes to his dinner. Anybody would die fighting to keep from starving, right?"

He smiled, still without facing me. "See, you said that quite well without the crude obscenities."

"Thank you, Colonel. But do you get my drift?"

"Of course." He shrugged. "Red Cloud apparently wants what everyone wants, simply to live in peace and provide for his people."

"There you are." I slapped my leg. "Finally someone gets the picture here. Colonel, the man feels like he's been talking to a stump. Where the hel—heck have you been? They should've sent you months ago."

"All he is actually asking is that we stay out of the land between the Black Hills and the Big Horn Range. Simply that we build no forts, cut no roads, down no trees, kill no game." He tossed a hand. "That sort of thing."

"Amen!" I pushed up my hat and let out a breath. This was all it really took, just one rational person who could listen and understand. I smiled at McDowell and watched him tug at his dangerous goatee in deep contemplation. "So . . . think you can help him out?"

He faced me with a warm "Jesus" smile across clean, sparkling sharp teeth. "Good will always prevail, anytime reasonable men sit down with honest intent."

* * *

". . . That's exactly how he said it, Jack. 'Good will always prevail, any—'"

"Red Cloud better sleep with his back against a wall and his hand over his mouth," Jack chuckled. "That's all I can tell ya."

"Come on, Jack, give the man a chance. I think he means it." I tapped my finger on my horse's mane. "And that'll get me off the hook about the rifles."

"You ain't been on the hook as far as Cloud's concerned. Don't ask me why, but that ole buzzard likes you. He knows you're just wrestling with your conscience. And he's right." Jack spit a stream. "If you'd made up your mind *not* to get them rifles, you'd've high-tailed it out of here before now. And if you was dead set on *getting* them, there ain't a rock this side of hell that would stand in your way." He spit another stream. "And I know it."

I cleared my throat. "Jack, do you have to cuss so damn much? Can't you talk intelli—"

"Hell no." He pulled his hat low on his forehead and grinned from beneath the wide brim. "That colonel has shined your handles plumb up to your elbows, ain't he?"

"Jack, somebody has to have the decency to see what's going on here. I believe he's different than Johnson, Fetterman, and that bunch."

"He ain't no different, he's just higher and slicker. That's called 'chain of command.' The others are field hands working the dirt. He's a cut above. It gets slicker as you go up. By the time you get to the White House, you can't even hold on to the railing."

"Alright, maybe he is, but I don't think so. We'll see when we get there."

I started to gig my horse away, but Bridger reined up beside us and started right in on Jack. "I remember once, just off the turn of the Canadian. We'd been hunting for—"

"Didn't I tell you not to mess with me?" Jack snarled like a dog.

"Come on, Jack," I said in a low voice. "It don't hurt to show some respect." On the other side of Jack, Shod sat slumped on his horse, his head bobbing up and down slowly. He was coming around.

"I've tried to make it clear." Jack spit a stream. "I don't like you,

Bridger. I don't like old folk, young folk, or people my age." He glared between Bridger and me, and nodded over toward Shod. "I don't like colored folk, white folk, Indians, or foreigners. I don't want to hear what you've done, might've done, or ever will do—"

Bridger reared back and laughed, pointing his finger. "That's just like Head-splitter. He was the same way!"

Jack looked up from under his hat and shook his head. "Nothing works on this feller." His hand drifted near his gun. I turned to Bridger. I didn't think Jack really would've shot him, but why take a chance?

"Mind if I ride with you to check on the scouts?"

"Not a'tall. It'll give me a chance to tell you how things used to be." I glanced at Jack; he shook his head and turned away as I followed Bridger up past the front of the column and into the woods.

Three hundred yards ahead, we swung up off the trail and met the Pawnee at the edge of a cliff overlooking a stretch of flatland Jack and I'd led Shod across two nights before. One of the Pawnee rose from his belly and rested on his haunches. We slid from our horses and approached him in a crouch. "Riders . . . white men." He pointed at a thin line of dust on the distant horizon.

"Yeah," said Bridger, studying the dust like a hawk. His eyes seemed to blot out everything but the thin line at the end of vision. "That be the ones tracking you and your party. I make it a half dozen. The Popes more'n likely." I noticed a difference in Bridger now that we'd gotten away from Jack and the army officers. Out here we were in his world, and he knew his world well enough to stay alive when most around him had long since fallen.

I squinted and strained my eyes against the sun's glare. I couldn't see anything but a fine brown swirl. "How do you know we were being followed?"

"Some things a body jest knows from being part of this country. We caught wind of you fellers while you thought you were slipping along beside us." He gave me a crafty grin. "Ain't bad for an old feller whose mind is stiff as hickory kindling, is it?"

I felt my face redden. "I said some things last night that I shouldn't have. I didn't know you were listening."

"I always am," he laughed, "riding or walking." He picked a tick off his shirtsleeve, examined it, then flipped it away. "From the color of that tick, I'd say winter's coming early this year."

"What about that bunch?" I nodded toward the wake of dust. "If they find us, I don't figure your brass Yankees will be much help."

"The Popes couldn't find their ass with both hands. But you're right about McDowell's bunch. They'd be dead in two days out here on their own . . . riding or walking. That's what keeps me and the Pawns here in beans and biscuits." Beside him the Pawnee scouts laughed and nodded.

I studied the wake of dust. "If you don't mind me asking. Why's a man like you leading these sorry bastards to Red Cloud? From what I've seen, it's a waste of time. He ain't going to give an inch."

"I know it, Red Cloud knows it too. This is my last chance to see some of my old friends at the army's expense. Once the railroad's finished, all the fun'll be over."

"Fun?"

"Well . . . let's jest call it 'something to do.' "

"Yeah, and the Indians end up losing their country."

Bridger chuckled. "Hold on now. I've seen more than you, and I'll tell you straight up, Indians have thrown away more'n they've ever lost."

I moved back in a crouch and stood up beside my horse. Bridger and the scouts moved back with me. He cut a plug of tobacco and passed the rest around. "Ask these Pawns." He nodded. "They'll tell you the same thing. I've seen hunting parties bring in a thousand buffalo tongues and trade them for a few barrels of whiskey right outside the gates of Laramie. I call that dumping in your own nest. Then they piss and moan that the white man is killing off the herds. Pee-thuey." He spit a stream.

I climbed up on my stolen Indian pony. Bridger slid into his saddle and reined over beside me. "I've seen many a chief trade his horses, guns, knives; hell . . . back in forty-one, Chief Bull Tail traded his daughters for a barrel of whiskey."

"That a fact?" I reined around and headed back down to the trail. I'd heard enough of Blanket Bridger for one day. "Makes you wonder why we sell it to them, don't it?"

"Another thing." He raised a finger. "I've seen 'em come in and get rifles and powder as a peace offering, then turn around the next day and kill the ones that gave them to 'em." He spit another stream. "I tell ya, signing a treaty with an Indian is like pissing straight up in a high wind. It'll splatter back in your face every time."

"So you're saying all this is the Indians' fault?"

"Why, no, where'd you get that notion? Hell, this is their country. They got a right to do how they want to in it. If we don't like it . . . we need to get out. I'm only telling you the truth of it. I've seen it all, riding or walking."

I gigged my horse forward to end the conversation, but Bridger stayed right beside me. "And punishing Indians, the way the army does, makes no more sense than kicking a dog for howling at the moon. The kicker gets a sore foot, the dog gets a sore ass, and the next time the moon's out, ain't a damned thing changed."

"So you're saying all Indians are liars and drunks and they can't be trusted."

Bridger considered it a second as a sly smile crawled across his face. "Yeah, that about sums it up. They're just like the rest of us."

◆✳ 30 ✳◆

"See?" said Jack, after I mentioned my talk with Bridger. "That's why I don't fool with the old fart. He *was* there and *has* seen it all. He's probably right about most of it. But who gives a blue damn?" He grinned and pushed his hat up. "I'm sight-seeing."

"Well, if the Popes catch up to us, you'll see a sight."

Jack chuckled. "We've got 'em by the short hair as long as we've got their money."

"It's the government's money," I heard Shod say in a weak voice.

"Well, look who's awake and preaching," I said, leaning forward and glancing at Shod. "You didn't care whose money it was when you tried to beat us out of it."

Jack unhooked his canteen and handed it to Shod. He took a long drink, poured a stream over his head, then winced as it ran down the cuts on his chest. "Thanks . . . both of you, for getting me out of there."

"Don't thank me. I wanted to stay and watch them gut you—"

"What's wrong with you anyway?" Jack folded his hands on his horse's neck and stared at Shod. "I never figured you for a double cross."

"I don't know." Shod shrugged his wide shoulders and sat slumped on the pony. "I must've lost my head, thinking about the money. You don't know what that money means to me . . ."

"You can save your sad song." I leaned forward again and stared at him. "Right now we've got the Pope Gang two hours behind us, and some pissed-off Shoshoni wondering who killed their cousins. But as soon as you're able to travel, you can go explain it all to them." I started to rein away.

"What about my pay?"

"Yeah, sure." I winked at Jack, and gigged my horse toward McDowell at the front of the column. "Leave an address; I'll be sure to mail it to you."

At the front of the column I reined up beside McDowell and Bridger. "Mister Bridger tells me we'll be heading into Red Cloud's camp by evening." McDowell spoke without taking his eyes off the banner. The wind had died down and now the flag hung down the pole in jagged stripes. "Perhaps you would like to ride in with Mister Bridger and announce our arrival."

"I reckon they already know we're close."

"Be that as it may. I think it would show well, since you obviously share some sort of commerce with the Indians."

I glanced at Bridger; he rolled his eyes. "Sure," I said, "I'm glad to help. By the way, what have you decided since we talked?"

"Oh, I agree with you completely. I think we have no interest here to substantiate our efforts. I can only recommend a complete and total withdrawal of our forces, and a well-intended reconciliation attempt between the Bureau of Indian Affairs, the secretary of the army, and, of course, the commander in chief." He cocked a rigid brow. "Satisfied?"

"Uh, yeah, I think so . . . if you just said you're going to get the hell out of here, then try to make peace."

"You're very astute." I saw a smug twitch of his dangerous goatee.

"If that's the case, why are you even going? Why not just get out, then send someone in after tempers have cooled?"

"I feel this is the appropriate time to make Chief Red Cloud aware of his options."

" 'His' options? You just said—"

"Indeed, and I mean it. We should withdraw. But in all fairness to the Sioux Nation, I feel we should offer some compensatory options to show good faith. We need to make recompense—"

"Colonel," I butted in, "can you say anything at all that I can understand? No offense, but I get a headache trying to listen to you."

"Of course . . . you would." He let out a patient breath. "We need to set up a system whereby this sort of situation doesn't happen again. We need to make it clear to both sides where the boundaries of Red Cloud's country begin and end. I'm afraid our people simply haven't understood."

"For one thing, you could have the government quit printing them stupid leaflets telling everybody to come up here . . . and not mentioning the fact that they're trespassing." I shook my head. "Poor dumb settlers. They hear how good it is. Nobody tells them they're going to get their heads opened by a tomahawk."

"There may have been a communication problem." He touched a gloved finger to his goatee. "I'm not sure. But I value your input and I'll certainly make note of it. During the meantime, I'm considering some guidelines that could help not only our westward expansion, but also help our red brothers' progress through this transition period."

I slapped my leg. "There's that damned word 'progress'—'gone crazy wanting more.' If that's what you're wanting to teach them, God help you if they ever learn it. If you think whiskey made them cockeyed, you don't want to see what greed does to them."

"Greed? Whiskey? Mister Beatty, what on earth are you babbling about?"

Before I could answer, one of the Pawnee came riding toward us at a brisk clip. Behind him, the Catahoula cur loped along carrying something in its mouth, then stopped and sat down in the middle of the trail as the Pawnee came to us, looking back over his shoulder.

McDowell raised a hand and the column snapped to a halt. Bridger and I jumped our horses forward and met the scout. "Clear Water Dog follow me, last five miles," said the scout. He seemed a little rattled; he glanced again over his shoulder.

"Don't worry," I said. "I know him. He just likes to hang around. He won't bother you."

"What's the problem up there?" said McDowell.

"Nothing, Colonel," Bridger called back to him. "We've got a Catahoula cur blocking the trail, is all."

"For goodness' sakes remove him, and let's continue on."

Jack came riding up. He reined in beside me and chuckled under his breath. "You heard him, Bridger. Kick that dog's ass out of the road so we can go on."

Bridger gave Jack a serious look. "Even ole Head-splitter

wouldn't stoop so low as to tell a man to kick a Catahoula."

Jack ducked his head with a sheepish grin. "Sorry, old-timer, I just lost my head for a second."

"What is the holdup?" McDowell stood up in his stirrups and gazed at us. Behind him, the officers and the rest of the column leaned sideways gazing toward us.

"Sorry, Colonel," I called back. "It's just a dog I know. I'll get him to move."

"See to it," the colonel replied.

I jumped my horse to the edge of the trail. "Come on, boy, over here." But the Catahoula just sat there, staring at the column in a low growl.

"What *is* the holdup?" McDowell's voice took on a sharp edge.

"Sorry, Colonel," I yelled. "But do you suppose we could go around him? He's pretty set in his ways. If we could just—"

"You have exactly one minute to get that dog out of the road, or I'll have him shot. We will not be held up by one stubborn wild animal. Do I make myself clear?" His voice sounded like the sizzling wick of a field cannon.

"Come on, boy," I said, jumping from my horse and into the road. "You're messing with the biggest, meanest, goddamnedest army in the world!" But he raised his hackles as I stepped toward him. I spun toward the column. A thick-backed sergeant had dismounted and stalked forward with a rifle raised. "Colonel! Don't let him fire that rifle or everybody that ain't in hell will be right here!" I let my hand drop to my pistol. I wasn't about to let him shoot the cur.

"Then I'll break his head open." The sergeant shoved me away as I tried to stop him.

"Don't!" I yelled, but it was too late. The sergeant drew back to smack the Catahoula with the rifle butt, and the dog shot straight up into his face like a streak of black lightning. "Help me, Jack!" I lunged into the rolling, snarling flurry of fur and uniform; but they rolled away. The Catahoula buried the soldier's face deep inside his powerful jaws and shook his head like tearing a melon from a vine. Blood flew.

"Stop that dog!" McDowell and his column flew from their saddles and ran toward us while the Catahoula slashed and snapped at the screaming sergeant. "Fire," shouted McDowell; but I grabbed the dog around his body and led him away with my gun drawn, cocked, and pointed. The soldier collapsed on his back, screaming to heaven, his face torn deep with both cheekbones shining. Beside me, Jack slid in with his pistol drawn. The soldiers froze.

"I'll drop you on my way down, Colonel! I swear to God!"

"Hold fire!" McDowell threw a hand in the air. "Get the medical kit!" he barked over his shoulder, and three soldiers ran back to the horses. "You'll answer for this," he yelled in a rage.

"Damn it, Colonel! I didn't bite him!" Jack and I kept our pistols pointed. I crouched over the Catahoula; he wagged his tail and licked his bloody tongue up my face. "I told you to go around! That's all we had to—"

"Everybody simmer," said Bridger in a low cautious voice. Him and the scouts stepped between us and the rifles as the three soldiers ran forward with a black medical bag. "Now, let's all keep our head and get this man attended to." Bridger pointed a finger at me. "Walk that cur away from here."

"Come on, boy." I led him away by the nap of his neck, crouched and still aiming my pistol. At the edge of the road, I nudged him into the sparse woods. He ran a few yards, turned, sat down wagging his tail and licking his bloody paw.

"Don't try to move him until you get him sewed up." McDowell turned from the soldiers bent over the sergeant. "And you!" He pointed at me as I walked forward. "I could have you shot!"

I dropped my pistol in my holster and saw Jack do the same. "For what, Colonel? I didn't tell the dog to bite him. I tried warning—"

"That's true, Colonel," Bridger butted in. "You can't blame this feller . . . riding or walking. Anybody with one eye and half sense knows not to fool with a brindle-Catahoula. They'll flat eat you up if you crowd 'em."

"That animal is wild and crazed, and deserves to die. He attacked that man for no reason!"

Bridger stepped over to where the Catahoula had been sitting in the road. "There's his reason." He bent, picked up a small bone, and pitched it near the colonel's shiny black boots. "We could've waited or gone around." He glanced at the sergeant's mangled face as a

soldier dabbed at it with a bloody gauze rag. "Now we'll do both
. . . with a man down . . . because a dog was scared we'd take his
supper." Bridger spit and ran his hand across his mouth. "I hope
you've learned something here, Colonel. If you don't, you never will
. . . riding or walking."

McDowell's face lost all color for a second, then surged back, fiery
red. His eyes glistened in rage. "Captain." His voice flickered between a whisper and a scream. "Leave these men here to tend to the
sergeant, and prepare the rest to move out."

Jack and I slipped quietly to our horses, mounted, and fell back
with Shod to the rear of the column. We rode wide around the blood
in the road and watched the sergeant's legs jerk in pain as a soldier
ran the needle through his torn cheek and tightened the thread. I
watched over my shoulder as the Catahoula slipped from the woods
to the road behind the soldiers. He snatched up the bone, shook off
the dust, and bounced away with his head in the air.

◆✳ 31 ✳◆

". . . Many moons have come and gone since I've seen my brother, Red Cloud." Bridger threw an arm in the air as Red Cloud took me by the shirtsleeve and pulled me to the side. He tossed a hand over his shoulder toward Bridger, who still sat on his horse and rambled on. "And my heart has been troubled," Bridger proclaimed, "for I have missed my friends, the Bad Faces . . ."

"Why you, bring him, here?" Red Cloud's hands made signs between us as he spoke in a low voice. "He was once a friend of the Sioux. Now he works for the army."

"I don't know nothing about his politics." I shrugged. "He said you and him were like brothers. He's here on a peace mission. They're about six miles back waiting to see if you'll talk. Did I do the wrong thing? They were coming anyway."

"I know, they come. We see them, for long time. See you with them. See Dog Who Points the Way, eat the soldier's face." He nodded toward Bridger. "But he, gets—" Red Cloud ran his hand down his face trying to find the word. His eyes asked me for help.

"Red? Sunburned?" The chief shook his head. "Embarrassed? Embarrassing!"

"Thank, you," said Red Cloud. "He tries, to act like, he knows everybody. He has been, doing it, for years. That is why, somebody has not cut off his head."

"I didn't know, Mister Cloud, or I wouldn't have rode in with him. If you like, I'll go back and tell them to leave."

"How've you fellers been?" I heard Bridger say to the braves gathered around him. "Ain't seen none of you in a coon's age . . ." His horse looked spooked, but he held it firm.

"As it is," Red Cloud tossed a hand. "I will meet, with them. We are out of coffee. Did they, bring coffee?"

"I'm sure. They never travel without it."

"Good." Red Cloud's eyes narrowed. "Where are my guns?"

"Well now." I cleared my throat. "We need to talk about that. See, we've had some problems with the Pope Gang—"

"And the Shoshoni." He pointed at my Indian pony.

"That's right." I nodded.

He pointed off to the string of horses grazing near the creek, the ones we'd stolen back from Fetterman. "And the bluecoats."

"Well . . . yeah, them too. You just wouldn't believe the trouble we've had."

"Is good, your enemies and mine, are the same."

"I didn't plan it, but that's how it is."

"But you gave your word. Crazy Horse and Band of Iron heard you say it. Now we want the guns."

"And I'll do the best I can—"

"You *will* get us guns." He turned away with his arms folded. "Now I will get ready, for talk. I will put on suit, and soft rope, that goes around my neck. I will wear the medal that shows the last time the Great White Chief broke his word." He spread a crafty grin. "Go and tell them, do not come, unless they bring coffee."

"What'd he say over there?" Bridger stood up in his stirrups and craned his neck as I walked toward him. "This bunch is so happy to see me, they won't let me get a word in edgewise."

"He said he'll talk, but only if they're furnishing the coffee."

"Did he say anything about me? Don't he want to say howdy?"

"Not exactly." I led my horse toward the string to trade it for one I could slip a saddle on.

Brown Horse fell in beside me with a friendly smile. "We did not know what to think when you and your friend left so quick."

"It's been crazy," I said. "Do you have a saddle I can borrow?"

"Borrow?" He looked confused.

"Can you give me a saddle?"

"Give?" He grinned.

"Okay." I ran my hands through my pocket and pulled out ten dollars and the string of beads Bridger gave me the night I met him.

Before I could say a word, Brown Horse snatched the beads and left the money in my hand. I shrugged. When it came to trading, who was I to set his values straight?

"I reckon Red Cloud was too busy to say howdy right then," said Bridger, trotting his horse along beside us. Brown Horse shot him a dark look and walked away to get his saddle. "We'll get a chance to talk about the good old days later." Bridger gazed around with a smile.

"Do you think it's wise, you coming here after being their friend and turning sides to the army?" Many angry eyes slid across Bridger as we made our way to the horses.

"Aw . . . they know it's just my way of keeping my hand in. I've been around long enough, riding or walking. They all know I'm apt to do most anything. Besides, you ain't the one to talk about being wise. You just traded a fine string of beads for a saddle you ain't even seen yet."

"What's the difference? How bad could it be for a string of beads?"

"Why you, walk with pain?" Red Cloud gazed at the dust up the side of me. Behind me, Bridger chuckled under his breath. I limped forward, leading my fresh horse.

"My saddle horn broke off."

"It made, you fall?"

"Naw." I ducked my head. "But when my stirrup broke, I grabbed the saddle horn . . ." Bridger snorted to keep from laughing.

"I see," said Red Cloud. He looked up and down my saddle. "Now both stirrups are broke."

"Yeah, I was kind of in a hurry." I reached up to the saddle to smooth down a strip of leather sticking up from the cantle. It came off in my hand.

"You gave, fine set of beads, to Brown Horse, for this saddle?"

"Like I said, Mister Cloud, I was hurrying."

"Better, slow down." I saw a trace of a firm smile in his solemn face.

" 'Scuse me, Chief," said Bridger, sliding down from his horse and almost jumping between us to get in his two cents. "I know you remember me. Bridger . . . Jim Bridger? Blanket Jim Bridger?"

"I do." Red Cloud folded his arms. "You brought in many blankets, to my people. Some of them, carried the great sickness."

I shot Bridger a glance. "So that's where you got the name Blanket."

"I never said I was no doctor." Bridger grinned. "I was in it for the money. If they were diseased, I wouldn't known it. Either way, they were damned pretty, weren't they?" He shot me a hard stare. "They call me Blanket because I live in the wild same as them, riding or walking."

Red Cloud turned from him to me. "Go, and bring in, the peace soldier. We will, drink coffee. We will talk of blankets, money, beads, and broken saddles. I will tell him why a dog protects its bone." I saw a gleam in his eyes. "If he preaches, I will not pray. If he gives me something, I will not take it." His face widened in a smile. "I will, say 'No.'" He leaned close to my ear. "Fugem-fugem-all," he whispered.

On the way back to McDowell's camp, we swung wide off the trail and circled atop a high ledge overlooking Tongue Valley. "I thought we best sidetrack," said Bridger, "and keep an eye on the riders we saw the other day. I don't reckon they'd chance riding this close to Red Cloud's village. But it would sure look bad on me if we got snuck up on."

I watched him scan the valley like a creature of prey. I couldn't believe how different he acted out in the wilds. Here he was master of his surroundings. Anywhere else, he struck me as a simple-minded old fool. I'd grown up on stories of people like Blanket Jim Bridger and Medicine Calf Beckwourth. It was hard for me to let go of the legend and see him as an old man who'd just about played out his string.

"Don't believe that story about the diseased blankets," he said, after we'd seen no sign of the riders and headed back to meet McDowell. "For I wouldn't do such a thing, riding or walking."

"I hope not," I said, riding along beside him with my legs dangling and a piece of stiff leather gigging me in the rump. "I can't think of anybody lower than a man who'd spread smallpox on a whole race of people, especially if he was supposed to be their friend."

"Yeah, but you got to admit, it would be a pretty smart trick." I watched his face as he stared straight ahead.

"I think it's cowardly, and evil."

"Back there it might be." His hand swept toward some distant place past the eastern horizon. "Up here, anything goes, riding or walking. This land belongs to the strongest and boldest. The 'meek' inherit it, but they get it right in their face, shovelful at a time." He threw back his head and cackled. I gigged my horse forward and bounced along in my rotted saddle until I met the Pawnee scouts a mile from camp.

Riding in ahead of Bridger, I stopped in a clearing off the trail where McDowell sat on a canvas folding stool reading the Bible. The rest of the troops milled around near the edge of the clearing while farther away, Jack sat dabbing a wet rag on Shod's back. Jack dropped the rag on Shod's shoulder and walked over as I stopped in front of McDowell. "How's the sergeant?"

"He'll be fine. It takes more than a few scratches to get a good soldier down."

"A few scratches? Jesus! The dog nearly ate him for supper—"

"I didn't expect you back so soon," McDowell cut in, with an I've-Just-Been-Reading-the-Bible smile.

"I don't think it was a wise idea to bring along Bridger, Colonel. Most of the Sioux ain't real happy about him working for the army."

McDowell shook his head and smiled wider. "You're forever the pessimist, aren't you?"

Jack walked up and stopped beside me as I spoke. "Red Cloud seems to think Bridger brought in a load of diseased blankets, years back."

"I heard that story too." McDowell waved a hand. "And David Crockett killed a bear when he was only three years old." He laughed and slapped his knee. "But come now. Do you suppose Bridger would be stupid enough to carry around a load of contaminated blankets? What would have kept him and his men from getting sick?"

I felt embarrassed. "He got'cha there," Jack chuckled. "You oughta know better than to open your mouth around the U.S. Army."

McDowell turned to Jack with a look of disdain. "Oh, am I to understand you have a grievance against the United States Army?"

"None you'd care to listen to." Jack hooked his thumb in his belt and started to turn away, but McDowell stood and turned right with him, his Bible open and hugged against his chest.

"Come now, don't be one of those who express some vague and general indictment, then refuses to elaborate with any specificity."

Jack chuckled. "If words were worth a nickel a ton, you'd be a millionaire."

"I see." McDowell bowed his head a second and flapped the opened Bible back and forth against his perfect tunic. "Because I don't say 'howdy partner' and spit and scratch my derriere when I speak, I, by some virtue of commonality known only by the two of you, can't possibly know what I'm doing."

Jack looked at me with a raised brow. "Do you understand any of that?"

I shrugged. "Just the 'howdy partner' part." I glanced around. "Shouldn't Bridger be getting here?"

"It may interest you both to know, there are some of us in the military who are deeply sympathetic to Red Cloud and his people."

Jack chuckled. "If you see Red Cloud chewing a bone in the middle of the road, I hope you've got enough sense to go around him."

McDowell's brows snapped tight, but he ignored Jack and cleared his throat. "As I told you, I will be recommending a complete withdrawal of our forces, and I'm sure President Johnson will be in complete agreement—"

"Hunh," said Jack. "Last I heard, that rotten bastard's 'bout to get his thieving ass thrown out in the street."

"How dare you!" McDowell exploded. "You loathsome, despicable . . ." He stepped forward, his hands slapping the open Bible against his chest like a hawk flapping its wings.

"Easy, Jack." I stepped between them.

Jack leaned around me with a crazy grin. "One more word,

soldier-boy, and I'll put a bullet twixt your Psalms and Proverbs."

"Hooo!" Bridger came sliding to a halt in a spray of dust and rocks. One of the Pawnee scouts slid in right behind him. "Big trouble coming, Colonel." Bridger sounded winded. Behind him, the troops already started reaching for their hats and rifles. "I spotted Standing Bear and over a hundred warriors rounding a turn in the valley."

"But we're under a peace symbol! Red Cloud knows we're coming."

"Standing Bear don't know it. We better light out'n here." Bridger glanced across Jack and me.

"He's right, Colonel. From what I've heard, Standing Bear is real ambitious about running the show."

Jack turned and ran to help Shod on his horse. Around us the soldiers watched anxiously, ready for the command to mount up.

"I had planned on arriving with a certain amount of military decorum, but I suppose we'll have to improvise as we go."

"Colonel," Bridger barked. "If we don't get going, we'll arrive on the end of a stick."

◆✳ 32 ✳◆

Our horses were winded and lathered as we rode into Red Cloud's camp. Dust covered the flag. McDowell and his officers tried to maintain their staunch military bearing, but sweat and dirt ran down their faces, giving them the look of sad clowns. Behind the officers, the troopers still glanced back over their shoulders. We'd spotted Standing Bear's braves along the ridgeline three different times on our way in. Now it occurred to me as we reined up our tired horses that they were there strictly to frighten us. It was Red Cloud's way of setting the stage for this little get-together. We came in on his terms. His camp became our refuge.

"Note the horses and arms," McDowell said quietly to the officer beside him. "This isn't the ill-equipped band of drifters depicted by last winter's reports from Laramie."

Since Bridger and I left, the herd of horses had been gathered closer and many were picketed throughout the camp. Battle shields hung from their blankets and saddles, and rifles lay across their backs, tied by strips of rawhide. Steam curled from many cooking pots, and the smell of boiling meat filled the air. Red Cloud knew how to decorate the stage.

As Brown Horse and Band of Iron greeted us, several young braves took our horses and began watering them from gourd dippers. Behind us, the troopers dismounted and stood beside their horses. "Welcome," said Band of Iron, using his hands in sign language as he spoke. "We will talk as food is prepared."

Two older women appeared from within a gathering crowd and stepped forward with three spotted puppies in their arms. One of them held out a puppy toward McDowell. He patted its head. "Yes, lovely little fellow."

"Pinch its ribs," said Bridger, near McDowell's ear.

McDowell cocked an eye and looked puzzled. "Is that some gesture of—"

"It's our supper." Bridger smiled. He shot me a guarded smile as McDowell's face turned pasty green. "She's asking your approval."

"Actually, I hadn't planned on staying for dinner. I don't wish to impose."

"It's a little greasy," Bridger teased, "but it's so tender, it'll melt in your mouth. Throw in a little sassafras and wild onion." Bridger smacked his lips. My stomach tried to hide behind my ribs. I would've given a large part of the money to stay and watch McDowell force his way through dinner, but as he and his officers gathered near Red Cloud's tent, Brown Horse stepped in beside me.

"My warriors and I will travel with you for a ways. Standing Bear will not harm you."

"Thanks." I nodded toward Jack and Shod near the rear of the column. "Will you see to it the big feller gets tended to? He can head out on his own when he's healed up some."

"Wait," said Band of Iron, stepping forward past McDowell and the officers. "You cannot leave until Red Cloud speaks to you."

McDowell and the officers turned toward me with a curious look. I smiled. "Pardon me, gents, while I visit my friend Mister Cloud."

McDowell shot me a cautious glance as I stepped toward Red Cloud's tepee. "I hope you realize the importance of this peace mission." He reached out a hand to my sleeve; I jerked away.

"Cloud and I don't talk war and peace. We talk religion and politics. Something you fellers couldn't do, without winding up in a fight."

Just as I stood up inside the tepee, Red Cloud stepped from the shadow beside the flap. He wore a firm smile. "I stand here and listen," he said in a low voice. "It is good, what you said. Now soldiers know, I have white friend. And it is good that I am repaying you for saving my life."

"Being my friend ain't exactly a plus, Mister Cloud." I eased down on an elk skin as Red Cloud circled the low flames and perched atop his pile of hides. It seemed higher than I'd ever seen it.

"I will say." His smile widened.

A feathered lance stuck up beside him and he wrapped his hand around it as he settled down on the hides. He struck back his chin as if posing for a picture. "Do I look powerful, like the white chief, beside the big river in the bucket of mud?"

I grinned. "You'll scare the hell out of this bunch, if that's what you're asking."

"Then maybe, they will listen." Red Cloud took a firm grip on the lance. He wore brand-new buckskin trousers, trimmed in red and black stitching, and a fancy white shirt with a pleated front beneath his breastplate of beads, silver bangles, and tiny feathers. His black hair glistened of grease, pulled straight back and dangling past his shoulders, nearly to his waist. A black formal coat lay smoothed out beside him. On top of it lay a shiny beaver-skin top hat. Next to it lay a sparkling war ax; next to it, an ornate pipe and pouch of tobacco. He looked like an ancient warlord sitting on his cache of treasure.

"Don't count on it, Mister Cloud. I believe McDowell is an honest man, but he only goes as far as his title can take him. Once it goes past him, his words won't mean spit. Remember what we talked about that night on the ridge. Whatever they're selling, it ain't worth buying."

Red Cloud nodded and gazed off past me. "I had a dream. In the dream, I saw you, bring me, many rifles. Your heart was troubled because many would die, in the Moon of the Cold. You left holding money in your hand that was covered with the blood."

"Whoa, Mister Cloud. Not to interrupt you, but as soon as I get your rifles from Dirty Jaw, Jack and I are Missouri-bound."

Red Cloud smiled patiently. "Then I have said enough. Sometimes, dreams are visions, sometimes only dreams."

"I reckon I won't be seeing you again, Mister Cloud. So I want to tell you, you've been a friend. I hope you and your people fare well in keeping your country. If there was any other way I could help—"

"Tell your people. Tell them of the Sioux Nation, what it is, and what it will always be. Tell them we are horses without bridles, bears without traps. Tell them we will not stand in a line or sit in a corner. Tell them, we will never live in the bucket of mud, but will die on the high plains, with our women in our arms and our babies on our backs." His eyes glistened in the low flames.

"I will," I said in a quiet voice. I watched as he stood up and put on the black coat and high top hat. He picked up a polished cane and swung it back under his arm. "I have spoke many times to the night, to learn how to speak to the white chiefs." He circled the fire as I stood up and offered my hand. "How am I doing?"

"Tell them like you just told me, Mister Cloud. Surely to God someone will hear you. If they don't, it's their loss."

"Watch out for the hair on your head as you travel my country." He smiled, taking my hand.

"Watch out for the shirt on your back when you deal with the soldiers."

◆＊ 33 ＊◆

"Do you s'pose McDowell will get Cloud to come to Laramie?" We sat watching Brown Horse and his warriors disappear into the scattered woodlands. Ten feet away, the Catahoula cur sat licking his belly and snapping at flies. The bald-faced gelding had followed us from Red Cloud's farm, feeding in short circles as we crossed the Bozeman Trail.

"I don't know, Jack. Red Cloud is a hard man to figure. But I feel like McDowell's heart is in the right place. If it ain't, I reckon Cloud will see it."

Jack turned, shaking his head. "You still don't get the picture up here, do you? McDowell probably has the best intentions in the world. All that does is make him more dangerous than the rest of these government snakes."

"Jack, you've gotta trust somebody. Somebody has to be able to take matters in hand and straighten out this mess."

"It ain't a matter of trust." He spit a stream. "It's a matter of things being gone too far. There ain't nothing going to settle it here but an all-out slaughter. Anything else anybody tries is just going to make it worse. It's like a runaway wagon with the brakes burnt out. Alls you can do is jump off or ride it 'til it crashes."

"Nothing like a cheerful attitude," I said as I turned my horse off the trail.

"I'm just saying what I know. McDowell wants to come in and make peace, but all he'll do is make things worse. The government wants out of this mess, but they ain't about to admit they've made a mistake."

"Either way, we're out of it. As soon as Dirty Jaw gets them rifles out of Laramie, I'll turn 'em over to Brown Horse outside of Crofton and we'll leave."

Jack chuckled, "I don't see why they couldn't do it themselves."

"I don't know, but as soon as it's over, we're leaving here with enough cash to stuff a mattress." I winked. "Riding or walking."

When we got to the clearing, I stayed back inside the scattered pines and covered Jack with my rifle. Only when he returned with the saddlebags did I stop scanning the trees and ridgeline and let out a breath. "I love it." He smiled as he opened the bags and let bundles of dollars spill out on the ground.

I took my blanket roll from behind my saddle and spun it out on the ground. We stacked the money neatly across the middle. I started to roll it up, when Jack snatched up three or four bundles and dropped them back in the saddlebags. I glanced up at him. He winked. "In case we get waylaid by Pope. It'll look better if he finds some of it."

"Good thinking," I said, hurrying with the bedroll. "We'll say we lost the rest crossing the Powder."

We mounted up and started out across the clearing, to stay away from the trail as long as we could. Halfway across, a shaky voice boomed out from the far edge of the clearing. "One more step and we'll blow your brains out!"

I glanced at Jack as we froze. He shrugged. "Reckon they got here late?" His hand drifted near his holster.

We heard a thrashing in the brush. "Get your hands up!" The voice sounded familiar, weak and trembling. "It's ours and we'll kill you for it."

"Jesus Christ." I let out a breath as Kid Cull and Run-around Joe came wallowing out of the brush. Jack's hand raised slightly from his holster. "Easy," I called to them. "We ain't looking for no trouble." Cull's hands shook as he pointed the shotgun. I hoped it wouldn't go off accidentally. "Don't you remember us?"

Run-around leaned forward and nearly fell. "Injuns . . . ?"

"No," I said. "We met on the trail a while back. Ya'll were drunk and gave us a couple canteens of 'wonderful stuff.' "

Cull stepped forward with the shotgun raised. "Now you figure on stealing the rest of it. Ain't that right?"

"Ar-my?" Joe belched out his words.

"Damn, Cull." I leaned forward. "We ain't after your whiskey. We've been looking for a friend of ours, got lost near here." I glanced at Jack.

"That's right," Jack backed me up. "Hell, if we wanted a drink, we know we'd be welcome. We wouldn't have to steal it."

"Circus?" Joe stared at the bald-faced gelding and the Catahoula cur as they roamed about the edge of the clearing. The Catahoula was muscling . . . looking slicker every day.

Cull let down the shotgun and shook his head. I glanced at Jack; he shook his head. "If we don't, they'll die out here."

"What's that?" Cull snapped the gun back to his shoulder. I raised a hand.

"I said, why don't you fellers throw in with us to Kearny? Tell you the truth, we're a little worried about Indians. We could use some help."

"Ain't you gonna sho-ot 'em?" said Run-around.

"Hell, I don't know," said Cull. He lowered his shotgun, snatched off his hat, and wiped it across his face. His hands trembled. Sweat covered his chest and shoulders. His knees shook so bad, we could hear his trousers flapping. "It's so damn confusing out here. This liquor's got me crazy as a June bug." He glanced back up as he propped the shotgun against his side. "Ya'll was running cattle up to Montany, weren't ya?"

"No." I grinned. "That was you two, remember? We was taking horses up to Kearny. Ya'll passed out on us."

"Now I remember," said Run-around. He stepped forward and wobbled against Cull. "They's the ones what killed that Indian."

"Yeah," said Cull, "and nearly got us scalped."

I shrugged. "We offered to take you with us. You wouldn't go."

Cull spread a one-tooth grin as I eased from my saddle and led my horse toward him. "It worked out. We gave 'em a jug and got 'em drunk. When they left here, they couldn't tell shit from shoe polish."

I handed him a canteen of water from my saddle, and he took it with a shaky hand. Water sloshed out of it as he raised it to his mouth, then passed it to Run-around. He let out a trembling breath.

"Turns out, they left us a scout to help us stay out of trouble. If you've lost your friend, he might could find him for you once he sobers up." He nodded toward the woods. "He's back there passed out, keeping an eye on our horses. Shoshoni is a purty good bunch, even if they do work for the army."

Jack slipped from his saddle and the four of us walked a quarter mile from the clearing to a clay overhang. Beneath it lay three broken jugs and a passed-out Indian who looked to be a hundred years old. Flies swarmed around him and a white streak of droppings ran down his shoulder where a bird had perched. It must've flew away as we came out of the brush. "He's dead," said Jack.

"Naw, he just smells like it. He's been down drunk for the past week. Once he's up and around, there ain't a better scout to be found—they call him One Drum Beat. Hell, he found a poor sumbitch been laying for a week with his ear gone and two fingers missing."

I shot Jack a glance. "Flowers?"

"Why not?" said Jack. "Nothing's simple up here. We start out to take care of business and wind up saddled with a bald horse, a crazy dog, two drunks, and a dead Indian."

That evening we sat around the low fire sipping coffee, waiting for the cover of darkness before heading out. Our intention was to swing wide of Fort Kearny and meet Dirty Jaw at Crofton. I figured if we could keep Cull and Joe away from the whiskey, it wouldn't hurt to have a couple extra guns in case we ran into trouble, and it would be better for them if we could get them out of Indian country. As far as what to do with One Drum Beat, I had no idea.

"What about this feller with a missing ear?" I said as we finished our coffee. "Where'd you find him?"

Cull wiped sweat and sipped at his coffee. Him and Run-around both kept licking their lips and glancing toward the jugs they'd tied to their horses. "Found him two weeks back, crawling up the side of a cliff. Beat found him, drug him back to us. We patched him up and poured him full of liquor. He left a few days ago, said he was retiring and heading south. Poor sum-bitch."

"That's good," I said, glancing at Jack. "I think we're going to retire ourselves when we get out of here." I stood and dusted my trousers.

We climbed to the top of the overhang as the sun cast long shadows across the darkening valley. Lying flat and scanning the distant line of scrub timber, we soon made out seven riders tracking the route we'd taken to the money. "Pope?" Jack rolled over on his back and gazed up.

"I don't think so." I squinted and studied the lead rider. "He looks familiar." I stared closer and saw the man turn his face up toward the cliffs beneath us. I let out a breath as recognition set in. "Jesus, Jack, it's Long Jake and his posse."

"Good. I was afraid we'd run out of something to do." Jack took out his pistol and checked the action.

Kid Cull crawled up the side of the cliff carrying a jug and stood straight up. "What're ya'll looking at?" Before I could warn him, a chunk of rock exploded at the edge of the cliff, near his feet. His face turned blue. "Hell's that?"

"Get down, you idiot!" I reached up for him; but he'd already dropped beside me as we heard the shot.

"Scopes," said Jack. "Next shot'll knock your head off. I admire a feller who goes with the latest in shooting gear."

"That's dangerous." I peeped above the edge and dropped back down as a rock exploded. "They don't know it's us. They could kill some innocent person."

"Up here?" Jack shook his head. "Not likely."

"What's going on?" Cull's voice trembled; he hugged the jug to his chest. "Are they Injuns?"

We turned and crawled toward the back of the cliff. "No," I said, "but there will be, quicker than you can blow a bubble in a bathtub. You might as well know the truth. There's a lotta folks pissed off at us up here."

"Why? Have ya'll broke the law?"

Jack chuckled as we inched down the overhang. "Not so's you could tell it from a long ways off. But if you wanta stay alive, you better crack that jug and get a clear head. If they fix them scopes on ya, you'll be heading for the last roundup."

"I'm just getting drunk here. I don't wanta die. Hell, I gotta wife and youngin!"

I saw that the shot had sobered him a little. As we slid the last few feet into camp, I stopped and grabbed him by the collar. "Listen, cowboy. Whether you like it or not, you're in this up to your eyeballs. Unless you think you can explain yourself through a rifle scope, you better work with us here, 'til we get to safety."

"But I ain't done nothing!" He pointed at Run-around and the Indian; they lay passed out. "None of us have!"

"Then you stay and tell 'em." I snatched the reins to my horse and swung up in the saddle.

"Wait!" Cull dropped the jug and started staggering in a confused circle. "We're going . . . we're going!" He grabbed Joe by the arm and tried pulling him to his feet. "Damn it, Run-around, get up."

Jack helped him drag the fat cowboy up and pour him into his saddle. I slid from my horse and did the same with One Drum Beat.

"You're gonna have to listen to me," I said to Cull. "I know you're still drunker than a hoot owl, but you'll have to pay attention and help us out."

Cull swallowed hard, glanced toward the jug of whiskey, and licked his trembling lips. "I'll try."

As we winded our way to the trail, I heard a voice from atop the cliff. "Crowe," yelled Parker Pope. "I'm taking back my money. Make it easy on yourself."

"Who's that?" Cull glanced back over his shoulder. Sweat poured down his forehead.

"That's just another sore loser," Jack chuckled.

"Eighty-twenty," yelled Pope, "that's my only offer." A shot echoed out across the valley as we hit the trail. We heard a scream from one of Pope's men.

"They've got scopes," yelled a voice from the cliffs behind us.

"Who does?" Pope's voice sounded rattled.

"I don't know, goddamn it! But I'm shot. Look at me!"

We'd pounded along the trail nearly a mile when the Catahoula came running back toward us from around a bend. An arrow whis-tled past him as he made the turn. Indians whooped as they chased him to us. Knowing Pope's gang wasn't far behind, instead of turning around, we veered off the trail and down into a dry creek bed, leaving Pope to run smack into a war party of Shoshoni, with Long Jake's riders coming up in the rear.

"Are all them people looking for you?" Cull's voice shook in rhythm to his trembling hands. The front of his shirt was wet with sweat. Run-around and One Drum Beat sat slumped in the saddle as we quietly followed the creek bed.

"Yeah, more or less." I glanced back over my shoulder toward the sound of rifles and the screams of dying men. "But notice they're not right now. As long as we can stay ahead of everybody, we'll be alright."

"Ya'll are outlaws, ain't 'cha?" Cull raised his hand as I stared at him. "Not that it's none of my business. I'm just trying to figure what I've gotten myself into."

"We'll talk about it when you're a little more sober." I gigged my horse and headed on up the streambed as darkness closed around us like a velvet glove.

"If I'm fixin' to die, I don't know as I really oughta be sober."

"That's up to you," I said, letting my horse have the lead along the loose footing as I gazed up at the moon through the ghostly arms of towering aspens and ancient pines. "But if you sober up and get a grip, maybe you'd have more say-so about staying alive." I smiled to myself and watched him bow his head. "Nobody likes a quitter," I said. "Especially us."

◆❋ 34 ❋◆

Early the next morning, we lay in the cover of scattered pines and watched the cavalry patrol cut across the trail toward the cliffs where the shooting had started the day before. I recognized Captain Fetterman at the head of the column, craning his neck as he held a hand on his sword handle. Beside him, Carrington rode along making notes in a small journal. Cull let out a breath. "I reckon we're saved now?"

"Not quite," Jack chuckled. "They're a little angry too. They have us confused with some fellers who stole all their horses."

"Lord, Lord." Cull shook his head. "Do ya'll live like this all the time?"

I grinned. "Naw, you just caught us on vacation."

When the cavalry disappeared over the edge of a rise, I slipped back to the horses and took out some dried shank and hard biscuits. Passing the food among the three of us—Joe and the old Indian lay propped against a tree with their heads leaned together—I worked up a low flame and fixed a quick pot of coffee.

"How can you think of food at a time like this?" Cull sipped the strong brew with steam curling up his face.

I winked at Jack. "We've gotta get your strength up. I expect we'll be hit hard today."

Cull snapped his eyes all around the land. "Who by? Injuns? Army? Who?"

"Hard to say. Could be all three." I leaned close. "Want a shot of 'wonderful stuff,' just to smooth out a little?"

"I never want to see that stuff again as long as I live. All it's done is got me in trouble; now I'm lucky if I don't die up here in this godforsaken place." He hung his head and stared at his boots.

By the time we swung around the two forks of Piney Creek to avoid the soldiers at Fort Kearny, Kid Cull's hands had settled down considerably. He became serious at listening and trying to understand. As he sobered, it seemed he became more interested in staying alive, or maybe just more afraid of dying. I rode up on him the evening before we started into Crofton, and saw him wiping dirt off a small pocket picture. "Sally and the boy," he said in a voice liquor-free but still not too strong. "You got a family, mister?" He still couldn't remember my name. I think he felt it was something he didn't want to remember in case he was later asked.

"No," I said, studying the land around us. "But don't worry, we ain't aiming to kill you. We're just planning on staying alive. Unless somebody gets in our way on the way out, we're leaving the Sioux Nation with everything we came in with."

"What're you paying?" He tried to look me in the eye, but the whiskey still had a hold on him.

"What am I paying?" I shook my head. "Your life if you do like you're told, your death if you don't. This ain't some wage-paying situation. You threw away your whole summer's pay on getting drunk. Don't try to make it up on us. You better ask yourself if you wanta die out here, or go back and face the woman and baby and be a man. Now, you wanta ask me again what we're paying?"

"Alright." He let out a breath. "Joe ain't gonna be much help, though; don't even expect it."

"That's okay. He's part of the deal. If we're all together, we stay together 'til we're out of the fire. We won't leave him behind, but you better try to sober him up if you can."

"What about One Drum Beat? He can't do nothing, but he don't deserve to die."

"Then keep him tied to his horse. The shape he's in, if he flies off, we'll have to figure the fall killed him."

He shook his head as I rode away quietly. I reined up beside Jack and gazed out across the western line. The sky was five layers of blue, streaked in gold. "He's sweating out a bad one, ain't he?" said Jack.

"Worst I've seen in a while. He's thinking everybody is out to kill him, and he deserves it because of his wife and baby, that he now thinks he'll never see again." I shook my head. "Then had the guts to ask what we're paying."

"Paying for what?" Jack turned and spit a stream.

"I don't know. He thinks we're riding into some kind of massacre or something."

"Did you tell him otherwise?"

"No, I just went along with him. That's all you can do. You can't talk sense to a hangover. Let him think it awhile; it might do him some good. Maybe it'll light a fire under his ass that'll send him back to Texas, back to Sally and little Thurmond, or whatever his kid's name is."

Jack cocked his head. "You ain't done nothing I don't know about, have you?"

"No, not that I can think of. The same people who would've killed us yesterday is the same ones who'd kill us today."

"Then it must just be his hangover. I've had 'em that bad."

"I hope so," I said. "I don't want him to be right, but if he thinks it awhile, it's one more gun looking out for us."

"We should've brought Shod." Jack spit another stream.

"That double crosser?"

"He told you why he did it. That's the same as apologizing."

"Apologize? He oughta be thanking God right now that we didn't kill him, and we should've. Or left him hanging from that tree."

"Look at it another way. We hired the poor bastard for a half dollar a day, him knowing we's stealing horses with both hands. Carrying a roll of money and a forged document that's so good, it fooled an army major. Drug him through Indian fights, gunfights, dogfights, got him shot and half-skinned . . ." Jack made an edge of his hand to divide the air. "Then . . . left him in the middle of an Indian battle camp, with that idiot Kermit, with a war going on and winter headed this way." Jack looked down and shook his head. "And . . . you wouldn't even *pay* him."

"He had nothing coming after what he did. There's such a thing as loyalty."

"Yeah." Jack spit out his wad of tobacco. "And you'd think his kind would know that after the past hundred years or so."

I stared at Jack a few seconds. "We've got enough money to buy Texas and have it painted. All I know is, he was 'bout to take it and cut out. If I've wronged the man, I don't see how. We made him a partner—"

"No we didn't. Not really. We just drew a smaller circle around ourselves and offered him more money—which he never got."

"The horse deal didn't work out, but I took him right in when I nailed the payroll money."

Jack shrugged. "Maybe he didn't figure we could handle it. Other things have gone to hell; maybe he feared this would."

"Well . . . if it'll help you, I promise to think about it some morning while I've got my boots propped up on a featherbed, waiting for the gaming room to open. I'll sort it all out and feel bad as hell, okay?"

Jack chuckled under his breath as I gigged my horse and rode away. "Hillbillies . . ."

Past midnight, we rode quietly the last two miles toward Crofton. I was surprised to see a faint glow of light when we stopped before riding in. By now I figured every rat had abandoned ship. Cull and Run-around reined up beside us, leading the old Indian's horse. One Drum Beat wobbled and made sounds like a death rattle. Behind him, I heard the bald-faced gelding; to our right, the Catahoula cur poked his nose in the air, sniffing toward Crofton.

"What kind of hell are we fixin' to ride into?" Cull asked in a low voice. Beside him, Run-around Joe sat silent as stone.

I glanced at Jack, took out my pistol, and clicked the action a few times. "There could be a thousand," I said, straight-faced.

"A thousand what?" Joe whispered.

Cull snapped his head toward him. "Indians, goddamn it! Now, keep your mouth shut and pay attention. We're in some awful serious shit here. I'm counting on ya."

Jack shook his head as we rode on. "Yeah," I said low, "I've heard that when they lift a man's scalp, it makes a sucking sound, like peeling a wet blanket from a mud floor."

"Lord God," Cull breathed.

We began hearing a steady clicking rhythm as we drew closer to the mud street of Crofton. It came from the glow of light, steady but broken, like a rattlesnake with hiccups. As we walked our horses onto the street, we heard a woman's laughter and the strum of a banjo, but above it, the constant clicking.

"That sounds like Queenie," said Jack. We glanced around in the darkness at the bare spots where shacks had stood. Most of the town had been torn apart and hauled away. All that remained was the saloon, three empty buildings, and the ragged tent. Two men stepped from the shadows beside the saloon as we rode toward the light spilling through the broken doors. They cradled rifles in their arms.

"Who're you people?" said a voice from beneath a wide-brimmed hat. They looked us over as the bald-faced gelding walked toward them. The Catahoula cur had disappeared.

"We're just back from Powder," I said, coming to a halt at ten feet. "We ran a string up to Fort Kearny."

"The hell's this?" I heard Joe whisper behind me.

"Shut up, pay attention," Cull whispered back. I heard Jack chuckle under his breath.

"Then I won't ask how's your trip," said the voice. The rifles drifted down. "Is he dead?" Both men stared at One Drum Beat.

"No, he's been drunk on trade whiskey. So's these two." I nodded toward Cull and Run-around as I reined up to the hitch rail. "So don't make any sudden move around them. They're still a little skittish."

"Lucky they're alive," said one of the men. "I've seen that stuff peel paint off a wagon." One of the men slipped back into the shadows as we followed the other into the saloon. We left One Drum Beat tied to his horse.

Through the gold-gray swirl of tobacco smoke and lamplight, I saw a banjo player tuning up, and next to him sat a toothless old man playing the spoons. At the center of the crowed bar stood a tall well-dressed man sipping a mug of beer. "Boss," said the rifleman, "this bunch just rode in from Kearny. Thought you'd want to meet 'em."

"Thank you, Bobby-Ray." The well-dressed man leaned toward us with a smile. "I hope you boys enjoy good music. We're getting ready to hear some."

"Music?" Cull spoke in a shaky voice. "Who can listen to music at a time—"

"I'm partial to good spoon and banjo," said Jack, "if it's done well."

The man tipped up his hat and smiled again. "Then you won't be disappointed." He looked Cull up and down, then nodded to me. "I'm Tillman, Frank Tillman, representing Rails West Security."

"Railroad?" I looked all around the crowded saloon. Rifles and bandoliers leaned everywhere. Queenie and her girls were slinging beer and shaking their wares in every direction.

"Yes, is that a problem, Mister . . . ?"

I snapped my eyes back to him. "Beatty . . . Jim Beatty. No, sir, no problem at all. I admire railroads . . . ride 'em every chance. I just can't get over so many people being here. I figured this place to be gone down the road."

"Progress, Mister Beatty." He beamed and hooked his thumb in his vest. "A few disenchanted Indians can't stop the will of the people."

"I reckon not." I saw one of the whores prop her foot on a feller's lap and rub her knee in his whiskers. "This here is Cull, Joe, and Smith. Like your man said, we're just passing through, back from Kearny."

"Quite a mess Carrington's made up there, isn't it?"

"He's got his hands full."

"Poor bastard. I heard he's starting another fort this week. And he hasn't even finished Kearny yet. They say you have to sleep with your horse to keep it from being stolen."

"I wouldn't know." I shook my head. "Do you mind me asking what you're doing up here? It's a hell of a ways from any rail work."

"Oh, just looking around. You know railroads. We like to keep an eye on the future."

"Got no liquor 'cept rye whiskey," shouted the bartender above the din of the crowd. "What'll ya have?"

"That'll do." I nodded.

"What'll do?"

"Rye'll do."

"What'll do?"

"Goddamn it!" Cull tried to grab the bartender. "Rye whiskey! Can't you hear? You stupid son of a bitch!"

"Easy, Kid." I grabbed Cull and pulled him away. Run-around threw an arm around his neck. Cull shook like a man with a terrible fever. Sweat poured down his face.

"What's wrong with you damn people?" He struggled against Joe's arm. "Don't you know we're all gonna die?" The saloon fell silent except for the rattling rhythm of the spoons.

"See here!" Tillman stepped back and laid his hand on his pistol.

"Don't mind him," I said. "He's been drunk on trade whiskey. He's got one of them 'gone crazy' hangovers." Some of Tillman's men had started to stand with their hands on their pistols. He waved them back down.

"I see." Tillman leaned close to me. "Thinks everybody is out to kill him?"

"That's the kind," I said. I saw Queenie come up to Jack, raise his hat, and ruffle his hair.

"Maybe he should go sleep it off." Tillman nodded toward the door. "I wouldn't want one of these men taking offense and blowing his head off."

"You're probably right." I threw back a shot of rye as soon as the bartender poured it. Hooking the bottle and glass, I turned to Run-around and nodded toward the door. "I reckon there's no one cares if we bed down in the livery barn?"

"Make yourself comfortable wherever you like. With the army gone, we're glad to have some extra guns around."

I'd turned to follow Joe and Cull when Tillman called out, "By the way, did you pass anyone on the trail?"

I shrugged. "No, but then we didn't stay on the trail much. We skirted in from the woods and ledges. Why? Are you expecting somebody?" I glanced once more quickly about the saloon. It struck me that this bunch was outfitted like a hanging posse.

Tillman smiled, but I noticed something guarded behind his narrowed eyes. "It always pays to know who's coming and going in this country."

Part VI
Indian Givers

◆❋ 35 ❋◆

The next morning, I awoke in the livery barn and saw Kid Cull staring out the window with his shotgun in his arms. He looked like a man with the world hung on his shoulders. He glanced at me as I stood up from a pile of hay, then back out the window as I walked over to him. "How much help will that bunch be?" He nodded in the direction of the saloon. "They won't be much, not after drinking all night." His voice was shaky with a bitter edge. I saw him slip the picture in his shirt pocket.

Behind us, Run-around Joe snored loud enough to loosen shingles. The old Indian lay sprawled out flat on his back with a thin cobweb stretched from his hand to his nose. Jack's blanket hadn't been slept on. I figured he'd gone off to Queenie late in the night. Outside the window, the bald-faced gelding walked around in a short circle. "And that horse is getting on my nerves something fierce," said Cull. "He's been walking in circles all night."

"Ain't you slept any?" I looked at his red-rimmed eyes.

"Some, maybe." He ran his shaking fingers back through his hair. "How the hell can ya sleep with the whole world ready to kill ya any second?"

I'd been washing my face in a rain barrel when Jack came strolling in, clean-shaved, wearing a freshly washed shirt and smelling of witch hazel. I just stared at him. He grinned. "But I thought about ya'll all night. You should've came along. Vera still thinks you're Wyatt Earp."

"You ain't, are you?" Cull turned from the window.

"It's a joke," I said, then turned to Jack. "Does she know anything we oughta know?"

249

"Yeah, and you ain't gonna like it." He poured water from his canteen and filled it with "wonderful stuff" from a jug sitting beside the old Indian. "Tillman and that bunch ain't here to lay rail, that's for damn sure. They're waiting for McDowell to bring Red Cloud to Laramie. They plan on waylaying them here and holding Red Cloud on some trumped-up charge 'til they can finish the rails running into Montana."

"You're shitting me. That could be over a year." I let the dipper of water spill from my hand. I heard Kid Cull mumble something about his wife and walk out the door.

"I wish I was." Jack shook his head. "I knew you wasn't going to take it real well."

"Take it well? Jack, that's the craziest thing I've ever heard of. It ain't even legal."

"Don't give me 'legal.' We're talking about Washington, plus army, plus railroad. That'll never come up 'legal.' "

"But what's it supposed to get them? It ain't gonna settle the Sioux. If anything, it'll make 'em madder."

"If you listen to whores, which I do, Queenie says one of McDowell's officers got drunk and told her they can cut a deal with one of the other chiefs. He told her it was the only way the army can come out without looking like a bunch of losers." He shrugged. "I reckon they're desperate."

"By God, I ain't gonna sit still and let it happen. We're gonna do something."

Jack shook his head. "Here we go."

"I mean it! Cloud's the only person who's treated us right since we got here. You think we can let this happen without doing something?"

"I was hoping you'd just write the president a nasty letter once we got back to Missouri." Jack turned up a swig from the canteen. "But I reckon I knew better."

I snatched the canteen. "Don't get started on this stuff. We're gonna need a clear head. We've gotta get word to Red Cloud."

"According to Queenie, if McDowell did his job right, they should be on their way right now. They would've left the day after we did, only they'll ride straight down the Bozeman. Hell, they could be here any time."

"McDowell! That rotten, smooth-talking son of a bitch." I swung the canteen in the air. "And I told Cloud I thought he could trust him."

"I told you so, about McDowell." Jack grabbed the canteen as I paced by him. "He's offering a wagonload of trade guns and powder, and a dozen carbines, just to get Red Cloud to come and talk. That's the hook to get him here. From here, the railroaders will take him into custody. That way if the plan goes sour, Washington won't catch the blame."

"Jesus, Jack. What's wrong with these bastards? Cloud's holding a signed treaty. Don't it mean anything?"

"He can wipe his ass on it. Other than that, I reckon not."

I glanced about us. A tiny spider walked along the thin web strung between One Drum Beat's nose and hand. Run-around Joe had quit snoring and turned facedown on the straw-piled floor.

"I'm riding out and telling Red Cloud." I turned toward the stall to get my horse. Jack grabbed me by the arm.

"Can't we just take our money and light the hell out of here? We came to make money and we've done it. We can always—"

He stopped talking. We turned toward the creaking door and watched Kid Cull walk in slowly with his hands tied before him. A trickle of blood ran down from a knot on his forehead. Behind him, three men stepped in with cocked rifles and fanned out across the barn. Tillman stepped in with a pistol pointed at Cull's head. Jack's hand drifted toward his holster. "One move"—Tillman grinned—"and I'll make a 'good' cowboy out of him."

I spread my hands, trying to play dumb. "What's going on?"

"Nothing, unless you cause it. We've got business to attend to. I just think it might be wise if we hold you boys awhile."

"What's going on here?" Cull's voice trembled. "I thought we's all on the same side."

Tillman shook him by the collar. "Shut up, cowboy." He waved his pistol toward us with a clean-toothed smile. "We'll have your guns, gentlemen."

I saw Jack's eyes turn dark; a twitch flickered across his cheek. "I never give up my gun. I wouldn't know how."

I stepped slowly away as the rifles took aim. I'd go for the one on the left of the door, then try for Tillman before he got a chance to kill Cull. In the corner of my eye, I saw the tiny spider hang by one leg, busily working the web.

Tillman laughed under his breath. "I had you pegged as a gunslinger." He spoke back over his shoulder. "Bobby-Ray?"

"Yeah, boss." A lanky feller with a crazy grin stepped into the doorway with an arm wrapped around Queenie. Her face was battered and bleeding; her head dangled limp toward her breasts. He raised the shiny razor in his right hand, drew back her head, and laid it firm against her throat.

"She shot her mouth off to you last night about our business. Now it's up to you whether she lives or dies."

Queenie's swollen eyes drifted to Jack; her voice was a hoarse whisper. "I'm . . . sorry." Jack took a step forward.

"I mean it," said Tillman. "He'll open her up."

"Bobby-Ray," said Jack, in a quiet voice. "Go on and cut her throat. I'll bet ten dollars I can put three right through her and blow your heart out before she hits the floor."

Queenie's eyes snapped open, "Jack . . . ?"

"You're bluffing," said Tillman.

"Am I, Bobby-Ray? Slice her open and let's find out."

"Jack!" Queenie's voice pleaded across swollen lips.

"Is he, boss?" Bobby-Ray's face twisted with fear. "I mean, I'll kill her, but I don't want to die!"

"Shut up! Of course he's bluffing."

"And I've got you, Tillman," I said, taking a step forward, "straight through Cull, before the rifles get me."

"Wait-just-one-goddamn-minute!" Cull's voice sounded like ice rattling in a metal bucket.

"Sorry, Queenie," said Jack, "but we all die someday."

Tillman's hand turned white around the knuckles as he pressed the pistol against Cull's head. His face turned to stone. "Alright, Bobby-Ray, cut her thro—"

"Wait!" Jack raised his hands just as a trickle of blood spilled over the edge of the razor. Bobby-Ray had to jerk his hand to stop. I let out a tense breath and raised my hands. Cull slumped against Tillman. The riflemen swept forward and lifted our pistols. Tillman uncocked his pistol and let it down. Bobby-Ray turned Queenie loose; she fell back against the wall, rubbing her throat. Jack chuckled under his breath. "You're a poker player, ain't ya, Tillman?"

Tillman smiled and shoved Cull away. "I'm familiar with the game." He straightened his suit coat and stepped forward. The riflemen stepped to the side. One stayed beside me to search for weapons.

Jack grinned and extended his hand. "No hard feelings?"

Tillman dropped his pistol in his holster and reached for Jack's hand. "Of course not—"

Jack's boot shot up into Tillman's balls so hard, it lifted him a foot off the floor. A rifleman drew back to bust Jack in the head, but I dove into his chest as Jack grabbed Tillman's hair and swung his head into a stall door. "Teach, you, to, cut, a, whore!" I caught a glimpse of Jack's fist flying up and down as I wallowed on the floor with rifle butts banging against my back.

"Damn it," shouted Cull. "We're s'posed to be on the same side." I tried rolling away and saw Jack's hand reach between two men trying to knock him out. I heard Queenie scream and cuss. Tillman was trying to crawl as Jack's hand reached for his face. Then the back of my head exploded.

". . . Ya'll some crazy sum-bitches, is all I can say." Bobby-Ray leaned against the inside of the barn door, cradling a rifle. Jack had just started to come to. He raised his head from the straw floor and looked around. "Alls we was gonna do is hold ya 'til we took the Injun. Now he's kicked Mister Tillman's nuts up into his windpipe. There ain't no telling what he'll do."

Jack rolled up beside me against the wall. He shot a glance toward my boot. I winked. "You better," he whispered, "after me getting my ass kicked to draw their attention."

"We're all sitting ducks here," said Cull, beside me. "We need to work together."

"Hey, no talking there."

Jack looked all around, then at Bobby-Ray. "What do you mean, 'no talking'? You think this is a damn schoolhouse?"

Bobby-Ray looked startled. "I'm just doing what I'm told—"

"Aw . . . I see." Jack rolled his eyes. "And somebody told you we couldn't talk? Is that what you're saying?"

"Well . . . naw, but—"

"Then keep your nose out of our business. You're here to guard us, not to tell us what to do."

I had to look away to keep from grinning. Jack was seeing how far we could go. He leaned forward, his hands tied and lying in his lap, blood and straw dried to his forehead. "Get me some water, so's I can get this blood off my face, boy."

Bobby-Ray shook his head. "I can't do it."

"Can't do it? Why, you sniveling little— I've already decided to kill you once Tillman turns us loose."

"Jack," I said, "it ain't his fault. He's just following orders."

"Ah . . . you got orders not to give me water? I'm killing ya, it's that simple, you hear me? As soon as it's over, you're a dead man. Nobody told you not to give us water. I'll ask Tillman myself. You better not be lying."

"I never said he told me I couldn't." Bobby-Ray looked like his mind was going in circles. Jack had him rattled.

"Then get me some water!" Jack kicked at the straw. Bobby-Ray moved quickly to the rain barrel, then to Jack with a dipper of water.

"We need to all stick together," said Cull, "for everybody's good." Run-around Joe still lay sleeping on the straw. Someone had tied his hands without waking him. The old Indian still lay flat with the spider building its web between his hand and nose.

"That's better," said Jack, cupping his tied hands and rubbing water around on his face. Bobby-Ray held the dipper ready as Jack washed.

"I don't want nobody thinking hard of me," said Bobby-Ray. "I'm just doing—"

"Forget it, kid." Jack looked up from behind his hands. "I just go killing crazy sometimes. I can't help it—"

"That's the truth," I chimed in. "I've seen him go nuts and kill *strangers* for no reason at all."

"See, I love that little whore, and you beating her up and all."

"But you was ready to kill her, to shoot me."

"See what I mean?" Jack shrugged. "I can't help it."

"I was just following orders." Bobby-Ray's eyes pleaded.

"It don't matter." Jack shrugged. "I reckon you're dead right along with us once this is over."

"What's he mean by that?" Cull snapped forward. I shot him a glance.

"What *do* you mean by that?" said Bobby-Ray.

"Don't be an idiot, boy," said Jack. "Do you think Tillman will let you live and be a witness to what's going on here? This is the kinda crime that'll get him hung twice."

"Aw . . . I never heard of no law against capturing an Injun."

"Where you from?" said Jack.

"Ohio."

"That explains it." Jack shook his head. "I ain't telling you nothing else. But we'll all soon be together in hell. You can count on it."

I glanced at Cull; his face was chalk white. Bobby-Ray walked back and leaned against the door, scratching his chin. "How stupid do you reckon he is?" I whispered to Jack.

"Hard to tell . . . somewhere twixt a stump and a cucumber. But if I can cut us loose, you gotta promise we'll light out of here and not look back."

I gazed at my horse over in a stall, still wearing the rotted saddle and the blanket filled with stacks of dollars. Jack nudged me. "Do you hear me?"

I looked Jack up and down; his face looked like ground meat gone bad. "You're beat all to hell, Jack. Are you gonna be alright?"

"Answer me, damn it." Jack's voice rose above a whisper. Bobby-Ray looked over from the door.

"Ya'll do me a favor and keep quiet if somebody comes in. I don't know if you're s'posed to be talking or not."

"Sure," said Jack. "You ask us to do something for you, but you ain't offering to do nothing for us."

"Leave him alone, Jack. He's as dead as we are once Tillman gets his hands on Red Cloud."

"What can *I* do for ya'll?" Bobby-Ray leaned up from the door.

"Well, for starters, you can get us a knife so's we can cut loose," said Jack. He knew I had the glades knife. He was just feeling him out. "Then when Tillman goes to kill you and us—"

Bobby-Ray turned quickly as the door opened behind him. "How's it going in here?" said Tillman. He walked in with a limp. His left eye was bloodshot and swollen. He handed Bobby-Ray a cigar. Bobby-Ray propped a foot on a pile of hay, stuck the cigar in his mouth, and let the rifle dangle across his knee.

"I owe you five dollars, Uncle Frank," he said to Tillman, with a firm smile. "You were right. He started in on me as soon as his eyes swung open."

I glanced at Jack; he shook his head and dropped back against the wall. Tillman stepped closer and looked down at us. Bobby-Ray laughed behind him. "He was just to the part where I should get them a knife, so they could cut loose and we could all get away when you try to kill us."

"That's fairly original." Tillman smiled. "Usually it's money they've got buried somewhere... All you have to do is let them lead you to it." Both of them laughed.

"It was worth a try," I said. "The fact is, you ain't letting us go, are you?"

"If I wanted you dead, why wouldn't I have already killed you?" He tapped Jack with the toe of his boot. "After what this bastard done, you'd have it coming."

"Because of the noise," I said. "You knew better than fire off them rifles and take a chance on somebody hearing."

Tillman cocked an eyebrow. "Hey, that's not bad for Missouri, Mister Crowe." He stepped back with a sly grin.

I shook my head. "Why does everybody confuse me with that feller?"

"Save it, Crowe. Long Jake Howard is up from Laramie. He's got an iron ball with your name on it. You're worth money dead *or* alive, so you better keep your mouth shut."

"Lord God!" Cull leaned forward. "Ain't we got enough to worry about with every Injun in the world surrounding us—"

Tillman nodded down at Cull as he turned back to the door. "There's *bad luck* wrapped in a cheap hangover."

When Tillman closed the door behind himself, I looked at Jack. "Twixt a stump and a cucumber, huh?"

"I ain't always right." Jack looked up at Bobby-Ray with a sheepish grin. "I'd like to know where you boys play poker, so I can make it a point not to go there."

"That's it," I said. "Now try some old-fashion brownnosing."

"Don't worry," Bobby-Ray chuckled, "you won't be around—"

"That does it," I said. "I'm offering him money."

"Shut up!" Jack plowed his elbow into my ribs.

Bobby-Ray pushed his hat up and rolled the cigar around in his mouth. "You boys don't quit, do you?"

"I don't know these fellers," said Cull, "I swear—"

"But it's the truth, Bobby-Ray." I nodded toward Jack's saddlebags hanging over a stall door. "See for yourself."

"You cowardly bastard!" Jack drew back a boot, spun, and planted it on my shoulder. I pitched over against Cull.

"Jack! What good is it if we're dead?"

Bobby-Ray sidestepped to the saddlebags. "Just out of curiosity."

" 'Cause I'd rather be dead with money than alive without it!" Jack drew back and kicked me again. Bobby-Ray turned the saddlebags upside down and dumped them on the straw floor. The stacks of bills landed in a large clump.

"Jesus Christ." Bobby-Ray leaned down, staring and wiping his hand on his knee. "There must be ten—fifteen thousand—"

"I hope you're satisfied!" Jack swung both tied hands; I ducked. "You sniveling coward!" I saw Cull stare at the money with his mouth hanging open.

"This is the payroll money Pope and his gang took." I watched the wheels turning in Bobby-Ray's eyes. "There was over eighty thousand in that robbery."

"That's right," I said, "and we've got all of it buried near—"

"That's it, damn ya!" Jack hurled himself against me. I tried to cover my face as he pounded me with his tied hands. I slung him away and planted my boot in his chest as he came back at me swinging.

"Hold it!" Bobby-Ray jumped forward, grabbing Jack's shoulder. The rifle dangled from his left hand.

"Get 'im off me!" I held Jack away with my boot as Bobby-Ray yanked him from behind. I felt both Jack's hands go into my boot, saw the quick flash, heard the snip of sharp steel, and watched Bobby-Ray's rifle fly away as he threw both hands beneath his chin. Blood gushed like a Roman fountain. I heard his teeth grinding behind drawn lips.

"That's how you play cutthroat, you sum-bitch." Jack lunged forward with the glades knife in both hands and lifted him up on the sunken blade.

"Lord-God-Lord-God." Cull rocked back and forth trembling. I threw out my hands—"Hit it"—and Jack slashed through the rope.

"What about me!" Jack threw out his hands as I ran over and pitched the timber latch across the barn door.

I ran back, grabbed the glades knife, and cut Jack's rope. "Get him." I nodded toward Cull, pitching Jack the knife as I reached down and scraped the money into the saddlebags with one hand and snatched up the rifle with my other.

"Please, God, no!" Jack threw his hand over Cull's mouth.

"He meant for me to cut you loose, idiot." Jack slashed through the ropes.

"What am I into here?" Cull glanced at the saddlebags of money. "Are you the Pope Gang?"

"No," I said, "but you'll wish we was if you don't settle down and get with us. We're trying to stay alive."

Jack peeled out of his bloody shirt and dipped it in the rain barrel. "My damn clean shirt . . . what a mess."

Cull swallowed hard; his face was drawn and sickly gray. "I just want out of here alive. Tell me what to do and I'll do it."

On the floor, Run-around Joe snorted and rolled over on his side. "Can ya'll keep it down a little?"

◆✳ 36 ✳◆

We rolled Bobby-Ray's body into an empty stall and tied the old Indian to a horse. A string of cobweb hung from his nose and fluttered in his breath. Run-around Joe mounted up and sat rubbing his face with both hands. "I'll be alright. Just don't get in front of me." Swapping my rotted saddle for a new one hanging on a stall door, I quickly swung it on a tall chestnut gelding and tied my blanket full of money behind it.

I'd just headed to open the back door when we heard someone knocking on the front. "Bobby-Ray, yooo-hoo, sweetheart. Let me in, you little devil. I can't stay mad at you . . ."

"It's Queenie," said Jack, peeping through a crack.

"Get her in here, before somebody sees her."

Jack opened the door a foot and snatched her through it. "You little animal," she giggled, then she saw it was Jack.

"What the hell are you doing here?" Jack slung her away from the door and shut it. Queenie looked around through swollen eyes. A bottle of rye hung from her hand; a gauze bandage circled her throat. Her eyes followed the trail of blood to Bobby-Ray's boots sticking out of a stall.

"I came to get you out." She raised her leg and pulled a forty-four from under her dress. "But I see you're just leaving."

"Thanks," said Jack, "but we worked it out." He reached for the pistol. Queenie pulled it back and cocked it.

"In that case, you dirty bastard"—she poked it straight in Jack's face; the tip of the barrel flattened his nose—"what the hell did you mean, 'go on and cut her throat, Bobby-Ray'? I even washed your stinking shirt."

"Get that gun off my nose!" Jack's voice sounded like he was talking through a tin can.

"Can't nobody work together here?" Cull pleaded.

"We ain't got time for no lovers' spat," I said, stepping forward with the rifle pointed at Queenie. "He didn't let them kill you, for Christ-sake."

"And if I had, it was just to protect the money." Jack tried a flat-nosed grin.

"What money?" Queenie cocked her head.

Jack stepped back an inch, then two, then a foot, and rubbed his nose as Queenie eased the pistol down to his chest. "Damn, honey. I've been meaning to tell ya, we got enough money buried out there to buy hell from the devil. We just got to get away to get to it." Jack glanced toward me.

"It's true, Queenie. You can't blame him . . . There was money involved."

"Well . . . I should *really* be pissed, but . . . can *I* have some?" She wrinkled her swollen nose and tried to wink.

"Why, hell yes!" Jack reached out, eased the pistol from her hand, and took the bottle of rye. "We're all friends here." Jack stuck the pistol down in his belt and pulled the cork from the bottle with his teeth. He spit it away. "But we need to get going."

"I'm going too." Queenie started toward a horse stall. Jack grabbed her arm.

"You can't go!"

She shook him loose. "The hell I can't. I ain't staying and getting blamed for killing Bobby-Ray. And I ain't letting you out of sight until I see some money in my hand. I'll scream loud enough to curl rope."

Run-around Joe let out a long yawn. "If we ain't going nowhere, I'm gonna lay back down."

"Jesus Christ, Jack, help her get a horse and let's get out of here." I looked around at our group and shook my head. The tiny spider hung at the end of the web string, swinging back and forth from the tip of One Drum Beat's nose with each breath. I went to the back door and peeped out through a crack. The back trail out of Crofton was overgrown with clumps of buffalo grass. Sunlight sparkled on scattered whiskey bottles.

I heard a slap behind me as I raised the timber bolt. "Get your hand off there," said Queenie. "I know how to straddle a horse."

"I bet you do," Jack chuckled under his breath.

We slipped silently out the back door and eased our horses through the grass, quiet as ghosts, toward the shelter of thin woodland fifty yards away. The bald-faced gelding circled the barn and trotted up beside us. For no reason at all, the horse threw back its hairless head and let out a shrill, echoing neigh. The Catahoula cur appeared out of nowhere and went into a fit of growling and barking as it snapped at the gelding's legs. I gigged my horse. "Run for it," I shouted. "You can't do nothing quiet around this goddamn bunch."

Near the woods line, I pulled to the side to let the others pass me. I reined around and threw the rifle to my shoulder as Tillman and three of his men ran out the back door and spotted us. One man took aim with a rifle, but Tillman shoved the barrel down. I let down my barrel and rode into the woods behind the rest. Jack reined back to me. "They won't shoot . . . but they're coming!"

"Hit the trail and ride like hell," Jack yelled to the others. The old Indian wobbled so bad, I thought he'd break his back as we cut through the woods and headed down to the trail. I rode in close, grabbed his reins, and led his horse at a hard run. Kid Cull was twenty yards ahead of the rest of us, raising a wake of dust.

A few miles down the trail we veered up a narrow path to the top of a red cliff and let our horses catch their breath as we looked back down on the trail. We saw no sign of Tillman's men, but I knew they couldn't be far behind. "Jack," I said, low enough to keep the others from hearing, "one of us is gonna have to leave this bunch behind if we expect to reach Red Cloud."

"You go." He nodded to the big chestnut gelding. "That's the best horse of the bunch. I'll get us out of sight and hold out 'til you come back."

"You sure? I can swap horses with you."

Jack reached over and pulled the rifle from my saddle scabbard.

"Naw, I'm a better shot, and you'll do better talking to Red Cloud anyway."

I reined up on the chestnut gelding to turn him. "I'll get back to you as soon as I can."

Swinging down to the trail, I gigged the tall gelding into a full run and gave him free rein. The horse stretched out and bellied down like the devil licked at his hoofs. It was nearly a half an hour later before he let down to a trot. By then we had rounded a turn beneath a cliff overhang and I saw a billow of dust over a distant low rise.

I drew the gelding to a walk as we topped the low rise. Sliding down from the saddle, I watched McDowell's party coming toward us at two hundred yards. The gelding walked in a circle blowing out his breath in a spray of white foam. In minutes, Bridger and one of the scouts jumped ahead and galloped toward me; I saw Red Cloud's top hat bobbing above the other riders just behind the waving flag.

"Didn't reckon on seeing you again, riding or walking," said Bridger, reining up sideways. "Why you pulling that horse down so hard?"

"I need to talk to Red Cloud," I said. I didn't know if Bridger was in on the setup or not. I couldn't chance telling him.

"Just make yourself at home." He grinned. "I believe that big feller is anxious to see you anyway."

I swung up on the gelding and rode back between Bridger and the scout. McDowell threw his hand in the air when we drew close, and the column snapped to a halt. Red Cloud sat silent as stone as McDowell gigged his horse forward. "Why are you still roaming around out here?"

"I need to talk to Mister Cloud." I wasn't sure where, how, or even *if* McDowell stood in the scheme, but I figured if I could get Red Cloud's ear for a minute, I could stop the whole crazy plan. I leaned out and stared past McDowell toward the column. "Mister Cloud," I shouted, "don't go into Crofton. It's a setup with the railroad."

McDowell bumped his horse against mine, grabbing the bridle. "What on earth are you talking about? Do you realize the difficulty I had getting him to come to Fort Laramie?"

I jerked my horse away. "Hear me, Chief? It's all one big double cross." Red Cloud leaned to one of his braves beside him. They both shrugged. Two officers rode up beside him as Shod and two soldiers gigged their horses up to us. "I want to talk to the chief," I said to McDowell. "Are you refusing to let me?"

"Before you speak to anyone, I suggest you first hear what Agent Shadowen has to say."

"Agent who?" I shot McDowell a puzzled look as Shod and the soldiers reined up. Shod whipped a small leather wallet from his pocket, and I saw sunlight sparkle on the small gold badge. "Mister Crowe," said Shod, "as an agent of the United States Secret Service, I'm placing you under arrest for theft of federal property, knowing and receiving stolen government property . . ."

I watched his lips move and heard his words, but somehow nothing made sense after the flash of the gold badge. I just stared at Shod with my mouth open as the two soldiers sidled up, took my reins, and patted me down for weapons. ". . . attempting to incite a riot among Indians, conspiring to sell firearms to the Indians . . ." He stopped and let the badge slump to his lap. "What's the use? You're just guilty . . . of everything that comes to mind."

"You've got the wrong man," I said, as the soldiers slapped a pair of cuffs around my wrists and tightened them. I felt I had to say something.

Bridger slapped his leg and cackled, "He's a pistol, riding or walking."

"And let me inform you," said McDowell, "you will hang right here if you do or say anything to interfere with this peace mission."

"Peace mission, hell! You're handing Red Cloud over to the railroad—" I swung my head toward Shod as a soldier took out a rawhide strip. "Shod, you've got to listen to me. I know you ain't in on this."

"Bring us a rope," McDowell barked at the soldiers.

"One second, Colonel." Shod raised a hand. "He's my prisoner. When he hangs, it will be at a federal penitentiary, not out here. It could take months just finding out his real name, if he has one."

"Then I strongly suggest you keep him quiet." McDowell swung his horse and cantered back to Red Cloud. I watched his hands explain things as the soldier reached to gag me. Red Cloud nodded.

"Shod, just listen to me one second. You're doing a terrible thing, riding Red Cloud into Crofton. There's a scheme to take him hostage. All the time we kept hearing about a reward. It was true—"

The rawhide strip slapped around my mouth; in a split second I knew how Ben Bone must've felt the night he tried to tell the truth to Mad Johnson. Shod eased his horse beside mine and pulled the glades knife from my boot. He leaned in so close, I saw my face in his dark pupils. "I've heard enough lies from you to last a lifetime. I don't think you even know when you're lying. But it's over now, so don't make me change my mind and kill you on the spot." He poked his spectacles up his nose. "We're not even going to Crofton, you fool. We're going to split off to wherever you've hidden the money. If we run into your friend, so much the better."

That afternoon, Shod released my gag as we sat down to a plate of jerked beef and canned peaches. Thirty yards away, McDowell had a canvas awning thrown up to shade Red Cloud, the officers, and himself. Shod and I sat on a rock. "I know I've lied to you," I said over a mouthful of peaches, "but no more than you have to me."

"That's different," he said. "I was performing my job as an agent of the government."

"I was performing mine as a horse thief. Funny how much the two have in common, ain't it?"

"I can put your gag back on, right now."

"I'm just making conversation. I can't get over you being a lawman." I shook my head. "How can you be a Secret Service agent when you people ain't even got your citizenship yet?"

"It's a secret." He grinned.

"Well . . . it ain't no secret that you're riding Red Cloud into a trap." Shod shot me a dark look; I threw up my cuffed hands. "Alright, I know I ain't supposed to keep saying it. But it's a fact. When we get to Crofton, you'll see. You'll feel like buying new boots and kicking yourself in the ass."

"Nobody is going to Crofton, especially us. After we eat, Kermit and I are taking you on a treasure hunt. I found the bodies of Pope's men where you or *somebody* ambushed them, but there's still Pope and his brothers, maybe more. My job was to find out who was giving Pope inside information on payroll shipments." He took a bite of beef and threw in half a peach behind it. "That's accomplished. You found it out the night you heard Mad Johnson talking to Pope in his tent. I should thank you for it." He grinned and chewed.

I rattled my handcuffs. "You have."

Shod shrugged. "I've given you every opportunity to get out of it, but you're like a crazed coyote. You just keep sniffing and foraging on." He shook his head. "I've never seen anything quite like you and your friend." He chuckled. "You'd both make good agents, if you could keep your saddle off other people's horses."

"You didn't mind accepting our friendship, deceiving us, making us think you were one of us."

"Don't hand me that. I was never more than 'hired help.' You never told me what you're really up to"—he tossed his head—"prowling around up here in the middle of an Indian war."

"That's where you're wrong. We came to run in horses, nothing else."

"I believe it now. I've seen that you're both actually crazy enough to do something like that. I probably thought it all along. But I'm not after you, never was. I just needed a cover for being here. I couldn't have gotten very far on my own. I knew when we met that if anybody would wind up in the thick of things, it would be you two. All I had to do was hook on and wait."

"Glad we could accommodate, Mister Shadowen." I remembered the day in Carrington's office when he told me he'd asked Washington to investigate the Pope Gang getting inside information. Now I felt foolish that I hadn't suspected Shod all along. Looking back, I saw that everything about him had been directed toward the Pope Gang, including charging the barn that first day in Crofton. "You're the reason Trapp wouldn't let us leave town, ain't ya? I bet it was your idea to have the horses confiscated."

He shrugged. "It would have ended right there. The Popes would have come for you; I'd have taken them down, clean and simple."

"That wouldn't have got you the money, or told you who their contact was."

"They would've talked. Not everyone is as hardheaded as you."

"Jesus." I shook my head.

"Riders coming," yelled Bridger, from the edge of camp. Shod stood, dusted his trousers, and gazed up the trail. When the horsemen became visible, he stepped over and pulled up my gag. "In case that's your friend." He smiled. I stood up and craned my neck. I could tell it was Tillman at the front of the four riders. His string tie fluttered in the breeze. I grunted and stomped the ground, feeling more and more like Ben Bone. "Keep still," said Shod, "or I'll crack your head." I settled right down.

Tillman and his men stopped outside the canvas awning, slid from their saddles, met Colonel McDowell wiping his moustache with a white linen napkin, and followed him over to us. "It seems these gentlemen are anxious to see you." Shod smiled. "I can't imagine why." I gazed past the approaching group and watched Red Cloud stand up from his meal and watch curiously. Beside him, one of the braves started to rise, but Red Cloud placed a hand to his shoulder, stopping him.

"That's him! That's the son of a bitch!" Tillman pulled out a forty-four and aimed it at me. I jumped behind Shod. "Step away, boy," Tillman bellowed. "I'm killing him, right here and now."

Shod stood firm. "Easy, sir. This man is a federal prisoner under my arrest. Put away the gun or you'll be arrested also."

Tillman swung his head toward McDowell. "What's this boy saying? Who the hell is he?"

"This *gentleman* is Agent—"

"I'm Jefferson Ellridge Shadowen, United States Secret Service. Do you have difficulty with that?" I saw Shod's neck and shoulders tighten.

Tillman's gun lowered; his jaw twitched. "No offense, boy. I just didn't know you were in on the plan—"

"Agent Shadowen is here investigating payroll robberies." McDowell spoke quickly. "He just happens to be riding with us—"

"What plan?" Shod's voice dropped lower.

I stepped around beside him and saw his nostrils flare. McDowell's face took on a pinched redness. "Our coming here has involved some carefully detailed coordination, Agent Shadowen. I assure you, we have scrutinized and evaluated every possible—"

"What plan?" Shod's voice kicked up a notch.

"Okay." McDowell fanned his hands. "We may have to detain Chief Red Cloud temporarily in Crofton for his own safety. Let me assure you, we will be extending every courtesy—"

I'd managed to work my gag loose. "I told you they're going to waylay him!"

Shod grabbed me by my handcuffs and slung me to the ground. "Open your mouth again and I'll put a bullet through you." He drew his pistol and pointed it toward me.

"And this weasel stole my horse and brand-new saddle." Tillman drew back a boot. Shod stepped between us. Tillman stepped back. "He also killed one of my men!"

"He's my prisoner," said Shod. "I don't doubt he stole your horse. He steals everybody's horse. But he's going with me. Unless you would prefer I travel with you to Crofton and see that everything goes smoothly with Red Cloud."

Tillman tried to sidestep Shod to get to me. McDowell intercepted him. "That will not be necessary, I assure you. I'm certain Mister Tillman's only interest is getting his horse and saddle back. Am I correct, Mister Tillman?"

"Damn it, Shod. You can't let them bastards take Cloud to Crofton—"

Shod cocked the pistol toward me. "One more word, Crowe."

I watched as one of Tillman's men walked over, took the reins to the chestnut gelding, and started back. "Take that flea-infested blanket off my saddle," Tillman barked.

The gunman untied my blanket full of money and threw it on the ground. The fall broke the leather ties and the blanket rolled open a foot; my heart nearly stopped. "If you'll take some good advice, you'll put a bullet through his head and roll him in a ditch." Tillman jerked the reins from his man's hand and turned to McDowell. "We've rounded up the rest of his group, all but one anyway. I'll expect you in Crofton tonight as planned."

"Of course," said McDowell. He turned to Shod. "I suggest you leave immediately. I don't want him around here trying to instigate trouble." He spun on his heel and walked away behind Tillman.

Bridger kneeled down and retied my blanket roll. "A feller needs his blanket, riding or walking," he said, pitching it to me.

"Thanks." I hugged it to me. "Well, Shod, there it is. Was I lying?" I watched Bridger walk away toward the Pawnee scouts. Shod stared as Tillman and his men mounted near the awning and turned back down the road. "I was right, wasn't I? They're gonna hold him prisoner."

"No," said Shod. He holstered his forty-four and gathered his gear. "For a minute I thought they were, but I should've known better. After seeing how the two of them acted together, it's apparent to me. They're not going to hold him prisoner, they're going to kill him."

I stared at him as the realization set in. He was right. I should've seen it all along. How would Standing Bear lead the Sioux as long as Red Cloud was still alive? Red Cloud was a strong leader. His warriors would hold out against the army for a year, maybe longer, if they knew he was alive and would be coming back. The railroad would be finished by then; and the government would be left with egg on its face.

Whatever the army and the railroad wanted to accomplish by having Standing Bear as chief had to be done quickly. Whatever land concessions they wanted from the Sioux had to be made before the rails reached across Montana. With Standing Bear in their pocket, they could wrap up a new treaty and squeeze as much land as they wanted.

"And you ain't gonna warn him?" I stared at Shod.

"Sure, Crowe, I'll warn him. I walk in there and tap a spoon against a coffee cup to get their attention—"

"So you're just going to let the leader of a whole nation die, so's you can trot off after the Popes?" I shook my head. "I respected you more as a horse wrangler."

"Horse *thief* is what you mean." He threw his gear up on his horse. Kermit came riding up slow on a gray dapple leading a barebacked army mule. "The fact is, you wouldn't have batted an eye if I'd hanged while working for you. So don't start expressing some deep concern for human life, Red Cloud's or anybody else. Sure you have the best intentions now, but it's difficult to believe a man once the metal has bitten his wrists."

I looked the mule over. "You can't expect me to ride this ridge-backed pack animal."

"You'll get used to it. You're adaptable. Make a saddle of your blanket roll."

◆✳ 37 ✳◆

Shod, Kermit, and I rode out past the rear of the resting column. I lay my blanket roll across my lap and tried to adjust myself to the grinding motion of the mule's backbone. I glanced over my shoulder as the soldiers and the canvas awning disappeared behind us. "Kermit," I said. "I'll trade you my hat, boots, this mule, and three whole dollars for that dapple gray." Kermit just stared straight ahead.

"Shut up, Crowe," said Shod. "The sooner you get tired of riding that rail-back, the sooner you'll lead us to the money."

"Hold your breath, Mister Shadowen, 'partner.' I'll grind my ass-bone up to my elbows before I'll take you anywhere but straight to hell. You're just as guilty as Tillman and his bunch. You're letting Red Cloud die just so you can make a showing for yourself up in Washington."

Shod grinned and stared straight ahead. "Keep it up, and I'll feed you to the Pope Gang before I kill them."

A mile behind the column, I heard the faint call of a night bird and watched Shod closely to see if he'd heard it too. I knew when Tillman had said they caught the rest of our bunch except one that Jack had managed to slip away. Shod's expression didn't change.

Another mile farther, Shod swung sharp off the trail and turned back in a wide circle. I looked around and saw he was heading back above the trail. "What's this? I thought you said we were heading back to the rock where the money's buried." Shod didn't answer. "I get it," I said. "All that talk about tracking the Pope Gang. You're scared you might really run into them." I was saying whatever came to my mind to try and find out his plans; but he rode on, silent as stone.

By the time we'd circled back above the spot where the column had stopped to eat, the trail was empty. We stayed in the scattered woods above, watched the wake of their dust in the distance, then began following them toward Crofton. "So you're heading in to help Red Cloud after all?" Shod just rode along without answering.

I spotted the glint of a rifle barrel on the slope above us as we entered a narrow terraced ravine. Figuring it was Jack taking position, I lowered my head and kept still about it. Then, ten yards into the shelter of pines, Shod's horse reared as a slug slapped into the ground near its hooves. The explosion echoed across the land. "Freeze, with your hands up," said a voice that wasn't Jack's.

I threw up my cuffed hands and the bedroll flipped off my lap and rolled down behind a rock. Shod and Kermit looked around as four riflemen eased slowly from behind cover and descended toward us. "We got the son of a bitches this time, boss!" one of Pope's brothers called over his shoulder. "Ease them pistols out and drop 'em."

I watched as Shod grudgingly raised his pistol with two fingers and let it fall. He slipped his rifle from the scabbard and pitched it away. Kermit threw away his shotgun. Pope's brother glanced over his shoulder. "That's it, Parker. Come on out." A few seconds passed as Pope's gunmen scanned the woods. "I says . . . Parker, come on out here." Only silence in the surrounding woods. Finally the gunman shrugged towards the woods. "What'n hell we s'posed to do now, Parker?"

I heard Jack chuckle as he stepped forward from the woods holding Parker Pope by the collar with a rifle jammed against his neck. He held the reins to his horse in his hand with his rifle. Pope had a red welt across his forehead. Blood trickled.

"You're the boss, boss," said Jack. "Tell 'em what to do. It's decision time here in the high country."

"Drop the guns," said Pope, as if ashamed. "Do what he tells ya."

The gunman looked confused. "Why? We've got the drop on 'em."

"Because, goddamn it," Pope breathed. "He's gonna kill me if you don't."

"Parker," said the gunman, "I don't mean to sound like a poor sport about it, but if he kills you, we'll still get the money, won't we?"

"Listen up, you dumb pecker-wood!" Jack stepped beside Pope with the rifle barrel still at his neck. "We ain't carrying the money with us. Do we look that stupid? Now, do like he says and drop the guns, or I'll give him this rifle and he'll shoot you."

"I don't know." The gunman shook his head slowly and took a step back. "I just can't see what it'll get me." He laid his thumb across the rifle hammer. I was ready to jump to the ground for Shod's gun any second. My eyes met Shod's as we both glanced toward the rifle on the ground. Kermit sat slumped with his hands high.

"You're my brother, for Christ sake," Parker pleaded.

"Still, I can't see what good it'd do for us to—"

In one motion, Jack slung Pope away and fired one shot through the gunman's chest as I leaped for Shod's rifle, caught it, and rolled away just as Shod slammed onto the ground behind me. I managed to cock the rifle and fire, but my handcuffs kept me from taking aim. Jack blazed away as I struggled to cock the rifle again. Before I could shoot, the gunmen scrambled away in Jack's hail of fire.

Shod dove for his revolver but was driven back beneath his spooked horse by two rifles. I scrambled to the pistol as Shod tried to keep from being stomped by his horse. Once I got the pistol in my hands, I poured fire into the closest rifleman and watched the other take off behind the cover of rocks. Shod started crawling toward me; I cocked the pistol in his face. "That's close enough, Mister Jefferson Ellridge Shadowen!" Shod just dropped on his chest and shook his head.

"It ain't my place to say," I heard Jack say to Parker Pope as I stood up, scanning the woods with Shod's pistol, "but if you ever start another gang, you oughta leave your family out of it. They ain't a real loyal bunch."

I glanced up at Kermit. "You can take your hands down now." He dropped his hands and stared off into the woods. I grinned at Shod and motioned him up with the pistol. "I think it's time we reorganize our travel arrangements."

"And we better do it quick," said Jack, shoving Pope over to the horses. "I figure Long Jake's gonna be sticking his nose in here about any minute now. If them Indians didn't kill him."

I held my hands out to Shod; he unlocked the cuffs. Snapping the cuffs around his wrists, I shoved him toward the mule. "Meet your new 'partner,' Mister Shadowen. The sooner you get tired of riding this ridge-back, the sooner you'll agree to help us save Red Cloud."

"Hold it," said Jack. "I ain't riding back to Crofton, if that's what you're thinking. I plan on taking the money and skinning straight back to Missouri."

"You mean you've got the money with you?" Pope sounded disheartened.

"No," said Jack, "and shut your mouth. After the way your bunch acted, you should be ashamed to talk to real outlaws." Jack winked at me. "I hope you buried it somewhere safe."

"I did, but I ain't digging it up 'til we've stopped Red Cloud from getting waylaid by Tillman and McDowell." I watched Jack glance around for the blanket roll.

"Listen." He pointed his finger. "My vacation is over as of today. I don't give a damn if they throw this whole Powder River bunch in one bucket and drop it down a well. I'm going home!"

I stepped over and picked up the blanket roll from behind a rock. Jack watched as I swung it up behind his saddle and tied it down. "You'll need something to sleep on. Take this." I just stared at him.

"And by God, I will." He started toward his horse, then stopped.

"Well, go on," I said. "I can handle it from here. Maybe I ain't nothing. Maybe I'm as no-account as everybody up here thinks I am." I shot Shod a glance. "And maybe I was crazy to ever get suckered into this mess . . . but Red Cloud's fixin' to die because he took my word about McDowell." I pounded my thumb against my chest. "That was *my* fault! And I'll *die* before I see it happen!"

"You'd give you life for Red Cloud . . . over this?" Jack swung his arm, taking in the country. "Then you are crazy! Hell, it ain't even yours . . . and it's a lost cause even if it was! We're leaving here rich!" He rubbed his thumb and forefinger together. "Cash! Greenbacks! That's what it's about. Now straighten up and—"

"It's about honor, Jack," I said in a voice turned quiet. "I gave my word without lying, for a change. I aim to keep it. It's just common decency, and I'm 'bout as common as it gets!"

Jack turned, leaned against his horse with both hands, shook his bowed head, and tapped his fingers on the saddle. I heard him chuckle and mumble something under his breath. Finally he turned and blew out a breath. "My vacation ain't really over 'til midnight tonight. I reckon that's enough time to clean things up." He shrugged. "I hate leaving a mess."

I glanced at Shod and thought I saw a trace of a smile before he looked away. Kermit sat scratching his head; Pope sneered and spit on the ground.

On the way back to Crofton, I ran things through my mind. I knew Jack was right, we should've taken the money and headed out; but I couldn't leave Powder River knowing I'd watched a good man go to his death for no reason except to cover up the army's mistake. Since the first day we'd arrived in Crofton—what seemed now like a long time ago—everyone I'd met had a different version of why the army was here, yet after hearing them all, I had no more understanding than I did when I started. I doubted if anyone really knew—doubted if anyone ever would.

Somehow in the progress, "gone crazy wanting more," everybody got caught up in the events and ignored the reasons. I reckoned that's all the devil ever needs to make his presence known. North of Fort Laramie and west of the Black Hills, Powder River was a world gone crazy, an old world fighting death and a new world struggling to be born.

Here was the kind of place that drew people like Ben Bone, Parker Pope, McDowell, Tillman, Bridger, Jack . . . and myself. Some came to change it, to tame it, to claim it, to bleed it dry. I felt a sudden sense of shame sweep over me as we stopped our horses overlooking the trail. Watching the sun set in a streak of blue and red, I pictured Red Cloud and his nation as something ancient and wounded, and tangled in the spokes of time. Whatever we were about to do here was only temporary; and for whatever reason we all thought we came, it dawned on me in a chill across my shoulders. We all came to kill it, each in our own way . . . or else stand on the sidelines and just watch it die.

"Having second thoughts?" Jack reined up beside me. He led Pope's horse by the reins and held a rope tied around the outlaw's neck. Behind him Shod trudged up on the mule. His feet nearly dragged the ground. Kermit rode beside him, slumped in the saddle.

"Naw, just thinking," I said. "When I spoke to Trapp that day in Crofton, he told me 'any fool could get to Powder River. The trick would be getting out.' Boy was he ever right."

Jack folded his arms across his saddle horn and spit a stream of tobacco. "I wouldn't put much store in it. He's got his head on a stick, and we're sitting on a sinful amount of good ole stolen money. Once we straighten out that bunch in Crofton and get Long Jake Howard off our heels."

I swallowed hard and stared at the road ahead. "I never figured I'd die like this. I always thought I'd get it in the back like Gyp Pope . . . riding away from something I'd done."

"If you want to change your mind and ride away from here right now, I'll not say a word about it. Red Cloud has won this war, but he'll never win another. If they don't kill him today, they'll kill him next week or the week after. We can still leave."

I stared at Jack with my jaw set tight.

"Just checking," he said with a raised hand.

I pushed up my hat as Shod stepped his mule beside me. "If you're smart, you'll set me free and let me help you. All I want is what I came for, Parker Pope and the stolen money. I feel as strongly about what's happening to Red Cloud as you do. That's why I circled back."

"Then you should've said so before the metal bit your wrists. It's hard to believe a man in a chain, remember?" I glared at him.

"Alright." He let out a breath. "I tormented you a little. Perhaps I shouldn't have. But let's put aside personal grievances and look at the facts. You need every gun you can get if you're going to take on McDowell and Tillman. I don't want to watch Red Cloud die just because you and I haven't exactly hit it off."

"That's putting it smooth and mild." I grinned and glanced at Parker Pope. "What about you, Pope? You think we oughta shake hands and make up . . . just outa your deep concern for Red Cloud?"

"Fuck you, Crowe." I saw a flash of his gold tooth as he sneered and spit at me. Behind him, Kermit sat with a wide-eyed blank expression. I looked at Kermit, shook my head, gigged my horse forward, and we started down the trail into Crofton.

We heard a thrashing in the brush beside us, and before either of us had time to draw our guns, the bald-faced gelding trotted up onto the trail, slinging his head back and forth and blowing out his breath. Behind him loped the Catahoula cur. They followed as we swung wide around the outskirts of town to look for Dirty Jaw and the wagonload of rifles. I had hopes that Dirty Jaw would throw in with us when he heard what was going on.

But when we met him on the road near Crofton and I told him about it, he laughed . . . actually laughed. "What's so funny?" I sat on my horse beside his wagon. "I hoped maybe you'd throw in with us."

He laughed again. "You're out of your mind if you think I'm facing the army and the railroad." Dirty Jaw released the brake on the wagon and started to slap the reins across the horses' backs. I jumped my horse in and grabbed the reins; he reached for a shotgun beside him. Jack drew and cocked his forty-four.

"Christ, Jaw! You're supposed to be his friend. He trusted you to bring his rifles to him. You ride with his warriors. Doesn't this mean anything to you?"

"Not a lick. I told you weeks back. I play it either way, and work for whoever is on top. If he gets killed, I guess he loses. In that case"—he gestured a salute—"*adiós*, Red Cloud."

I threw loose the reins. "Then get out of here. I guess you're stuck with a load of rifles."

"We made a deal. You're supposed to pay me on delivery."

"And I will. The deal was, you'd deliver them to me in Crofton. So I'll see you there. *Adiós,* Mister Dirty Jaw."

"Wait. We didn't figure on Crofton being crawling with army and railroaders. I'm delivering the rifles right here."

"That's fine . . . but I'm giving you the money in Crofton. That's how it is, flat out. If you don't like it, write your goddamn congressman." We turned and started away.

"Look . . . I'll give you one day. If Cloud's still alive when the smoke settles, I'll bring 'em in; if not . . . I'm gone."

We rode away quietly and stopped at the creek behind Crofton. As the horses watered, I gazed at the thin glow of light from the rough-cut saloon, heard the plunking banjo and rattle of spoons, and felt loneliness close around me.

"Look at it this way," said Jack, standing beside his horse, cleaning his rifle. "As much far-handed crap as we've pulled, what's the odds of us getting killed doing something decent for somebody?" He gazed away for a second. "It'd have to be better than a million to one."

"Thanks, Jack. I feel a lot better now."

"Gentlemen," said Shod. "You better consider my offer. I get Pope and the money. Both of you go free, and Red Cloud lives. After the fighting starts, it'll be too late to negotiate."

"That's mighty generous of you, Mister Shadowen. But there's no way in hell we're giving up the money." I shot Jack a glance. "It ain't in our nature. And no more deals. I'm sick of deals. Deals is what's caused all this." I checked my pistol and spun it on my finger to calm my nerves. "Army deals, railroad deals . . ." I watched the pistol spin and shimmer in the moonlight, like the hand of fate spinning the wheel of time. "Deals, deals, deals."

"Besides, all our friends would talk bad about us if we gave up the money," Jack said. He took out his pistol and checked the action by holding it close to his ear and turning it a cylinder at a time. When he'd finished, I heard the soft click of metal against leather as he slipped it loosely back into his holster. He cleared his throat and let out a long breath, and we just sat there in silence, watching the bald-faced gelding pick at a clump of grass and scrape its hoof. The Catahoula ventured forward quietly, sat down at the edge of the creek, and gazed out through the gentle night.

◆❋ 38 ❋◆

A couple of hours before daylight, we handcuffed Shod around the trunk of a cottonwood tree, hog-tied and gagged Parker Pope, and rolled him into a clump of bushes along the creek. With our reins in hand, we waded the shallow creek and crept through the buffalo grass and broken bottles behind the livery barn, leaving Kermit stationed with our horses inside the tree line.

Twenty yards from the barn, we lay quiet as ghosts listening for any sound of guards and training our eyes toward the mud street. I felt something crawling up beside us and swung around with my pistol. The Catahoula cur whined softly, wagging its tail back and forth in the grass with its head lowered. "Damn it," I whispered, "I knew I should've tied him. Next, I reckon that hairless horse will come charging in."

"Leave him be," Jack whispered in reply. "If they hear any noise, they'll think it's him."

When we were satisfied that no one was patrolling the rear door, I patted the dog's head and snuck forward. Jack threw an arm over the dog to keep it with him. At the corner of the barn, I eased up onto my feet and found a crack wide enough to peep through. In the fading glow of a lamp, Cull, Run-around, and One Drum Beat lay in a pile of hay against the wall with their hands tied, just like before. Cull's eyes searched the flickering darkness. Run-around and One Drum Beat snored quietly. Inside the front door, one of Tillman's men sat on a barrel with a shotgun across his lap.

Looking back toward Jack, I waved my arm slowly in the air; but when he didn't come forward, I risked a soft night bird call, and in seconds he crawled slowly through the grass. The Catahoula followed. I shook my head. Ten feet behind him, I could make out the outline of the bald-faced gelding, grazing in a short circle, swishing its tail.

We heard the splatter of heavy boots coming toward us from the mud street, and in a second we'd scooted around the far corner of the barn. The Catahoula disappeared. "That you, Bert?" said a voice from inside the barn.

"Yeah, it is," said a flat Texas twang, as the man leaned against the back door and puffed on a cigarette. I glanced at Jack and threw up my hands; he shrugged.

"When they bringing over that Injun?" The voice in the barn sounded tired.

"Hell, I don't know. They're still trying to get him to sign a new treaty or some shit. I told Ernie to shoot him in the head and sign it himself, but *no*, they're going to fool around all night, then end up doing it anyway." He chuckled and blew a long stream of smoke.

We lay a long time in the darkness beside the barn, watching him smoke as I tried to figure our next move. I was on the verge of standing up and just shooting him when once again we heard boots splattering across the street. This time we heard the front door swing open and crouched back down.

"Damn," said the voice inside the front door, "what the hell did you hit him with?"

"Had to hit him twice," said another voice. "He's tougher than a pine knot." We heard them thrashing around inside as I found another crack to peep through.

Two other men and the front door guard dragged Red Cloud's limp body across the floor and pitched him against the wall beside Kid Cull. His hands were cuffed and his ankles shackled. Cull drew away and stared at the knocked-out Indian. "He ain't gonna flare up and try to kill me, is he?" Cull sounded shaky. The men laughed and walked back to the door.

"Why don't we just pop him?" The guard leaned back against the door.

"That's Standing Bear's job, come morning," said one of the men. "Tillman wants it done in front of witnesses. And he wants it Indian style, so's nobody else gets the blame."

"That's a crock," said the guard. "Shoot him and be done with it, I say."

"You just stay awake. We'll send over some more men now that we got the Injun here." The two men stepped back through the door.

"Good. Tell 'em to bring some coffee." The door creaked shut.

As soon as their footsteps faded across the street, I stood up and started to slip around the corner of the barn; but the Catahoula appeared and ran up to the rear guard, wagging his tail. We snapped flat against the barn and held our breath. "Jimmy," said the Texas twang. "Come back here and look at this dog. He's meaner-looking than your wife."

"I don't wanta see no damn dog."

"Good boy." He leaned down to pat the dog. I crept around behind him while he had his head down; and just as he turned to look up, I smacked him in the face with the rifle butt. Jack had snuck off to the front door.

"The hell's that noise?" said the guard inside.

"What noise, Jimmy?" I spoke low in a Texas twang as I took the knocked-out guard's pistol and bullet belt. The Catahoula sniffed the man's face. In a second, I heard Jack knock quietly on the front.

"Brung you some coffee," I heard him say.

"Good." I heard the front door creak, then a quick lick and a heavy thud.

"What's going on?" said Cull as Jack ran through the barn and raised the rear timber latch. The bald-faced gelding shot through the back door and straight into a stall. "It's ya'll, ain't it?"

We dragged the rear guard inside. Jack tied and gagged him; I ran to Cull and split his rope with my glades knife. "Where's Queenie?" I glanced around.

"They turned her loose." Cull shook his head. "They said it served no good purpose keeping her locked up when she could—"

"I understand," I said. "Just so's they didn't hurt her."

"I thought ya'll had hightailed without us."

"Give him a hand." I nodded toward Jack; Cull scrambled to him. "Chief," I said, "wake up." I shook Red Cloud by the shoulders. He looked up from beneath a thick knot on his forehead.

His eyes swam, but he recognized me. "Where's . . . my guns?"

Beside him, Run-around stirred. "Now what?" His voice sounded cross.

"It's us, Joe! Give me a hand; we gotta get him out of here!"

I heard a knock on the door and froze. "Open up, Jimmy, if you want this damn coffee." I glanced at Jack. He reached down, snatched the guard's hat from the floor, and put it on. With his head bowed, he eased open the door.

"Boss and some of the others are on their way. Here's a fresh pot." The man stepped inside, saw me, and stopped. Jack grabbed the pot of coffee with one hand and smacked him across the jaw with the pistol barrel. The man staggered, reaching for his gun; Cull, standing beside the door, reached in with the shotgun butt and busted him in the back of the head. A shot went off right in the man's holster as he fell.

"Come on! Let's go!" I pulled Red Cloud to his feet. Joe helped me loop his arms over my shoulders and we started for the back door. Jack slapped the timber latch shut on the front door.

"What's going on over there?" I heard Tillman's voice boom, as we ran to the rear. "Quick, surround it!" We heard boots running around the barn. We started out with Red Cloud; a shot slammed into the door.

"Damn it!" Joe pulled Red Cloud's arms up from over my shoulders and slung him away as I slammed the door and threw down the latch. Three more shots slapped the back wall. I spun toward Jack as he jumped away from flying splinters.

"Hold your fire!" I heard Tillman bellow. I glanced around. Cull stood behind a post with the guard's shotgun pointed at the front door; his knees shook. Jack stood in the middle of the floor with a rifle. "Who's in there? Crowe? Is that you?" I ran to the front and peeped through a crack. Tillman and six men crouched behind a wagon and a woodpile. Others came running in from all directions.

I spun toward Jack. "It looks bad!"

"Figures." Jack shrugged and walked to the coffeepot on the floor; somewhere a rooster crowed. "Glad I didn't throw this away. It's gonna be one of them long mornings."

* * *

"Tell him to go to hell." Jack sat on a nail keg in the middle of the floor, sipping the last of the coffee. It'd been over a half hour. Twice they'd tried to shoot us out, then they'd started talking.

"My friend says 'go to hell.' He says your coffee's cold."

"Weak, too." Red Cloud nodded beside me. The knot on his head was the size of a goose egg. He struck a firm pose and waved his arms slowly about the barn. "This is going well."

I leaned back from the door. "No, Mister Cloud, I think we're gonna die here . . . but maybe if you tell 'em you'll sign that damn treaty, it'll let their guard down enough that we can make a break for it."

"I . . . won't sign." Red Cloud sliced his cuffed hands through the air; his jaws tightened.

"I know, but you can tell them you will."

"Why lie? That's what they do. Look where they are. They are caught in their own trap. We are ready to devour them."

I leaned forward and peeped through the crack. McDowell had showed up; his troops were scattered out across the street with rifles. He stood behind the wagon next to Tillman. I shook my head. "We must be looking at this from different angles, Chief."

"Soon Standing Bear will sweep down and destroy them. Blood will run like streams from the great mountains. Dirty Jaw will bring me rifles. I will repay you for saving my life. We will drive our enemies from our country and live in peace."

"Jack," I said, "am I missing something here?"

Jack shook his head and sipped the coffee. "I like his version better, but I've got my doubts."

"Crowe," McDowell called out. "We're running out of patience. If you don't come out, our only alternative is to burn you out."

"Do it, you butter-mouthed son of a bitch! I swear to God I'll kill you before you get a chance to kill the chief."

"Why do you persist in thinking we're going to assassinate him?" McDowell stepped from behind the wagon with his arms spread; I fired a shot through the crack. He jumped back behind the wagon as the bullet thumped into it.

"Damn it, missed!" I slapped the pistol against my leg.

"Why don't you quit shooting," said Jack. "You can't hit nothing."

Cull called down from the hayloft, "They're lighting torches down the street!"

"Great," I breathed. "Ya'll alright up there?" I glanced up, and Joe poked his head down.

"I'd feel better if I had a gun."

"What the hell." I pitched him the pistol and a belt of bullets. "Don't shoot your foot off." I still had the other guard's rifle. Both guards sat wide-eyed and trembling where we'd tied them to a post. Earlier, I'd told Tillman we would kill them if he didn't let us go; he'd laughed.

"Jack? Yooo-hoo," Queenie called from the other side of the street. "Why don't you come on out, hon? I'll kiss it where it hurts . . ."

"Tell her I'm busy," Jack chuckled.

"He said he's busy." I turned to Jack. "Are you going to get up and do something today?"

Jack stood and walked near the front door. "Tillman, McDowell. If ya'll don't let us go . . . I'll beat the hell out of ya!" Two shots slapped into the door. Jack ducked away, and shrugged. "There, now what do you want from me? There ain't a damn thing to do but wait 'til they fire us up, then go out shooting. No point getting all worked up 'til then."

"This man, makes sense." Red Cloud nodded. "When Standing Bear comes, we will—"

"Chief!" I slammed my hat to the floor. "He's gonna kill ya! Why can't you get that through your head? There ain't gonna be no rifles and there ain't gonna be streams of blood, except ours!"

His eyes flashed, his jaw tightened. He stepped toward me. "Easy, Chief," said Jack. "He gets a little tense in these kinds of situations. He'll settle down once they go to killing us."

"I understand," said Cloud. He stared at me. "Why do you come to free me, if you are afraid to die?"

"Here they come with the torches," yelled Cull.

"Aw hell, Chief, I don't want get into all that. I'm here, they're out there." I waved the rifle. "You're a good feller—"

"Right down the street!" Cull's voice trembled.

"I couldn't leave, not after saying you could trust McDowell."

"I see. So now you want to die with me."

"It ain't so much that I want to—"

"But you are willing—"

"Do you hear me?" Cull screamed.

"I hear you, goddamn it! What am I supposed to do about it?"

Jack bit off a chew of tobacco, shook his head, and cocked his rifle. "You could be a little more polite," he chuckled. "They didn't ask to be here, you know."

"Holy God! Now there's Injuns coming, too!" Cull flew out of the loft screaming. His shotgun sailed through the air. Joe flew out behind him and grabbed him as he headed for the back door. They wallowed on the floor.

"Good," said Red Cloud. "Standing Bear will save us."

"Hold up with those torches," yelled Tillman. I jumped over and grabbed up the shotgun.

"I'm killing him and McDowell at the same time. Open that door, Jack, and cover me; that's all I ask!"

"That's the spirit!" Jack shot Red Cloud a grin. "I told you he'd settle down."

"Red Cloud," shouted Tillman, "one of your chiefs is here. He wants you to come out and talk." The sound of many hoofs faded to a halt. Horses nickered.

"Get the door, Jack! Tillman's first."

"Wait," said Red Cloud. "I will talk with Standing Bear."

"No! That's what this is all about. He's here to kill you and take over." I pointed the rifle at Red Cloud. "You ain't going out there!"

Red Cloud looked puzzled. "You will shoot me, to protect me?"

"It's his war," said Jack. "He can do what he wants to."

I lowered the rifle. "Chief, if you go out there, he'll kill you. I can't stop you, but damn it, this was all done to save you. Now you're throwing all our lives away for nothing."

"Standing Bear is a bold war chief, who wants much power. If he leads my people, he will lead them well. If I must die today, it is because it is time for another to take over the war. These are things the spirit tells us, if we listen."

"I say we throw open the door and shoot our way through them. If we make it, it's because the spirit wants us to; if we don't, we'll all die trying. Ain't that just as good as your way?"

Red Cloud smiled and turned to Jack. "He would've been a good warrior." He nodded and made signs with his hands. Jack reached out and slipped the timber latch.

◆❋ 39 ❋◆

Daylight spilled through the door as Jack stepped back into Red Cloud's shadow. Cull and Joe crept up beside me. I handed Cull his shotgun. His hands were steady. "Who should we shoot at?" he asked, glancing around slowly. We looked past the door at mounted Indians, soldiers lining the far side of the street, and Tillman's men cowered behind woodpiles, wagons, and water troughs.

"I don't know . . ." I shook my head. "Whoever you want to, I reckon." My voice sounded low and strange to me. Red Cloud walked out into the sunlight like a lamb to slaughter. "Just don't shoot me . . . if you can help it," I added, glancing between Cull and Run-around Joe. "Sorry I brung ya'll in on this."

"You oughta be," said Run-around.

"Be quiet, Joe." Cull's voice was calm. "Let's just do the best we can."

Red Cloud stopped for a second in the sunlight, then walked over and stared up at Standing Bear atop a tall roan. Standing Bear was seated in a shiny new cavalry saddle with a muzzle loader slung over his shoulder and a bow across his lap with an arrow in it. Behind him, thirty or more warriors held rein on their skittish horses. "They say, you will kill me, and become chief of the Sioux." Red Cloud's voice was strong, without fear. Standing Bear's only reply was a smug twitch of his jaw. The street fell under a tense silence.

McDowell ended the silence by clearing his throat with a nervous chuckle. "Gentlemen, who knows how these rumors get started?" He shot Tillman a glance. Tillman shrugged. "But let me assure everyone. We have no intention of harming anyone. We've only held you here overnight to insure your safety before riding on to Fort Laramie."

Red Cloud faced McDowell and raised his cuffed hands. McDowell looked more and more nervous. "That was a terrible mistake, Chief Red Cloud. We're taking those off you this instant. Perhaps if we sit down and iron out our communication difficulties, we could continue on to Laramie." He pivoted on his heel toward Tillman. "Mister Tillman, release Chief Red Cloud." I stood tense, ready to throw down any second.

"Of course," said Tillman. McDowell snapped back toward us. Cull and Joe had fanned out slowly across the front of the barn.

"And you gentlemen. *Please* lay down your guns and let us behave like rational adults."

Jack chuckled and spit a stream. "What's he think—we're a bunch of kids?" Red Cloud stepped into the middle of the street, and Tillman leaned down and unlocked his shackles. I stayed tense.

Red Cloud turned to us. "Listen to Chief McDowell and lay down your guns. This is a Sioux matter."

"Sorry, Chief," said Jack. "It's bad luck laying down your gun."

McDowell's face swelled red. "Sergeant, if these men try anything, shoot them down like dogs!"

"That goes for you men too," said Tillman, standing and pitching away the shackles. He reached out and started unlocking Red Cloud's handcuffs. "They're interfering with an Indian and government effort here. We're offering them a chance to leave. If they refuse, we owe them nothing."

For a second I wondered if we were in the wrong, if maybe all we had to do was drop our guns and go home, if maybe it was all some terrible misunderstanding. "Jack, are we—"

"Don't buy it," he said out of the corner of his mouth.

"I repeat," said McDowell, "this is a government matter and you are out of order here."

"Well . . . Standing Bear," called Tillman as he pitched away the handcuffs, "congratulations." He backed away from Red Cloud three feet. "You're about to become the chief—" I saw Standing Bear's bow come up from his lap. I started swinging my rifle up.

"—of the whole—" Red Cloud stared straight into Standing Bear's eyes as the bowstring pulled back tight. He dropped his hands to his sides as if welcoming death. I swung the rifle toward Standing Bear but saw I was too late. The arrow whistled. "—Sioux Nat—!" Tillman's hands flew up, grabbing the feathered end of the arrow sticking from his throat. The tip of it stuck out the back of his neck and seemed to pull him backward and down, as if pointing his way to hell. He slapped the ground with his eyes crossed; his face turned from blue to purple.

"Good shot," said Red Cloud, making signs to Standing Bear; and for a second the whole world seemed to draw its breath and hold it.

Two soldiers stepped forward staring at Tillman's body. Jack and I took a step back toward the barn door; a drum pounded in my head. McDowell threw out his arms like a savior waiting for his cross. "Wait!" His eyes snapped wide in confusion and fear. "I had no idea—" Then Red Cloud disappeared as if into thin air; and hell exploded.

McDowell took off down the middle of the street with arrows whistling past him. I took off right behind him, firing at him as bullets shot past me. "You, son, of, a, bitch." I punctuated each word with another shot but only managed to knock his hat off. Behind us, I heard Indians whooping and men screaming. McDowell struggled with his holster as he ran. As he rounded the corner of the alley beside the saloon, I tried to stop and take aim; but my shot only tore a chunk of wood off the corner as he went around it. Now I knew he'd have his pistol out, so I crouched as I ran forward.

I stopped suddenly as McDowell came wobbling backward out of the alley, his pistol dangling in his hand; the blood-smeared point of a cavalry sword stuck out his back. Bridger came walking out slowly. Rope dangled from his wrists. They must've had him tied. A rawhide gag hung loose from his chin. He followed like a stalking wolf as McDowell stumbled backward with a stunned look. "I'll be no part of such treachery, riding or walking." And McDowell fell to the dirt with the sword handle sparkling in the sun.

I turned and ran back toward the barn to help Jack. Two of Tillman's men came running toward me along the boardwalk. An arrow took one down; the other kneeled and took aim at ten yards.

I threw up the rifle and pulled the trigger. It just snapped, out of bullets. I knew he had me.

I started to jump away, but saw a big black hand wearing a broken handcuff reach out of the doorway and grab him by the neck. He tried to scream as Shod dangled him in the air and snatched the rifle from his hand. I ran on, waving my rifle like a club.

I heard Shod firing the man's rifle behind me as I leaped over the water trough and broke the rifle stock over a man's head. Beside him, Shod's bullet hit a man in the chest, and I snatched his pistol and kept going. The cavalry were retreating under a hail of arrows and rifle fire as I rolled through the barn door with bullets slapping the ground and tearing off chunks of wood. Tillman's men were well covered. The Indians chased the soldiers.

"Close the door," shouted Jack. I rolled to the side, swung the door half-closed, then jumped away as bullets streaked through it. One Drum Beat stood up in the straw rubbing his eyes. I shoved him down. "Where the hell're they going?" Jack motioned toward the Indians.

"They're chasing the cavalry."

"What about us?" Cull lay behind a bale of hay reloading a pistol. Joe lay beside him squeezing a wounded arm.

"Why don't they just leave?" he yelled. "They've got no more business here."

"I don't know! Why does everybody keep asking me all this stuff?"

Shod came rolling through the door, knocking it wide open. "Why did you close the door on me?"

"Where'd he come from?" Jack shot Shod a glance, then fired through a crack.

"Who the hell is *he*?" Cull yelled above the rifles.

"Damn it! Everybody shut up!" I jumped over, pulling my bandanna loose and making a quick tourniquet for Joe's arm. "Hold it tight."

For a second the firing stopped. I turned toward the door. "Crowe," said one of the men. "Give yourself up and the rest can walk out of here. We know there's a reward for you. We're gonna make something out of this mess."

Jack shook his head. "I'll be damned."

"Send him out here," said another voice. "No need in all of you dying."

"I'll clear this up," said Shod. He crawled around behind the door, closing it as he spoke. "You men listen up out there." He raised his badge and held it past the door as he closed it. "I'm an agent with the United States Secret Service. This man is my prisoner. Now, leave here immediately." Shots pounded the door. The badge exploded in a spray of blood. One round split the door and knocked Shod backward. Jack jumped over and dragged him to safety as blood ran from a graze across his head.

"Secret Service your black ass," yelled a voice.

"And I'm Santa Claus," said another. "Five minutes and we'll burn you out of there. Give 'im up."

"My finger is gone," I heard Shod say as Jack wiped blood from his face.

"You're alright," said Jack.

"I know." Shod held up his left hand. His third finger was gone at the first knuckle. "But look, it's gone." Blood ran down his hand.

"That's okay. It'll grow back," Jack said seriously.

"Fingers don't grow back," Shod snapped, squeezing his wrist.

"Who is he?" Cull watched Shod tend to his bloody hand.

"Ya'll were drunk when you met him, but he's with us."

"Is he really whatever he said he is?"

"I reckon."

"And we're all his prisoners?"

"No . . . just me, but not really. I mean . . . just forget it, and no more questions, okay?"

"Three minutes," said the voice.

I looked around at Shod, Jack, the two cowboys, and the old Indian. The two guards still sat tied to the post, scared and shaking. One had a long splinter sticking in his leg. If they burned us out, we'd all die. I couldn't see the point.

"Listen up out there. I'm coming out."

"No you ain't," said Jack. "Not if I have to knock you in the head."

I crawled over to him and Shod. "I ain't going to give myself up. But if I take off, they'll follow me and give you a chance to get away." I turned to Shod. "Is Kermit still back there with the horses?" Shod's spectacles lay in the hay beside him. I snatched them up and shoved them in my pocket without him seeing a thing.

"Yeah," said Shod, leaning up on his elbows, "but I moved him back a hundred yards in case there was trouble. You'll never get through to him, though. There's three men still guarding the back door. I saw them when I came through."

"I can blast out of here on the bald-face while Jack gives me some cover."

"No way," said Jack. "That crooked-backed son of a bitch will fall down, and you know it."

"Not from here to Kermit. I can change horses and leave 'em sitting. Meanwhile ya'll go and I'll catch up to you."

"I don't like it." Jack spit a stream.

"I'm going, and that's that. I just need you to cover me."

I found an old saddle lying inside an empty stall, took it and pitched it on the gelding. The horse jumped around like it'd been years since anything had been on his back. "This ain't gonna work," said Jack.

"One minute," said a voice outside.

I pulled the gelding from the stall and swung up quickly. The horse went crazy, running and kicking all around the barn. "Open the door," I yelled, barely holding on as the gelding swung past the front door and drew shots from outside.

"He's making a run for it!" I heard boots pounding around the barn as Jack swung open the door and I charged out. Two riflemen sprang up as I tore across the grass toward the tree line. I heard a shot and saw one fall as I plowed right over the other. His rifle went off and cut a graze across my shoulder. "Get your horses," I heard someone yell behind me, but I knew I'd be well away by the time they started. I pounded out through the tree line.

When I slid to a halt twenty feet from Kermit, he just stayed sitting on a rock with his head in his hands. "Come on, Kermit, I gotta move out. Take the other horses up near the barn and wait for Jack's signal." I started to swing down when I heard the pistol cock close to my head. I snapped toward it and saw the flash of Parker Pope's gold tooth behind a tiny derringer. I froze.

"You just keep stepping in shit, don't you?" He reached out, took the pistol from my belt, and cocked it in his other hand. I glanced at his horse; it was Jack's, with both the blanket roll and saddlebags full of cash. I listened for horses behind me but heard none.

"There's a posse right behind me. If they catch me, they catch you. You're wanted too."

"I don't hear nothing. Now, let's go."

"I'll have to change horses. This one has a crooked back. He'll give out and fall." I listened for the riders behind me. Nothing.

"Quit stalling." He pointed the gun closer.

"I ain't stalling. It's the truth. I don't want to get caught no more than you do. You heard the ruckus." Still no sound from Crofton. "They're right behind me."

He bit his lip for a second. "Alright, hurry up."

I slid from the saddle and pitched Kermit the reins. He caught them without getting up. Grabbing the biggest horse of the bunch, I swung up. Just as I did, I heard Indians yelling in the distance and the sound of gunfire from Crofton; but no riders. "Sounds like the posse ran into trouble." Pope grinned. "Now it's all going my way."

I eased my horse close to his, and he raised the pistol to my face. I let out a breath. "I'm glad somebody's happy. I sure ain't." I stared him straight in the eyes. "Are you gonna kill me after I take you to the money?"

"I oughta, after ya'll running my gang off. But naw, not unless I have to." His grin broadened. "All I want's the money. At least I won't have to share it. Hell, we're in the same business. You just got outsmarted, is all."

"What do you mean?"

He stepped his horse almost against mine and held up the derringer. "You can think about this for the rest of your life." He broke open the derringer and laughed in my face. "It's empty."

I laughed along with him. "Want to hear something else funny?"

He nodded with me, holding the pistol firm. "What?"

"So's mine." I laughed and slapped my leg. His grin disappeared; his neck stiffened. His eyes darted to the pistol, and in that split second I shoved his gun hand in the air. At the same time, I whipped out the glades knife with my left hand and cracked him across the nose with the brass handle. He fell to the ground like a bundle of rags. Kermit jumped forward, grabbed the pistol, and pitched it to me.

"Why, thank you, Kermit." I reckon my surprise showed on my face. He just nodded.

Pope struggled to his feet, holding his nose. "Goddamn it, Crowe. You broke my damn nose."

I shook my head. "You're too stupid to be an outlaw. You oughta go back to school or something."

He jumped behind Kermit and threw his arm around his throat. "Aw yeah? One move and I'll cut his head off, I swear I will."

Kermit's eyes sprang open. I leaned forward and shrugged. "What with?"

Pope's eyes darted around, then back to mine. "I've got a knife in my boot, same as you. Now, drop the gun!"

"Give it up, Pope." I shook my head. "It's been a long day and it still ain't over."

He let go with a sheepish grin. "Did I have you there for a second?"

"No."

"Gonna kill me?"

"No. It's just something for you to think about the rest of *your* life."

"I don't suppose you'd give me part of the money . . . say, ten thousand? That leaves you an awful lot."

"No. You know that ain't how it works. Now, take that mule if you want it and get out of here."

"You ain't gonna shoot me in the back, like my brother Gyp?"

"Huh-uh, just go."

Pope walked to the mule, wiping blood on the back of his hand. He took the reins and turned to me. "You going to tell anybody about this?" He waved his hand around the clearing.

"Not if you don't."

He hesitated a second. "Are you really Miller Crowe, the horseman for the James Gang?"

"Would I admit it if I was?"

"I understand." I saw a flash of a gold tooth as he slid up the mule and let out a breath. "I was just wondering if they might be hiring."

"I wouldn't know." I shook my head. "For what it's worth, if I was you, I'd work on my skills some. You'd never make it in Missouri."

"I wish you'd let me have some of my money . . . five thousand maybe?"

"I won't, so go away." I almost felt sorry for him as he turned with his head down and started for the woods. "Parker," I called out. He turned. "I'm sorry about killing Gyp. I truly am."

"That's the way this business goes," he said. "But I didn't mean what I said that day about not giving a shit that you killed him."

"I know you didn't. He was your brother."

"I was just sounding off, trying to look good for the gang."

"I understand."

"This is a hard business." He shrugged. "But I don't have to tell you that."

I smiled a tired smile and watched him ride away on the mule. "No, you sure don't," I said under my breath.

When I heard brush breaking behind me, I turned quickly with my pistol pointed. "Don't pop no cap on me," I heard Jim Bridger say as he rode into the clearing on one fine-looking army horse and leading another behind him. He cackled and slapped his leg. "That was some rip-snorter if I do say so."

I lowered my pistol. "I'm glad you weren't in with McDowell," I said. "For a while I had my doubts."

"Me? With that bunch? Why, I'd be insulted if I wasn't having so much fun. I swear . . . it was like the old days back there for a while." But his smile turned down on the corners. "Except for the treachery, that is." He spit and shook his head. "This new breed of soldiers don't know how to have fun."

I just stared at him. "So now you're leaving?"

"Yep. Got a couple good horses and a fine rifle. Figured I'd make a sweep west before heading back . . . kick up my heels one more time before they tie me to a rocking chair. Want to go with me?"

I almost laughed. "No, thanks. I'm heading back to Missouri, soon as I finish up here."

Bridger gazed off and smiled. "Missouri. Now, that used to be a fine place—"

"Still is," I said.

He smiled. "To you young fellers, I reckon it'll do. I like a little more room and a little less folks myself." He narrowed a gaze into my eyes. "You ain't gonna mention me gut-hooking McDowell, are ya?"

"I couldn't care less," I said. "You oughta get a medal. I can't believe the army would stoop to such a thing."

"It ain't the army," he said. "They's just ole boys like ourselves. It's the wheels behind it . . . over there." He pointed a finger east. I imagined for a split second that it was dead on the mark to the front door of the White House. "Time was, when a common feller like me could ride right in, tell 'em what was wrong and how to fix it." He spit. "Not anymore, not unless I was carrying a tote-sack of money or had a powerful bunch of friends. I tell ya, government's out of control."

"Well . . . I got no time to talk politics," I said. "Nothing I can do about it anyway. I'm just an outlaw . . . an outsider." I turned my horse away from the clearing and back toward Crofton.

"Ha! That's what all you young fellers say. So I reckon that makes it true." He called out as Kermit and I disappeared into the woods. "If you think of it . . . tell old Red Cloud I did what I could, alright?"

"He probably already knows it," I called back over my shoulder.

◆✳ 40 ✳◆

On the short ride back to Crofton, Kermit and I heard the squeaking freight wagon coming through the brush beside us. "Wait up," called Dirty Jaw. We reined up as he topped a low rise and rolled in beside us. "I saw some of Bear's men chasing some cavalry out across the valley. Looks like we're still cooking on the rifle deal." He grinned.

"You're a piece of work," I said, gigging my horse forward and leading the bald-faced gelding.

"It's just business. You should understand that. How'd Red Cloud come out of it?"

"Alive and kicking." I shook my head. "It was strange. You really had to be there."

He laughed. "Nothing surprises me about that old man. You know, he was once captured by some Shoshoni and watched them cut strips off his legs and cook 'em for supper."

"Go on now . . ."

"No lie. They say later on he caught their chief, cut his heart out, and took a bite of it."

"That's enough. I don't want to hear it."

"He'll have something special for both of us, you know. Me for bringing in these rifles, you for handling the deal."

I looked at Jaw and rubbed the back of my neck. "Why do you suppose he had me do this? I mean, anybody could've met you and handed you the money. Why me?"

"You can't tell about these old blanket Indians. He mighta had a dream, saw a vision." He shrugged. "Maybe he wants to prove a point. Hell, who knows? . . . Probably has something to do with you saving his life."

"Well, I didn't do it for a reward. The man was wounded."

"Why'd you save his bacon this time?" Jaw spit. "You didn't owe it to him. You could've been long gone before anybody knew you set him up for the railroad. You might even get a little cash—"

"I reckon it's something you wouldn't understand," I said, tapping my horse forward and leading the bald-faced gelding.

Dirty Jaw laughed and slapped the reins. "Suit yourself. I'll be just as big a hero as you, and I didn't even risk getting killed."

When we climbed up on the road into Crofton, Kermit and I trotted in ahead of the wagon. We reined our horses to a walk as I looked around at the bodies strewn along the shell of a town. Evidently Tillman's men had ran smack into Red Cloud and Standing Bear as the Indians came back for us. Ahead of us, Jack and Red Cloud stood on the boardwalk outside the saloon and watched us ride forward.

"Mister Cloud was just telling me," Jack said, "that he wants people to know what went on here, so's they can see he ain't the bad guy the army's made him out to be."

"Good idea. There ain't an American north or south that'd hold with this kind of double-dealing."

I swung off my horse and hitched it and the bald-faced gelding to a post. I turned back to them as Kermit slid down from his saddle and wandered around the street. "The fact is—"

"Where are, my rifles?" Red Cloud faced me with his arms folded. I pushed up my hat and grinned.

"I'm glad you asked, Mister Cloud. They're right up the road, headed this way."

Red Cloud cocked his head, smiled, and bounced up on his big roan. "I'll be, right back."

Three braves fell in beside him as he galloped to the edge of town. "I'm glad to get that off my back," I said. "Where's Shod and the cowboys?"

"They're inside licking their wounds. You missed quite a stir here."

"I bet." I glanced once more around the street. The bodies of Tillman and McDowell were missing. Standing Bear trotted his horse around the side of the livery barn and up to us.

The horse reared as he stopped and looked down at me. "I have watched you wander back and forth in my country, and asked myself why Red Cloud would not let me kill you. He said you are dumb but your heart is right."

"I reckon that's a compliment, kind of."

"I have never seen one man steal as many horses."

"I've kept busy, that's true."

"Why did you think I would kill my brother Red Cloud to become chief?"

I glanced at Jack and cleared my throat, glanced up the road and wished Red Cloud hadn't rode away. "Well . . . a lot of people thought you would do most anything to become chief of all the Sioux. I reckon if they hadn't thought it, Tillman wouldn't have offered you the deal."

A smile twitched at his narrow lips. "He asked me if I thought it would be *wise* business to kill Red Cloud and take over. I told him it would. I did not *say* I would do it. How can a man lead his country by becoming chief through trickery and deceit? What kind of country would he lead? Where would he lead it? What kind of people would follow?"

I let out a breath. "You've got a point, but believe it or not, Chief, it happens every day. They call it 'politics.' "

"Pile of what?"

"Never mind." I waved my hand. "It's a way of doing whatever you *want* to, and saying you *had* to . . . in order to *get* to where you *need* to . . . to, lead others?" I glanced at Jack and shrugged. "Help me out here."

He shook his head. "I've got time to talk to that banjo player while you straighten out the world."

"Do what?" I looked at Jack, but he turned and walked away.

"Then we have nothing to fear from such foolish people," said Standing Bear, still attending to our conversation atop his prancing white horse as Jack walked into the saloon.

I raised my brow. "If I were you, I'd be scared, very scared. You don't know them like I do."

He reared his horse and shot me a disgusted glance before riding off to Red Cloud. "White men . . ."

I walked into the saloon and saw Shod leaning on the bar holding a wet rag to his head. Without his eyeglasses, his eyes looked beady and weak. His left hand was wrapped in a bloody bandanna. Beside him, two Sioux warriors leaned on the bar riffling a deck of cards and looking at the pictures. One had a bloody war axe lying beside his elbow. The bartender stood behind the bar with a nervous smile and a long trickle of sweat running down his forehead. "So," I heard him say, "you gentlemen in town for long?"

Kid Cull and Run-around Joe sat at a table sweating and holding their heads; Joe had a heavy bandage around his arm. Cull seemed tense and ready to jump up screaming. One Drum Beat was up and around, pinching at one of the whores and dangling a bottle of rye whiskey. At the far end of the bar, Jack stood arguing with the banjo player. "It don't take but two or three strings to play most songs, and I know it. You're just being hardheaded."

"Jack," I said. "If we're through here, I wouldn't mind heading back to Missouri." I saw two spoons hanging from his hand.

"I'm just trying to work up a little music here." Jack pointed at the banjo player. "But he acts like I ain't professional enough to suit him."

"No, no, that's not it at all. I've broken two strings—"

"Where's Pope?" I heard Shod's voice, and turned around. His eyes looked tiny without the spectacles. They seemed to swim around the room. "Have you seen my spectacles?"

"Pope's dead." I shrugged. "And no, I haven't seen your spectacles. You're supposed to look out for your own personal stuff. I left Pope's body near the creek."

"I'll have to see it . . . when we go for the money."

"Sure." I shrugged. "But how can you see it without your glasses?" I grinned and clapped my hands. "Everybody listen up. Have any of you seen this man's spectacles? He can't seem to find them." I'd already decided. If I could tear Jack away from his musical interest, I would ask Red Cloud to hold Shod's glasses long enough for Jack and me to get a good head start. I harbored no ill feelings now that things were winding down. It's easy to forgive when you're rich.

"Damn you, Crowe!"

"Why, Agent Shadowen. That's the first time I've heard you cuss."

Shod's weak eyes darted about the room. "You'd drive a holy man to cursing. You're still under arrest!" His eyes tried to locate me.

"Sure." I winked at Jack, but he was busy slapping the spoons against his leg. "But how will you get us back without bumping into trees . . ."

Queenie walked through the door and put a hand to her hip. "Cloud wants you outside," she said to me. "Somebody should teach that old turd some manners."

I walked past her as Jack started behind me. "What'd he do?" asked Jack, rattling the spoons against the palm of his hand.

"I just tried to tickle his crotch . . . you know, just being friendly? You wouldn't believe what he said!"

"The nerve," Jack chuckled under his breath.

Outside, Red Cloud, Standing Bear, and four warriors sat on horses and stared as I stepped out the door. Standing Bear's bow lay across his lap. Beside them, Dirty Jaw sat on the wagon seat wearing a proud smile. "Where is, the money for the rifles?" Red Cloud leaned forward in his cavalry saddle.

I reached inside my shirt and pulled the stack of gun money from behind my belt. It was damp with sweat. "That's where you've been carrying it?" Jack looked concerned.

I riffled through it. "Yeah, why? Something wrong?"

"It don't seem safe. What if we'd run into trouble?"

I just stared at him as I handed the money up to Red Cloud.

He backed his horse and stepped it beside the wagon. Pitching it down to Dirty Jaw, he smiled and made sign. "You wanted to ride with my warriors and I said you must prove what you are. You have."

Dirty Jaw riffled the stack of money, took out a bill, examined it, and popped it between his fingers. "It wasn't easy, Chief, let me tell you." Jaw shot me a glance and pretended to wipe sweat from his brow.

"Some said, I could not trust you, but they were wrong. I told them you would do what it took to bring me rifles if there was pretty picture money for you." Red Cloud spread a proud smile. "I was right." He motioned his warriors in from the street as Jaw held the dollar bill before him. "See this," Red Cloud called out. "This is the reward for any Sioux warrior who helps his people—" Jaw beamed as if holding up an award plaque. The arrow whistled straight through the dollar bill, pinned it to his chest, and nailed him to the back of the wagon seat. "—for a handful of pretty pictures." Red Cloud finished his sentence with a frown of contempt.

"Jesus!" I winced. Dirty Jaw let the stack of money spill from his hands. The band broke as it hit the wagon wheel; bills fluttered along the street. Two whores jumped into the mud, screaming, snatching, giggling . . .

Dirty Jaw's eyes turned into two question marks, then traveled to a far place and quit asking. His hands fell from the arrow and relaxed in his lap. "Good shot." Red Cloud spoke and made sign to Standing Bear. He reached out, broke off the arrow, and slid the bill off the stub. Waving it over his head, "The pretty picture is not strong. It's medicine is not real. Arrows go through it, blood colors it . . ." He stepped his horse around the wagon and stopped before me. I swallowed hard as everyone but Jack stepped away. "And men of honor do not let it come between them." He stared deep into my eyes.

"This man came to bring horses to our enemies. He loves these pretty pictures." Again he waved the bloody bill; again I saw his contempt as he looked at it. "He came to make money from our sorrow."

"Easy, Chief," said Jack with his hand near his pistol. I glanced at him and saw his crazy grin—the wildcat showing its fangs. I figured he'd go first for Standing Bear. I'd try for Red Cloud, as bad as I hated to, then we'd fall back inside and do what we could.

I heard a creaking sound on the boardwalk and caught a glimpse of Shod stepping quietly beside me. He whispered out the corner of his mouth, "You'll have to tell me where to shoot. I can't see a thing."

Standing Bear's horse slung its head and stomped a hoof. A feather fluttered in its mane. Bear stared at me, wearing the same grin as Jack; but his fangs didn't show.

"But I took this man's horses and I asked him to bring me rifles," Red Cloud continued. "At first he said 'Yes' because he was sick on pup stew." My belly growled just hearing him say it. "Then he said

'No' because he saw what our warriors did to his people." Red Cloud turned back to me with a proud smile; but I'd seen what that smile did to Jaw. I let my hand drift closer to my holster.

"When the soldiers—" Red Cloud stopped and searched my eyes for the right word.

I shrugged tensely. "Screwed?"

"When the soldiers 'screwed' him out of the horse money, he stole all their horses and their money and came back to me."

The braves nodded among themselves. I thought it a good sign; but then Bear raised his bow and propped it straight up from his lap. "Now I reward him for saving my life." I almost threw down as Red Cloud reached forward and handed me the bloody bill. I reached to take it and he held on a second. He made a crafty smile and twitched his head toward Bear. "We had you, going there, didn't we?"

I let out a breath and almost rocked forward. "That ain't no way to do a feller, Chief." I looked at the bloody bill and held it up—away from my chest just to make me feel better. "Thank you, thank you very much." I waved a still-trembling hand as the warriors whooped and cheered.

I leaned forward toward Red Cloud and spoke just between the two of us. "I still don't know why you had me bring them rifles. Anybody could've—"

"It was a gift for you saving my life." His eyes took on a crafty slant. "Honor." Red Cloud laid his fist against his chest. "You needed to give your word, and keep it. You needed someone to take your word, and believe it."

"Well . . ." I rubbed my jaw; I didn't know what to say. I looked again at the dollar, then back at Red Cloud.

His voice dropped to a low chant. "Until a man finds something he will die for, he is a man with no reason for being alive."

His words flashed across my shoulders like cold lightning as I pictured the same words from the mouth of Cletis Avery, the week before he died.

"I've heard that before," I said softly, feeling as if a wise hand had reached and touched me from a long ways off.

"I know," Red Cloud said, and he paused a second, looking deeper into my spirit than anyone ever had, then or since. "But now you know what it means." He smiled and backed his horse as I stood there dumbfounded.

"Once again you've managed to impress everyone," Shod breathed beside me. But I didn't even answer. I watched Red Cloud slip from his horse, and I followed him into the saloon.

Inside the saloon, some of the braves brought in Tillman's and McDowell's bodies and pitched them on the floor. The braves glanced toward the bartender; he wiped a towel across his forehead and nervously polished a shot glass. "I just serve refreshments." He tried to grin. "I don't see nothing."

Red Cloud looked down at the bodies and pointed at each as he spoke. "Business." His finger hovered over Tillman's corpse. McDowell lay with arms outspread as if ready for a cross. "Government." He pointed at McDowell as a fly crawled across the dead colonel's nose. "It is done. All of the white man's medicine has been destroyed. They have come at me with their 'progress.' They have gone crazy wanting more, and they leave here with nothing, not even their life."

The braves nodded; one stepped forward, grabbed Tillman by the hair, and drew a knife. Red Cloud stopped him with the wave of a hand. "There is no honor in taking the hair of such men as these." He turned to me with a firm smile. "They talked, but I did not listen. They preached, but I would not pray. Now there is nothing left for the white man to do but surrender. When the Moon of the Cold comes and sweeps snow under the tepee, we will have our land back and keep it from now on. I will travel to the big river by the bucket of mud and tell all who will listen that we are here. That we will always be here."

"I hate to bust it up," Queenie yelled from the street, "but there's enough cavalry coming to break the bed slats."

Kid Cull jumped up, knocking the table over. "I can't stand it no more! Yiiii . . ." He ran screaming through a glass window; in a second we heard his horse's hoofbeats headed out of town.

"Poor feller," said Jack. "I reckon he just sobered up too much all at once."

"Now, I go." Red Cloud and his warriors started for the door.

"Wait, Chief." I stepped before him. "You knew all this, exactly how it would be, right? Knew Standing wouldn't kill you and knew I'd come to warn you, right? That's right, ain't it?"

"I had to come get the rifles," Red Cloud said. "What safer way than with the army?"

I slapped my forehead. "Jesus!"

Red Cloud laughed and placed his hand on my chest. "You came here empty, not knowing why." He tapped my chest firm but gently. "Leave here full. Guard the gift I gave you. Keep it strong. Go with *honor.*" He turned toward the door.

"But, Chief, wait!" I started after him. I don't know why.

"No time." Red Cloud threw his words over his shoulder on his way out. "Write me a letter."

"A letter? Damn it, Chief—"

Red Cloud glanced back and winked as he and the braves disappeared through the door, and in a second they were gone. I stood and watched them fade into the sparkling sunlight. Looking around the empty street, I tried to think of something to say, or think, or do. Finally I turned as Jack gathered his rifle and snatched up a bottle of rye. "Put this on my tab," he called over his shoulder to the bartender. "We better get out of here ourselves."

"What tab?" The bartender shrugged with his palms up.

"You're not going anywhere," Shod bellowed. He turned and fell over the upturned table. Joe and One Drum Beat helped him to his feet. He slung them away. "Crowe!" But I followed Jack through the door, jumped from the boardwalk, and looked around for the horse with the blanket roll.

"Come on," Jack shouted, already in the saddle and backing his horse.

"Jack! The money's gone!" I kept turning in circles looking for my horse. "It's gone, goddamn it! My horse . . . and the money!" Next to where my horse should've been, Cull's sorrel mare stood at the hitch post calmly gnawing its bit. I stood looking at it with my arms spread and my mouth hanging open. It shook out its mane and nickered right in my face.

"Alls I can say is, Kid ain't no horse thief." Joe shook his head as we rode along the back trail out of Crofton. "No, sir. If he took it, it's just on a'count of he's scared shitless. You ought not tormented him so bad." Beside him, One Drum Beat nodded in agreement. The Catahoula loped along with us, followed by the bald-faced gelding.

"Shut up, Joe, or I'll kill ya." I was strung tighter than a cheap fiddle. Behind us, I heard the voice of Captain Fetterman bringing his column to a halt as we slipped out of town. "You better hope and pray we find him," I said.

"Hell, you can have my horse." Joe patted his horse's shoulder. "I don't want no hard feelings. A horse is a horse. I'll even throw in one of these jugs if it'll square things."

We followed Cull's tracks until they faded into a rock slope. Evening turned gray as we sat gazing across a flat stretch of grassland at a tiny cloud of dust on the distant horizon. "He'll be in Texas before he ever slows down." I glanced at Jack. "We'll never catch up to him."

Jack spit a stream. "I'm starting to think this whole trip ain't nothing but a headache. I wish I'd stayed home and just read some travel books about the Orient. Or maybe gone south to the shores and ate a fish."

"If you let us go, I'll tell him you want your horse back just as soon as I see him. I swear I will."

I glanced at Jack; he shrugged and lowered his head. I looked at Run-around Joe and One Drum Beat, and nodded my head. "Give us a jug and get the hell out of here."

"I shore do thank ya." Joe let out a breath. "And I mean it about telling him. I really do. You'll see. He'll send that horse right back. He will."

One Drum Beat laid his hand on his heart. "I will speak of you for a long time to come, of all the great battles we fought side by side. I will tell of our courage and of how we pursued our enemies—"

I drew my pistol. "Get out of here!"

Jack and I sat watching in silence until Run-around Joe and One Drum Beat became two thin streams of dust in the red glow of evening sunlight.

"Can't speak for you, but it's sure been one hell of a vacation for me," Jack chuckled. I heard the cork pop from the jug of whiskey and turned toward Jack just as he threw back a drink and let out a sigh.

"Is that stuff as bad as I recall it being?" I slumped in my saddle and pushed up my hat.

"Yep," Jack said, stifling a belch, "only it's aged some since the last time you tried it."

"Good." I reached over and took the jug, tipped it in a toast to the vanishing cowboy and Indian on the distant horizon, and threw back a swallow.

Part VII
American Balladeers

✦✳ 41 ✳✦

I opened my eyes the next morning with a terrible pounding inside my head. My stomach felt like I'd spent the night swallowing hot rocks. The Catahoula cur sat beside me, poking his wet nose in my face and making long licks up the side of my head. I heard a dark quiet laugh and raised up on my elbows. Parker Pope sat on a rock with the jug between his feet and a rifle pointed at us. I saw sunlight flash on his gold tooth.

"Jack," I said in a near whisper. "Wake up. We've got company." A few feet from Pope, I saw Long Jake's body lying facedown in the dirt. A wide puddle of blood spread beneath his throat.

"Leave me alone!" Jack growled, rolled over, and slung his arm over his face.

"He can't help you." Pope smiled. "I snuck his gun. Yours too." He patted his waist where he'd stuck our weapons. "You probably want to know how I found you."

"I don't really give a damn, Pope." I rubbed my pounding head.

"Well . . . I just tracked this sum-bitch and he led me right to you. Most of his bunch got wiped out by the Shoshoni. He would've killed you, but I slipped in and cut his throat."

"So what? Does that make you a big-time outlaw? Killing Jake Howard ain't nothing."

Pope looked surprised. "I always heard he was really something, big gun out of Kansas."

"Whatever you say." I shrugged and glanced around the camp. I needed an edge, some way to get the drop on him. I glanced at my right boot but only saw my dirty foot sticking up. Beside me, Jack snored.

"Give it up, Crowe. I even took off your boot and threw your knife over the ledge. There ain't nothing you can do but give me the money." He cocked the rifle. "So where is it?"

At the sound of the rifle cocking, Jack snapped up from his blanket and slapped his empty holster. He staggered around bleary-eyed. "I tell ya, boys." Pope stood up, pointing the rifle. "I was pretty slick getting the drop on ya like this."

"Pull that trigger and you'll bring every lunatic in Powder River down on us."

"What's going on?" Jack dropped back down and rubbed his eyes.

"I ain't stupid. I'll tie ya up and skin ya 'til one of you tells me where it is."

"Hell with it." Jack yawned and lay back down. "It's in my saddlebags, what's left of it. The rest is on its way to Texas just as hard as it can ride."

Pope stepped to the horses without taking his eyes from us. "I bet the James Gang would be real glad to get a feller like me riding with them, once they hear of this."

"Sure, right, Pope. This will go down in history." I shook my head and mumbled under my breath. "Stupid bastard."

Pope slung the saddlebags over his shoulder, untied our horses, and shooed them away. He walked back to a scrub bush, untied his horse, and stepped to the edge of the overhang. He jerked our guns from his belt and threw them out into the air. "I ain't gonna kill ya. I want ya to have to think about this a long time. I want ya to remember who it was—"

An explosion belched from behind a tree and Pope spun like a lopsided top. The saddlebags fell to the ground as Pope flew out off the ledge. Jack and I jumped to run. "Don't make a move, goddamn yas!" We turned slowly into the crazy, grinning face of Ben Bone behind a smoking double-barreled shotgun.

Pope's horse galloped away as Bone stepped forward and hefted the saddlebags. "Fuck with ole Ben long enough, and you wind up getting the Bone." He cackled; we stood staring. "You sons a bitches thought you'd seen the last of me? Let me tell ya both, my luck just took a straight-up change!" He shook the saddlebags and laughed louder.

"I don't wants spoil this for you, Bone, but that shotgun just brought in everybody from here to the Canadian Rockies. Kill us, and you ain't got a chance, especially without a horse."

"Aw-haw-haw! I've got a horse. Yes-sir!" He backed to the edge of the brush, reached around the tree, and pulled the reins on the bald-faced gelding. The horse bounced into the clearing like it was ready to run a race.

"I hate to tell you, Bone, but that horse has a crooked spine. He won't go two miles without sitting down—"

"Shut up, you lying bastard. I watched you ride him out from Crofton the other day like the devil was on your ass. You ain't tricking me."

"But, Bone—"

"Leave him alone," Jack chuckled. "Can't you see his losing streak is over? We're the ones you need to worry about here."

Bone swung the saddlebags up behind the worn-out saddle and tied it down with one hand while he kept us covered. "I always liked you better than this sum-bitch," he said to Jack. "Since I've only got one shot, I ain't gonna kill you." He swung up in the saddle and aimed the shotgun at me. "But him—"

The gelding reared high and the gun fired straight up in the air. "Get him!" Jack and I dove forward, but the gelding spun and headed down toward the trail like a Thoroughbred. Sprawled on my stomach, I picked up a handful of dirt and threw it. "Goddamn it! We ain't had no luck for the longest time."

A few minutes later, we sat looking out over the ledge, sipping from the jug of "wonderful stuff," and watching Bone's dust as he pounded across the valley below. "There goes the last of our money." Jack raised the jug and took a long swallow.

From the cover of brush fifty yards to Bone's right, I saw the band of Sioux dart forward in pursuit. I nudged Jack and took the jug. "Look at this, talking about luck." We watched Bone slapping the reins as the Indians drew closer; but the harder he slapped, the slower the gelding ran. By the time the Sioux were within ten yards, the gelding wound down to a slow walk. Bone gigged and whipped like he was at a full run. We could hear him hollering. Then as the

Indians circled him, the gelding reared high, came down slowly, and sat down like a tired old man relaxing in an armchair. The horse just turned its head back and forth calmly, watching the Indians trot up around him. "I tried to tell him," I said under my breath. "Reckon that's Brown Horse's bunch?" We passed the jug back and forth as they drug him from the gelding. They tied a long rope around his feet and took off, dragging him back to the cover of the brush.

"Brown Horse, White Horse, Black Horse, what's the difference?" Jack stood and dusted the seat of his trousers. "They'll skin him, whoever they are."

"Yeah." I stood up and limped around on my one boot. "We better get on out of here before somebody else shows up." No sooner than I said it, I heard the heavy thud of a hoof and looked up at Big Shod sitting atop a buckskin mare. In one hand he held a rifle propped straight up from his saddle, in the other he held a long-stemmed reading glass. "I'll be damned." I just threw up my arms.

"Where's Pope and the money?" He gigged his horse forward, looking around at Jake Howard's body and the bloody mess at the edge of the cliff. Jack sat down with the jug in his lap and just stared out across the valley.

"Pope is laying somewhere over this ledge with his head blown off. The money is down there with Ben Bone and a band of Sioux warriors. I reckon they'll be skinning him if they ain't already." Kermit Bone stepped his horse out of the brush, over to the edge, and gazed down. One of the Indians had taken the saddle and bridle from the gelding; it grazed in a short circle with wind whipping its mane and tail.

"I thought you told me yesterday that Pope was dead." Shod stepped his horse around the campsite.

"Just look down there and tell me how lively he looks to you." Shod shook his head. "You're never without an answer."

"And you're never without a smart mouth." I reached down and started rolling up my shirtsleeves. "Are we under arrest?"

Shod watched me through the reading glass. "Why? Are you getting ready to wash clothes . . . or do dishes?"

"I'm getting ready to kick your ass, you big son of a bitch. Are we under arrest or not?" Beside me Jack chuckled under his breath.

"What difference would it make, as far as us fighting?"

"You can't just answer a question, can you?"

"Certainly I can. Can you?"

"See? See what I mean?" I began circling him, ready to fight.

"The answer is no. You're not under arrest." He pointed a long finger at me. "And I'm not going to fight you, you fool. If you persist. If you try to force me into it. I promise, I'll pick you up and throw you out there." He thumbed toward the valley.

I let out a breath, gazed over the edge of the cliff. "You're lucky I've got a headache."

"Who killed Long Jake?"

"Pope."

"And Bone killed Pope?"

"Right, that's what I said."

"Now the Indians are killing Bone?"

"Yep." I glanced toward Kermit. "Sorry, Kermit. I tried to tell him—"

"Fuck him," said Kermit, in a deep strong voice. All three of us snapped our heads toward him. It was the first time any of us had heard him speak. "He's done nothing but hack me around my whole damned life, call me an idiot, let others call me an idiot . . ." We heard a long echoing scream from the valley. "They can't kill him slow enough to suit me." As he turned away, I thought I saw tears in his eyes.

"Well . . . what now, Mister Shadowen? You're calling the shots."

"I'm through here." Shod shoved his rifle in his scabbard. "I talked with Carrington in Crofton, told him what had happened with Red Cloud. He wants to act like the whole incident never happened."

"Yeah, I bet he was in on it."

"No. Carrington's not that kind. He's a straight-up 'by the book' soldier. McDowell was a different kind of cat altogether. It's the ones like McDowell who cause this sort of thing. It's some crazy 'win at any cost' policy." Carrington is simply a day-to-day soldier, wading from one mess to the next."

"So you won't report what went on here?"

"No." He shook his head. "Who would believe it anyway? Besides, you've come out smelling like a rose. I told Carrington and Fetterman that you were skinned and gutted by a war party of Sioux. So, if you are Miller Crowe, here's a chance for you to go straight. If you're smart, you'll take it."

I cocked my head. "You did that for me? Why?"

Shod grinned as Jack stood up and stepped forward with the jug. "As long as there's people like you running loose, there's plenty of work for people like me."

I laughed with him. I took the jug from Jack, started to raise it, and stopped. "No kidding now, why'd you do it?"

Shod shrugged. "To be honest, I really don't know."

"Hear that, Jack?" Again I started to raise the jug; again I stopped.

"Actually, I saw the difficulty you had over the way the Indians are being treated here. I also saw the way you tried to make sense of it, not that you ever did." He let out a breath. "I believe if there had been a way to help straighten out this mess, you would've given it a try. It wasn't just about the money."

I laughed. "You're wrong there. There's nothing turns my wheels more than a good bag of—"

"Save it, Crowe, Beatty, Jesse James . . . whoever you are. I'm sure if you talk long enough, you'll make me change my mind and shoot you." He reached out for the jug; I gave it to him, and watched him turn back a big swallow. He handed it back as he struggled to catch his breath. I took it and tossed back a long swig.

"I think we might've proved something here." My voice came out ragged the first try. I cleared my throat.

"What?" Shod took the jug again.

"Well, you know, people like you and people like me, being able to work together to do what's right. I mean somehow we've all gotta learn to pull together, or the likes of Tillman and McDowell end up running everything."

"You might be right."

"I am right. Now, admit it. We worked damn well together when it came to saving each other's hide. You'd do it again in a minute, wouldn't you?"

"We did work together alright. But as far as doing it again"—he stopped and gazed out across the sky—"I'd rather be dipped in boiling lard."

"Me too," I laughed, "but I mean if we didn't have *that* choice."

Shod grabbed his saddle horn and swung up. Kermit stepped his horse over beside him and they started off down the trail. "Wait," I called out. They stopped and looked back as I limped to them. I took Shod's spectacles out of my pocket and pitched them to him. "I found these along the trail." He hooked them behind his ears and handed Kermit the reading glass.

Kermit looked at me through the thick glass. His eye looked three times its size. "Good-bye, Mister Beatty," he said behind the enlarged eye.

I don't know how far we'd walked that day before coming upon two well-dressed young men riding fine horses. When they rode up, I stood there supporting my bare foot with a walking stick while Jack wobbled beside me, hugging the jug of "wonderful stuff." "What in the world happened to you boys?" One of the men leaned down and studied us close. "Are you wounded? Where's your boot?"

I just shook my head. "It's one long sad story. You don't want to hear it. How far are we from Laramie?"

"Too far to be walking. What's happened to your horses?"

I glanced at Jack. "Indians stole 'em. A bunch of Shoshoni."

"I find that odd," said the taller one with a drooping moustache. "They're supposed to be working for the army."

I shrugged. "Believe what you will."

"You're not part of Long Jake Howard's posse, are you?"

"No. We're all that's left of a sight-seeing tour. We came here on vacation. Didn't know there was a war."

They both rubbed their mouths to hide their smiles. "I'm sorry," said the taller one. He reached down a hand. "How can we help you? My name is Earp . . . Wyatt Earp. This is my friend." He didn't mention his friend's name. "We're up from Kansas. Apparently some scoundrel has been using my name in a most degrading manner. It's hard enough establishing a reputation of honesty and decency without some scoundrel—"

"I'm here to kill them," said Earp's friend. He looked like he could barely contain himself just thinking about it.

"You gentlemen haven't heard anything about it, have you?"

I scratched my chin. "Yes, come to think of it. There was a short little feller traveling on one horse with an Indian girl. He called himself Wyatt Earp." I waved my hand. "But heck, he left and headed for Fort Laramie over a month ago. Said he worked for some religious organization."

"They glanced at each other. "I saw him," said Earp. "I knew something wasn't right about that fat little snake." His eyes turned dark and cold. "Is there anything we can do for you? If not, I'm afraid we're in somewhat of a hurry here."

"No, we'll be alright." The Catahoula cur appeared beside me, and I reached down to pat his head. The two of them stared at each other and then back at the dog.

"Do you know C. W. Flowers?"

Again I scratched my chin. "I recollect the name, but I can't say from where."

"What's your dog's name?" Earp's eyes looked crafty.

"Oh, he ain't my dog. He's just been hanging around with us. He's just a stray, I reckon."

"Huh-uh." Earp's friend leaned forward. "That dog's no stray. He's belonged to C. W. Flowers for years. I'd recognize him anywhere."

I glanced at Jack, hoping they hadn't noticed my mouth drop open. "But he's never looked that good before," said Earp. "Getting away from Flowers must agree with him."

Earp's friend nodded and pushed his hat up. "Flowers never half fed him, smacked him around. I'm surprised that dog didn't turn on him. They'll do that, you know. Catahoulas are the best dogs in the world if you treat them right. But they've got a wild streak in them that won't tolerate abuse. They're like Indians. Never mistreat one. For God's sake . . . don't ever kick one."

"I've heard that," I said.

The jug was nearly empty by the time we reached a spot where the trail turned into a wide dirt road. I limped along while Jack rattled the spoons against the palms of his hands. "Why don't you throw them things away? You ain't musically inclined."

"I've always wanted to learn. Listen to this." He started rattling them again, as if playing for an audience.

I shook my head. "Jack, I came here on a slick riding mare, leading a fine string of horses, with plenty of operating capital. I had brand-new shooting gear and a glades knife . . . and good boots." I looked at him; he kept rattling. "After stealing, robbing, fighting . . . killing, sneaking . . . lying . . . running, hiding . . . nearly getting killed more times than I've got fingers and toes." Jack stopped for a second; I took a breath.

"I'm leaving on foot, with one boot . . . no money . . . no gun." I looked at Jack. He chuckled and rattled louder. "An empty jug . . . a hangover . . . and one bloody dollar . . . with a hole in it." I stopped and grabbed the spoons when I realized my voice was starting to keep time to the rattling.

"Why'd you stop?" Jack jerked them away, laughed, and pushed his hat up. "That was sounding pretty good."

"Buenas Noches," said a voice, as we walked around a turn and came face-to-face with a Mexican leading a long string of horses. We stepped off the side of the road and just stared as the horses filed past us. Two more wranglers rode past; they eyed us close and watched over their shoulders as we stood gawking. "What's wrong with them?" said one to the other.

"I don't know, but something has them pissed off."

"Sí, whisky-loco." The Mexican laughed and pointed at our jug.

I waved my stick in the air as if conjuring a storm cloud. "You staring at us . . . hunh? Are ya?" I was a little drunk.

Jack laughed. "Don't stare at us, goddamn ya!"

I cupped my hand to my mouth as they rode around the turn, still looking back. "Think you're something with your *fine* goddamn horses? Well, let me tell you—" I turned to Jack laughing and wiping my eyes. "Just watch . . . I bet you." I held my finger in the air, anticipating. In a second, one of the wranglers came back around the turn and stopped before us. "See?" I grinned at Jack.

"You boys doing alright?" The young feller leaned down and looked us over.

"Never better," I laughed. "Where'd ya get them horses?"

He managed a straight face. "I'm Stedman . . . Carl Stedman. I'm a dealer out of Louisville. I'm taking a string up to Powder River, all the way to Fort Kearny—for the army."

I glanced at Jack, then back to the young man. "You'll never get through without a requisition. You got one?"

"No." He rubbed his chin without taking his eyes from mine. "But these are fine animals and I hear they need horses—"

"Boy, are you in luck!" I reached inside my shirt, flipped out the wrinkled paper, and waved it back and forth.

Jack chuckled under his breath. "Outlaws . . ."

We sat bareback atop two well-groomed horses, upon a ridge, and watched the long string of horses wind around to the narrow trail and disappear up toward Powder River. We'd looked the horses over for any brands and markings. Stedman swore they were not stolen, but he didn't quite recall where they came from. The Catahoula sat on the ground beside me, sniffing the air and watching their trail of dust. "You know"—Jack pushed up his hat and took a bite of tobacco he'd bummed from the Mexican—"I'm gonna miss Big Shod. I liked that sum-bitch from the get-go."

"Well . . ." I watched the dust begin to settle. "I didn't at first, but he turned out to be a top hand. I reckon he's one of a kind."

"Now, why is it, back when you thought he was robbing us, you said 'they're all just alike.' Now that he's been a friend, he's 'one of a kind.' "

I felt my face redden. "I can't help it. I reckon we're all just what we are." I glanced down at the Catahoula. "Ain't that right, ole Dog That Points the Way?" The dog snapped his head up toward me with the strangest look—I mean a *confused,* bewildered look. He flipped up to his feet, shook himself so hard his ears rattled, stared at me a second with a low growl, then tore out toward Red Cloud's farm like the devil was behind him.

"What got into him?"

"Damned if I know." I scratched my jaw. "Something I said, evidently." We watched him disappear into the settling dust of the horses.

"What the hell were we doing out there?" I said to Jack in a hushed voice.

"You know . . . just doing it." He shrugged and spit a stream.

"Doing what?"

"Sight-seeing," he chuckled, and let out a breath.

I watched a hawk rise up from nowhere and ascend effortlessly northward. I watched for a few seconds until he became a black dot in the evening sky. From where he soared, he could see the valley of the Tongue and the two forks of the Powder in a mere toss of his head, or at least I liked thinking he could.

"No, Jack." I shook my head. "I'm serious. This has been something strange and crazy. Don't joke. What the hell were we doing up there?"

"Who says I'm joking?" Jack glanced at me from beneath his hat brim. "I told you before, 'sight-seeing ain't nothing to joke about.' It's what a feller has to do, if he ever wants to know what any of this means." He swung an arm to take in the whole of the high plains. "We've been 'seeing America.' Ain't it a precious thing. She's a fine young whore, tight-bellied, wild, greedy, and lusting to live. God"—his eyes got misty—"I love this big beautiful bitch!"

"Aw . . . you're drunk." I breathed in the cool air and thought of Red Cloud and his farm, wondered who would live and die in the Moon of the Cold, and who would be left to feast on warm puppies and tell the story in the Moon When Snow Drifts Into the Teepee. Who would tell it . . . how would it be heard?

"Besides." Jack chuckled under his breath, threw away the empty jug, and gigged his horse. "What else was there to do all summer?"

Sunlight faded, casting a long shadow across Powder River, across Red Cloud's world. I turned my horse and fell in beside Jack as he took out the spoons and rattled them against his leg. "Now, how'd that go? 'I CAME HERE ON A FINE HORSE.'" Jack sang his drunken heart out to the wide evening sky . . .

◆ ❋ Epilogue ❋ ◆

Over the years I kept an ear toward Powder River; but to tell the truth, the first couple of weeks at home, all I wanted was to be by myself awhile, lie around, eat, sleep—just think about things. Maybe I was just worn-out; I don't know.

During Christmas week, I heard that Captain William J. Fetterman had been killed in an unauthorized attack on two thousand Sioux, Cheyenne, and Arapaho warriors. As fate would have it, there were eighty troops in his command—exactly the number he said he needed to wipe out the whole Sioux Nation. When I heard it I almost laughed; but I remembered the face of that dumb kid who'd wanted to be a horse soldier, and, well . . . dying ain't funny.

Shortly after that, I read that Colonel Carrington had been relieved of command, and a year and a half later the whole Powder River occupation force left the forts abandoned. Red Cloud burned Fort Phil Kearny to the ground . . . and won his war. The *only* war the Indians ever won.

I've always guarded the gift Red Cloud gave me, the gift of honor, for I've come to realize that without it, a man has little else. Maybe that's what I'd really gone looking for at Powder River. I'd lost a lot of things in the last year of the great civil conflict, and I reckon honor and self-respect were among 'em. Red Cloud must've seen it, and knew that I could not show him honor without some of it rubbing off on me.

Powder River was the last holdout against a world "gone crazy wanting more," and for a time I really thought progress had won. But for people with honor, with self-respect, it ain't about who wins or loses; it's about one hand to another, spirit to spirit, heart to heart, and who can hold their head the highest when the smoke clears and the dust settles. For in the end that's all any of us get, "riding or walking."

I didn't go to Powder River as I once thought, to bleed it, rob it, or to watch it die. I went to feel it, breath it, and let it cleanse me. Maybe that's why we all were there, but just couldn't realize it . . . and that's a shame.

I thought so much about Red Cloud over the years that once I sat down and wrote him a letter just like he told me to. I addressed it in care of the Tongue River Indian Village, and as crazy as it sounds, six weeks later I got an answer. It was from one of his chiefs; and it informed me that Red Cloud could not answer the letter himself, as he was presently in Washington, D.C., speaking to Congress and the Indian Bureau on behalf of all the tribes between the Black Hills and the Big Horn Mountains. There was a suggestion that I could reach him by telephone at the Globe Hotel, but I couldn't bring myself to call him there. I'd heard Red Cloud loved talking on telephones, but I preferred remembering him as I'd last seen him . . . atop a wild plains pony leaving town.

I never saw Jefferson Ellridge Shadowen again, and I reckon it's just as well. We could've never been around one another very long without ending up in a fight. I heard two different accounts of what became of him. One story had it that he'd drifted down to Texas, practiced law after quitting the government, and wound up getting killed trying to save a little white girl from a runaway wagon. God bless him if that story was true.

But then another story said he'd been fired from the government, took to drinking, killed a white man in a fair fight, and a band of hooded night riders hung him without a trial. If that story was true, then . . . God bless him even more.

As for Kermit Bone, I never heard of him again. I would've liked to see him years later just to see how he turned out. I thought it peculiar that he'd kept his mouth shut through all that went on, and in spite of everybody else calling me Crowe, he left that day looking at me through that reading glass and called me Mister Beatty. Who knows? I did run into two other people from Powder River a few years later. It was Queenie and a feller I didn't recognize right off.

I'd been gambling in a fancy gaming parlor in New Orleans when I heard a familiar voice behind me. "Yooo-hoo, remember me?" I watched her wave as she stepped forward smiling. She wore a diamond necklace and ruby earrings that looked to weigh a pound each. The gentleman with her stood to the side holding a tall top hat and carrying a gold-tipped cane.

"Sure I do." I shook her hand and nodded toward her gentleman friend. "Can I buy ya'll a drink?"

"Your money is no good here, my friend." He stepped forward and snapped his fingers at the bartender. "See to it this gentleman doesn't pay for anything else while he's here."

I glanced at Queenie. She giggled and leaned close to me. "He can afford it . . . he owns the place."

I glanced around at the fine tapestries, crystal, brass, and the silver inlaid bar-top. "He looks familiar, but I just can't place him."

"Of course you can't," he said, overhearing me as he held out the long-stemmed glass of wine. "It's been a long time. But you, sir, are the very reason I'm on top of the world today." He smiled, giving me another chance to recognize him.

"I'm sorry." I shrugged. "I'm really at a loss here."

"I met you on my way out of Powder River? The war?" He stopped and waited again.

"Jesus," I breathed, as I added a scraggly beard and a pound of dust to his face, rolled back years of good food, fine wine, and fancy living. "The settler? You're the feller I gave horses to, to pull your wagon?" I pointed my finger. "I'll be damned."

"That's me!" He spread his arms as if to go into a song. "And following your advice is what brought me into all this." He waved his hands about the place.

"My advice?"

"Excuse me, gents. I've heard this story a thousand times." Queenie turned toward a roulette wheel.

"Remember? You told me I'd have a better chance at getting rich on a New Orleans gaming table than I'd have at staying alive in Powder River." He threw back a laugh. "And you were right. What a dumb bastard I was."

I laughed with him a second, then stopped. "But you weren't

dumb. Not for wanting to live there. I've missed that crazy place something awful." I nodded and wiped my finger across my lip. "Naw sir. But what about your wife . . . your youngins?"

"Oh, them. Well . . . we just grew apart after I struck it big, if you know what I mean." He shrugged. "Oh, I see the children now and then; they're fine . . . youngest is going on ten."

"Your wife?" I pictured the rough hands I'd seen that day as they reached over and comforted him. Surely to goodness there was something better for her. If not, I would've been justified in killing him.

"Oh, she's fine too." I wondered if he'd read my mind. "She had it rough awhile—the divorce and all. But them ole Pennsylvania gals, hell, you couldn't kill one with a stick. Now she's fatter than a house cat and living the life of ease."

"That's good." I took a sip.

"Yes, she married one of the Texas cattle barons, Joseph Philipé, of Cull, Philipé, and Beat, biggest beef brokers in Dallas, got land holdings you couldn't cover with both hands on a map. You've heard of them, I'm sure . . ."

I said the names as if in a trance. "Kid Cull . . . Run-around Joe . . . One Drum Beat."

"Yes, I believe that's what they used to call themselves. They struck it rich in Powder River! God knows how; of course, I'd never ask." He leaned forward and winked. "I ran into some stolen horses myself, but I kept my mouth shut, hunh?" He gigged me. "Didn't I?"

I grinned, but my heart wasn't in it.

Later that night, maybe closer to morning, I stood alone on the shoreline of the Mississippi and listened to gentle waves slap the bank beneath my feet, slow and steady like the heartbeat of God. Behind me in the distance, I heard a man cuss and a woman scream. A bottle broke; a dog barked, and soon the same voices laughed like fools. "America . . ." I whispered under my breath as I remembered Jack's drunken words. "Goddamn her, Jack, I love her too. We all do. Why won't she just love us all in return?" I shook my head. "While there's still enough of her to go around."

I looked up at sparkling sky, at diamonds pitched across black velvet, so clean it swirled in its depth and darkness. I followed a trails of stars northwestward; stopped my eyes and mind at a point I knew lay above Red Cloud's farm. I knew it because God's heart-beat grew stronger beneath my feet, here where all the rivers flowed as one. I felt my throat tighten and blinked my eyes to clear my vision. I thought of broken saddles, lost money, war, lies, death, and deception; and of how good it must feel to think of none of these things. I sniffed, ran my finger beneath my nose, and thought of things that seemed to matter, of dogs you couldn't kick, of crippled horses set free, and of spirits that couldn't be broken. For a second, I understood what went on at Powder River, that strange place where fools turned into heroes and heroes turned to fools. I tried to grasp the thought, but in another second it was gone, disappeared to a place where I knew I couldn't follow.

I reached down, picked up a rock, and tossed it out above the river. I listened, but never heard it land. "Fugem, Mister Cloud," I laughed, and whispered to the wind, the water, and the sky, as if reciting a chant, raising a cheer, or swearing a curse, or uttering a prayer. "Fugem," I said again, and ran my finger beneath my eye. "Fugem-fugem-all."